Tongues of Serpents

Tongues of Serpents

NAOMI NOVIK

BALLANTINE BOOKS · NEW YORK

Copyright © 2010 by Temeraire LLC

All rights reserved.

Published in the United States by Del Rey,
an imprint of The Random House Publishing Group,
a division of Random House, Inc., New York.

DEL REY is a registered trademark and the Del Rey colophon
is a trademark of Random House, Inc.

Map © Mapping Specialists Ltd.

Library of Congress Cataloging-in-Publication Data
Novik, Naomi.
Tongues of serpents / Naomi Novik.
p. cm. — (Temeraire)
ISBN 978-0-345-49689-8 (alk. paper)
1. Great Britain. Royal Navy—Officers—Fiction.
2. Penal colonies—Australia—Fiction.   3. Napoleonic Wars,
1800–1815—Fiction.   4. Dragons—Fiction.   I. Title
PS3614.O93T68 2010
813'.6—dc22   2010012934

Printed in the United States of America on acid-free paper

www.delreybooks.com

2 4 6 8 9 7 5 3 1

First Edition

For my father, Samuel Novik,
who also came over the sea to another country

ACKNOWLEDGMENTS

I am hugely grateful to my longtime beta readers Georgina Paterson and Vanessa Len, who not only tromped all over the Blue Mountains with me, but helped me work out the plot for the last three forthcoming books of the Temeraire series over lunch in Sydney. Possibly drinks were involved also? (To determine whether or not this was a good thing, you will have to wait for me to write them.)

Many thanks for beta-reading also to Meredith Lynne and Alison Feeney, and to the wonderful Terri Oberkamper for all her help; and I am so thrilled to once again have Dominic Harman's amazing cover art! Much love and gratitude to my fantastic editor, Betsy Mitchell, at Del Rey and my wonderful agent, Cynthia Manson, and a special thank-you to Rachel Kind, who has shepherded my books all over the world. Rachel, my crammed-full bookshelves might not be grateful, but I am!

And most of all to Charles, who gives me daily more gifts than words can ever adequately convey.

From the preface to

An Inland Journey in Terra Australis in the year 1809

by Sipho Tsuluka Dlamini

[LONDON, 1819]

I have taken the liberty of marking the route of our journey upon a simplified version of the most extraordinary and beautiful map of the continent published by the late Mr. Matthew Flinders, of the *Investigator*, in his work *A voyage to Terra Australis*, omitting the soundings and those geographical features of the coastline which have therein been more thoroughly examined.

I must apologize to the reader for the incompleteness and undoubted inaccuracies of my annotations, which do not adequately represent the native holdings nor the variety and number of the tribes; I can only offer as my excuse that these observations were made at a young age, during a journey with no translator or guide, and my opportunities for research were regrettably limited and have not since been improved upon . . .

However, I think my information sufficient to illustrate the entire folly, which at present seems to dominate conversation regarding the interior, of asserting the presence of a vast central inland sea, either fresh or salt, which should conveniently lend itself to farming. The lake which I have marked upon the map was the only sizeable body of water which we encountered upon our journey, and proved only seasonally potable. That the extraordinary aridity of the weather which we encountered, barring a handful of brief and unproductive storms, is rather a regular condition than an unusual case, is a supposition borne out not only by the testimony of all the natives with whom we had conversation, but by the most peculiarly adapted behavior of the local fauna, as my record will further demonstrate.

Java

Flores

Timor

SOLOMON ISLANDS

ARCHIPELAGO OF LOUISIADE

New Caledonia

Great Barrier Reef

Torres Strait

Gulf of Carpentaria

NEW SOUTH WALES

BLUE MOUNTAINS

Wiradjuri

Sydney

VAN DIEMEN'S LAND

Bass Strait

Spencer Gulf

Gulf of St. Vincent

Head of the Great Australian Bight

Maljangapa

salt lake

Uluru (*monolith*)

Larrakia

Pitjantjatjara

10° S

20° S

30° S

110° E

120° E

130° E

140° E

150° E

160° E

I

Chapter 1

HERE WERE FEW STREETS in the main port of Sydney which deserved the name, besides the one main thoroughfare, and even that bare packed dirt, lined only with a handful of small and wretched buildings that formed all the permanence of the colony. Tharkay turned off from this and led the way down a cramped, irregularly arranged alley-way between two wooden-slat buildings to a courtyard full of men drinking, in surly attitudes, under no roof but a tarpaulin.

Along one side of the courtyard, the further from the kitchens, the convicts sat in their drab and faded duck trousers, dusty from the fields and quarries and weighted down with fatigue; along the other, small parties of men from the New South Wales Corps watched with candidly unfriendly faces as Laurence and his companions seated themselves at a small table near the edge of the establishment.

Besides their being strangers, Granby's coat drew the eye: bottle-green was not in the common way, and though he had put off the worst excesses of gold braid and buttons with which Iskierka insisted upon adorning him, the embroidery at cuffs and collar could not be so easily detached. Laurence wore plain brown, himself: to make a pretense of standing in the Aerial Corps now was wholly out of the question, of course, and if his dress raised questions concerning his situation, that was certainly no less than honest, as neither he nor anyone else had yet managed to work out what that ought in any practical sense to be.

"I suppose this fellow will be here soon enough," Granby said, unhappily; he had insisted on coming, but not from any approval of the scheme.

"I fixed the hour at six," Tharkay answered, and then turned his head: one of the younger officers had risen from the tables and was coming towards them.

Eight months aboard ship with no duties of his own and shipmates nearly united in their determination to show disdain had prepared Laurence for the scene which, with almost tiresome similarity, unfolded yet again. The insult itself was irritating for demanding some answer, more than anything else; it had not the power to wound in the mouth of a coarse young boor, stinking of rum and visibly unworthy to stand among even the shabby ranks of a military force alternately called the Rum Corps. Laurence regarded Lieutenant Agreuth only with distaste, and said briefly, "Sir, you are drunk; go back to your table, and leave us at ours."

There the similarity ended, however: "I don't see why I," Agreuth said, his tongue tangling awkwardly, so he had to stop and repeat himself, speaking with excessive care, "why I should listen to anything out of a piss-pot whoreson traitor's fucking mouth—"

Laurence stared, and heard the tirade with mounting incredulity; he would have expected the gutter language out of a dockyard pickpocket in a temper, and hardly knew how to hear it from an officer. Granby had evidently less difficulty, and sprang to his feet saying, "By God, you will apologize, or for halfpence I will have you flogged through the streets."

"I would like to see you try it," Agreuth said, and leaning over spat into Granby's glass; Laurence stood too late to catch Granby's arm from throwing it into Agreuth's face.

That was of course an end to even the barest hope or pretense of civility; Laurence instead pulled Granby back by his arm, out of the way of Agreuth's wildly swinging fist, and letting go struck back with the same hand, clenched, as it came again at his face.

He did not hold back; if brawling was outrageous, it looked inevitable, and he would as soon have it over with quickly. So the blow was armed with all the strength built up from childhood on rope-lines and harness, and Laurence knocked Agreuth directly upon the jaw: the lieutenant lifted half-an-inch from the ground, his head tipping back and leading the rest of his frame. Stumbling a few steps as he came down, he pitched face-front onto the floor straight through the neighboring table, to the accompaniment of several shattering glasses and the stink of cheap rum.

That might have been enough, but Agreuth's companions, though

officers and some of them older and more sober than he, showed no reluctance in flinging themselves at once into the fray thus begun. The
men at the overturned table, sailors on an East India merchantman,
were as quick to take offense at the disruption of their drinking; and a
mingled crowd of sailors and laborers and soldiers, all better than
three-quarters of the way drunk, and a great scarcity of women, as
compared to what would have been found in nearly every other dockyard house of the world which Laurence knew, was a powder-keg
ready for the slow-match in any case. The rum had not finished sinking
between the paving-stones before men were rising from their chairs all
around them.

Another officer of the New South Wales Corps threw himself on
Laurence: a bigger man than Agreuth, sodden and heavy with liquor.
Laurence twisted himself loose and heaved him down onto the floor,
shoving him as well as could be managed under the table. Tharkay was
already with a practical air seizing the bottle of rum by the neck, and
when another man lunged—this one wholly unconnected with Agreuth, and by all appearances simply pleased to fight anyone at all—
Tharkay clubbed him upon the temple swiftly.

Granby had been seized upon by three men at once: two of them,
Agreuth's fellows, for spite, and one who was trying his best only to get
at the jeweled sword and belt around Granby's waist. Laurence struck
the pickpocket on the wrist, and seizing him by the scruff of the collar
flung him stumbling across the courtyard; Granby exclaimed, then, and
turning back Laurence found him ducking from a knife, dirty and rust-
speckled, being stabbed at his eyes.

"By God, have you taken all leave of your senses?" Laurence said,
and seized upon the knife-wielder's hand with both his own, twisting
the blade away, while Granby efficiently knocked down the third man
and turned back to help him. The melee was spreading rapidly now,
helped along by Tharkay, who was coolly throwing the toppled chairs
across the room, knocking over still more of the tables, and flinging
glasses of rum into the faces of the custom as they rose indignantly.

Laurence and Granby and Tharkay were only three together,
and thanks to the advance of the New South Wales officers well-
surrounded, leaving the irritated men no other target but those same
officers; a target on which the convicts in particular seemed not loath
to vent their spleen. This was not a very coherently directed fury, however, and when the officer before Laurence had been clubbed down

with a heavy stool, the choleric assailant behind him swung it with equal fervor at Laurence himself.

Laurence slipped upon the wet floorboards, catching the stool away from his face, and went to one knee in a puddle. He shoved the man's leg out from under him, and was rewarded with the full weight of man and stool landing upon his shoulder, so they went sprawling together upon the floor.

Splinters drove into Laurence's side, where his shirt had ridden up from his breeches and come wholly loose, and the big convict, swearing at him, struck him on the side of his face with a clenched fist. Laurence tasted blood as his lip tore upon his tooth, a dizzying haze over his sight. They were rolling across the floor, and Laurence had no very clear recollection of the next few moments; he was pounding at the other man savagely, a blow with every turn, knocking his head against the boards over and over. It was a vicious, animal struggle, insensible of both feeling and thought; he knew only distantly as he was kicked, by accident, or struck against the wall or some overturned piece of furniture.

The limp unconsciousness of his opponent freed him at last from the frenzy, and Laurence with an effort opened his clenched hand and let go the man's hair, and pushed himself up from the floor, staggering. They had fetched up against the wooden counter before the kitchen. Laurence reaching up clutched at the edge and pulled himself to his feet, aware more than he wished to be, all at once, of a deep stabbing pain in his side, and stinging cuts in his cheek and his hands. He fumbled at his face and pulled free a long sliver of broken glass, tossing it upon the counter.

The fighting had begun already to die down, oddly quick to Laurence's instinctive sense of an action; the participants lacked the appetite of a real engagement, where there was anything of worth to be gained. Laurence limping across the room made it to Granby's side: Agreuth and one of his fellow officers had clawed their way back up onto their feet and were yet grappling weakly with him in a corner, vicious but half-exhausted, so they were swaying back and forth more than wrestling.

Coming in, Laurence heaved Granby free, and leaning on each other they stumbled out of the courtyard and into the narrow, stinking alley-way outside, which yet seemed fresh out from under the makeshift tarpaulin; a fine misting rain was falling. Laurence leaned gratefully against the far wall made cool and light by the coating of dew, ignoring with a practiced stomach the man a few steps away who was heaving the contents of his belly into the gutters. A couple of women coming down the alley-way lifted their skirts over the trickle of muck and continued past them all without hesitation, not even looking in at the disturbance of the tavern courtyard.

"My God, you look a fright," Granby said, dismally.

"I have no doubt," Laurence said, gingerly touching at his face. "And I have two ribs cracked, I dare say. I am sorry to say, John, you are not in much better case."

"No, I am sure not," Granby said. "We will have to take a room somewhere, if anyplace will let us through the door, to wash up; what Iskierka would do seeing me in such a state, I have no notion."

Laurence had a very good notion what Iskierka would do, and also Temeraire, and between them there would not be much left of the colony to speak of afterwards.

"Well," Tharkay said, joining them as he wrapped his neckcloth around his own bloodied hand, "I believe I saw our man look into the establishment, a little while ago, but I am afraid he thought better of coming in under the circumstances. I will have to inquire after him to arrange another meeting."

"No," Laurence said, blotting his lip and cheek with his handkerchief. "No, I thank you; I think we can dispense with his information. I have seen all I need to, in order to form an opinion of the discipline of the colony, and its military force."

Temeraire sighed and toyed with the last bites of kangaroo stew—the meat had a pleasantly gamy sort of flavor, not unlike deer, and he had found it at first a very satisfying change from fish, after the long sea-voyage. But he could only really call it palatable when cooked rare, which did not offer much variety; in stew it became quite stringy and tiresome, especially as the supply of spice left even more to be desired.

There were some very nice cattle in a pen which he could see, from his vantage upon the harbor promontory, but evidently they were much too dear here for the Corps to provide. And Temeraire of course could not propose such an expense to Laurence, not when he had been responsible for the loss of Laurence's fortune; instead Temeraire had silenced all his mild complaints about the lack of variety: but sadly Gong

Su had taken this as encouragement, and it had been nothing but kangaroo morning and night, four days running—not even a bit of tunny.

"I do not see why we mayn't at least go hunting further along," Iskierka said, even while licking out her own bowl indecorously—she quite refused to learn anything resembling polite manners. "This is a large country, and it stands to reason there ought to be something more worth eating if we looked. Perhaps there are some of those elephants which you have been on and on about; I should like to try one of those."

Temeraire would have given a great deal for a delicious elephant, seasoned with a generous amount of pepper and perhaps some sage, but Iskierka was never to be encouraged in anything whatsoever. "You are very welcome to go flying away anywhere you like," he said, "and to surely get quite lost. No one has any notion of what this countryside is like, past the mountains, and there is no one in it, either, to ask for directions: not people or dragons."

"That is very silly," Iskierka said. "I do not say these kangaroos are very good eating, because they are not, and there are not enough of them, either; but they are certainly no worse than what we had in Scotland during the last campaign, so it is stuff to say there is no one living here; why wouldn't there be? I dare say there are plenty of dragons here, only they are somewhere else, eating much better than we are."

This struck Temeraire as not an unlikely possibility, and he made a note to discuss it privately with Laurence, later; which recalled him to Laurence's absence, and thence to the advancing hour. "Roland," he called, with a little anxiety—of course Laurence did not need nursemaiding, but he had promised to return before the supper hour, and read a little more of the novel which he had acquired in town the day before—"Roland, is it not past five?"

"Lord, yes, it must be almost six," Emily Roland answered, putting down her sword; she and Demane were fencing a little, in the yard. She patted her face down with a tugged-free tail of her shirt, and ran to the promontory edge to call down to the sailors below, and came back to say, "No, I am wrong: it is a quarter past seven: how strange the day is so long, when it is almost Christmas!"

"It is not strange at all," Demane said. "It is only strange that you keep insisting it must be winter here only because it is in England."

"But where is Granby, if it is so late?" Iskierka said, prickling up at once, overhearing. "He did not mean to go anywhere particularly nice, he assured me, or I should never have let him go looking so shabby."

Temeraire flared his ruff a little, taking this to heart; he felt it keenly that Laurence should go about in nothing but a plain gentleman's coat, without even a little bit of braid or golden buttons. He would gladly have improved Laurence's appearance if he had any chance of doing so; but Laurence still had refused to sell Temeraire's talon-sheaths for him, and even if he had, Temeraire had not yet seen anything in this part of the world which would have suited him as appropriate.

"Perhaps I had better go and look for Laurence," Temeraire said. "I am sure he cannot have meant to stay away so long."

"I am going to go and look for Granby, too," Iskierka announced.

"Well, we cannot both go," Temeraire said irritably. "Someone must stay with the eggs." He cast a quick, judgmental eye over the three eggs in their protective nests of swaddling blankets, and the small canopy set over them, made of sailcloth. He was a little dissatisfied by their situation: a nice coal brazier, he thought, would not have gone amiss even in this warm weather, and perhaps some softer cloth to go directly against the shell; and it did not suit him that the canopy was so low he could not put his head underneath it, to sniff at the eggs and see how hard their shells had become.

There had been a little difficulty over them, after disembarking: some of the officers of the Corps who had been sent along had tried to object to Temeraire's keeping the eggs by him, as though they would be better able to protect them, which was stuff; and they had made some sort of noise about Laurence trying to kidnap the eggs, which Temeraire had snorted off.

"Laurence does not want any other dragon, as he has *me*," Temeraire had said, "and as for kidnapping, I would like to know whose notion it was to take the eggs halfway across the world on the ocean, with storms and sea-serpents everywhere, and to this odd place that is not even a proper country, with no dragons; it was certainly not mine."

"Mr. Laurence is going directly to hard labor, like all the rest of the prisoners," Lieutenant Forthing had said, quite stupidly, as though Temeraire were allowing any such thing to happen.

"That is quite enough, Mr. Forthing," Granby had said, overhearing, and coming upon them. "I wonder that you would make any such ill-advised remark; I pray you take no notice of it at all, Temeraire, none at all."

"Oh! I do not in the least," Temeraire answered, "or any of these other complaints; it is all nonsense, when what you mean is," he added to Forthing and his associates, "you would like to keep the eggs by you, so that they should not know any better when they hatch, but think they must go at once into harness, and that they must take whichever of you wins them by chance: I heard you talk of drawing lots last night in the gunroom, so you needn't try and deny it. I will certainly have none of it, and I expect neither will the eggs, of any of you."

He had of course carried his point, and the eggs, away to their present relative safety and comfort, but Temeraire had no illusions as to the trustworthiness of people who could make such spitefully false remarks; he did not doubt that they would creep up and snatch the eggs away if he gave them even the least chance. He slept curled about the tent, therefore, and Laurence had put Roland and Demane and Sipho on watch, also.

The responsibility was proving sadly confining, however, particularly as Iskierka was not to be trusted with the eggs for any length of time. Fortunately the town was very small, and the promontory visible from nearly any point within it if one only stretched out one's neck to look, so Temeraire felt he might risk it, only long enough to find Laurence and bring him back. Of course Temeraire was sure no one would be absurd enough to try and treat Laurence with any disrespect, but it could not be denied that men were inclined to do unaccountable things from time to time, and Forthing's remark stirred uneasily in the back of his head.

It was true, if one wished to be very particular about such things, that Laurence was a convicted felon: convicted of treason, and his sentence commuted to transportation only at the behest of Lord Wellington, after the last campaign in England. But that sentence had been fulfilled, in Temeraire's opinion: no-one could deny that Laurence had now been transported, and the experience had been quite as much punishment as anyone could have wished.

The unhappy *Allegiance* had been packed to the portholes with still-more-unhappy convicts, who had been kept chained wrist-and-ankle all the day, and stank quite dreadfully whenever they were brought out for exercise in their clanking lines, some of them hanging limp in the restraints. It seemed quite like slavery, to Temeraire; he did not see why it should make so vast a difference as Laurence said, only because a law-court had said the poor convicts had stolen something: after all, anyone might take a sheep or a cow, if it were neglected by its owner and not kept under watch.

Certainly it made the ship as bad as any slaving vessel: the smell rose up through the planking of the deck, and the wind brought it forward to the dragondeck almost without surcease; even the aroma of boiling salt pork, from the galley below, could not erase it. And Temeraire had learned by accident, perhaps a month out on their journey, that Laurence was quartered directly by the gaol, where it must have been far worse.

Laurence had dismissed the notion of making any complaint, however. "I do very well, my dear," he had said, "as I have the whole liberty of the dragondeck for my days and the pleasanter nights, which not even the ship's officers have. It would be unfair in the extreme, when I have not their labor, for me to be demanding some better situation: someone else would have to shift places to give me another."

So it had been a very unpleasant transportation indeed, and now they were here, which no-one could enjoy, either. Aside from the question of kangaroos, there were not very many people at all, and nothing like a proper town. Temeraire was used to seeing wretched quarters for dragons, in England, but here people did not sleep much better than the clearings in any covert, many of them in tents or makeshift little buildings which did not stay up when one flew over them, not even very low, and instead toppled over and spilled out the squalling inhabitants to make a great fuss.

And there was no fighting to be had at all, either. Several letters and newspapers had reached them along the way, when quicker frigates passed the laboring bulk of the *Allegiance*. It was very disheartening to Temeraire to have Laurence read to him how Napoleon was reported to be fighting again, in Spain this time, and sacking cities all along the coast, and Lien surely with him: and meanwhile here they were on the other side of the world, uselessly. It was not in the least fair, Temeraire thought disgruntledly, that Lien, who did not think Celestials ought to fight ever, should have all the war to herself while he sat here nursing eggs.

There had not even been a small engagement at sea, for consolation: they had once seen a French privateer, off at a distance, but the small vessel had set every scrap of sail and vanished away at a heeling pace. Iskierka had given chase anyway—alone, as Laurence pointed out to Temeraire he could not leave the eggs for such a fruitless adventure—and to Temeraire's satisfaction, after a few hours she had been forced to return empty-handed.

The French would certainly not attack Sydney, either: not when there was nothing to be won but kangaroos and hovels. Temeraire did not see what they were to do here, at all; the eggs were to be seen to their hatching, but that could not be far off, he felt sure, and then there would be nothing to do but sit about and stare out to sea, as far as he could tell.

The people were all either engaged in farming, which was not very interesting, or were convicts, who it seemed to Temeraire marched out for no reason in the morning and then marched back at night. He had flown after a party of them one day, just to see, and they were only going to a quarry to cut out bits of stone, and then bringing the bits of stone back to town in waggon-carts, which seemed quite absurd and inefficient to him: he could have carried five cartloads in a single flight of perhaps ten minutes, but when he had landed to offer his assistance, the convicts had all run away, and the soldiers had come to complain to Laurence stiffly afterwards.

They certainly did not like Laurence; one of them had been very rude, and said, "For fivepence I would have you down at the quarries, too," at which Temeraire put his head down and said, "For *twopence* I will have you in the ocean; what have you done, I should like to know, when Laurence has won a great many battles with me, and we drove Napoleon off; and you have only been sitting here. You have not even managed to raise a respectable number of cows."

Temeraire now felt perhaps that jibe had been a little injudicious; or perhaps he ought not have let Laurence go into town, after all, when there were people who wished to put him into quarries. "I will go and look for Laurence and Granby," he said to Iskierka, "and you will stay here: if you go, you will likely set something on fire, anyway."

"I will not set anything on fire!" Iskierka said. "Unless it needs setting on fire, to get Granby out."

"That is just what I mean," Temeraire said. "How, pray tell, would setting something on fire do any good at all?"

"If no-one would tell me where he was," Iskierka said, "I am quite sure that if I set something on fire and told them I would set the rest on fire, too, they would come about: so there."

"Yes," Temeraire said, "and in the meanwhile, very likely he would be in whatever house you had set on fire, and be hurt: and if not, the fire would jump along to the nearby buildings whether you liked it to or not, and he would be in one of those. Whereas I will just take the roof off a building, and then I can look inside and lift them out, if they are in there, and people will tell me anyway."

"I can take a roof off a building, too!" Iskierka said. "You are only jealous, because someone is more likely to want to take Granby, because he has more gold on him and is much more fine."

Temeraire swelled with indignation and breath, and would have expelled them both in a rush, but Roland interrupted urgently, saying, "Oh, don't quarrel! Look, here they are all coming back, right as rain: that is them on the road, I am sure."

Temeraire whipped his head around: three small figures had just emerged from the small cluster of buildings which made the town, and were on the narrow cattle-track which came towards the promontory.

Temeraire's and Iskierka's heads were raised high, looking down towards them; Laurence raised a hand and waved vigorously, despite the twinge in his ribs, which a bath and a little rough bandaging had not gone very far to alleviate; that injury, however, could be concealed. "There; at least we will not have them down here in the streets," Granby said, lowering his own arm, and wincing a little; he probed gingerly at his shoulder.

It was still a near-run thing when they had got up to the promontory— a slow progress, and Laurence's legs wished to quiver on occasion, before they had reached the top and could sit on the makeshift benches. Temeraire sniffed, and then lowered his head abruptly and said, "You are hurt; you are bleeding," with urgent anxiety.

"It is nothing to concern you; I am afraid we only had a little accident in the town," Laurence said, guiltily preferring a certain degree of deceit to the inevitable complications of Temeraire's indignation.

"So, dearest, you see it is just as well I wore my old coat," Granby said to Iskierka, in a stroke of inspiration, "as it has got dirty and torn, which you would have minded if I had on something nicer."

Iskierka was thus diverted to a contemplation of his clothing, instead of his bruises, and promptly pronounced it a natural consequence of the surroundings. "If you will go into a low, wretched place like that town, one cannot expect anything better," she said, "and I do not see why we are staying here, at all; I think we had better go straight back to England."

Chapter 2

"I AM NOT SURPRISED in the least," Bligh said later that evening, when they had left Riley's table and gone to the quarterdeck for coffee and cigars, "not in the least; you see exactly how it is now, Captain Laurence, with these whoreson dogs and Merinos."

His language was not much better than that of the aforementioned dogs, and neither could Laurence much prefer his company. He did not like to think so of the King's governor and a Navy officer, and particularly not one so much a notable seaman: his feat of navigating three thousand miles of open ocean in only a ship's launch, when left adrift by the *Bounty,* was still a prodigy.

Laurence had looked at least to respect, if not to like; but the *Allegiance* had stopped to take on water in Van Diemen's Land, and there found the governor they had confidently expected to meet in Sydney, deposed by the Rum Corps and living in a resentful exile. He had a thin, soured mouth, perhaps the consequence of his difficulties; a broad forehead exposed by his receding hair; and delicate, anxious features beneath it, which did not very well correspond with the intemperate language he was given to unleash on those not uncommon occasions when he felt himself thwarted.

He had no recourse but to harangue passing Navy officers with demands to restore him to his post, but all of those prudent gentlemen, to date, had chosen to stay well out of the affair while the news took the long sea-road back to England for an official response. This, Laurence supposed, had been neglected in the upheaval of Napoleon's invasion and its aftermath; nothing else could account for so great a delay. But no fresh orders had come, nor a replacement governor, and meanwhile in Sydney the New South Wales Corps, and those men of property who had promoted their coup, grew all the more entrenched.

The very night the *Allegiance* put into the harbor, Bligh had himself rowed out to consult with Captain Riley; he had very nearly asked himself to dinner, and directed the conversation with perfect disregard for Riley's privilege; though as a Navy man himself he could not be ignorant of the custom.

"A year now, and no answer," Bligh had said in a cloud of spittle and fury, waving his hand to Riley's steward to send the bottle round to him again. "A full year gone, Captain, and meanwhile in Sydney these scurrilous worms yet inculcate all the populace with licentiousness and sedition: it is nothing to them, nothing, if every child born to woman on these shores should be a bastard and a bugger and a drunken leech, so long as they do a little work upon their farms, and lie quiet under the yoke: *Let the rum flow* is their only maxim, the liquor their only coin. and god." He did not, however, stint himself of the wine, near-vinegared though it was, nor the last dregs of Riley's port; ate well, also, as might a man living mostly on hardtack and a little occasional game.

Laurence, silent, rolling the stem of his glass between his fingers, had been unable to feel some sympathy: a little less self-restraint, and he might have railed with as much fervor against the cowardice and stupidity which had united to send Temeraire into exile. He, too, wished to be restored, if not to rank or to society at least to a place where they might be useful; and not to merely sit here on the far side of the world upon a barren rock, and complain unto Heaven.

But now Bligh's downfall might as easily be his own: his one hope of return had been a pardon from the colony's governor, for himself and Temeraire; or at least enough of a good report to reassure those in England whose fears and narrow interest had seen them sent away.

It had always been a scant hope, threadbare; but Jane Roland certainly wished for the return of Britain's one Celestial, when she had Lien to contend with on the enemy's side. Laurence might have some hope that the nearly superstitious fear of the breed which had sprung up, after the dreadful carnage of Lien's attack upon the Navy at the battle of Shoeburyness, was beginning to subside, and cooler minds to regret the impulse which had sent away so valuable a weapon.

At least, so she had written, encouragingly; and had advised him, *I may have a prayer of sending the* Viceroy *to fetch you home, when she*

*has been refit; only for God's sake be obliging to the Governor, if you
please; and I will thank you not to make any more great noise of yourself: it would be just as well if there is not a word to be said of you in
the next reports from the colony, good or evil, but that you have been
meek as milk.*

Of that, however, there was certainly no hope, from the moment
when Bligh had blotted his lips and thrown down his napkin and said,
"I will not mince words, Captain Riley: I hope you see your duty clear
under the present circumstances, and you as well, Captain Granby," he
added.

This was, of course, to carry Bligh back to Sydney, there to threaten
the colony with bombardment or pillage, at which the ringleaders
MacArthur and Johnston would be handed over for judgment. "And to
be summarily hanged like the mutinous scoundrels they are, I trust,"
Bligh said. "It is the only possible repair for the harm which they have
done: by God, I should like to see their worm-eaten corpses on display
a year and more, for the edification of their fellows; then we may have
a little discipline again."

"Well, I shan't," Granby had answered, incautiously blunt after the
free-flowing wine, "and," he added to Laurence and Riley privately, afterwards, "I don't see as we have any business telling the colony they
shall have him back: it seems to me after a fellow has been mutinied
against three or four times, there is something to it besides bad luck."

"Then you shall take me aboard," Bligh said, scowling, when Riley
had also made his—more polite—refusal. "I will return with you to England, and there present the case directly; so far, I trust, you cannot
deny me," he asserted, with some truth: such a refusal would have been
most dangerous politically to Riley, whose position was less assured
than Granby's, and unprotected by any significant interest. But Bligh's
real intention, certainly, was to return not to England but to the colony,
in their company and under Riley's protection, with the power meanwhile of continuing his attempts at persuasion however long they
should remain there in port.

It was not to be supposed that Laurence could put himself at
Bligh's service, in that gentleman's present mood, without at once being
ordered to restore him to his office and to turn Temeraire upon the
rebels. If such a course might have served Laurence's self-interest, it
was wholly inimical to his every feeling. He had allowed himself and
Temeraire to be so used once, in the war—by Wellington, against the

French invaders, in Britain's greatest extremity; it had still left the blackest taste in his mouth, and he would never again so submit.

Yet equally, if Laurence put himself at the service of the New South Wales Corps, he became nearly an assistant to mutiny. It required no great political gifts to know this was of all accusations the one which he could least afford to sustain, and the one which would be most readily believed and seized upon by his enemies and Temeraire's, to deny them any hope of return.

"I do not see the difficulty; there is no reason why you should surrender to anyone," Temeraire said obstinately, when Laurence had in some anxiety raised the subject with him aboard ship as they made the trip from Van Diemen's Land to Sydney: the last leg of their long voyage, which Laurence formerly would have advanced with pleasure, and now with far more pleasure would have delayed. "We have done perfectly well all this time at sea, and we will do perfectly well now, even if a few tiresome people have been rude."

"Legally, I have been in Captain Riley's charge, and may remain so a little longer," Laurence answered. "But that cannot answer for very long: ordinarily he ought to discharge me to the authorities with the rest of the prisoners."

"Whyever must he? Riley is a sensible person," Temeraire said, "and if you must surrender to someone, he is certainly better than Bligh. I cannot like anyone who will insist on interrupting us at our reading, four times, only because he wishes to tell you yet again how wicked the colonists are and how much rum they drink: why that should be of any interest to anyone I am sure I do not know."

"My dear, Riley will not long remain with us," Laurence said. "A dragon transport cannot simply sit in harbor; this is the first time one has been spared to this part of the world, and that only to deliver us. When she has been scraped, and the mizzen topmast replaced, from that blow we had near the Cape, they will go; I am sure Riley expects fresh orders very nearly from the next ship into harbor behind us."

"Oh," Temeraire said, a little downcast, "and we will stay, I suppose."

"Yes," Laurence said, quietly. "—I am sorry."

And without transport, Temeraire would be quite truly a prisoner of their new situation: there were few ships, and none of merchant class, which could carry a dragon of Temeraire's size, and no flying route which could safely see him to any other part of the world. A light courier, built for endurance, perhaps might manage it in extremis with a well-informed navigator, clear weather, and luck, setting down on some deserted and rocky atolls for a rest; but the Aerial Corps did not risk even them on any regular mission to the colony, and Temeraire could never follow such a course without the utmost danger.

And Granby and Iskierka would go as well, when Riley did, to avoid a similar entrapment; leaving Temeraire quite isolated from his own kind, save for the three prospective hatchlings who were as yet an unknown quantity.

"Well, *that* is nothing to be sorry for," Temeraire said, rather darkly eyeing Iskierka, who at present was asleep and exhaling quantities of steam from her spikes upon his flank, which gathered into fat droplets and rolled off to soak the deck beneath him. "Not," he added, "that I would object to company; it would be pleasant to see Maximus again, and Lily, and I would like to know how Perscitia is getting on with her pavilion; but I am sure they will write to me when we are settled, and as for *her,* she may go away anytime she likes."

Laurence felt Temeraire might find it a heavier penalty than he yet knew. Yet the prospect of these miseries, which had heretofore on their journey greatly occupied his concerns, seemed petty in comparison to the disaster of the situation that now awaited them: trapped in the roles of convict and kingmaker both, and without any means of escape, save if they chose to sacrifice all intercourse with society and take themselves off into the wilderness.

"Pray do not worry, Laurence," Temeraire said stoutly. "I am sure we will find it a very interesting place, and anyway," he added, "at least there will be something nicer to eat."

Their reception, however, had if anything only given more credence to Bligh's representations, and Laurence's anxiety. The *Allegiance* could not be said to have crept up on the colony: she had entered the mouth of the harbor at eleven in the morning on a brilliantly clear day, with only the barest breath of wind to bring her along. After eight months at sea, all of them might have been pardoned for impatience, but no one could be immune to the almost shocking loveliness of the immense harbor: one bay after another curving off the main channel, and the thickly forested slopes running down to the water, interspersed with stretches of golden sand.

So Riley did not order out the boats for rowing, or even try to spread a little more sail; he let the men mostly hang along the rail, looking at the new country before them while the *Allegiance* stately glided among the smaller shipping like a great finwhale among clouds of baitfish. Nearly three hours of slow, clear sailing before they lowered the anchor, then, but still there was no welcome come to meet them.

"I will fire a salute, I suppose," Riley said, doubtfully; and the guns roared out. Many of the colonists in their dusty streets turned to look, but still no answer came, until after another two hours at last Riley put a boat over the side, and sent Lord Purbeck, his first lieutenant, ashore.

Purbeck returned shortly to report he had spoken with Major Johnston, the present chief of the New South Wales Corps, but that gentleman refused to come aboard so long as Bligh was present: the intelligence of Bligh's return had evidently reached Sydney in advance, likely by some smaller, quicker ship making the same passage from Van Diemen's Land.

"We had better go see him ourselves, then," Granby said, quite unconscious of the appalled looks Laurence and Riley directed at him, at the proposal that Riley, a Navy captain, should lower himself to call upon an Army major, who had behaved so outrageously and ungentlemanlike. Granby did not notice, but added, "It don't excuse him, but I would not have put it past that fellow Bligh to send word ahead himself that we were here to put him back in his place," sadly plausible; and to make matters worse, there was little alternative. Their stores were running low, and that was no small matter with the hold crammed full of convicts, and the deck weighted down with dragons.

Riley went stiffly, with a full complement of Marines, and invited Laurence and Granby both to accompany him. "It may not be regular, but neither is anything else about this damned mess," he said to Laurence, "and I am afraid you will need to get the measure of the fellow, more than any of us."

It was not long in coming: "If you mean to try and put that cowering snake over us again, I hope you are ready to stay, and swallow his brass with us," Johnston said, "for an you go away, we'll have him out again in a trice; for my part, I will answer for what I have done to anyone who has a right to ask, which isn't any of you."

These were the first words uttered, preceding even introduction, as soon as they had been shown into his presence: not into an office, but only the antechamber in the single long building which served for barracks and headquarters both.

"What that has to do with hailing a King's ship properly when it comes into harbor, I would like to know," Granby said heatedly, responding in kind, "and I don't care twopence for Bligh or you, either, until I have provision for my dragon; which you had better care about, too, unless you like her to help herself."

This exchange had not made the welcome grow particularly warmer: even apart from the suspicion of their assisting Bligh, Johnston was evidently uneasy for all his bluster, as well might he and his fellows be with their present arrangements, at once illegal and unsettled, with so long a silence from England. Laurence might have felt some sympathy for that unease, under other circumstances: the *Allegiance* and her dragon passengers came into the colony as an unknown factor, and with the power of disrupting all the established order.

But the first sight of the colony had already shocked him very much: in this beautiful and lush country, to find such a general sense of malaise and disorder, women and men staggering-drunk in the streets even before the sun had set, and for most of the inhabitants thin ramshackle huts and tents the only shelters. Even these were occupied irregularly: as they walked towards their unsatisfactory meeting, and passed one such establishment with no door whatsoever, Laurence glanced and was very shocked to see within a man and a woman copulating energetically, he still half in military uniform, while another man snored sodden upon the floor and a child sat dirty and snuffling in the corner.

More distressing still was the bloody human wreckage on display at the military headquarters, where an enthusiastic flogger seemed to scarcely pause between his customers, a line of men shackled and sullen, waiting for fifty lashes or a hundred—evidently their idea here of light punishment.

"If I would not soon have a mutiny of my own," Riley said, half under his breath, as they returned to the *Allegiance,* "I would not let my men come ashore here for anything; Sodom and Gomorrah are nothing to it."

Three subsequent weeks in the colony had done very little to improve Laurence's opinion of its present or its former management. There was nothing in Bligh himself which could be found sympathetic: in language and manner he was abrupt and abrasive, and where his attempts to assert authority were balked, he turned instead to a campaign of ill-managed cajolery, equal parts insincere flattery and irritated outbursts, which did little to conceal his private conviction of his absolute righteousness.

But this was worse than any ordinary mutiny: he had been the royal governor, and the very soldiers responsible for carrying out his orders had betrayed him. Riley and Granby continuing obdurate, and likely soon to be gone, Bligh had fixed upon Laurence as his most promising avenue of appeal, and refused to be deterred; daily now he would harangue Laurence on the ill-management of the colony, the certain evils flowing from permitting such an illegitimate arrangement to continue.

"Have Temeraire throw him overboard," Tharkay had suggested laconically, when Laurence had escaped to his quarters for a little relief and piquet, despite the nearly stifling heat belowdecks: the open window let in only a still-hotter breeze. "He can fish him out again after," he added, as an afterthought.

"I very much doubt if anything so mild as ocean water would prove effective at dousing that gentleman's ardor for any prolonged time," Laurence said, indulging from temper in a little sarcasm: Bligh had gone so far today as to overtly speak of his right, if restored, to grant full pardon, and Laurence had been forced to quit him mid-sentence to avoid taking insult at this species of attempted bribery. "It might nearly be easier," he added more tiredly, the moment of heat past, "if I did not find some justice in his accusations."

For the evils of the colony's arrangements were very great, even witnessed at the remove of their shipboard life. Laurence had understood that the convicts were generally given sentences of labor, which being accomplished without further instance of disorder yielded their emancipation and the right to a grant of land: a thoughtful design envisioned by the first governor, intended to render them and the country both settled. But over the course of the subsequent two decades, this had remained little more than a design, and in practice nearly all the men of property were the officers of the New South Wales Corps or their former fellows.

The convicts at best they used as cheap labor; at worst, as chattel. Without prospects or connections to make them either interested in their future or ashamed of their behavior, and trapped in a country that was a prison which needed no walls, the convicts were easily bribed to both labor and their own pacification with cheap rum, brought in at a handsome profit by the soldiers, and in such a way those who ought to have enforced order instead contributed to its decay, with no care for the disorder and self-destruction they thus engendered.

"Or at least, so Bligh has argued, incessantly, and everything which I have seen bears him out," Laurence said. "But Tenzing, I cannot trust myself; I fear that I *wish* the complaints to be just, rather than *know* they are so. I am sorry to say it would be convenient to have an excuse to restore him."

"There is capot, I am afraid," Tharkay said, putting down his last card. "If you insist on achieving justice and not only convenience, you would learn more from speaking with some local citizen, a settled man, with nothing to complain of in his treatment on either side."

"If such a man is to be found, I can see no reason he would willingly confide his opinion, in so delicate a matter," Laurence said, throwing in, and gathering the cards up to sort out afresh.

"I have letters of introduction to some few of the local factors," Tharkay said, a piece of news to Laurence, who wondered; so far as he knew, Tharkay had come to New South Wales merely to indulge an inveterate wanderlust; but of course he could not intrude upon Tharkay's privacy with a direct question.

"If you like," Tharkay had continued, "I can make inquiries; and as for reason, if there is discontent enough to form the grounds for your decision, I would imagine that same discontent sufficient motive to speak."

The attempt to pursue this excellent advice now having ended in public ignominy, however, Bligh was only too eager to take advantage and press Laurence further for action. "Dogs, Captain Laurence, dogs and cowardly sheep, all of them," Bligh said, ignoring yet again Laurence's attempt to correct his address to *Mr. Laurence;* it would suit Bligh better, Laurence in exasperation supposed, to be restored by a military officer, and not a private citizen.

Bligh contined, "I imagine you can hardly disagree with me now. It is impossible you should disagree with me. It is the direct consequence of their outrageous usurpation of the King's authority. What respect,

what discipline, can possibly be maintained under a leadership so
wholly devoid of just and legal foundation, so utterly lost to loyalty
and—"

Here Bligh paused, perhaps reconsidering an appeal to the virtues
of obedience, in the light of Laurence's reputation; throwing his tiller
over, however, Bligh without losing much time said instead, "—and to
decency; allow me to assure you this infamous kind of behavior is general throughout the military ranks of the colony, indulged and indeed
encouraged by their leaders."

Fatigue and a soreness at once physical and of the spirit had by
now cut Laurence's temper short: he had endured dinner in increasing
discomfort, his ribs grown swollen and very tender beneath the
makeshift bandage; his hands ached a great deal, and what was worse,
to no purpose: nothing gained but a sense of disgust. He was very willing to think ill of the colony's leadership, of Johnston and MacArthur,
but Bligh had not recommended himself, and his nearly gleeful satisfaction was too crassly, too visibly opportunistic.

Laurence put down his coffee-cup with some force on the steward's
tray. "I must wonder, sir," he said, "how you would expect to govern,
when you should be forced to rely upon those same soldiers whom you
presently so disdain; having removed their ringleaders, who have preferred them to an extreme and given them so much license, how would
you conciliate their loyalty, having been restored at the hands of one
whom they already see as an outlaw?"

"Oh! You give too much credit," Bligh said, dismissively, "to their
loyalty, and too little to their sense; they must know, of course, that
MacArthur and Johnston are doomed. The length of the sea-voyage,
the troubles in England, these alone have preserved them; but the hang-
man's noose waits for them both, and as the time draws near, the advantages of their preferment lose their luster. Some reassurances—some
concessions—of course they may keep their land grants, and those ap-
pointments not made too ill may remain—"

He made a few more general remarks of this sort, with no better
course of action envisioned on Bligh's part, so far as Laurence could
see, than to levy a series of new but only cosmetic restrictions, which
should certainly only inflame men irritated by the overthrow, by an
outsider and an enemy, of their tolerated if not necessarily chosen leadership.

"Then I hardly see," Laurence said, not very politely, "precisely how you would repair these evils you condemn, which I cannot see were amended during your first administration; nor is Temeraire, as you seem to imagine, some sort of magical cannon which may be turned on anyone you like."

"If with this collection of mealy-mouthed objections you will excuse yourself from obliging me, Mr. Laurence," Bligh answered, deep color spotting in the hollows of his cheeks, "I must count it another disappointment, and mark it against your character, such as that is," this with an acrid and unpleasant edge; and he left the quarterdeck with his lips pressed tight and angry.

If Bligh followed in his usual mode, however, he would soon repent of his hasty words and seek another interview; Laurence knew it very well, and his feelings were sufficiently lacerated already that he did not care to be forced to endure the pretense of an apology, undoubtedly to be followed by a fresh renewal of those same arguments he had already heard and rejected.

He had meant to sleep aboard the ship, whose atmosphere had been greatly improved: the convicts having been delivered to the dubious embrace of the colony, Riley had set every one of his men to pumping the lower decks clean, sluicing out the filth and miasm left by several hundred men and women who had been afforded only the barest minimum of exercise and liberty essential to health. Smudges of smoke had been arranged throughout, and then a fresh round of pumping undertaken.

With the physical contamination and the hovering and perpetual aura of misery thus erased, Laurence's small quarters now made a comfortable if not luxurious residence by his standards, formed in his youth by the dimensions of a midshipman's cot. Meanwhile the small shelter on the dragons' promontory remained unroofed and as yet lacked its final wall, but Laurence felt bruised more in spirit than in body, and the weather held dry; he went below only to collect a few articles, and quitted the ship to seek refuge in Temeraire's company.

In this mood, he was by no means prepared to be accosted on the track back up to the promontory by a gentleman on horseback, of aquiline face and by the standards of the colony elegantly dressed, who leaned from his horse and demanded, "Am I speaking with Mr. Laurence?"

"You have the advantage of me," Laurence said, a little rudely in his own turn; but he was not inclined to regret his curtness when the man said, "I am John MacArthur; I should like a word."

There was little question he was the architect of the entire rebellion; and though he had arranged to be appointed Colonial Secretary, he had so far not even given Riley the courtesy of a call. "You choose odd circumstances for your request, sir," Laurence said, "and I do not propose to stand speaking in the dust of the street. You are welcome to accompany me to the covert, if you like; although I would advise you to leave your horse."

He was a little surprised to find MacArthur willing to hand his reins to the groom, and dismount to walk with him. "I hear you had a little difficulty in the town to-day," MacArthur said. "—I am very sorry it should have happened.

"You must know, Mr. Laurence, we have had a light hand on the rein here; a light hand, and it has answered beautifully, beyond all reasonable hopes. Our colony does not show to advantage, you may perhaps think, coming from London; but I wonder what you would think if you had been here in our first few years. I came in the year 'ninety; will you credit it, that there were not a thousand acres under cultivation, and no supply? We nearly starved, one and all, three times."

He stopped and held out a hand, which trembled a little. "They have been so, since that first winter," he said, and resumed walking.

"Your perseverance is to be admired," Laurence said, "and that of your fellows."

"If nothing else, that for certain sure," MacArthur said. "But it has not been by chance, or any easy road, that we have found success; only through the foresight of wise leadership and the strength of determined men. This is a country for a determined man, Mr. Laurence. I came here a lieutenant, with not a lick of property to my name; now I have ten thousand acres. I do not brag," he added. "Any man can do here what I have done. This is a fine country."

There was an emphasis on *any man,* which Laurence found distasteful in the extreme; he read the slinking bribery in MacArthur's pretty speech as easily as he had in Bligh's whispers of pardon, and he pressed his lips together and stretched his pace.

MacArthur perceived his mistake, perhaps; he increased his own to match and said, to shift the subject, "But what does Government send us? You have been a Navy officer yourself, Mr. Laurence; you have had the dregs of the prison-hulks pressed into service; you know what I am speaking of. Such men are not formed for respectability. They can only be used, and managed, and to do it requires rum and the lash—it is the very understanding of the service. I am afraid it has made us all a little coarse here, however; we are ill-served by the proportion of our numbers. I wonder how you would have liked a crew of a hundred, five and ninety of them gaol-birds, and not five able seamen to your name."

"Sir, you are correct in this much: I have had a little difficulty, earlier in the day," Laurence said, pausing in the road; his ribs ached sharply in his side, "so I will be frank; you might have had conversation of myself, or of Captain Riley or Captain Granby, as it pleased you, these last three weeks, for the courtesy of a request. May I ask you to be a little more brief?"

"Your reproach is a just one," MacArthur said, "and I will not tire you further to-night; if you will do me the kindness of returning my visit in the morning at the barracks?"

"Forgive me," Laurence said dryly, "but I find I am not presently inclined to pay calls in this society; as yet I find the courtesies beyond my grasp."

"Then perhaps I may pay you another call," MacArthur suggested, if with slightly pressed lips, and to this Laurence could only incline his head.

"I cannot look forward to the visit with any pleasure," Laurence said, "but if he comes, we ought to receive him."

"So long as he is not insulting, and does not try to put you in a quarry, he may come, if he likes," Temeraire said, making a concession, while privately determining he would keep a very close eye upon this MacArthur person; for his own part, he saw no reason to offer any courtesy at all to someone who was master of a place so wretchedly organized, and acquainted with so many ill-mannered people. Governor Bligh was not a very pleasant person, perhaps, but at least he did not seem to think it in the ordinary course of things for gentlemen to be knocked down in the street in mysterious accidents.

MacArthur did come, shortly after they had breakfasted. He drew up rather abruptly, reaching the top of the hill; Laurence had not yet seen him, but Temeraire had been looking over at the town—sixteen sheep were being driven into a pen, very handsome sheep—and he saw MacArthur pause, and halt, and look as though he might go away again.

Temeraire might have let him do so, and had a quiet morning of reading, but he had not enjoyed his meal and in a peevish humor said, "In my opinion it is quite rude to come into someone's residence only to stare at them, and turn pale, and go, as if there were something peculiar in them, and not in such absurd behavior. I do not know why you bothered to climb the hill at all, if you are such a great coward; it is not as though you did not know that I was here."

"Why, in my opinion, you are a great rascal," MacArthur said, purpling up his neck. "What do you mean by calling me a coward, because I need to catch my breath."

"Stuff," Temeraire said roundly, "you were frightened."

"I do not say that a man hasn't a right to be taken aback a moment, when he sees a beast the size of a frigate waiting to eat him," MacArthur said, "but I am damned if I will swallow this; you do not see me running away, do you?"

"I would not eat a person," Temeraire said, revolted, "and you needn't be disgusting, even if you do have no manners," to which Laurence coming around said, "So spake the pot," rather dryly.

He added, "Will you come and sit down, Mr. MacArthur? I regret I cannot offer you anything better than coffee or chocolate, and I must advise against the coffee," and Temeraire rather regretfully saw he had missed the opportunity to be rid of this unpleasant visitor.

MacArthur kept turning his head, to look at Temeraire, and remarked, "They don't look so big, from below," as he stirred his chocolate so many times it must have grown quite cold. Temeraire was quite fond of chocolate, but he could not have that, either; not properly, without enough milk, and the expense so dear; it was not worth only having the tiniest taste, which only made one want more. He sighed.

"Quite prodigious," MacArthur repeated, looking at Temeraire again. "He must take a great deal of feeding."

"We are managing," Laurence said politely. "The game is conveniently plentiful, and they do not seem to be used to being hunted from aloft."

Temeraire considered that if MacArthur was here, he might at least be of some use. "Is there anything else to hunt, nearby?" he inquired.

"Not of course," he added untruthfully, "that anyone could complain of kangaroo."

"I am surprised if you have found any of those in twenty miles as the crow goes," MacArthur said. "We pretty near et up the lot, in the first few years."

"Well, we have been getting them around the Nepean River, and in the mountains," Temeraire said, and MacArthur's head jerked up from his cup so abruptly that the spoon he had left inside it tipped over and spattered his white breeches with chocolate.

He did not seem to notice that he had made a sad mull of his clothing, but said thoughtfully, "The Blue Mountains? Why, I suppose you can fly all over them, can't you?"

"We *have* flown all over them," Temeraire said, rather despondently, "and there is nothing but kangaroo, and those rabbits that have no ears, which are too small to be worth eating."

"I would have been glad of a wombat or a dozen often enough, myself," MacArthur said, "but it is true we do not have proper game in this country, I am sorry to say I know from experience: too lean by half; you cannot keep up to fighting-weight on it, and there is not enough grazing yet for cattle. We have not found a way through the mountains, you know," he added. "We are quite hemmed in."

"It is a pity no-one has tried keeping elephants," Temeraire said.

"Ha ha, keeping elephants, very good," MacArthur said, as if this were some sort of a joke. "Do elephants make good eating?"

"Excellently good," Temeraire said. "I have not had an elephant since we were in Africa: I do not think I have tasted anything quite so good as a properly cooked elephant; outside of China, that is," he added loyally, "where I do not think they can raise them. But it seems as though this would be perfectly good country for them: it is certainly as hot as ever it was in Africa, where they raised them. Anyway we will need more food for the hatchlings, soon."

"Well, I have brought sheep, but I did not much think of bringing over elephants," MacArthur said, looking at the three eggs with an altered expression. "How much would a dragon eat, do you suppose, in the way of cattle?"

"Maximus will eat two cows when he can get them, in a day," Temeraire said, "but I do not think that is very healthy; I would not eat more than one, unless of course I have been fighting, or flying far; or if I were very particularly hungry."

"Two cows a day, and soon to be five of you?" MacArthur said. "The Lord safe preserve us."

"If this has brought you to a better understanding of the necessity of addressing the situation, sir," Laurence said, rather pointedly Temeraire thought, "I must be grateful for your visit; we have had very little cooperation heretofore in making our arrangements from Major Johnston."

MacArthur put down his chocolate-cup. "I was speaking last night, I think," he said, "of what a man can make of himself, in this country; it is a subject dear to my heart, and I hope I did not ramble on it too long. It is a hard thing, you will understand, Mr. Laurence, to see a country like this: begging for hands, for the plowshare and the till, and no-one to work it but an army of the worst slackabouts born of woman lying about, complaining if they are given less than their day's half-gallon of rum, and they would take it at ten in the morning, if they could get it.

"In the Corps, we may not be very pretty, but we know how to work; I believe the Aerial Corps, too, might be given such a character by some," MacArthur went on. "And we know how to make men work. Whatever has been built in this country, we ha'e built it, and to have a—perhaps I had better hold my tongue; I think you have been shipmates with Governor Bligh?"

"I would not say we were *shipmates*," Temeraire put in; he did not care to be saddled with such a relationship. "He came aboard our ship, but no-one much wanted him; only one must be polite."

Laurence looked a bit rueful, and MacArthur, smiling, said, "Well, I won't say anything against the gentleman, only perhaps he was no too fond of our ways. The which," he added, "certainly can be improved upon, Mr. Laurence, I do not deny it; but no man likes to be corrected by come-lately."

"When come-lately is sent by the King," Laurence said, "one may dislike, and yet endure."

"Very good sense; but good sense has limits, sir, limits," MacArthur said, "where it comes up hard against honor: some things a man of courage cannot bear, and damn the consequences."

Laurence did not say anything; Laurence was quite silent. After a moment, MacArthur added, "I do not mean to make you excuses: I have sent my eldest on to England, though I could spare him ill, and he must make my case to their Lordships. But I will tell you, I do not tremble, sir, for fear of the answer; I sleep the night through."

Temeraire became conscious gradually, while he spoke, of being poked; Emily was at his side, tugging energetically on his wing-tip. "Temeraire!" she hissed up to him. "I oughtn't go right up with that fellow there, he is sure to see I am a girl; but we must tell the captain, there is a ship come from England—"

"I see her!" Temeraire answered, looking over into the harbor: a trim, handsome little frigate of perhaps twenty-four guns: she was drawn up not far from the *Allegiance,* riding easily at anchor. "Laurence," he said, leaning over, "there is a ship come from England, Roland says: it is the *Beatrice,* I think."

MacArthur stopped speaking, abruptly.

Emily tugged again. "That is not the news," she said, impatient. "Captain Rankin is on it."

"Oh! whyever should *he* have come?" Temeraire said, his ruff pricking up. "Is he a convict?" Without waiting for an answer, he turned his head to the other side. "And Roland says that Rankin is here, on the ship: that dreadful fellow from Loch Laggan. You may certainly put *him* in a quarry," he added to MacArthur. "I cannot think of anyone who deserves it more, the way he treated poor Levitas."

"Oh, why won't you listen," Roland cried. "He ain't a convict at all; he has come for one of the eggs."

Chapter 3

"OWING TO THE MODE of our last communication, it is quite impossible Mr. Laurence and I should have any intercourse. —I hope I may not be thought difficult," Rankin said, his crisp and aristocratic vowels carrying quite clearly, over the deck of the *Allegiance*; his transport the *Beatrice* had already gone away again, with no more news for the colony: she had left only two months after the *Allegiance* herself, and the news of the rebellion had not yet reached Government. "But it is generally accepted, I believe, that the dragondeck is reserved for officers of the Corps; and if the gentleman is quartered towards the stern, I see no reason why any inconvenient scenes should arise."

"I see no reason why I shouldn't push his nose in for him," Granby said, under his breath, joining Laurence on the leeward side of the quarterdeck, where passengers were ordinarily allowed liberty. "The worst of it," he added, "is I can't see any way clear to refusing him: the orders are plain black on white, he is to be put to Wringe's egg. What a damned waste."

Laurence nodded a little; he, too, had had a letter, if not in an official capacity. . . . *though nothing would I like better than if he should get himself sunk in the Ocean on his way to you*, Jane had written.

> *. . . but his damnd Family have been squalling at their Lordships for nigh on Five Years now, and he had the infernal Bad Luck—mine, that is—of finding himself in Scotland, lately, when we were so overset: went up with one of the Ferals out of Arkady's pack, saw a little fighting, and mannaged to get himself wounded again.*
>
> *So I must give him a Beast, or at least a Chance of one,*

*and Someone must put up with him thereafter; as I am about
to have twenty-six hatchlings to feed and likely enough a War
in Spain, I don't scruple to say, Better You Than Me.*

This last was emphatically full of capitals, and underlined.

*I have made the Excuse, that this is the first Egg we have
had out of the Ferals, and his having Experience of them in
the field, should be an Advantage in its Training.*

*I was tolrably transparent, I think, but a Title does
wonderful things, Laurence: I should have contrivved one
much sooner if I had known its Use. Gentlemen who swore at
me like fishwives sixmonth ago are become sweet as milk, all
because the Regent has signed some scrap of paper for me,
and nod their Heads and say Yes, Very Good, when before
they would have argued to Doomsday if I should say, It is
coming on to rain. Also it is a great benefit they none of them
know whether to say Milady or Sir, and as soon as they have
arrived at a Decision, they change it again. I only hope they
may not make me a Duchess to make themselves easy by
saying Your Grace; it would not suit half so well.*

*I am very obligd to your Mother, by the bye: she wrote,
when she saw my name had come out in Debrett's—as
J. Roland, very discreet—and had me to a nice, sociable little
Dinner, with every Cabinet Minister she could contrive to lay
hands on, I gather: all very shocked, as they had brought their
Wives, but they could not say so much as Boo with Her
Ladyship at the foot of the Table as if Butter would not Melt
in her mouth, and the Ladies did not mind inn the Least,
when they understood I was an Officer, and not some
Vauxhall Comedienne. I found them sensible Creatures all of
them, and I think perhaps I have got quite the wrong Notion
about them, as a Class; I expect I ought to be cultivating
them. I don't mind Society half so much if I may wear
Trousers, and they were very kind, and left me their Cards.*

*We are trundling along well enough otherwise and getting
back into some Order: feeding dragons on Mash and Mutton
Stew is a damn'd site cheaper, Thank God, if the older ones
do complain; Excidium is all Sighs and loud Reminiscences of*

fresh Cattle, and Temeraire's name is not much lov'd among them, for having given us the Technique.

I will say a word in your Ear for him: I am uneasy about this Business in Spain. Bonaparte ain't a Fool, and why he should wreck a dozen cities, on the southern Coast, fresh from the ruin of his Invasion, I cannot understand. Mulgrave thinks he means to take Spain and to stop us from supplying them from the Sea, but for that, he ought to be burning them in Portugal, instead.

If Temeraire should think it some Stratagem of Lien's, I would be glad to know of it, even late as the Intelligence must come: it is very strange to think, Laurence, that I cannot hope for an Answer in under ten Months and a year and a half the more likely. Now we have lost the Capetown port to those African fellows, the couriers cannot even go to India, and meet your letter halfway.

For Consolation, if you should find yourself overcome with Passion and happen to accidentally drop Rankin down a Cliff, or by some Mischance run him through, at least I will not hear of it for as long, and anyway you are already transportd, which I must call a great Convenience for Murder. But I do not mean to Hint, although it is a great Pity to waste an Egg upon him, even one of our poor unwanted Stepchildren.

I hope Emily has not got into too many Scrapes; tho she cannot officially be your Ensign, I am sure you will oblige me by keeping her from any really reckless Behaviour, and do not let Rankin come the Scrub over her, if he have the Gall: I have seen enough to know he is just the sort of Rotter who would try off Airs of False Pity for her Sacrifice and other non Sense.

The three eggs which had been sent with them to begin the experiment were not, by the lights of Britain's breeders, any great prizes: one a dirt-common Yellow Reaper, sent over because there were seventeen such eggs in the breeding grounds waiting; the second a disappointing and extremely stunted little thing which had unaccountably been produced out of a Parnassian and a Chequered Nettle, both heavyweights. The last and most promising of the three, large and handsomely mottled and striated, was the offspring of Arkady, the feral leader, and Wringe, the best fighter of his pack.

There was no great enthusiasm for this egg in Britain, where the breeders for the most part viewed the newly recruited ferals as demons sent to wreak havoc and destruction upon their carefully designed lines; so it had been sent away. But it had quickly become the settled thing among the aviators who had been sent along as candidates for the new hatchlings to anticipate great things of the egg. "It stands to reason," Laurence had overheard more than one officer say to another, "if that Wringe one should have got so big out in the wild, this one should do a good deal better with proper feeding, and training; and no one could complain of the ferals' fighting spirit."

Those young officers were now in something of a quandary, which Laurence was not above grimly enjoying, a little: they had been firm and united in their disdain, both for his personal treason and for what they saw as his failure to manage Temeraire properly. But now Rankin had come to supplant one of them, and claim the best egg for himself; he was their most bitter enemy, and Temeraire's recalcitrance their best hope of denying him.

"He mayn't have it at all," Temeraire had said at once, when he had been informed of the proposed arrangement, "and if he likes, he can come up here and try and take it; I should be very pleased to discuss it with him," darkly, in a way which bade fair to answer all of Jane's hopes.

"My dear," Laurence said, having lowered his letter, "I like the prospect as little as you; but if he should be denied even the chance, and return to England thwarted, we have only deferred the evil: he will certainly be put to another egg, there, where you may be certain the poor hatchling will have less opportunity to refuse. And the blame will certainly devolve upon Granby: the orders are for him, and the responsibility to carry them out."

"I am certainly not having Granby take the blame for anything," Iskierka said, raising her head, "and I do not see what the problem is, anyway; the egg will be hatched, by then, and why should it be any business of ours what it does after that? It can take him or not, as it pleases."

Iskierka herself had hatched already breathing fire, and with all the disobliging and determined character anyone could have imagined; she would certainly have had no difficulty in rejecting any unworthy candidate. Most hatchlings did not come from the shell with quite the same mettle, however, and the Aerial Corps had developed many a technique and lure to ensure the successful harnessing of the beasts. Rankin had certainly prepared himself well: he had come over from the *Beatrice* with not only his two chests of personal baggage, but a pile of leather harness, some chainmail netting, and a sort of heavy leather hood.

"You throw it over the hatchling's head as it comes out of the shell, if you are out of doors," Granby said, when Laurence now inquired, "and then it cannot fly away; when you take it off, the light dazzles their eyes, and then if you lay some meat in front of them, they are pretty sure to let you put the harness on, if you will only let them eat. And some fellows like it, because they say it makes them easier to handle; if you ask me," he added, bitterly, "all it makes them is shy: they are never certain of their ground, after."

"I wonder if you might be able to put me in the way of some cattle-merchant," Rankin was saying, to Riley and Lord Purbeck. "I intend to provide for the hatchling's first meal from my personal funds."

"Surely he can be restrained in some way," Laurence said, low. He was not yet beyond the heat of righteous anger kindled all those years before, when they had been unwilling witness to the cruelty of Rankin's treatment of his first dragon. Rankin was the sort of aviator beloved of the Navy Board: in his estimation as in theirs, dragons were merely a resource and a dangerous one, to be managed and restrained and used to their limits; it was the same philosophy which had rendered it not only tolerable but desirable to contemplate destroying ten thousand of the French beasts through the underhanded sneaking method of infection.

Where Rankin might have been kind to Levitas, he had been indifferent; where indifferent, deliberately cruel, all in the name of keeping his poor beast so downtrodden as to have no spirit to object to any demands made upon him. When Levitas had with desperate courage brought them back the warning of Napoleon's first attempt to cross the Channel, in the year 'five, and been mortally wounded in that effort, Rankin had left his dragon alone and slowly dying in a small and miserable clearing, while he sought comfort for his own lesser injuries.

It was a mode of service which had gone thoroughly out of fashion in the last century among most aviators, who increasingly preferred to better preserve the spirit of their partners; the Government did not always agree, however, and Rankin was of an ancient dragon-keeping family, who had preserved their own habits and methods and passed these along to the scions sent into the Corps, at an age sufficiently delayed for these to be impressed upon them firmly, along with a conviction of their own superiority to the general run of aviators.

"He cannot be permitted to ruin the creature," Laurence said. "We might at least bar him from use of the hood—"

"Interfere with a hatching?" Granby cried, looking at Laurence sidelong and dismayed. "No: he has a right to make the best go of it he can, however he likes. Though if he can't manage it in fifteen minutes, someone else can have a try," he added, an attempt at consolation, "and you may be sure fifteen minutes is all the time he will have; that is all I can do."

"That is not all that *I* can do," Temeraire said, mantling, "and I am not going to sit about letting him throw nets and chains and hoods on the hatchling: I do not care if it is not in the shell anymore. In my opinion, it is still quite *near* being an egg."

He realized this was an irregular way of looking at the matter, but after all, if the hatchling had not yet eaten anything, and if perhaps a bit of egg were still stuck to its hide, one could not be *sure* that it was ready to manage on its own, and so it was still one's responsibility. "Anyway," he added, "I do not like him at all, and I don't see that he has any right to be a captain again; just let him try and come here, and I will knock him down for it."

"You are not doing anything which Granby would not like!" Iskierka said, jetting out a bit of steam.

"As though you had anything to say to it," Temeraire said, coolly. "Anyway, you do things which Granby does not like every day."

"Only," Iskierka said, "when it is particularly important," a monstrous lie, "and anyway, that is quite different. You might think of Granby, since you are always on about how I do not take proper care of him: I am not having *him* made not a captain, like you have done with Laurence, only because you are being absurd again and worrying about hatched dragons," she added, which thrust hit home quite successfully; Temeraire flinched involuntarily, and put back his ruff.

"Why," Iskierka continued, "I have seen this Rankin person: he is smaller than a pony, even. I could have burnt him up to a cinder as soon as I cracked the shell."

"If he wanted *you*," Temeraire said, "he might have you, and welcome," but this was only a feeble bit of quarreling, and not really a just argument; he put his head down and stared at the eggs unhappily.

"And," he said to Laurence, a little later, "if the egg does not take him, I suppose he will want to try the second, and then the third; I am sure he will not just go, when he has come all this way where no-one wants him, only to be difficult."

"Only to have another dragon; but so far as that goes, I am afraid you may be right," Laurence said, low. "But there is not much we can do about it, my dear, if we do not care to put Granby in a very awkward position; and make our own the worse. The eggs are not formally in our care at all, but his."

"But Arkady charged me with *his*," Temeraire said, "and I gave my word; surely that makes me interested."

Laurence paused and agreed somberly, "That does put another complexion on the matter," but it did not offer any other solution, except squashing Rankin, which would have been quite unfair, as a matter of relative size, and which Laurence insisted was not to be contemplated, despite Admiral Roland's letter.

Laurence did not dissuade Temeraire with much enthusiasm; he would not have greatly minded Rankin's being squashed under other circumstances, and the present situation would have rendered the event not only painless but highly desirable. His sentiments in the matter were only the more exacerbated the following morning, when Riley called upon them: Laurence had preferred to pass another irregular night up on the promontory in his small tent, still more comfortable a berth than remaining aboard ship, when he now must be careful only to visit the quarterdeck, and not go forward.

For Rankin was of course perfectly correct in the point of etiquette, and they were both barred from the field of honor, which was the only other suitable redress Rankin could have demanded for Laurence's actions in their last meeting. Laurence could not be sorry in the least for having handled Rankin so violently, but neither could he force himself into Rankin's presence, nor pursue the quarrel to which Rankin could not make answer, and retain any pretensions to the character of a gentleman.

"And I cannot blame you for it, either," Riley said, "but it left me in an awkward position. I had to have him to dinner, and Bligh, too, or look rather shabby; and I am wretchedly sorry, Laurence: is this egg likely to be something out of the common way? Because what must the cawker do ten minutes after we are at table but declare Bligh has been monstrous used by a pack of mutinous dogs, and it ought not be borne."

"Oh, damn him," Laurence said, unguarded in savage exasperation. "No, Tom, so far as the egg goes; not if you mean of an order to pick a quarrel with Temeraire; but that has nothing to do with the case. We cannot set upon a British dragon, if it is as small as a Winchester. Are we to have a pitched battle in the harbor? I cannot conceive what he is thinking."

"Oh, I will tell you *that,*" Riley said. "He is thinking he means to have the beast, will-you, nill-you. I beg you to imagine how our passenger took it: Bligh at once informed me he considers it my duty to ensure the Admiralty's orders as regards the egg are carried out; and that he will be sure to write their Lordships to express his opinion, and convey that he has made me so aware."

And the very last thing desirable to Riley at the present date was any suggestion of disobedience or recalcitrance, and all the more so if there were any sign it should be provoked by Laurence or even amenable to him. Their connection had already injured Riley's credit with their Lordships to a severe extent, and he served now, as did all Laurence's former associates, under a veil of suspicion. Bligh might not carry his point so far as his re-establishment in the colony, and his ill-management might invite the scorn rather than the sympathy of the Admiralty; that did not mean the Navy Board would not accept with the other hand any charges Bligh laid at Riley's door.

All the more so, Laurence knew, that they had been given fresh cause to regard Temeraire, and any personage even remotely associated with him, with suspicion: Temeraire had received a letter also, in the post carried by the *Beatrice;* from Perscitia, who had evidently somehow acquired a scribe.

We have finished the Pavilion already—

"Oh!" Temeraire said sadly, "and I am not there to see it."

—and begun on a second; we were puzzled where we should get the funds, as it is amazing how quickly Money goes. The Government tried to persuade us all to go back to the Breeding Grounds and leave off building: when we were almost quite finished, if you can imagine it. So the promised Supply has been very late and slow, and when they do send us any Cattle they are thin and not tasty, so we have had to buy Food of our own, and it is very dear at present; also Requiescat will eat like A Glutton, of course.

But we contrived: Majestatis suggested we should send Lloyd to Dover, to inquire after carting work, and we have worked out that men will pay a great deal just for us to carry things to London, and other Towns, as we can do it much more quickly than Horses; and I have worked out a very nice Method by which one can calculate the most efficient Way to go among all of them, taking on some goods and leaving off others; only it grows quite tiresome to calculate if one wishes to go to more than five or six Places.

There was a little noise about our coming and going— nobody much minded when it was just the Winchesters, or even the Reapers; but of course, Requiescat can carry so very much more—even if he is too lazy to go further than Dover to London and back—and Ballista and Majestatis and the other Heavy-weights, and after all, it is not as though we do not fit into the Coverts, so we really saw no reason they should not go, too. But then Government grew upset—when they might have given us proper Food, to begin with, and we should never have needed to trouble ourselves!—and they tried to make a Quarrel, and set some harnessed dragons in the Covert and told them to keep us out of it.

They were out of Scotland, I think; we did not know them, particularly, but Ballista said to them it was no sense squabbling over something so silly: for look, the Government had just put them in the Covert, because they did not want us in the Covert, even though they were just as big; and anyway there was plenty of Room, and we were only passing through. They all thought that was quite sensible, once she gave them a

*few of our Cows to be friendly; it seems Cows are very dear
in the coverts, too, and nobody gets them very often anymore,
even the harnessed beasts.*

There was besides this communiqué a good deal of gossip about
the relations among the dragons, which Laurence read to Temeraire
only half-attending; between Perscitia's lines he could easily read the
frantic reports racing through Whitehall: unharnessed heavy-weights
descending as they wished into every great city of Britain, terrifying the
populace and wrecking the business of ordinary carters to boot; and
bribing their harnessed fellows with the greatest of ease, despite all the
certain persuasions and efforts of those dragons' captains.

"That is a great pity about Gladius and Cantarella having a falling-
out," Temeraire said, "for I was sure they would have made a splendid
egg; also I do not like Queritoris very much, for he was always making
a fuss about carrying soldiers, when we all had to do it; so very tiresome, for everyone, but complaining did not make it any better. Laurence, do you suppose we might carry things for people, here, and so be
paid? Only, no," he interrupted his own thought, rather downcast,
"for there is only this one town, and no other to carry things to; how I
wish we were home!"

Laurence had wished it, too, but silently folded away the letter
which killed his hopes of return aborning; it yet crackled in his coat
pocket now, as he answered Riley, "I am sorry you should have had the
unpleasantness of his threats; we will of course not ask you to interfere,
Tom; nor, I hope, put you in any awkward position."

"Well, I hope I am not so much a scrub as to come here and ask
you out of the side of my mouth to have a care, for my own sake,"
Riley said. "I am pretty well found in prize-money, after all, and if I am
set ashore, at least I can take my little fellow home, and not worry my
life away wondering what absurd thing Catherine is doing with him."
This, a little bitterly: he had *not* received a letter from Captain Harcourt.

"But this could easily grow to be a more serious matter than a mere
quarrel," Laurence said soberly to Temeraire, after Riley had left, "if
Bligh chooses to make it a charge of disobedience, and their Lordships
pleased to have an excuse for a court-martial; I can easily imagine it."

"I can, too," Temeraire said, "and I am sure we oughtn't let him
hurt Riley, or Granby, either; but we cannot let Rankin hurt the egg,

either. Laurence, I have made Roland and Demane bring the egg out, just long enough so I might look at it, and I think it is going to hatch very soon; can we not take it away?"

"Away?" Laurence said; there was nowhere to go.

"Oh, into the countryside," Temeraire said, "only until it has hatched, I mean; and then we can come back again, and it may choose among the officers if it likes. Or if you thought better," he added, "we might take one or two of the best of them, instead, so it might choose among them directly: but no-one who would mean to try and use a *hood,* or a *net.*"

It was a scheme which Laurence ought at once have rejected, but he surprised himself by thinking soberly that so blatant a maneuver would, at least, be a stroke bold enough to ensure blame could be set only to their own much-overdrawn account. Granby and Riley, left behind and unable to trace their whereabouts, could not so easily be complained of as Granby and Riley standing idly by, in the face of some interference carried out immediately before them.

It was scarcely calculated to win him approval from their Lordships; certainly none from Bligh, but there was, Laurence with a little dark humor acknowledged, something liberating in having nothing whatsoever of which he might be robbed by the law: not even hope. He looked at the egg, himself: he did not hold himself up as an expert, but the shell was certainly harder than it had been, aboard ship, and with that same brittle, slightly thinning quality which he remembered a little from Temeraire's hatching, and Iskierka's.

"We could take no one else with us," Laurence said, "at least, not consenting; and there would be something curious in abducting an aviator to make him a captain: the fellow could not help but be doubted, afterwards."

"Well, to be perfectly honest I think it just as well not to take any of them," Temeraire said. "I do not think much of the lot: they were all quite unpleasant, on the ship, and they *will* think they have a right to the eggs, even though they had nothing to do with making them, and I have been taking care of them all this while. They have nothing to recommend them, any more than Rankin does: I don't suppose the hatchling will want any of them."

"We are in too much disgrace, my dear, to expect to see any of them display to advantage," Laurence said, "but Lieutenant Forthing at least is held a good officer, Granby tells me, and fought with courage at the battle of Shoeburyness."

"Oh, he is the worst of them!" Temeraire said, immediately censorious, though Laurence did not quite know what had provoked such a degree of heat, "and I don't care if we are in disgrace; that is no excuse for behaving like a scrub. Besides," Temeraire added, "he is wretchedly untidy: strings coming out of his coat, and his trousers patched; even Rankin does not look *ragged*."

"Rankin," Laurence said, "is the third son of an earl, and can afford to be nice in his clothing; I am afraid Mr. Forthing was a foundling in the dockyards at Dover, and taken on for creeping into the coverts as a child to sleep next to the dragons: he has no kin in the world."

"He might still *brush* his coat," Temeraire said, obstinately. "No: I should quite prefer no-one at all, to him; I am sure Arkady would be quite disgusted with me if I should allow it." He leaned over to look at the egg, and put out his thin forked tongue to touch the shell.

"I cannot quarrel with you on this point, if he has left the egg in your charge," Laurence said. "The judgment must be yours. In any case, it would be difficult to manage. We must also contrive some covering, for the egg; and—"

"Oh," Temeraire said, "oh, no, whatever are you doing?"

Laurence paused in confusion. "I beg your pardon?"

"No, Laurence; I am speaking to the egg," Temeraire said, raising his head with an expression of consternation, his ruff flattened against his neck. "It is hatching; however are we to get it away, now?"

"Only remember, you must put up with him for a little while," Temeraire informed the egg, as it rocked a little more, "as otherwise he can make no end of trouble for everyone, but it will only be a few minutes, and then you may choose someone else, or to have no one at all. And if he puts anything on you which you do not like, only wait a moment, and I will take it away directly. You might," he added a little exasperated, "have waited in the shell a *little* longer, until we had gone away and you were quite safe: anyone would think you were not listening to me at all."

"Captain Granby, if you would be so good as to remove the egg from the prospect of any more interference," Rankin said, as he and the party of officers came up the track and onto the promontory, "I would be grateful; if it would suit you, I should like to arrange the hatching here," indicating the place where he stood, quite near the track and a distance from the promontory's edge.

Temeraire flared out his ruff: Rankin indeed had the leather hood which Laurence had spoken of, and a heavy net with chains, such as Temeraire had once been held down with, shipboard during a typhoon; he had not liked it at all. "Remember, only a moment," he hissed at the egg, and then reluctantly let the aviators take it away: at least they were very careful, carrying it.

When it was in place, Rankin detailed a couple of the younger officers, midshipmen, to stand on the other side of the egg with the mesh netting, as though they would entangle the poor hatchling if it should try and fly away. To add insult to injury, a boy was leading a handsome sheep on a string behind him, and as soon as the first crack had appeared, Rankin nodded, and two men butchered it into a tub—a lovely hot smell of fresh blood—and brought it over. Temeraire thought it quite unfair—one was so hungry, breaking the shell; it would be so very difficult to resist—and wondered if perhaps he ought take the meat away.

"Granby," Iskierka said, pricking up her spikes as she also observed, "I do not see why we should not have bought a sheep or two, ourselves; or a cow. I am sure we have enough money."

"It wouldn't be polite, dear one," Granby said.

"I don't see why," Iskierka said. "Temeraire might have money, too, if he were as clever at taking prizes as I am; it is not my fault he shouldn't have arranged things better, and I needn't eat kangaroo to make up for it."

"Pray let's discuss it later," Granby said, hastily. "The egg is hatching, anyway."

The shell did not crack neatly, Temeraire noted with a critical eye; instead it fractured off in bits and pieces, and then the hatchling finally smashed its way out in a very messy burst, shaking itself loose. It was not very pretty, either, in his opinion: it was grey all over like Wringe, save for two very broad red streaks of color sweeping from the breastbone and under the wing-joints to trail out in spots along the backbone into its long, skinny tail.

"Good conformation," Granby said to Laurence, under his breath, "—blast it! Shoulders as strong as you could like."

The hatchling was quite heavily built forward, Temeraire supposed; and it had very clever snatching front claws, which it used almost at once: Rankin stepped forward with two quick steps, holding the hood; but to Temeraire's delight, the hatchling snapped out its wrists and seizing hold dragged it away from him and said, "No, I won't have any of that," and setting its teeth in the other end tore it quite apart with a slash of its talons.

It flung the pieces down on the ground, with an air of satisfaction. "There; now take it away, and give me the meat."

Rankin recovered, despite this setback, and said, "You may have it as soon as you have put on the harness."

"You needn't, at all," Temeraire put in, ignoring the looks of disapprobation which the aviators flung at him. "You can take yourself a perfectly tasty kangaroo, anytime you like."

"Well, I don't like; what I like is the smell of that meat over there," the hatchling said, and put its head over on its side consideringly. "As for you: you are an earl's son, is it?" it inquired of Rankin intently. "An especially *good* earl?"

Rankin looked a little taken aback, and said after a pause, "My father's creation dates from the twelfth century."

"Yes, but, is he rich?" the hatchling said.

"I hope," Rankin said, "that I may not be so impolite as to speak crassly of my family's circumstances."

"Well, that may be pretty-spoken, but it don't tell me anything useful," the hatchling said. "Does he have any cows?"

Rankin hesitated, visibly torn, and then said, "I believe there are some dairy farms on his estates—several hundred head among them, I imagine."

"Good, good," the dragonet said, approvingly. "Well, let us have a look at this harness, and as long as you are busy being polite, you might give me a taste while I am thinking it over; I do like your hair," it added; Temeraire did have to admit Rankin's was of a particularly appealing shade of yellow which looked a little like gold in the sunlight, "and your coat, although that fellow has nicer buttons," meaning Granby, "but I suppose you can have some like that put on?"

"But you do not want him, at all!" Temeraire said. "He is an extremely unpleasant person, and neglected Levitas dreadfully, although Levitas was forever trying to please him, and then Levitas died, and it was all his doing."

"Yes, so you have said, over and over, while I was getting ready to come out; and all I have to say is, this Levitas fellow sounds a right bore," the dragonet said, "and I shall like to have a captain who is the son of an earl, and rich, too; I don't aim to be eating kangaroo day-in and day-out, thank you; or hurrying about catching prizes for myself, either. But that," he added, looking at the harness which Rankin was with a slightly uncertain air proffering, "is not nice enough by half: those buckles are dirty, it looks to me."

"They are certainly dirty," Temeraire put in urgently, "and so was Levitas's harness, all the while: quite covered with dirt, and Rankin would not even let him bathe."

"This is only a temporary harness," Rankin said, adding tentatively, "and I shall have a nicer made for you, chased with gold," in what Temeraire felt was a quite shameful bargaining sort of manner.

"Ah, now that sounds more like," the dragonet said.

"And I shall give you a name, straightaway," Rankin added, with more firmness. "We shall call you *Serenitus*—"

"I have been thinking *Conquistador*, myself," the dragonet interrupted him, "or perhaps *Caesar;* only as I understand it, the conquistadores came out of it with a good deal more gold."

"No-one is going to call you *Caesar*," Temeraire said, revolted. "You are only going to be a middle-weight, anyway, if you are that big: Wringe is not even as big as a Reaper."

"You never know," the dragonet said, unphazed. "It is better to be prepared. I think *Caesar* will suit me very well, now I think about it a little more."

"Well, I wash my hands of it all," Temeraire said to Laurence, afterwards, in more than a little aggravation, watching Caesar—oh! how ridiculous—eating a *second* sheep; Rankin had sent out for it, after Caesar had eaten all the first one, down to the scraps, and suggested with a very transparent air that perhaps eating quite a lot while he was fresh-hatched would help him to grow bigger. "And I do not believe that at all," he added.

"Well, my dear, they seem to me admirably suited," Laurence said dryly. "Only I am damned if I know what we are to do now."

Chapter 4

"*L*AURENCE, I HOPE you will forgive me," Granby said, low, while across the way Caesar continued his depredations upon the live-stock which Rankin had evidently intended for his first week of feed-ings. "I didn't mean to say a word, unless he should manage to harness the beast; but he has, and there is no way around it—you must let me go-between, and make up the quarrel."

"I beg your pardon?" Laurence said, doubtfully, certain he had misunderstood; but Granby shook his head and said, "I know it's not what you are used to; but pray don't be stiff-necked about it: there can't be two captains in a covert at dagger-ends forever and anon, and you can't fight him; so it must be made up, whatever you think of the blighted wretch," he added, rather failing at conciliation.

It was by no means what Laurence was used to; the thought of of-fering Rankin anything so like apology, for an act which had been richly merited by his behavior, and which Laurence would gladly have drawn swords to justify, appalled more than he could easily bear.

"You needn't think of it that way," Granby said, "for it's only that you have the heavier beast, you know: that is the rule. It's for you to make the first gesture; he can't, without looking shy. And it don't sig-nify you aren't a captain anymore in the official way, because that doesn't make Temeraire vanish into the air."

Laurence could not be so easily reconciled, despite all the obvious sense in this policy, to a gesture which to him partook of the worst part of both withdrawal and deceit. "For I do not withdraw, John; I cannot withdraw in the least. It would be rankest falsehood for me to pretend in any way to regret my actions, or any offense which was given by them; and under the circumstances, such a withdrawal must bear a character of self-interest which I must despise."

"Lord, I am not saying you must truckle to the fellow!" Granby said, with a look half affection and half exasperation. "Nothing of the sort; you only need to let me go forward, and have a word with him, and then you shan't speak of it again, either of you: that is all. No-one will think any less of you: the contrary, for it would be rotten for the dragonet, you know. If you are giving his captain the go-by, it must make a quarrel between him and Temeraire, too, and you can't say that is fair."

This argument had too much justice for Laurence to ignore; he managed barely to make himself nod, once, by way of granting permission, and looked the other way when Rankin joined Granby's table that night, in a small hostelry, for the dinner which should honor his promotion. Granby cast a worried look at him, sidelong, and said to Rankin, in tones of slightly excessive heartiness, "I am afraid Caesar means to lead you something of a merry chase, sir; a most determined beast."

Granby, who had more knowledge of the management of a determined if not obstreperous beast than any ten men, might have been pardoned for some degree of private satisfaction in this remark. "If it is any consolation," he had said to Laurence, earlier, rather more frankly, "the little beast is his just deserts, anyway: how I will laugh to see him dragged hither and yon, protesting all he likes that Caesar must obey. *That* creature won't take being shot off in a corner and left to rot."

Laurence could not wholly take amusement in any part of the circumstances which forced him to endure Rankin's company; but he did not deny a certain grim satisfaction, which became incredulous when Rankin answered, coolly, "You are very mistaken, Captain Granby; I anticipate nothing of the sort.

"That there has been some mismanagement of the egg, I cannot dispute," Rankin added, "nor that his hatching did not give cause for concerns such as you have described: but I have been most heartened since those first moments to find Caesar a most complaisant creature by nature. Indeed, it is not too far to say I think him a most remarkable beast, quite out of the common way in intelligence and in tractability."

Laurence forgot his feelings in bemusement and Granby looked equally at a loss for response, when so far as they had seen, Caesar had spent the afternoon demonstrating only an insistent gluttony. Perhaps Rankin chose to deceive himself, rather than think himself overmatched, Laurence wondered; but Rankin added, with a self-satisfaction that seemed past mere wishful thinking, "I have already begun instructing him on better principles, and I have every hope of shaping him into the attentive and obedient beast which must be the ambition of every aviator. Already he begins to partake of my sentiments and understanding as he ought, and to value my opinion over all others."

"Well," Granby said doubtfully, then, "Mr. Forthing, the bottle stands by you," and the conversation limped away into a fresh direction; but in the morning Laurence was astonished to find Rankin at the promontory, with a book, to attend Caesar's breakfast. He seated himself at Caesar's side and began to read to the dragonet as the beast ate: an aviation manual of some sort, Laurence collected from what he overheard, although the language was very peculiar.

"Oh, he has never dug up that antique thing," Granby said, with disgust, and added, "It is from the Tudor age, I think; all about how to manage a dragon. We read it in school, but I cannot think of anyone who gives it a thought anymore."

Caesar listened very attentively, however, while he gnawed on a bone, and said earnestly, "My dear captain, I cannot disagree at all, it seems very sensible indeed; pray do you think I ought to try and manage another sheep? I take it quite to heart, what the book says about the importance of early feeding. If it accords with your judgment, of course: I am wholly willing to be guided by your superior experience; but I must say I find I am so much better able to attend when I am quite full."

"This," Iskierka said, "is what comes of worrying about hatchlings."

Temeraire did not think that was very just: he had not worried about Caesar for very *long*, certainly, and at the present moment he would not have given one scrap of liver for all Caesar's health and happiness; not, of course, that Caesar seemed to be in any short supply of either. In one week he had eaten nine sheep, an entire cow, a tunny, and even three kangaroos, after Rankin had been forced to reconsider the speed at which he was depleting his funds.

That would have been quite enough to make the dragonet intolerable, particularly the smacking, gloating way in which he took his gluttonous meals, but apart from these offensive habits, he *would* strut, and wake one up out of a pleasant drowse in the midday heat by singing out loudly, "Oh, my captain is coming to see me," and he would with very great satisfaction inform Rankin that he was looking very fine, that day, and make a pointed note of every bit of gold or decoration which he wore.

The one consolation which Temeraire had promised himself, Rankin's certain neglect, which should also ensure his absence, did not materialize: instead Rankin was *forever* coming, and so Temeraire had to endure not only Caesar, but Rankin also, and hear his irritating voice all the day, reading out from this absurd book full of nonsense about how one ought to never ask questions of one's captain, and spend all one's time practicing formation-maneuvers.

"I cannot understand in the least," Temeraire complained, "why when he had the very nicest of dragons, he was never to be seen; and now one cannot be rid of him. I have even hinted a little that he might take himself off, in the afternoons when it is so very hot and one wishes only to sleep, but he will never go."

"I imagine he had a better chance of society more to his liking, in Britain," Laurence said. "He was a courier-captain on light duty, and might easily visit friends of his social order; he has never been a particular favorite, among other aviators."

"No, I am sure he has not," Temeraire said, disgustedly.

Meanwhile there was no end of trouble to be seen, because the company Rankin *did* keep, aside from Caesar, was Governor Bligh, whom Temeraire had now classed a thoroughly unpleasant sort of person: not surprising when one considered he was part of Government. Bligh certainly had some notion that when Caesar was a little more grown, Rankin would help put him back in his post; Temeraire had even overheard Rankin discussing the matter with Caesar.

"Oh, certainly," Caesar said, "I will always be happy to oblige you, my dear captain; and Governor Bligh. It is of the first importance that our colony—" *Our colony,* Temeraire fumed silently. "—that our colony should have the finest leadership. I understand," he added, "that governors have quite a great deal of power, isn't it? They may give grants of land?"

Rankin paused and said, "—yes; unclaimed land is in the governor's gift."

"Just so, just so," Caesar said. "I understand it takes a great deal of land to raise cattle, and sheep; I am sure Governor Bligh must be well aware of it."

"A clever beast," Laurence said dryly, when Temeraire with indignation had repeated this exchange to him. "I am afraid, my dear, we may find ourselves quite at a stand."

"Laurence," Temeraire said, shocked, "Laurence, surely you do not imagine he could beat *me*. If ever he tried to cause us any difficulty—"

"If you were ever to come on to blows," Laurence said, "we should already be well in the soup; such a conflict must at all costs be avoided. Even in defeat, he might easily do you a terrible injury, and to run such a risk, for the reward only of making yourself more an outlaw and terrifying to the local populace, cannot be a rational choice. Consider that every week now brings us closer to word from England, and I trust the establishment of a new order."

"Which," Temeraire said, "is likely to be just as bad as Bligh, I expect."

"So long as we are not responsible for either its establishment or its destruction," Laurence said, grimly, "and neither its hated enemy nor its cosseted ally, our situation can only be improved."

"I do not see very well how," Temeraire said, brooding over the matter; he was not quite certain he saw it the same way. "Laurence, if we must stay here for some time—?" He paused, interrogatively.

Laurence did not immediately answer. "I am afraid so," he said, at last, quietly. "The waste of your abilities is very nearly criminal, my dear, and Jane will do her best by us, of course; but with matters as they are amongst the unharnessed beasts in England, and such reports as Bligh is already likely to make of us, I must not counsel you to hope for a quick recall."

Temeraire could not fail to see that Laurence was quite downcast by his own words. "Why, I am sure it will be perfectly pleasant to remain awhile," Temeraire said, stoutly, making sure to tuck his wings to his sides in a complaisant sort of way. "Only if we *are* to remain," he did not allow any disappointment to color his words, "then it seems to me that Caesar is right on this one point: we *ought* have better leadership, who can arrange it so we can have proper food, and everything nice—perhaps even a pavilion, with some shade and water, against all this heat. We might even build some roads as wide as in China, and put the pavilions directly in the town; just like a properly civilized country."

"We cannot hope to promote such a project, however desirable, without the support of civil authority; you cannot force the change wholesale," Laurence said; he paused and added, low, "We might make such a bargain with Bligh, I expect; he cannot be insensible of your much greater strength, and he knows he requires at least our complaisance, even if he has Rankin's aid."

"But Laurence, I do not like Bligh at all," Temeraire said. "I have quite settled it that he is a bounder: he will say anything, and do anything, and be friendly to anyone, only to be back as governor; but I do not think it is because he wishes so much to do anything pleasant or nice for anyone."

"No, he wishes only to be vindicated, I believe," Laurence answered, "—and revenged. Not without cause," he added, "but—" He stopped and shook his head. "There would be a species of tyranny in it, when they have ruled so long and without argument from the citizenry."

Temeraire brooded on further afterwards, that afternoon, while Caesar discussed enthusiastically with Rankin plans for an elaborate cattle farm, quite exploding Temeraire's hopes of napping. He was beginning to understand strongly the sentiment that beggars could not be choosers. No one would ever have *chosen* to be trapped here; but now he must make the best of it, for himself and for Laurence. Temeraire dismally recognized that he had solaced himself, by thinking that Iskierka was only a wretched pirate, really, and her excesses for Granby in poor taste, which Laurence would not have liked, anyway. But now here was Rankin, too, also wearing gold buttons, and *he* was a captain still, as Laurence ought have been. There was no thinking two ways about it: Temeraire had not taken proper care of him; he had quite mismanaged the situation.

"Demane," Temeraire said, lifting his head, and speaking in the Xhosa language, so Rankin could not sneak and overhear, nor Caesar; Demane looked up from where he was figuring sums with Roland—or rather, giving his sums to Sipho to figure for him, while he instead cleaned yet another old flintlock; he had acquired another four in the town, lately. "Demane, do you remember that fellow who was here the other day, MacArthur? Will you go into town and find out where he lives; and take him a message?"

"I cannot but feel I have—I am—mismanaging the situation," Laurence said somberly, tapping his hand restlessly upon the table until he noticed his own fidgeting, which even then required an effort to cease.

From wishing only to have the decision taken out of his own hands, Laurence now found he did not think he could be easy in his mind to watch the colony's leaders deposed and, as he increasingly thought Bligh's intention, executed without even awaiting word from England. "But if Rankin should move in his support, I cannot avoid the decision: either we must stand by or intervene. I hope," he added ruefully, "that I am not so petty as to have more sympathy for Johnston and MacArthur, and the less for Bligh, only because Rankin has ranged himself alongside him."

"You might have a worse reason," Tharkay said. "At least you cannot call the decision self-interested; his restoration would be more to your advantage."

"Not unless it is by my own doing," Laurence said, "which I cannot reconcile with a sense of justice; and I doubt even that would serve," he added, pessimism sharp in his mouth. "Even to act must rouse fresh suspicions; we are damned in either direction, when all they want of us is quiet obedience."

"If you will pardon my saying so," Tharkay said, "you will never satisfy them on that point: the last thing you or Temeraire will ever give anyone is quiet obedience. Have you considered it might be better not to try?"

Laurence would have liked to protest this remark: he believed in the discipline of the service, and still felt himself at heart a serving-officer; if he had been forced beyond the bounds of proper submission to authority, it had been most unwillingly. But denial froze in his throat; that excuse was worth precisely the value that their Lordships would have put upon it, which was none.

Tharkay left him to wrestle with it a moment, then added, "There are alternatives, if you wished to consider them."

"To sit here on the far side of the world, seeing Temeraire wholly wasted on the business of breeding, and condemned to tedium and the absence of all society?" Laurence said, tiredly. "We might, I suppose, do some work for the colony: ferry goods, and assist with the construction of roads—"

"You might go to sea," Tharkay said, and Laurence looked at him in surprise. "No, I am not speaking fancifully. You remember, perhaps, Avram Maden?"

Laurence nodded, a little surprised: he had not heard the merchant's name from Tharkay since they had left Istanbul, nor that of Maden's daughter; and Laurence had himself avoided any mention of either for fear of giving pain. "I must consider myself yet in his debt; I hope he does well—he did not come under any suspicion, after our escape?"

"No; I believe we made a sufficiently dramatic exit to satisfy the Turks without their seeking for conspirators." Tharkay paused, and then his mouth twisted a little. "He has been lately presented with his first grandson," he added.

"Ah," Laurence said, and reached over to fill Tharkay's glass.

Tharkay raised it to him silently and drank. A minute passed, then leaving the subject with nothing more said, he abruptly added, "I am engaged to perform a service for the directors of the East India Company, at his request; and as I understand it, several of those gentlemen are interested in outfitting privateers, to strike at the French trade in the Pacific."

"Yes?" Laurence said politely, wondering how this should apply to his situation. What service those merchant lords might require, in this still-small port, Laurence could not understand, though it explained at least why Tharkay had come—and then he realized, startling back a little in his chair, that Tharkay meant this as a suggestion.

"I could scarcely fit Temeraire on a privateer," he said, wondering a little that Tharkay could imagine it done: it was not as though he had not seen Temeraire.

"Without having broached the subject with the gentlemen in question," Tharkay said, "I will nevertheless go so far as to assure you that the practicalities would be managed, if you were willing. Ships can be built to carry dragons, where interest exists; and a dragon who can sink any vessel afloat must command interest."

He spoke with certainty; and Laurence could take his point. A dragon could never ordinarily be obtained for such a purpose; as yet they were the exclusive province of the state. They and the first-rates and transports which could bear a dragon were devoted to blockade-duty, and to naval warfare, not to the quick and stinging pursuit of the enemy's shipping. Temeraire would be unopposed, and a privateer so armed would be virtually at liberty to take any ship which it encountered.

Laurence did not know how to answer. There was nothing dishonorable in privateering—nothing dishonorable in the least. He had known several men formerly of the Navy to embark on the enterprise, and he had not diminished in respect for them at all.

"I doubt the Government would deny you a letter of marque," Tharkay said.

"No," Laurence said. It would surely suit their Lordships admirably. Temeraire wreaking a wholesale destruction among French shipping would be a great improvement over Temeraire sitting idly in New South Wales, with none of the risks attendant on bringing him back to the front and once again into the company of other impressionable beasts, which he might lure into sedition.

"I will not urge it on you," Tharkay said. "If you should care for the introduction, however, I would be at your service."

"But that sounds quite splendid," Temeraire said, with real enthusiasm, when Laurence had laid the proposal before him in only the barest terms. "I am sure we should take any number of prizes; Iskierka should have nothing on it. How long do you suppose it would be, for them to build us a ship?"

Laurence only with difficulty persuaded him to consider it as anything other than a settled thing; Temeraire was already inclined to be making plans for the use of his future wealth. "You could not wish to remain here, instead?" Temeraire said. "Not, of course, that I mean to suggest there is anything wrong here," he added unconvincingly.

The mornings and late evenings were now the only and scarcely bearable times of day, and they had begun to stretch them with early rising and late nights; the sun was only just up, spilling a broad swath of light across the water running into all the bays of the harbor, making them glow out brilliantly white against the dark curve of the land rising away, blackish green and silent. Temeraire had not eaten in two days: the stretch was not markedly unhealthy, given his inaction, but Laurence feared it was due largely to a secret disdain for his food, the regrettable consequence of Temeraire's having grown nice in his tastes, a grave danger for a military man—and there Laurence was forced again to the recollection that they were neither of them military, any longer.

Even so, there was an advantage to a stronger stomach: he himself, subject to shipboard provisions during the most ravenous years of his life, could subsist on weeviled biscuit and salt pork indefinitely; even though he had not often had to endure those conditions. Temeraire had too early in his life developed a finicky palate; Gong Su had done what was in his power, but he had made quite clear one could not turn a lean, scrub-fed game animal, half bone and sinew and anatomical oddities, into a fat and nicely marbled piece of beef; Laurence was considering if his finances could stretch to the provision of some cattle, at least for a treat.

"There is Caesar's breakfast," Temeraire said, with a sigh, as the mournful lowing of a cow came towards them from the bottom of the hill; but when it was brought up, by an only slightly less reluctant youth, he delivered it not to Caesar but to them, stammering compliments of Mr. MacArthur, and for Laurence there was an invitation card, asking him to supper.

"I wonder he should make such a gesture," Laurence said, rather taken aback; one thing for MacArthur to bring himself to the covert—however irregularly organized, still in the nature of an official outpost—and quite another to invite Laurence to his home, in mixed company likely overseen by his wife. "I wonder at it indeed; unless," he added, low, "he has had some intelligence of Rankin's interest in Bligh's case: that might make sufficient motive even for this."

"Umm," Temeraire said indistinctly, nibbling around a substantial thigh-bone; his attention was fixed notably on Gong Su's enthusiastic preparations: the cow had been butchered, and was going into the earth with what greenstuffs had passed muster, and some cracked wheat; even Caesar had peeled open an eye and was looking over with covert interest.

The hour was fixed sufficiently late they could wait until the heat of the day had passed and travel at the beginning of twilight; Temeraire, having made a splendid meal, carried Laurence aloft into the softening but yet unbroken blue: no clouds, yet again, all the day. What would have made an hour's journey on horse, across rough country, was an easy ten minutes' flight dragon-back, and there was a wide fallow field open near the house, where Temeraire could set down.

"Pray thank him for my cow," Temeraire said, contentedly settling himself to nap. "It was very handsome of him, and I do not think he is a coward anymore, after all."

Laurence crossed the field to the house, and paused to knock the dirt from his boots before he stepped into the lane: he had worn trousers, and Hessians, more suitable to flying; but in concession to the invitation, he had made an effort with his cravat, and put on his better coat. A groom came out, and looked about confused for Laurence's horse before pointing him to the door: the house was comfortable but not especially grand, built practically and made for work, but there was an elegance and taste in the arrangements.

He was shown into the salon, and a company heavily slanted: only four women to seven men, most of those in officers' uniforms; one of the women rose, as Mr. MacArthur came to join him, and he presented her to Laurence as his wife, Elizabeth.

"I hope you will forgive the informality of our society, Mr. Laurence," she said, when he had bowed over her hand. "We are grown sadly careless in this wild country, and the heat crushes all aspirations to stiffness. I hope you did not have a very tiring ride."

"Not at all; Temeraire brought me," Laurence said. "He is in your southwest field; I trust it no inconvenience."

"Why, none," she said, though her eyes had widened, and one of the officers said, "Do you mean you have that monster sitting out in the yard?"

"That monster's sharpest weapon is his tongue," MacArthur said. "I am pretty well cut to ribbons yet: did the cow sweeten him at all?"

"As much as you might like, sir," Laurence said, dryly. "—you have quite hit on the point of weakness."

The supper was, for all the ulterior motives likely to have been its inspiration, a comfortable and civilized affair: Laurence had not quite known what to expect, from the colonial society, but Mrs. MacArthur was plainly a woman of some character, and though indeed never striving for a formality which both the climate and the situation of the colony would have rendered tiresome and a little absurd, she directed the style of their gathering nevertheless. She could not have a balanced table, so she served the meal in two courses, inviting her guests to refresh themselves in between with a little walking in the gardens, illuminated with lamps, and rearranging the seating on their return to partner the ladies afresh.

The meal was thoughtfully suited to the weather as well: a cool soup of fresh cucumber and mint, meat served in jellied aspic, beef very thinly carved from the joint, lightly boiled chicken; and instead of pudding an array of cakes, with pots of jam, and excellent, fragrant tea; all served on porcelain of the very highest quality, the one real extravagance Laurence remarked: dishes of white and that particularly delicate shade of blue which could not be achieved by any European art, and the strength of real quality.

He noticed it to his hostess with compliments; to his surprise she looked a little crestfallen, and said, "Oh, you have found out *my* weakness, Mr. Laurence; I could not resist them, although I know very well I oughtn't: they must be smuggled, of course."

"Do not say it aloud!" MacArthur cried. "So long as you do not know it for certain, you may ha'e your dishes, and we our tea; and long may the rascals thrive."

One of the many charges Bligh had laid at the rebels' door had been the practice of smuggling: the back alleys and trading houses of Sydney were flooded with goods from China, which from the price alone one could tell had evaded the East India Company's monopoly on such trade. "And I expect he would blame us for the drought, too, if he heard me say I thought the weather would hold clear another month," MacArthur said, offering a glass of port, when the ladies had left them.

"I don't say we have never brought in some goods which a governor might not approve of," he continued, "but I am speaking of rum, which we must have; you cannot get a man to work here, except you fill his glass, and with more than you can pour at five shillings the bottle. A damned folly, too: a pickled liver cannot tell good dark West Indian rum from the Bengali stuff. But we cannot even bring in that, now: there is not a smell of any kind of goods, from Africa, since the Cape was lost.

"As for the China goods, by God! If I could make a profit selling China ware at two pounds a box in Sydney, with all the cost and risk of freight, I would be packing it on ships for England, instead, and die rich as Croesus. There are fellows making a pretty penny selling it on, I believe, even when they can only buy it one box at a time."

There was a general murmur of agreement, and some anecdotes of trading agreements followed: it seemed to Laurence the officers all were tradesmen also, in some measure, and the tradesmen all former officers, and many of them landed as well: they made no distinction amongst themselves, and perhaps could not have, if there were not men of business enough established in the colony to provide opportunities for investment, or their rough-and-tumble fortunes not yet sufficiently realized in coin to take advantage of them.

MacArthur drew him aside, as the cigars were offered around and lit, and to the open doors looking into the gardens: squeaking small bats were flying now in clouds around the trees where earlier they had slept, hanging. "I am grateful to you for coming," he said. "We gave you little enough reason to do so."

"You are a good host, sir," Laurence said, "and it is a welcome I had not looked for."

"Governor Bligh would call me a traitor, so far as that goes: has done oft enough, I imagine," MacArthur said, "and would hang me for it, too. I will not pretend, sir, to be anything less than deeply interested, under the circumstances. I said to you, I believe, that I am ready to stand judgment for my acts; and so I am, but I don't care to be marched to the scaffold *before* it is handed down."

Laurence looked out at the gardens a little grimly—wilting in the heat and yet still restful to look upon, neatly arranged, and beyond them the wide spreading fields. He was conscious that MacArthur's establishment made a powerful argument in support of his claim to have made something of himself, and in an isolate and difficult country to have carried forward the banner of civilization: uniting all the taste and respectability which was absent from the sad and rackety condition of the town. So long from England and longer yet from any respectability, Laurence could feel the force of that argument all the more strongly.

"Sir," he answered, "I can well understand your desire; but forgive me, I will not commit myself, and moreover Temeraire, to any course of action in advance. I have a reputation which may make me seem more a friend to rebellion than I am by any willing choice; and for that part, my assistance might not be an unmitigated boon to you, if you had it."

"And, if you will allow me to be blunt," MacArthur said, "for your part, you would be in a pretty position, standing in the way of seeing Governor Bligh restored, if a frigate should come in a couple of weeks, declare us the worst unhanged scoundrels south of the line, and the governor to be put back into place at gun-point. No, sir; I do not ask any man, so unconnected to me as you are, to put his neck on the chopping-block with mine; but if you are amenable enough to listen, I had rather propose to you a means of evading the issue entirely."

He drew Laurence into his study, and on the desk drew out the maps of the colony, and the penning mountain range about it, a great labyrinthine mass of gorges and peaks, only vaguely sketched. "All our purposes can march together," MacArthur said. "You wish to be well out of the affair; just so: I wish you out of it also, and every other dragon in the place with you, at least long enough for our doom to arrive. It cannot be long now, when the last frigate brought the post only a month behind our news."

His proposal was an expedition whose purpose should be to find a crossing over the Blue Mountains, and establish a cattle-drive road from the colony to the open territory beyond, "where," he continued, "you may set up this covert your beasts will require, and take yourselves all the land you might like: I cannot see how anyone can complain, when you have opened the passage yourselves.

"Captain Granby is senior, I think," he added, "and can I suppose order this Captain Rankin on such a mission: if this new creature means to go on eating as he has begun, it seems to me you had all better be thinking of how to feed him, particularly as you have two more hatchlings to come."

"I am afraid it must keep you here a little longer," Laurence said, rather diffident in making the suggestion: he could not like asking Granby to enter into such a stratagem, however practical.

He felt himself caught between shoals and a lee-shore, in an unfamiliar channel: MacArthur's machinations were no more noble than Bligh's in their ends, and likely less; even if in their forthrightness more appealing, and with the benefit of MacArthur's greater charm of person. And they were neither of them looking beyond the parochial boundaries of their quarrel, to the titanic struggle creeping ever more widely over the world. If either of them gave a thought to the war, Laurence could not discover it, and though they might gladly make him any promises which would make of him the useful ally they desired, they neither of them recognized in any real way the colossal folly of wasting Temeraire in this isolate part of the world.

It was enough to make him look again at Tharkay's suggestion: Laurence could easily long for the sea-wind in his face and the open ocean, and at least the comfort of doing *some* rather than *no* good, even if that small and diversionary. Something in his heart curled away from the mercenary life; but he was not certain he ought let that stand in his way, and Temeraire's. If there was no honor in it, neither could he see any here, at best errand-runners for an indifferent overseer, and at worst pawns in a selfish squabbling.

MacArthur's proposal offered, however, at least a temporary escape from all these alternatives; if it could not answer for long, Laurence was at present in the mood to be satisfied with small blessings. "But I would not in the least press it upon you," he added, "and I hope you will not act in any way contrary to your judgment, nor—"

Nor, he meant to add, *in excessive haste,* but Granby broke in on him before he could. "For God's sake let us go first thing in the morning," Granby said, passionately. "I have been living in mortal terror every day I should wake up and find myself a hundred miles into the interior: she keeps talking of going to look for elephants. What I am to do if Rankin will not come, though, I cannot tell you. No one can argue Iskierka isn't in a different class, but I have no official orders to be here, where he does; and seniority is a sad puzzle: he was a captain first, even if he hasn't had a dragon for years."

"I suggest you do not concern yourselves until the event," Tharkay said, "if it should arise," and shrugged when Rankin, to Laurence's private surprise, made no objections either to the project or to Granby's assertion of rank. "Bligh's support was desirable to him when he thought you might try to deny him the egg," Tharkay said. "Now he can only gain very little and risk much by committing himself; I imagine he is perfectly satisfied to have you provide him a convenient excuse to withdraw, particularly when Granby must soon depart and restore his precedence."

Laurence could of course not look upon the expedition with anything like pleasure, save the meager sort involved in escaping a worse outcome. There was nothing attractive in the prospect of shepherding

a gang of convicts, and a month in Rankin's company would have been
a most effective punishment in quarters less confined than a small encampment; for insult to add upon these injuries, he might also expect
the hostility of the rest of the aviators.

"I know they have made clods of themselves, but you had better
have at least one officer," Granby said, scratching out a haphazard list
of the aviators on the back of a napkin, in his shipboard cabin, as he
chose which men to assign to Temeraire and to Iskierka, as temporary
crews. Laurence of course had been stripped of his subordinates with
his rank, and Iskierka had left her own back in Britain when she had
decamped without permission to follow them, taking only Granby.
"Will you take Forthing?"

"Temeraire has taken him a little in dislike, I find," Laurence said.

"Yes, I know," Granby said. "I should like to give Forthing a
chance to make it up with him; otherwise we will have a job of it to
persuade Temeraire to let him make a try for one of the eggs. Not that
Forthing is any less a clod than the rest, but at least he is a competent
clod. Most of the rest are the flotsam of the Corps as much as the eggs
are. That fellow Blincoln is pleased with himself if he manages to round
up half-a-dozen men to put away harness in good order; and I suppose
he may as well be, because it don't happen very often."

Laurence nodded. "We will take Fellowes and Dorset, of course;
and Roland and Demane can manage the rest, I expect," he said. "We
ought not take more men than necessary; there can be no need to burden the dragons."

"I hope," Tharkay said, "that I may form one of your party, as
well, if it is not inconvenient."

They looked at him with surprise. After a moment, Laurence said,
"Certainly, if you like," forcibly repressing his curiosity; Granby said,
"But Lord above, whyever for? We will end with pickaxing our way
through solid rock for a month in the worst heat of summer, and there
is not a blessed soul out there to be found: unless we see some of the
natives, and with three dragons I am pretty sure we won't."

Tharkay paused, and then said quietly, "You will be surveying first,
from aloft; if there is a route in use, that will offer the best chance of
seeing it."

"If there were a route in use, we shouldn't have to build one,"
Granby said.

"I am not expecting to find a road suitable for general use," Tharkay said. "A mule-track at most, I should think."

"But—" Laurence said, and only barely restrained himself; Granby also had stopped, with an open mouth: but it was too plain Tharkay did not choose to volunteer more; he might easily have done so. "Oh, if you like, then," Granby said awkwardly, after a moment, looking at Laurence.

"We should be glad of your company," Laurence said, with a bow, and only later, privately to Temeraire, expressed his confusion.

"Maybe he is looking for the smugglers," Temeraire said, unconcernedly, nibbling up another portion of sheep stuffed with raisins and grains: MacArthur had sent another present that morning, letting no grass grow. Laurence stared. "Well, if someone has a secret road and has not said anything to anyone about it," Temeraire offered, having swallowed, "it stands to reason they must be hiding it for cause; and you were just telling me of all these goods from China which are coming in."

"It would be a very peculiar way to bring goods into a port city," Laurence said, doubtfully, but he recalled Tharkay had engaged himself in service to the directors of the East India Company: at Maden's request, he might well have undertaken such a task, even if it did not seem a likely explanation for his wishing to accompany their party.

"But anyone could think of searching the ships and the dockyards, to catch them," Temeraire said, and Laurence after a little more consideration had to acknowledge that if the intention was ultimately to ship the goods on to England, the arrangement was ideal: slip the goods into the markets unsuspected, and then any legitimate captain might openly purchase them and carry them onward.

"They must be landing them in a convenient bay, then, somewhere further up the coast," Laurence said, "and taking them around by land; but it would be a most circuitous route, through unsettled and dangerous countryside."

"There is nothing very dangerous when there is nothing but kangaroos about," Temeraire said dismissively.

They decamped in accord with Granby's fondest wishes, the very next morning, with all the speed and disorder usual to the Aerial Corps and more when traveling so light: the bulk of their baggage was made of simple pickaxes and hammers and shovels, instead of bombshells and gunpowder, and the few tents which would be their shelter. The mountains were richly green despite the summer, even seen from a distance; they might rely on finding sufficient water without trying to carry very much of it as supply, and with a few sacks of biscuit and barrels of salt pork they were ready to depart.

The work gang had been assembled with equal haste: some dozen convicts, having been promised their liberty in exchange for this one service, were herded with difficulty up to the promontory and thence into Temeraire's belly-rigging. They were an odd, ill-favored assortment of men, for the most part thin and leathery, with a peculiar similarity to their faces perhaps born of suffering and their preferred mode of consolation: fine traceworks of broken red capillaries about the base of their noses, and eyes shot through with blood.

There were a few men who looked a little more suited to the work which lay ahead: a Jonas Green, who might himself have been cut none-too-neatly out of rock, with bulk in his shoulders and his arms; he alone of the convicts was not drunk when they came up to the promontory. A Robert Maynard was rather more fat than substantial, and no one could have accused *him* of abstinence, but he had reportedly a little skill at stonemasonry, and his hands showed the evidence: callused hard as iron and large out of all proportion, thick-fingered.

"You had better not mistake him," MacArthur said, handing over the manifest of men. "Transported for pickpocketing. He cannot do much harm out in the wilderness, but I would advise you keep your purses close when you are coming back."

Though they were nearly one and all a little intoxicated, and the hour early enough to yet be dark when they had been marched up to the promontory, the convicts balked at dragon transport, seeing Temeraire's head swinging towards them through the foggy dimness, and were inclined to withdraw at once.

"It's more than you can ask a man," one almost fragile, reedy-voiced fellow said: Jack Telly, sad-eyed and disappointed in his face, his stunted person incongruous with the aggression of his protest. "I can swing a pick all day and all night, and will, too, but I ain't to be thrown in a dragon's belly without so much as a by-your-leave."

The general agreement with this sentiment resisted all logic and was only overcome with sufficient doses of rum and cajolery to leave the men in a more or less stupefied state—not unlike the methods used for transporting cattle, Laurence with some resignation noted—before they could at last be marched aboard. Green alone refused the bribery, with a shake of his head when offered a glass; he was one of the convicts who had only lately been brought over in the *Allegiance,* and climbed aboard rather with no confidence but a stoic resignation: as though he did not care very greatly if he were to be fed to a dragon.

Forthing saw the loading managed efficiently under Temeraire's darkling gaze and said, "I believe we are ready, Mr. Laurence," a little stiffly but without open discourtesy: Granby, Laurence thought, had made him a few pointed remarks, on the subject of his prospects and how likely these were to be advanced through behavior which should irritate the dragon overseeing the remaining eggs that were all his hope of promotion.

"The eggs are quite secure?" Temeraire said, nosing down at his own belly, where they had been snugged in: he had utterly refused to leave them behind, even in Riley's care.

"No: for Bligh is still aboard the ship," Temeraire had said, "and apart from any other mischief he might do them, if one should hatch, I should not be at all surprised if Bligh should try and take it for *himself,* since Rankin is not going to oblige him after all. I would not worry ordinarily, but plainly the sea-voyage has affected the eggs badly: that is the only explanation for Caesar, in my opinion," with great disapproval.

"Pray be sure that the little one is in properly," Temeraire added now. "It would be quite dreadful if it were to slip out."

"The netting is tight, and the padding will not shift," Laurence said, pulling against the thick hawsers of the belly-netting with his hand, and leaning his weight against it, without much yielding. "And we cannot have any fear of the temperature falling too far. Try away, if you will."

Temeraire reared himself up on his hindquarters and shook; not with quite the usual vigor, as he had too much care for the eggs, but enough to be sure nothing was ready to tumble free or break loose. "All lies well," he said.

"If you are quite ready," Iskierka said, "perhaps we might leave in reasonable time, instead of sitting about for hours."

"*Some* of us," Temeraire returned smartly, "are carrying things, instead of being quite useless; and if you would not mind being careless with the eggs, I would."

Iskierka could not easily be used for transport: her spikes, which jetted steam almost perpetually, rendered her hazardous to all but trained men and packages securely wrapped in oilcloth; so she was a good deal more unburdened, carrying only Granby and her makeshift skeleton crew.

"I don't see why we must be in such a hurry," Caesar said, disconsolately, to take the opposing position; he was not inclined to do much of anything yet but sleep and eat, in the way of new hatchlings, and did not seem much affected by the boredom which had rendered Iskierka an imminent danger. "We might leave tomorrow; or when it is less hot."

"That," Temeraire said, "will not be for three months; now stop complaining, and let us be off."

For all the apprehension of difficulty and tedium, Laurence could not yet repress a sensation of pleasure in climbing aboard Temeraire's back, the familiar and solid snap of the metal carabiners locking in his hands, securely fixed on to the harness-rings; the sense of a crew, however small, moving about behind him; other beasts in company. And then the great coiling leap upwards: Temeraire's wings snapping outstretched to cup the rushing hot air, endless blue above welcoming and glitter on the water below.

The *Allegiance* and all Sydney herself were reduced to charming picturesque, the dusty roads become gold ribbons from the air, and beyond the city's bounds the neat squares of cultivated fields and orchards unrolling before them like a spreading carpet; and the dragons' shadows fell upon them like cut-out silhouettes, rising over the hills, with the mountains rising in their blue haze in the distance.

Chapter 5

❧

THE SENSATION GREW only gradually: the settled fields yielding to unbroken wilderness, stands of ancient timber, eucalypts with their oddly sharp fragrance rising if they landed, and the last hunting tracks fading away beneath the leaf cover. They crossed the Nepean and followed a small nameless tributary winding slow and westward into the mountains, hoping to find somewhere at its end a pass through: but there was none. Instead they came one day after another to another high, rising cliff wall: ragged sandstone, fresh yellow and old stained grey, climbing in heaps of pebbles and cracked boulders to where at last the face rose away sheer.

There was the quality of a hedge-maze to the gorges. The sun appeared only late and vanished early, hidden behind the rearing walls of rock. At first they had been glad of the deep lingering shadows, the cooler air about the river, but with the passing days Laurence was conscious of a building unease as they retreated once more along their course and tried yet another branching of the stream, with only the same fruitless result. They had not yet made forty miles from Sydney, as the dragon flew, and yet they had traversed ten times that distance, it seemed, going back and forth.

It was not merely the lack of civilization; it was the absence of all human life. The country felt wholly untenanted, not empty but abandoned. They had once at night seen a distant fire; in the morning, they had gone on foot nearer to investigate, hoping to meet some native who might perhaps be solicited as a guide; but in the deep crowding thicket they did not find even enough remains of a camp to be sure of what they had seen, or to learn if there were another living soul anywhere within a day's flight; even Tharkay's skill could uncover no certain sign. Upon the stone, from time to time, they found markings: handprints in white ochre, or in red; but these were old and weather-worn, for years perhaps, and spoke only of some distant occupation.

"Dead, of the plague and of the pox," O'Dea said, when Laurence had observed as much to Tharkay, wondering why the country should have been abandoned: O'Dea was an older convict, and a man grown grizzled and sodden through hard years, though not uneducated. "It came upon them hard, the early years after we came, and we saw them die in Sydney town: their bodies came floating into the harbor, spotted sepulchrous white, and their fires burned low and went out; now they are gone, and only their curses linger."

He was an Irishman and a former lawyer, taken up in the troubles in 'ninety-eight, and under life-sentence; this expedition had offered his first and perhaps his only chance of liberty since he had been fetched to the colony fifteen years before, and while he had solaced himself liber-ally with rum in the intervening span, he had not wholly lost either his spirit, or a gift for inconvenient poetry.

With too much matter here for it to work upon: Laurence did not doubt his explanation, though it might be exaggerated; he had glimpsed in Sydney some of the natives, walking through the town or plying their canoes in the harbor, seeming unconcerned with the colony's life rather than either party or inimical to it. But few in num-ber, and here stood the markings for evidence that this country had once been peopled, enough to bring men to this isolate place—not only once but often, for the most recent marks were layered upon older—and now was deserted. There was something bleak and lonely in the fading handprints upon the walls, which vanished into the twilight as they retreated away down the gorge: a claim and a memorial all at once, which seemed a symbol of the land itself denying them pas-sage.

From there on, the disquiet grew among them; the stillness itself made a mute reproach. Temeraire was not immune, either. "I do not understand why we have not yet found a way," he said. "Whenever we have flown up over the mountaintops, it looks as though this gorge and that one should meet, beneath the trees, and then we come down again and suddenly we have gone the wrong way, or else the gorges do not meet at all, and there is a great heap of rock waiting; and everything looks the same. I do not like it in the least, and it seems to me quite un-canny we should mistake our way so often."

Large game was not plentiful, and what they found the dragons had to eat; Caesar complained of his much-reduced menu, incessantly, until the general oppression began to make itself felt to him as well, and then he wished only to be gone. "There is nothing good in this place, and I am sure no cows would like to come here, either," he said. "We had much better get a grant of land nearer the city, where it was so sunny and pleasant; not here where one cannot even see past the trees."

They were obliged to spend some time each day finding water, although from their lack of success in finding a route, they were often able to fall back to their former camp by the river. The fifth day of their surveying attempt, however, ended in more confusion. From the air, they thought two valleys had conjoined, if only by a narrow passage, which could barely have admitted men on foot to pass, single-file. "I will settle for that, gladly," Granby said. "It can be widened, and perhaps once we have found one route, we can find another, if we look in the other direction."

"And more to the point, while we look, we can in the meantime put the men to work, which should hardly be delayed another hour," Rankin said, with a cold look over his shoulder at the string of convicts who had not yet roused themselves from around their rough and makeshift camp, though the morning was well advanced. "So far they have nothing to occupy them but idleness and rum, and I am sure we may expect trouble from leaving such men prey to restlessness and wild fancies."

Those wild fancies were rampant not only amongst the convicts, by now. "I hope, sir," Fellowes, his staid and hard-headed ground-crew master, and ordinarily a sensible fellow, said to Laurence under his breath, "I hope you will have a care, walking that pass; I am sure we have not had so much bad luck for no reason."

"I do not like it, either," Temeraire said. "Perhaps I might try and break it open wider, myself, before you should go; I have found the divine wind answers quite well for breaking rock."

"And for bringing half the cliff wall down upon our heads, certainly," Rankin interjected.

"It may come down upon *your* head, and no-one mind in the least," Temeraire flared, but this criticism was unfortunately sound, and barred the experiment: the soft sandstone walls would crumble a little even from a leather-gloved hand rubbed vigorously across their face, and everywhere the rock rose above the tree-line stood the scars of small landslides and collapses.

The ground of the pass was uneven and shifted easily beneath their feet, gravel and rock slipping where new grass and undergrowth had yet to take secure hold, though there was also enough greenery risen calf-high to hide the canyon floor and make their passage more difficult. They could only go single-file, and the rock thrust up on either side crowding near, so that looking up, squinting, one saw only a narrow strip of sky stark against the dark walls; Laurence had the sensation that the cliffs leaned in towards them.

The wind also was crammed in narrowly, and whistled a little where it passed over sharp edges or crevasses in the rock; a loose slope challenged them awhile in climbing, and Laurence slipped badly on the other side, sliding with a tumble of loose pebbles, sand creeping into all his clothing; falling backwards he caught himself awkwardly on his hands, which sank wrist-deep into the gravel as he slid a little further.

He managed to halt his skidding progress, and lying a little dazed in the spill of stones around him saw directly in front of him another overhang in the cliff, the height of several men from the ground, marked with the ochre signs: handprints and a faded painting. A very narrow and steep ledge protruded from the cliff face which might have served as a track to reach it, for an exceptionally skilled climber.

Laurence struggled up to his feet, and only then saw there was no way forward: they had yet again come to the end of a gorge, without breaking through. There was only a small grassy clearing within almost curved walls of rock, spiky-leaved plants like ivy and a few sapling trees protruding almost horizontal from cracks, and the overhang standing above with the quality of an empty sentinel post.

Granby came in a more controlled slide down the gravel slope beside him, saw at once the dead end, and did not say anything. A few pebbles rolled a little further along from his feet, rattling, and then stopped. There was a palpable silence, all sound muffled and deadened by the encircling rock and the high slope of loose stones.

"Another false start, then?" Rankin said irritably, from the summit of the slope, breaking the silence and yet not the queer power of the place, cathedral in quality. Even he was not insensible to it: his words fell into the space and died without echoing, and he did not speak again.

It was not so easy to get out of the clearing as to get in; Granby managed it, at the price of scraped palms, but Rankin had in the end to brace against the wall and reach down a hand for Laurence to scramble up the slope and out again. Rankin himself balanced easily despite the unsteady ground: he was, Laurence could not deny, an aviator born to the life; his training had started nearer to the cradle than even the age of seven, when most boys were taken into the service.

They returned somberly along the narrow passage, quiet with failure and discomfort; it was a longer and hotter walk retracing their steps, the sun having climbed overhead, and Laurence was weary and damp with sweat before they had returned to the waiting dragons. "No," Laurence said briefly, to Temeraire's raised head, "there is no passage. We must return to the river."

"It's cursed country," Jack Telly announced loud and sourly, over the disheartened groans and objections of the other convicts as Lieutenant Blincoln made a desultory effort to marshal them for loading, "and I don't see why there is any call for a road into it; if we ain't all to be found like dried-up husks ten years hence we had better be going back to town. And I ha'nt a drink all morning."

"That is quite enough, Mr. Telly; you will have one when we have made camp by the river, if you are not having strokes for malingering," Forthing said, and with a clout of a stick roused Maynard and Hob Wessex, who had not even taken their hats off their faces.

He went to prod Jonas Green also, lying curled in the shade of a tree, but Green, who had so far been the most reliable of the men, did not stir but only moaned; and after prodding again, Forthing turned to Laurence and said, low, "Sir, if you would—"

Across the clearing, Rankin looked away from Caesar's side, where he had been adjusting a strap, and said frowning, "What are you about, there? Get that man up."

Forthing hesitated, and by then the men were looking over; Green yet had not moved. "He's not drunk, sir," he said.

Laurence stepped over and looked down: Green was curled around himself with sweat sprung out all over his body, soaked through his shirt in great dark stains; when they turned him over, his hand was swollen large and reddened around two small black punctures.

*   *   *

Dorset made an inspection—though a dragon-surgeon, he was the nearest thing to a physician among them; he shook his head. "A snake perhaps, or a spider: it is quite impossible to tell."

"What ought be done?" Laurence asked.

"I will take most detailed notes on the progression," Dorset said. "I understand there are several highly venomous species recognized already in this part of the world; it will be of great interest to the Royal Society."

"Yes, but what are we to do for the poor blighter in the meantime?" Granby exclaimed.

"Oh; I can bind up the arm, but I imagine the venom has already spread," Dorset said absently, his fingers on the man's pulse. "He may not die; it is entirely dependent upon the degree of venom, and his natural resistance."

"Water, I imagine," Tharkay said, a more practical compassion; but Green moaned wordless and incoherently when touched, and vomited up all he was given before they had managed to lift him into the belly-rigging. His condition silenced the noisiest complaints, from respect, but a low muttering grew as they went back aboard: it seemed fresh proof of the hostility of the country which surrounded them.

Perhaps through this distraction, or only from fatigue, they turned at some point wrongly; or so Laurence supposed, when after an hour they had not yet found again their former camp or the river. The sound of running water could be heard, but the canyons brought distant echoes near, now and again, and even from high aloft they could only see impenetrable green, and the alternating pattern of flat clifftops rising and the tree-choked valleys between.

It was very hot. Abruptly and without warning, Caesar set down, tiring all at once. He fit himself into a little shade at the edge of a clearing and curled small, for once without any noise or complaint; he only shut his eyes and lay breathing heavily. Rankin dismounted and stood by his head frowning while Dorset, the surgeon, climbed down from Temeraire's back to make his inspections. Dorset looked into Caesar's mouth and nostrils, then pushed his spectacles up into place again as he rose. "There is as yet no serious condition, in my judgment, but he is overheated; and has not had enough water: at this stage of his growth he does not yet possess those reserves which should make him able to bear more privation."

"Well, we haven't any water here, so there is no use his lying down now," Iskierka said, callously, nudging at Caesar's flank with her nose; he did not stir, except to flick the long narrow end of his tail. "I am thirsty, too; and not getting less so while we sit here."

Rankin snapped, "Captain Granby, you will restrain your beast, if you please. I will not take Caesar flying about wildly in this heat again; we will have to wait until after dark."

"Except my beast, if you like, has it aright: we haven't water here, and we aren't going to find some more easily in the dark," Granby said. "Precious soon he will need that more than rest. Could we get him up on Temeraire's back?"

Temeraire put back his ruff, but reluctantly said to Laurence, "Oh; I suppose I can carry him, if I must; but I think we had much better let everyone down, and go and find water first. Once we know where it is, we may come back and fetch them all, when it is cooler and not so unpleasant to be loaded down."

Laurence shook his head. "I had rather not part company," he said, "when we have already seen we can so easily mistake our way; we have grown too complacent, in thinking that we need only go aloft to find our path again. I feel as though we have turned around three times in the last quarter-of-an-hour, for all the sun has not shifted."

"It seems to me," Iskierka said, "that the trouble is all these trees, everywhere; I might burn off some of them, and then we could see where the river is, perhaps."

"After four days of a firestorm, we would not very much care, however," Rankin said cuttingly.

The trees were not of a sort which would be easily amenable to burning, either, nor to being knocked down: these were not small scrubby creatures, despite their queerly peeling trunks, but old giants, prime timber; Laurence had seen half-a-dozen which could have made the *Allegiance* a new mainmast. Even Temeraire's strength could not have quickly uprooted one, and a single tree falling would scarcely have made any notable diminishment in the cover.

They determined at last to wait a little while: the sun was climbing to its zenith, white-hot and hammering directly down upon them. The day grew yet more still; the faint breath of wind brought no relief, only a dry, papery feeling to one's skin, lips cracking and white.

They unloaded the dragons and Rankin, turning to the convicts, ordered them to break off young tree-branches, and rip up some of the undergrowth, to lay over Caesar's hide to deepen the shade and give a little vegetal coolness from what water remained within the limbs. The men only resentfully obliged him, then with more attention treated Jonas Green in the same manner: he had been lowered to lie in the darkest shade, and Dorset was dosing him with a small cup of water.

The rest of the convicts returned to their own torpor beneath the trees. Rankin paced for a short time, as if considering whether to try and stir them back to work; but the heat presently defeated him, and he went to sit against one of the tall eucalypts, across from his dragon, his eyes closed. Green moaned occasionally, and stirred; he was yet sweating copiously, and when he roused he could not speak, but only mumbled a few words thickly and crumpled back to sleep.

Temeraire sighed a little, without much noise: he and Iskierka were awkwardly situated in the smallish clearing, having wound themselves into place among the towering spires of the oldest trees, and he could not be wholly shaded from the intensity of the sun; nor could he spread out his wings as he was often wont to do when excessively hot. He did what he could to shade his head, his neck nearly doubled back upon itself, curling partly around a tree, and then he, too, closed his eyes. Sitting not against him but near-by, Laurence also slept; or something like sleep, not half so restful: a sensation not of peace but of drifting, unmoored, the world turning away from beneath them and the sun piercing the leaf cover now and again to stab.

At length it fell beyond the other rim of the gorge, and they had a little more shade: but the lassitude was not easily shaken off, and instead deepened for a little while, so when Laurence had at last roused himself, with an effort, the day was wearing away and late: it was past six, he thought, at the very least, and perhaps later. There was a smell of roasting meat, which had brought him out of that well of uneasy sleep: Demane had half-a-dozen wombats on skewers, over a small, neat fire, and had already given a small cup of the blood to his brother to drink.

"I am not hungry," Temeraire said, opening his eyes, "but I would not in the least mind a drink of water: pray let us go find the river now; and then I do not suppose I would mind a bite of wombat, even though they are not really worth eating."

"Then get your own," Demane said, rather indignantly. "They are very worth eating, to me. Finish that," he added, to Sipho, who was showing no marked enthusiasm for his treat.

"It is hot, and it tastes very ill," Sipho said, but quelled by a look accepted his unhappy fate and tipped back the rest of the cup; several of the convicts, also woken by the smell of the cooking meat, watched with more envy than sympathy; every man's mouth was dry as sand.

"Might send the boy to fetch some more," Telly said, eyeing Demane, who glared in offense and turned his back.

"We had better make a go of finding the stream again, I suppose," Granby said, "—we won't have more light than we do now."

They already had little, and that quickly diminishing. Though fortunately they had not unloaded wholly, but only shifted the baggage so Temeraire might lie down, it must all be resecured, particularly the eggs; and then Caesar had to be persuaded to climb up onto Temeraire's back.

"I do not see why I must ride on him; it is very hot and unpleasant," Caesar grumbled; he had roused enough with the coolness to be difficult. "I think I had much better stay here, and you may go and fetch some water and bring it back; and then I will feel like flying again."

"It will be a good deal more hot and unpleasant for *me*," Temeraire said, "so you may cease caterwauling: it will be no treat to carry you, and I think it is a great pity you should have been allowed to be such a glutton that you are grown fat with no good purpose; I am sure that is why you have tired so quickly."

This was unjust, coming from a beast who himself had grown to perhaps five times his hatching weight in the space of a week, and Caesar was inclined to resent it; but Iskierka's temper was at once shorter and more violent. Having reached its ends, she did not bother with recrimination, and only jetted a thin stream of flame directly at Caesar's hindquarters; which as a form of persuasion worked to admirable effect, as he scrambled forward promptly.

"Ow!" Temeraire said, jerking his own singed tail away, and hunching his wings away from Caesar's claws. "That is not at all helpful, in the least; and will you stop catching at me? I am not to be climbed like a hill."

Their departure so delayed, the light was very nearly gone before they were aloft again: only the gorge walls holding a little reflected brightness, the trees a solid dark mass beneath, blanketing the ground. Lacking any certainty of their way, they continued along the line of the gorge, eastward away from the vanishing sun, hoping in such a way to retrace part of their course; the sound of water tormented them, once in a while, coming so clear that Temeraire would raise his head and prick forward his ruff.

From time to time, Iskierka would set down, where there was a little opening, and thrust her head beneath the cover: but there was no sign of water. The stars had slowly begun to come out, and Laurence looking up realized in dismay from the Southern Cross that they had somehow turned again: they were traveling north-west, instead. "Temeraire," he said, "set down: there, in the space at the base of that cliff."

"What the devil are you doing?" Rankin demanded; sharp with anxiety.

"We have lost our way, again," Laurence said. "We cannot keep flying in circles and exhaust them: better we should rest until the stars come more clear."

Temeraire was indeed very hot and fatigued; where Laurence touched the hide with his bare hand, after they had landed, it felt nearly feverish: blood pumped vigorously along the great swollen vein curving down from the wing-joint. "I do not feel ill; only so thirsty," Temeraire said.

Caesar was also worse: somnolent again and still, barely twitching when Rankin touched his head. They had only a few cans of water left among them; Temeraire held up the dragonet's head carefully with a talon, and they tipped what little they had inside. They could not do more than moisten his tongue and mouth, but it at least perhaps gave a sensation of relief; he seemed to lie easier, afterwards.

"Let's have a little rum, then," Jack Telly said, whining; and with some reluctance Laurence approved Blincoln's doling it out to the men in small cups: the worst possible medicine for their present condition, considered as a matter of health, and yet as a matter of discipline the most necessary; they were grown restive in direct proportion to the increasing torpor of the dragons, and the folly of discomfort might easily drive them to desertion and flight into the wilds of the forest, however more unlikely they were to find relief or water on their own.

"I suppose we might dig to a little water," Granby said. "We aren't in a desert, at least."

They had the shovels, and Iskierka was persuaded to oblige as well; but the ground was too porous: they managed to sink a hole some ten feet down, and a few inches of water filled in, but it ran quickly away, and the sides collapsed too easily to hold. Every man had a handful of water, soaked up in handkerchiefs and wrung out into the mouth; they soaked a few more again and laid them over poor Jonas Green's face, to give him a little relief; and then they were forced to give it up: they could not even fill a cup or a can.

The sky was yet obscured by clouds, which only infrequently broke long enough to show the stars. "We ought to have listened to Temeraire from the first," Laurence said quietly. "In the morning, I think we must unload him and separate; we cannot hope for more than another day of searching from him or Iskierka, without we find them water."

"And when you have found any water, how do you propose to find your way back?" Rankin said. "If you do, of course; that certainly would simplify the problem."

"Oh, honestly," Granby said, a more measured if less formal response than Laurence would have liked to make, when Temeraire had spent so much of his strength already in carting Caesar about. Rankin compressed his mouth, and did not apologize, but neither did he attempt to continue this line of inquiry; he looked over at Caesar instead, with real anxiety: he could not, Laurence supposed, ever hope to have another beast, if he lost this one as well; and perhaps he had learnt to value the privilege more, after finding himself out of harness.

"In the morning, we'll have Iskierka set a fire going, a little way up the gorge," Granby said. "If we break up one of these old monsters, we can make a bonfire they will see in Sydney, I dare say: then we can find our way back. For my part," he added, "I mean to try crossing some of these ridges, instead of going along the gorges: I don't know if we have gone back anywhere near the way we came, and I think skipping along sideways we are more like to find some kind of water, even if it isn't that same blasted stream."

"I have very little say in the matter, I find," Rankin said, coldly. "I trust the rest of us will not have been murdered by our company before you return; I suppose at least I can let them at the rum, if it comes to that." He rose and went to Caesar's head, and cast himself alongside to sleep.

"I don't like to be coarse," Granby said to Laurence, "but if I did, I would be," a sentiment Laurence shared: he could not help but contemplate with some unhappiness the prospect of long years immured in the colony, with Rankin the senior captain, and with the support of both military rank and family influence, back in England: it could not make for a comfortable or a quiet future.

That, however, whatever vicious phantasies Rankin might entertain, had not the least bearing on their present circumstances. In the morning they must find water, or the dragons would perish: another stretch beneath the sun's height, in heat this implacable, with no relief, would leave them too wrung-out to fly even a little distance. "If we cannot find anything before noon," Laurence said, "we must try and sink a proper well; if we line the sides with tree-bark, perhaps, and widen the whole, enough that we can get inside and dig."

Granby nodded a little; they did not need to speak of the alternative.

They separated, to sleep beside their own dragons; but Laurence found sleep did not come; he was not tired enough, after their long half-involuntary rest during the heat of the day. He sat instead beside Temeraire's jaw, where the heat radiating from his body did not come too strongly; the night air was still close and thick and hot. The moon rose, at length, and shone from behind a thin veil of clouds, haloed brilliantly in shades of pale pearl-grey and white.

It was very queer to be amid this verdant and standing forest, the ground soft and rich beneath their hands, and still so desperately thirsty when plainly there was plentiful water somewhere near; something almost like deliberate torment in it. Laurence did not care for superstition; he did not yield to it now, but he felt it not unreasonable to be conscious of how ill-fitted they were to be in this country, a lack of understanding and of place.

"They say," he heard Jack Telly telling the others, low, "that you can fetch up all the way to China, on the other side of the mountains: and get work on a merchantman, and back to England if you like. I spoke to a fellow got up there and back, a year ago."

"A charming notion, do you not think?" Tharkay said to Laurence; he had come to sit beside him.

"Have you heard it before?" Laurence asked.

Tharkay nodded. "It is rather popular in the port, and made all the more so for these goods coming in; although I think they imagine something more in the line of Xanadu than Canton."

The convicts were taking it in turns to give Green a few drops of water from the handkerchief-squeezings and to fan him, despite their almost satisfied airs of pessimism. "He is sure to die, and he will not be the last man of us to go, either, you may be sure of it," O'Dea said, tenderly wiping his brow.

At length, Laurence stretched himself on the ground, rather out of duty than a real desire to sleep. The leaves were thick blotches overhead: for backdrop, the moon had sunk deeper into cloudbank, imbuing the sky with a general pallor instead of the pitch-black of a clear night. The silence, the heat, remained. Laurence thought perhaps he slept a little; but he had no sense of time passing when he opened his eyes. There was a strange low moaning, but it was not Jonas Green, as he first thought: it was a song, somewhere in the distance.

Laurence remained prone a moment, then abruptly sat up as the noise broke fully into his mind. Several other of the men were sitting up already, tense and listening, their eyes showing white in the corners. They could not make words out, but the rise and fall and rise of the drumming came clearly, over and over: and over it an unnatural and repetitive rattle like dried leaves shaking in wind. It died away even while they listened; then began once more afresh.

"That is a very strange sound," Temeraire said, drowsily, without opening his eyes. "Whoever can be making it? It sounds as though they did not feel very well; or perhaps were angry."

This interpretation plainly did not recommend itself to the listening convicts. "Pray do not disturb yourself," Laurence said, loud enough to carry over the noise, and reach their ears. "It cannot be of concern to us in your company, and you had much better get as much rest as you can."

Temeraire did not answer, except to sigh a little breath and sleep again. Laurence put a hand on his muzzle, and turned back to his pallet; beside it Tharkay's lay empty, and his small pack gone with him.

Laurence lay down again, mostly to give an example to the men which should reassure; he did not feel very much like sleep, with that strange inhuman music still lingering. It felt of a piece with all the rest, the alien cry of an alien land.

There were more low whispers, inarticulate yet uneasy, until abruptly Rankin's voice rang out in its drawling, ironic vowels, "I am sorry to have to ask you gentlemen to be so good as to reserve your presentiments of disaster for morning: I am not competent to endure the hysterics without the fortification of a night's rest and strong coffee."

The cold contempt did what sympathy, perhaps, would not have: it silenced them. The strange moaning song died away once more, fading into the dry air. Laurence watched the leaves stirring overhead, and again time slid away from him; he opened his eyes this time to a touch

upon his shoulder, and pushed himself up to look at Tharkay, who silently handed him a canteen, full and dripping wet.

"Thank Heaven," Laurence said, low; and looked a question at Tharkay, why he had not roused all the camp for the discovery.

"I did not find our singers," Tharkay said, "but their tracks, I believe: there is a way over the ridge to another river, and its banks are not impassable. I have found only the fewest signs of passage, but the trail is not unused. I think it may answer your search—and perhaps mine, also."

"The—smugglers?" Laurence said, slowly, relying on Temeraire's intuition.

Tharkay paused and said, "I imagine you find I have been very close; although perhaps not so close as I might have prided myself upon."

"You may congratulate yourself as much as you like," Laurence said ruefully, "—my intelligence is borrowed: Temeraire worked out the whole, not myself, and that only by guessing. But I cannot see I have the least right to demand candor from you on the subject of your private affairs. I am sufficiently in your debt," he added, "that I hope you know I would be glad of an opportunity to make some return; and you need not make me explanations."

Tharkay smiled, glinting a little even in the dark. "You are kind to make me such an offer; I can well imagine how little you would like in practice to lend yourself so blindly to another man's course."

Very true, Laurence was forced to admit, "but despite that, I will not withdraw," he said, "and if you prefer to keep your silence, I beg you to believe I will not press you."

"I do not propose to entertain myself unnecessarily," Tharkay said, "though I will ask you to come aside with me: I have been silent all this while shipboard only because I am not content with the genteel fiction of privacy when separated by only a plank of wood from a hundred idle ears, and I am no more so here in an open forest, surrounded by men who may only pretend to sleep."

Chapter 6

"Yes," Tharkay said, "I am looking for the smugglers."

They had walked a short distance into the trees, pressing down the undergrowth; pebbles shifting underfoot and the creak of branches pushed aside assured them no one should be following without their hearing it.

"The East India Company," Tharkay continued, "is losing some fifty thousand pounds per annum to their work, and they fear worse to come; much worse. So far the illegal trade is only a trickle, but it is a steady trickle they cannot close up, and widening."

Laurence nodded. "And the goods are not coming in by sea?"

"More to the point," Tharkay said, "the goods are not leaving by Canton." Laurence stared. "You begin to understand the degree of their concern, I think."

"How can they be certain?" Laurence said. "The port is fantastically busy; some shipments must be able to evade their monopoly."

Tharkay said, "When the smuggling first began to be noticed, a little more than a year ago, word was sent to the offices in Canton to make a note of all ships coming through the port, with the intention of tracing the source: similar efforts have been made before, of course, although they were puzzled by a method so indirect as funneling the goods through Sydney—"

"The operation must eat nearly all the profit of it," Laurence said.

"So they imagined," Tharkay said, "and did not at first take it very seriously; they expected to find at the bottom of it only some enthusiast, who was willing to spend a pound to save sixpence: there is very little which inspires creativity so much as government tariffs and licenses. But the ships and their cargo are accounted for, nearly every one. There are a handful of cases—" He shrugged a little, dismissing these. "Nothing which could account for the steady flow of goods; which is only increasing."

"They fear, then, that the Chinese have opened another port," Laurence said, "to some other nation."

"Perhaps not officially," Tharkay said. "But if the officials of some port city should choose to turn a blind eye to the occasional foreign vessel; for instance, if they should be persuaded by one with sympathy for some foreign nation—"

"Lien," Laurence said immediately, "and Napoleon would care nothing for the profit; not so long as he could undermine our trade."

Tharkay nodded. "It all fits together very nicely," he said. "The French funnel cheap goods to our markets, undercutting the East India Company—"

Trade was Britain's lifeblood: it bore the cost of the merchant marine which trained her seamen and her shipbuilders; it brought in the gold and silver which funded her allies, and put armies on the Continent to stand in the way of Bonaparte's dominion. "If prices fell badly enough, they might cause a panic in the Exchange," Laurence said. "But would anyone in China risk so obliging Lien?"

She had been disgraced in China with the death of her former companion, Prince Yongxing: he had been chief of that conservative faction which had preferred to have nothing to do with the nations of the West, either in commerce or in politics. They had schemed to supplant Crown Prince Mianning, himself privately a sympathizer with the more liberal slant of his court; their design having been uncovered and thwarted, and Yongxing himself slain, Lien had chosen exile in France, divorcing herself from her former home in hopes of finding Napoleon an effective instrument of revenge.

Tharkay shrugged. "You know as well as do I the reverence with which Celestials are viewed, and Yongxing's political allies were only defeated, not eradicated. In the intervening years, they may have regrouped."

"It seems just the sort of thing Lien would do," Temeraire said, shaking his tendrils free of water, having drunk his fill, and enjoying the sentiment of righteous disdain. "She and Yongxing were so angry that China should have any trade with the West, and tried to do so many wicked things all in the name of preventing it; and now she has changed her notion and is looking for more."

Laurence paused, and doubtfully said, "I had not considered that her philosophy was so opposed to opening the borders of China, in its principles; it is incongruous, a little," then fell silent.

"That is just what I mean," Temeraire said. "She is perfectly happy to throw all of that over, if only it will hurt us: just her sort of unpleasantness. Laurence, I do not mean to complain," he added, "for this water is very nice—so fresh and crisp!—but I *am* hungry."

Tharkay's little creek had led them, with only half-an-hour's flight, to the river into which it merged: wide and clear, and lined along both banks with tall, tall pines. The river flowed in the wrong direction for their needs, south towards Sydney instead of away, and anyway it was full of rocks and very shallow in places; but there was room to walk along its banks, and Tharkay was of the opinion that if they should follow it upstream, they might well find it beginning somewhere in a pass, on the other side of the mountains.

Temeraire thought it an excellent idea to stay close to the river, in any case; one grew so very parched, much more quickly than one might have expected, and then of course there was Caesar—

He cast a disgusted look over: Caesar had needed to be carried to the river, even after they had given him two canteens full of water, and told him there was more to be had, even more cool and refreshing; it had not stirred him to make any effort. He had only said, "I don't care to fly, just yet; Temeraire may take me," in the most casual way, and sighed even when asked to climb up onto Temeraire's back. And when they had finally brought him to the river, he had climbed down and, before anyone could stop him, walked straight on off the bank to immerse himself, so everyone else who wished to drink or to fill a canteen had to use a less convenient place further upstream.

Even the poor sick convict Jonas Green had done better: he had roused up quite heroically when given a full cup, and said, "Damn me if I will die, after all: let me have some more!" and although he trembled dreadfully when he tried to stand, he hobbled over with two men helping him, and sat by the bank until he had managed to wash himself all over, and his wretchedly stinking clothing also, all of which he spread beside him on some flat stones, in the sunlight, to dry.

Caesar, on the other hand, had to be reminded to drink; and then not allowed to drink too much; and then prodded sharply to get out of the water, so others might bathe; even though he was so small yet that a little while lying in the river had sufficed to see him clean. He had sighed and hinted that he wanted scrubbing, when all he needed to do was flatten himself a little to have the water rush over his back with no help. Rankin had at once ordered several of the convicts to oblige him, which meant they were all tired and disinclined to help when Temeraire wished to be bathed a little, too, and needed someone to carry buckets up to his back to pour the water over.

Temeraire sighed and made the best of what Demane and Roland could do, meanwhile dabbling his nose in the deepest part of the river, and tipping his head up so the water would run down his neck. "You might wash down the eggs, too," he added, "with a soft rag, if you please, and not very hard, only to be sure the shells are clean."

Lieutenant Forthing was very quick to join in this work, Temeraire noted disapprovingly, and made sure to keep close watch upon him and ensure Forthing did not try and speak to the eggs, to make them any inappropriate promises or brag of himself. "That is enough; it is clean, so you may have done," Temeraire said, when Forthing had wiped away the dust on the larger egg, the Yellow Reaper; he was not so eager to linger while working on the very little one, at least.

"Temeraire," Tharkay said to him, when they had all drunk their fill, and settled for a comfortable rest in the shade, while the sun worked past its height, "do you see any signs of fire, along the river, more distantly?"

Temeraire did not mind leaping aloft for a little while, now there was water, and hovering looked as closely as he could in either direction, so far as he could see before the river twisted out of sight around a curve, and plunged away into a canyon the other way, but there was no sign of any person at all, "and also," he said, coming back down, "I am sorry to say, no sign of any game. I hope I have not been too ungrateful, about the kangaroos."

"That may make us a little uncomfortable, but it is some encouragement to me if the game has been frightened off," Tharkay said, and turned towards the camp.

"So you propose to erect a road alongside the river," Rankin was saying to Laurence, "which will meander in every direction, to the certain unnecessary expense of twenty miles out of fifty, no doubt, and having been built in the midst of summer and drought will be flooded at the first rains; and this, before we have even traced it to its conclusion."

"Captain Rankin," Laurence said, in that very level and restrained way which meant he was particularly angry, "if you have uncovered a more certain passage, overnight, I would be glad to hear of it. In the meantime, we are charged to build a road—"

"We are not charged to waste our days wandering in an uncomfortable wilderness to no good purpose, sitting idly by and shepherding these men along, to we know not what end," Rankin said. "And I *have* made use of a night's reflection to better comprehend what anyone of sense," he stressed, pointedly, "might have observed, from our flights yesterday: there is no reason why these gorges should make a passage at all, and as they evidently choose to collapse at very little provocation, even if we should find one, we could not rely on its perpetuity. We are wandering in a maze that has no exit. We had far better go up on the heights, and find a crossing along the ridges."

"So that every cow can be marched a thousand feet into the air, and a thousand feet down again, before they come to market," Granby said. "Precious clever sort of route that would make."

The day was just as stifling and unpleasant, and they were all hungry, and inclined to argue; as they did not mean to walk any further at present, there was nothing else to do, and it was too hot even to sleep.

"Seems to me we might stay by the water and be comfortable," Jack Telly said, never shy of putting in his own opinion.

"Much to no one's surprise," Rankin snapped. "I imagine we would see two hours' work in a day, and the rest spent in idling and drunken stupors."

Temeraire, for his part, privately thought that at least the ridges, being so much higher, would be cooler and more pleasant; one might have a chance of some wind, and at least one would not be staring into these rock walls on every side: so confining. But of course, he would not say anything which might support Rankin, who did not deserve such a mark of distinction; as he had made the suggestion, it could be of no use whatsoever.

"May I propose," Tharkay said, "that when the sun has eased, we instead follow the course of the river to its culmination and see what advantage this route affords; we need not immediately begin construction."

This seemed quite sensible; but Rankin did not answer Tharkay, and indeed he turned his back, without a word, and walked away to sit with Caesar: not even the slightest inclination of his head, to acknowledge he had been spoken to, and Tharkay had not been the least bit impolite. "I do not understand what business Rankin has, behaving so rudely," Temeraire said to Laurence afterwards, while they began to collect the baggage once again.

"None; although I imagine he takes Tharkay's descent for his excuse," Laurence said, looking up the course of the river. "You are quite sure you saw no-one on the banks?" he asked. "If you should see any-one—we would be glad to speak the natives, if they were the singers last night; they might well be able to tell us if we have taken a reasonable route."

"No, there was no-one, but I will certainly look again when we are up," Temeraire said, remembering belatedly the odd music; he had been so very drowsy and uncomfortable last night that it had all seemed very nearly a dream, or at least far away. "That was a very interesting kind of song; I have never heard anything like, or that language, at all. But whatever about Tharkay's descent can Rankin object to? After all, it is not as though he were not hatched yet, and no one knows what he might turn out be."

"His mother was Nepalese," Laurence said, "and there was some irregularity about the marriage, I understand; I find Rankin is given to think a great deal of birth, and not enough of character."

He did not try to keep quiet: he and Granby were inclined to resent Rankin's insult, and Temeraire did not mind joining them in the sentiment; so everyone was very stiff and formal as they packed everything up. Caesar sighed heavily, and made many reluctant noises about flying, and let his head and tail and wings drag limp towards the ground as he pushed himself up; and then Dorset went over and examined him and said, "He may fly, but he should carry no weight; you may not ride, Captain Rankin."

Caesar sat back on his haunches and said, "I can carry him! He is *my* captain," indignantly, all signs of limp torpor gone in a flash, but Dorset was implacable, so Temeraire would have to endure carrying Rankin again, and Laurence did not look at all pleased, either.

To add insult to injury, when Laurence quietly inquired further, Dorset said, "No, no; he is capable of carrying, perfectly capable; but he is bidding fair to develop into a malingerer, and an early lesson such as this is like to have a good effect."

For his part, Temeraire thought that correcting Caesar's bad habits was so thoroughly lost a cause that it could not justify any such efforts, when they led to situations so unpleasant to other innocent parties; but Laurence did not like to contradict a surgeon. So up Rankin came again, boarding with Laurence at the very end because of his rank, and as a guest; and instead Tharkay went to fly with Iskierka, which did not suit anyone except her. Though Tharkay was not his, precisely, Temeraire had grown used enough to his company to feel a sense of some responsibility, a degree of justified interest; and Tharkay could not in the least prefer to ride upon Iskierka, who was exceedingly hot and damp in her person, and so unreliable.

They had been working in the hot sun, so that when it dropped again below the gorge walls they were ready to take advantage of the chance, and to fly onward at once. It was not pleasant flying, despite the lack of direct sun: they had to keep close within the narrow canyon walls, uninteresting and covered with scrubby dried-out grass and shrubs gone pale as wheat.

The river running over the rocks had a strange, steady noise; not loud enough to be called a roar, it seemed more a part of the same queer silence which seemed to envelop the gorges. It was not a sound one could listen to; it rather wished to swallow up all other noises, so Temeraire could scarcely even hear his own wings beating.

Caesar kept insisting on flying too close, where he could keep an eye on Rankin, even though it was his own fault he was not allowed to carry his own captain, and as though anyone else would have wanted Rankin, anyway, Temeraire thought. Caesar *would* clip him, coming too close to the wings, and once he even fouled Temeraire's wing-joint with the tip of one claw.

Temeraire had been drifting a little, almost sleeping as he flew; the scratch startled him unpleasantly aware again, and conscious of his surroundings. "Ow!" he said, sharply. "That is quite enough; you will keep further off, if you cannot mind where you are putting your claws," he added, and snapped at Caesar's tail for warning; Caesar tipped his wings back and dodged hastily, but took the lesson and made a little more of a safe distance between them.

Temeraire settled himself back into the tedium of long flying, but in so doing, noticed a flash of color below. "Laurence," he said, looking over his shoulder as he paused, hovering, "I think that is a bit of broken plate, there, if I am not mistaken."

"Whatever is of interest in some flotsam?" Rankin said; Laurence asked Temeraire to set them down, and when Iskierka had come down also, he and Tharkay considered the fragments: it was certainly a very lovely example of Qingbai ware, broken up; a sad waste, Temeraire thought, and the smugglers had ought to have been more careful.

They went aloft again afterwards, flying quite low, where they might be shaded from the sun. The river curved away from them upstream, into a series of gorges, and Temeraire had settled it in his own head they would be flying until nightfall, when he made the last turn and stopping abruptly nearly made Iskierka and Caesar both pile into him; they could not hover as he did.

"What are you doing?" Iskierka demanded, and then beating up over him said, "Oh, *there,*" with immense satisfaction, as though she had done anything useful to bring them to this point. The river plunged on through the trees below them, but up ahead the timber petered out, and a broad field of rich green growth, very small, spread out across the floor of a wide green valley, framed but not cramped by rising mountains.

There was a murmur of pleasure and satisfaction among all the men—"I have rarely seen such splendid farming country," Laurence said to Temeraire, "or at least so it looks."

Temeraire himself was far more preoccupied with the startling evidence they had not been the first to make the crossing, after all; before him, in the field, stood a small and placid herd of cattle, their coats gone shaggy and ragged, munching upon the grass.

"Oh! I cannot think of anything I like better than stewed beef," Temeraire said, leaning over the cooking meat to inhale its vapours, "or at least, when it is so particularly good." Gong Su had contrived with his assistance to cut out a little hollow of water from the river, into which a fine, fat specimen of the herd had gone along with many stones Iskierka had heated, for the dragons' dinner; and the soup was doled out in bowlfuls to the men, to eat with their salt pork and biscuit.

Laurence took a cup of the broth and some biscuit himself, and walked out a little distance into the valley: the earth was soft and springy beneath his feet, unmarred by rocks or stumps, and the leathery smell of the cattle as familiar to him as breathing. He might almost have been on his father's estates again in Nottinghamshire, but for the glorious rearing escarpments of sandstone, yellow and grey and red, which framed the wide comfortable bowl of the valley floor.

When Temeraire had eaten, they went aloft together to the heights and cleared away a little space amid the vegetation. The long, thickly forested slopes curved downward to the valley floor like wide-spread green skirts, then thinning out into grassy plains: timber and grazing land as well, and the valley stretched a considerable length, ample to any use. The river's banks needed only to be widened a little, and the mouth of the valley cut, to allow for a most convenient road with easy supply of fresh water for driving cattle.

"If one should put up a pavilion here," Temeraire said, a little wistfully, "I do not think anyone could ask for a finer prospect: look at those falls over there; and all the cattle would be in view."

If a great deal of labor would be required to realize such a project, dragon strength could make light work of that. Temeraire might fell the timber they required, and manage the stone as they quarried it, even while the men were set to cutting the road back to Sydney, Laurence thought. And when they had finished, there would be no great difficulty to bring back more cattle along it: the valley could certainly sustain a herd of thrice the size, at least—enough to support even four dragons, if the beasts should supplement their diet with game.

Laurence put down his glass, half-amused to discover in himself so much inclination towards this peculiar sort of domesticity, when he thought how eagerly he had fled from any such work as a boy and spurned with contempt the management of estates, or anything so quiet and unadventurous as a comfortable living; in the face of his father's impatience and punishment both. He had never seen any honor to be won on fields such as these; now it seemed to him the cleanest place which he had seen in life.

"The trail continues westward," Tharkay told him, when they had returned to the valley floor, "and I am left none the wiser as to its source. It must meet the coast, somewhere, to be taking on goods from the ships; but I expected to find the path curving, or doubling back upon itself, sooner than this."

"Now that you are certain the goods have come this way," Laurence said, "might your search not be more fruitful if you sailed along the coast to examine what nearby harbors, not so distant from the trailhead, should suffice to host a merchant vessel? Or," he added, "you might leave a sentinel over the trail, and see who will appear."

"No-one will appear," Tharkay said, "now that we have come to occupy the valley with three dragons; we might as well be knights on errantry, blowing horns as we go. I expect you will be staying," he added, half a question.

Laurence paused. "It is certainly an ideal situation for a covert," he said slowly, and looked at Temeraire. "Could you be happy with such a home?" he asked. "I know it can offer none of the advantages of a more improved location."

"Oh! as for improvements, we may make our own," Temeraire said, "and I dare say, once the eggs are hatched, we will make a great deal of progress; particularly as these trees and stones are not anyone's property, and we do not need to buy them before we make use of them. I must say," he added, "while it *is* strange there are no dragons here, it is very convenient not to always be wondering if something you happen to look at is already someone else's territory, and they will be upset that you have taken one of their cows."

He seemed as delighted with the prospect as ever he had with privateering; and later, as the sun dipped below the escarpments, and they settled to sleep, Temeraire expounded drowsily on his thoughts, adding, "We will certainly put up a splendid pavilion out of this fragrant wood, and some of this yellow rock; and Laurence, when we have done so, and increased the herd, why, I would put this territory against any in the world.

"And perhaps Maximus or Lily might yet come and visit, or we might have an artist come and work up a painting of it, which we might send to them to look at; and another to send to my mother, also. I am sure she would be curious to see it, and it cannot fail to please. I do not think we have seen a valley like this in China: there are very many interesting places there, of course; and the city cannot be compared, but one might be very well content here, I think."

Laurence could not encourage him to hope for dragon visitors, but he was glad nevertheless to see Temeraire so contented. The men had built a small fire for the comfort of its light; the temperature had fallen in the dark to a milder degree, and, settled on Temeraire's forearm, Laurence was conscious himself of a great weight lifted from his shoulders: if politics should deny them the chance to be of use in any material way in the war, there was at least work here to be done which he could not disdain, and the hope of building something rather than tearing away, to no purpose.

The steady rush of Temeraire's measured breathing made a constant like the ocean lapping the side of a ship; the wind breathed through the trees. Laurence slept, as solidly as he ever had in life, and roused to Temeraire snorting with displeasure and raising his head: Iskierka had nipped him on the back of the neck.

"Whatever is the matter?" Temeraire said irritably. "I was having a very pleasant dream; you need not have interrupted me."

"There is no time to be sleeping!" Iskierka said. "—The egg is gone."

II

Chapter 7

"**MY DEAR**," Laurence said, keeping his hand on Temeraire's forearm by way of both comfort and urging restraint, "we cannot be haring into the countryside unguided: aloft you cannot follow a trail, and with the quantity of timber in this country even the most unhandy thief can evade you for the price of hiding concealed the day, and traveling at night."

"We cannot be sitting here while they are carrying the egg off to who knows what fate," Temeraire said, his tail lashing so rapidly that Laurence feared he might do someone an injury; he was certainly wreaking destruction wholesale upon the vegetation in its path.

The stunted little egg sat lonesome on its nest of dry leaves and branches, the empty space beside it mutely reproachful: evidently forced to choose amongst prizes, the thieves had taken the larger Yellow Reaper egg, and left the runt behind.

Laurence had rarely seen Temeraire so roused, or Iskierka: a threat to himself or Granby offered the nearest comparison, and Laurence thought this might exceed even that passion: the greatest effort was visibly required to restrain them from immediate action, however purposeless; and Iskierka had already burnt up three trees by way of venting her feelings.

"Pray keep in mind," Granby said urgently, "that the thieves will take the very best care of the egg: they haven't stolen it to do it harm, they want a dragon of their own, plainly; although," he added more quietly to Laurence, as they went to consult with Tharkay, who had already set about examining the trail, "I don't know whatever for: I have never heard of men, ordinary men that is, wanting anything to do with a dragon."

"If Tharkay's supposition is right," Laurence said, "these may not be ordinary smugglers; if Napoleon has gone to such lengths to undermine our trade, they may as likely be French soldiers as mere profiteers."

"Even so, what would they want with an egg, here?" Granby said. "They can't mean to set up a covert of their own; it isn't as though the French have any prayer of holding a colony here, their navy being what it is, and ours being what it is."

"Why do pirates steal ships?" Tharkay said, without looking up from the ground. "They hardly need to establish a covert to make use of a dragon; they need only to evade you, and hunt enough game to feed it. A good, reliable, middle-weight beast would suit them admirably, I imagine: a transport for their goods better than a mule-train, and which leaves no trail on the ground to be followed."

What few traces he had found of the smugglers led onward to the north-west; little to give them hope, but all the intelligence Temeraire required to cast off all restraint. "Let us go at once, then; what if they are taking the egg back to the coast, to a ship? Or they might drop it, or cause it some hurt; they are certainly not properly trained aviators, and they do not have a dragon with them. What if they do not feed it when it has hatched, and only try and chain it? Oh! There are a thousand dreadful things which might be happening to it even now."

"And we are certainly not going to find it sitting *here*," Iskierka put in, which was true, but a species of logic which put an end to any rational design of the pursuit: the two of them *would* be off, at once, and when Caesar, evidently not yet inclined to so protective a view of his hypothetical year-mate, began to complain, Iskierka caught him by the ruff of his neck, shook him, and none too gently dragged him squalling and protesting up onto Temeraire's back: they refused point-blank to be constrained by his slower pace.

Laurence expected some protest from Rankin; but he made none, and Granby only shook his head and ordered his handful of men aboard. "Mr. Laurence," Forthing said, a little formally, when Laurence turned, "we have the egg ready to go aboard, if Temeraire should please: I have taken the liberty of swaddling it with more padding, and Mr. Fellowes believes we may rig it hammock-fashion, that it should not suffer from any shaking which the pursuit might make necessary."

"That is very good," Temeraire said, swinging his head around to inspect the arrangements, the first sign of approval he had offered For-thing; he nosed the well-wrapped egg a little to confirm and then squat-ted himself awkwardly that the fittings might be lashed to the breast-bands of his abbreviated harness, and to the broader band be-hind the wings, and the egg thus cradled gently rocking against his chest.

There were some sidelong and hostile looks towards Forthing and this operation, from the few officers who had accompanied Granby: if they had grudged a little before that Forthing should be situated so near the eggs, and have the best prospects of securing for himself the captaincy of the preferable Yellow Reaper, Laurence could well imag-ine their feelings now. They had all swallowed an assignment to a re-mote and undesirable posting, with few chances of seeing all-important combat or of advancement, with the only consolation the prospect of promotion for men who could not have hoped for the step otherwise.

Laurence did not think they would find the lost egg. Tharkay's ex-pression, looking at the trail, had not been sanguine, even if discretion had prevented him from conveying a discouraging opinion in the hear-ing of the excessively interested dragons. The smugglers must know their course, and anticipate pursuit: they had already found themselves at least this one route through the wilderness, and likely knew other passages.

So there was one chance only left, the stunted egg: undesirable by comparison yet priceless now, and to make matters worse, this must substantially worsen the breeding prospects of the new colony. Jane meant to send them more eggs, Laurence knew, but these three had been intended as the foundation, and the Yellow Reaper perhaps the most critical. If the egg had hatched a sire, who might be bred against many other lines, Jane would have sent a wider variety of the eggs of many more desirable breeds, for which men already here and estab-lished in service could aim to be preferred. If the egg had hatched a dam, the aviators likely hoped that a lack of alternatives might incline Temeraire to affection.

Whatever they might think of Temeraire's personal habits of free-thinking, these they generally credited, Laurence knew, to his own ac-count: when, he was dryly amused to think, the reverse was by far the truth of the matter. They certainly none of them had any objections to Temeraire's capabilities from a military perspective.

"A cross with a Reaper would be just the thing," Laurence had overheard, more than once—marrying Temeraire's virtues with the tractability and general good humor traditional to the Reaper breed, which had made it so widely preferred for service.

But there would certainly be no hope of a crossing between Temeraire and the little creature that would come out of the final egg: and therefore likely no hope of any mating at all until more eggs arrived, unless the runt proved female, and willing to be interested in Caesar—who had not risen in the estimation of the aviators since his hatching; the possibility did not excite great anticipation.

But there was nothing to be done. The Reaper egg was gone, and likely beyond all hope, even though they should have to go and search: Temeraire's and Iskierka's spirits could not bear otherwise. Only the slow grinding of time and failure would ease their grief and the disappointment to manageable levels. "We may hope, I suppose," Laurence said to Tharkay quietly, as they parted to go aboard, "that this search will at least be of some use in your quest: if we do overshoot the smugglers, at least we can follow the trail to its culmination, and the source of their goods, which if it is a harbor of any consequence will not be easily replaced, when we have denied it to them with regular patrols."

"From my perspective, nothing could be better," Tharkay said. "My fee was for tracing the smugglers' methods; it would not extend to the hire of dragons and a company of men to hunt them down, nor certainly to their destruction: but I imagine the greatest difficulty will be cutting a few of them out for questioning, if our friends continue in their present sentiments."

Tharkay went to join Granby; Laurence swung himself up to Temeraire's back without ceremony, and latched on to the harness at the back; Rankin was already hooked on and speaking quietly with the sulky Caesar.

"If *you* wish it, my dear captain, of course I will oblige, even though I am sure I don't see what the fuss is," Caesar said, "or why we should be bundled about like bag and baggage, when we might just as easily stay here and keep watch over the cows."

He said it quietly, though, and Temeraire ignored him entirely, only swinging his head briefly about to say, "Laurence, you are quite secure?" and cast a glittering eye over the rest of his passengers: the slitted pupil was open unnaturally wide, with almost a hint of red glowing within, the reflection of the lowering sun.

"I am," Laurence said, and they were airborne: the valley and its green curves falling away, away, and the sandstone cliffs; its serenity already a distant memory, and the drumming of wings like the beat for the turning of the capstan, bringing the anchor up.

The greatest danger, of course, Temeraire realized even through the distancing haze of fury, was they should overshoot the thieves, and miss them entirely: the men were carrying the egg, which should be a difficult burden for them, if they did not have waggons—Tharkay thought they did not—and of course, they were walking upon the ground in so tiresome a way, having to work through the brush.

"We cannot only fly straight after them on the trail," he told Iskierka. "Otherwise, we should soon go much further than they could possibly be, and meanwhile I am sure they should have hidden themselves somewhere aside, and be waiting for us to pass. We must be sure they are not in any countryside before we fly on out of it."

"I think we must fly sweeps," Laurence said, and sketched for them the pattern: they should keep the trail in the center of their course, and fly first zigging west, and then north, in arcs like a swinging broom.

Iskierka jetted steam from her spikes, restlessly. "How far do you think they might manage, to the side of the trail?" she asked. "If we go flying off all over the place, they will get ahead of us after all; and they might have horses, even if they don't have waggons."

They decided after some debate on a span of five miles in either direction, and continuing north-west began the flying pattern. It was hard, distressing flying—every bit of pale stone that caught the eye made Temeraire's heart leap uncomfortably in his chest, lest it should be the smooth creamy-pale shell, speckled black; so he was reminded at every turn of their dreadfully urgent purpose, and his head ached, too, from staring fixedly down at the ground.

Iskierka, who did not have so many people to carry, dived over and over towards some flash of movement—and over and over came away only with some useless bit of game, a wretched kangaroo or one of the stringy-legged cassowaries. She shared with Temeraire, at least, so they might eat as they flew and thus waste no further time; and she was, he could not deny, very quick to see the little flashes of movement.

It was comforting, not to be quite alone in the search; Iskierka was wrongheaded and irresponsible in almost every particular, and no one could enjoy her company, but in this one instance where they were of united mind and purpose, he might acknowledge her a valuable presence. On occasion—very few occasions, of course—she even saw something which he himself had not just yet noticed.

"Is that—" he began, and Iskierka dived at once: there was a knot of trees and low, coarse shrubbery, where he thought he had seen a glimmer of movement. She blasted the stand with fire, a quick hot roaring which did not properly catch in the greenery, but would have stunned any enemy within, and then tore into the trees: saplings and bushes cast aside into a singed heap, while she thrust her head within and searched, reaching in her talons to claw and snatch at the ground.

And withdrew: she had a few small rodents collected in a handful of dirt, asphyxiated dead and barely each of them a bite. They ate them anyway, raw and uncleaned. It was of a piece with the sensation Temeraire recognized, of being removed from a place of conscious thought: but then, at present thought was not necessary, nor desirable; and neither was anything like sensibility. They needed only fly, and seek, and hunt so far as was needed to sustain life: he could not be very sorry to be reduced to an animal state, at present, when he must suffer otherwise a fresh dose of self-recrimination.

Iskierka, he had to admit, had not accused him. She might have said, *What were you about, to let the egg be left unguarded?* Or she might have reproached him for sleeping, or sleeping so soundly, that someone had managed to spirit it away. She had not. Of course, Temeraire might have answered back with the same charge; but he had kept charge of the eggs all the long way from Britain: Iskierka had not had a full share in looking after them. He had not let her have it; and if he had, he was miserably forced to consider, perhaps she *would* have been more wary, or more alert; perhaps she would *not* have let the egg be taken.

He had much rather not think at all, than think along such lines. He tore into his little wombats for what virtue they had: they were thin and lean, but each one a small hot bite of juice, revitalizing.

"Are you hungry, Laurence?" Temeraire asked, surfacing only so far from his intent preoccupation.

"No; we do well enough with biscuit, have no fear on that score," Laurence said, "but my dear, we cannot keep searching for very much longer tonight. The light is failing."

"We can make torches," Iskierka said, and turning set her claws into one of the larger eucalypts, shaking it back and forth until at last its roots came loose; a torrent of fire ignited the tree-top and made an oily flame, pungent and queerly medicinal in smell.

But it was not quite so easy as it might have sounded to throw the light properly onto the ground, and when Iskierka had made a torch for Temeraire, he found that holding it was awkward, particularly as he had to be careful of the last little egg hanging forward on his breast, and the convicts slung below in his netting, whenever the wind pushed the fire towards his belly.

He saw the torchlight flicker in reflection, on something on the ground, and turned quite by instinct; cries warned him, and he jerked the torch abruptly aside, but in so doing singed his talons painfully, and dropped it. He half-reached for the falling torch, but then he reconsidered: and went instead for that small reflection, while he yet could place where it had come from.

But he only landed upon stone, and clawing away found only more. Iskierka brought her light over, and it shone abruptly in red and green and pearlescent fire, on a narrow vein his scraping had exposed in the rock.

"Opal," Tharkay said. The stone was beautiful, and under any other circumstance Temeraire would have greeted the discovery with the utmost pleasure: he could feel nothing for it now, nothing in the least, but only the sharp and bitter disappointment of failure and regret.

"I am very sorry; I beg you will not press on again. You cannot help but miss more than you find, with this method," Laurence said quietly. "The nights are grown short, in this part of the world; dawn will come soon, and you must have some rest in any case. Better to sleep a little while, and rise at the earliest traces of light."

The fallen torch was burning down to embers, a little distance off, the only gleam of light anywhere around; all the night seemed very black but for the spray of stars above, and that last orange glow. Iskierka with a low hiss of frustration and wrath flung her own torch aside, and cast herself down in a restless, coiling tumble to sleep.

Temeraire stayed only long enough to be unloaded, although he said, "No; you may leave it there, and the harness; I find I can sleep quite well with it on after all," when they would have taken off the little egg. He felt very weary suddenly, although he would not have stopped, not for anything, if only there had been any way of continu-

ing the search. He arranged himself carefully on the ground, propped
up a little and with the last egg bracketed within his arms, where no
one could have come at it without disturbing him.

It did not quite answer, though; uneasily he realized he was used to
people clambering over him; so small and light as they were, he might
never notice. He decided he should only rest. But sleep stole treacher-
ously over him: his head drooped, his eyelids sank shut, and then the
wind shifted, or a branch rubbed along his wing, and he managed to
jerk awake again; he nosed anxiously at the egg and made sure all was
well, and then the enemy sleep was creeping up again.

He was so tired; and then Laurence, dear Laurence, put a hand on
his forearm and climbed over, to sit beside the egg. "Pray get as much
rest as you can," he said. "I can sleep tomorrow when you must be flying."

"Thank you, Laurence; it should be the greatest comfort to me,"
Temeraire said gratefully, and sleep might be allowed to come at last;
he closed his eyes on the deeply reassuring sight of the gleam of Laurence's drawn sword, lying across his knees to be sharpened, and fell at
once into slumber.

In the morning, however, the sustaining wrath had fled. All that remained was a grey, grinding misery, the sensation of failure mingled
with the certainty that however futile, the search must continue, until
the egg's final fate—dreadful though it was likely to be—should be
known. Temeraire nosed at the last, littlest egg to comfort himself: it
had begun to harden, he thought, and would soon cease to be in danger; the event could not come quickly enough to suit him.

"You might hurry, if you liked," he told the egg quietly, "although
certainly not so you do yourself any harm; only if you felt hungry, perhaps, or ready to try a little flying, you might come out sooner rather
than late."

Iskierka was pacing, meanwhile: a restless abbreviated movement
back and forth, so her long and coiling tail lagged behind when she
made her turns, and continued in her original direction for a while,
until she lashed it up behind her again. "Well?" she said. "Let us be
going; it is light again."

It was not yet quite light; there was just enough of a paler quality to the sky to see her shape silhouetted black against the horizon, and the faint white clouds of steam issuing from her spikes. But the men had still to be got aboard: the sun was near the horizon as they finally leapt back aloft, and in their climb they broke into the sunlight before it had struck the land.

They had a little while searching before they found the trail itself again, and were obliged to land several times that Tharkay might look for signs. The repeated delays were extremely wearing to the spirit, but Temeraire held back the complaints which he might have wanted to make; he could see that their insistence on continuing to search, into the night, had made it quite impossible for Tharkay to keep any sight of the trail. He could not be unreasonable, he told himself, and added to Iskierka at the fourth such pause, "And the chances of finding the egg must be so much smaller if we should lose the trail entirely; it is only sensible, and we are not wasting time, really, but gaining it."

"Yes, yes," Iskierka said. "Is he not done yet? Whyever must it take so long, only to peer at the ground; and why must there be so many trees here?"

"As long as they *are* here, you might let me down to rest under them; I am very hot again," Caesar put in, from Temeraire's back, where he had been sternly instructed to remain; naturally, just to make more of a nuisance of himself, he had put on another five or six stone of weight overnight, Temeraire thought.

It was very inconvenient to be hunting over such forested country: they had crossed now over the mountains, and there were everywhere trees, so one might look as far as one liked without seeing a break in them, except for the river below flowing south- and westward, away from the ocean. "It must flow to the southern coast, or empty into some lake or inland sea, I suppose," Laurence said, looking at them, and at his spread-out maps of the coastline of the continent, sadly incomplete.

"That would be something to look forward to, I suppose," Granby said, wiping his sleeve across his forehead. "I would not mind coming across a lake. These smugglers must have water somewhere along their road?" he added.

It was very hard to endure the slow pace, the endless trees slipping by, the river winding away from them. Iskierka was of the opinion they had better be done with it, and fly onward straight; and Temeraire found it a grave struggle to persuade her otherwise: he had to argue with himself and not only her, even though Laurence and Granby were so very certain.

Temeraire tried to fly as cautiously and slowly as he might, but several days went by without a sign, and Tharkay began insisting for all their efforts they had overshot and must go back. Temeraire could not quite believe it—they had been going so very slowly—but Laurence at last persuaded him to pause, one morning before they had gone aloft, to let him draw out a diagramme, showing him the fastest pace the thieves could have made: and Temeraire could not deny it; they had gone too far.

They had another three days flying back over the same ground, retreating to the last traces they had found and repeating their search, before at last Tharkay allowed them to continue further: but he had found nothing new. Temeraire landed dully for water that afternoon by the river, full of despair; he could not help but drink thirstily, but he did not feel he deserved it.

"Laurence," Tharkay said, rising, "a word, if you please." Temeraire pricked up his ruff, and valiantly resisted the temptation to eavesdrop; whatever could Tharkay be saying, which he should not like the rest of them to hear? And Laurence looked quite serious, when he said it; of course one could not go prying into a secret conversation, but—

"I cannot hear them at all," Iskierka said. "Granby, go and tell us what they are saying."

"Well, I shan't," Granby said firmly, "and you shan't go nearer, either; you have enough sins to your account with adding on the vice of listening."

But then Laurence came back and said, very gently, "My dear, I must ask you to exert the greatest restraint, and to persuade Iskierka to do the same, before I should—" and Temeraire stricken said, "Oh—oh, he has found—a bit of the egg—"

"No," Laurence said, "no, my dear; quite the contrary, but you must not disturb the trail, nor lose it. Tharkay thinks they were here, only last night, and that they kept the egg here on this low hillock of sand: but he cannot be certain—"

"They are near, then!" Iskierka exclaimed, rearing up on her hind legs.

"Stop, stop!" Temeraire said, and leaping pinned down several of her coils to the ground. "You must not flap and stir the ground, otherwise he will lose everything; we must wait. Tharkay, can you tell at all where they have gone?"

His wings wished to tremble with excitement; all the grimy sense of despair quite swept away. They had *not* failed: the thieves had not got clear with their prize. "Why, we have only been flying a few hours this morning," Temeraire said, exultantly, "and stopping so often; surely we must find them and catch them up before to-day is spent, after all. And you are quite sure, I hope, that the egg was well when they were here?" he asked. "Was it near their campfire, perhaps, could you tell?"

"I have already provided you the best part of a phantasy," Tharkay said, "to speculate the egg was here at all," but that was only his dry way, Temeraire decided.

Iskierka was all for going at once, with all speed on a direct course, but Granby and Laurence were insistent on the subject: they had to keep flying their sweeps, for the thieves likely should know by now that they were being so closely pursued. "It is very inconvenient that we should be so large, and they so small," Temeraire said to Laurence unhappily, "for I dare say they are hiding somewhere in the trees looking at us this same instant, thinking, *There they are, and they cannot see us at all!* in a very unpleasant gloating way."

"I will go so far as to assure you," Laurence said, "that if the thieves are anywhere and under any sort of cover imaginable, where they can see you and the treatment you have been meting out to the surrounding vegetation, they are not in the least inclined either to gloating or laughter. Prayer might be more to the point."

Temeraire could no longer complain at all whenever Tharkay wished them to stop again, and neither could Iskierka; instead they peered over his shoulder, at whatever speck of dirt or dust he might be inspecting, and tried to work out whatever traces he had found. Temeraire saw nothing at all, himself, although he nodded and tried to look wise when Tharkay should point at some perfectly indistinguishable patch of ground and call it a footprint, or at an unremarkable bush and call it a trace of passage.

A few days later, still at the creeping sluggish pace, they had struck away into open country away from the river, only creeks and smaller tributaries left: traveling north-west. The forests were clearing out of the way into scrubby grassland, so Temeraire could not mind the dust, however much there was of it: which was a great deal; he coughed and sneezed as he flew, and when they stopped for the nights.

Laurence was anxious on the subject of water. Temeraire could not let such small concerns distract him, and though it was certainly not as convenient to leave behind the river, if the smugglers had done so, then there must be water. "That does not mean we may find it as easily as have they, my dear," Laurence said, when the last little stream dried away and fell behind them as they flew, "and you must consider: a small party of men may carry their own supply of water for several days, where we have not that luxury."

"But there is so much less cover, too," Temeraire said, "and so it must be easier to *see* the water even from quite far away, and the thieves, too; if only we can find them, we needn't worry about anything else."

"*We'd* best worry about it, I warrant," Jack Telly said to the other men, from the belly-netting. "If there's water found, there's some gullets as it'll go down first, and maybe none left for the rest of us."

Temeraire snorted in disdain at this. "And there is a perfectly nice water-hole directly there," he added, "so you need not complain."

It was easy to see: a faint silvery gleam amid the dusty country, ringed invitingly by many shrubs and a few thin trees, and after they had drunk, Tharkay called their attention to the small hill a little way off, where at the summit he had found the mid-day camp where the thieves had paused to eat a little.

Tharkay said, "I imagine they had a fire, here," pointing at a bare patch of ground, with a little mess of twigs perhaps. Temeraire sniffed unobtrusively at this last after Tharkay had stood to move to another part of the camp, but he could not even make out any smell of smoke until he put out his tongue, and then he thought he just barely might have a sense of faintly burnt wood.

But then, then, then, Tharkay said, "—and the egg was here," and Temeraire turning saw it very plainly: there was a nest of leaves and grasses scraped quite close together, around a little framework of thin branches, and the nest had a smooth, curved hollow depressed within it, just the right size and shape to hold an egg: Temeraire might have scraped together something very like for the same purpose.

"You have brought us up on their heels out of ten thousand acres of wilderness," Laurence said. "—I should not have credited it."

Tharkay shook his head. "You may praise me when we have them in hand, and I do not see them; do you?"

Temeraire went aloft, for them all to peer about, and indeed he could not see any sign of anyone walking in any direction—there was a little dust going up a few hills over, but that was only some cassowaries running, and in the distance a few wild dogs. "But we *must* be close, if they ate here so lately," he said, rallying his spirits as he landed.

"I do not care to be discouraging," Tharkay said to Laurence, "but they seem to know this country uncommonly well. There is no hesitation in their trail—no false starts. They ate quickly—they had food with them, or knew where nearby to get it. They came directly to this camp, knowing there would be water here; and they did not have the advantage of an aerial view."

"I hope I may not be called over-optimistic," Laurence said, "but I will indulge in a little more confidence, even so: they may know their route, but they cannot know the countryside well enough to stray very far from it, and we have the advantage of being able to cover it in wide swaths."

"We had better use that advantage, then," Temeraire said. "Pray let everyone come back aboard." The convicts reluctantly came up and out of the shade to go back into the belly-netting, even Caesar was prodded up whining, and then Lieutenant Forthing said, "Where has that blasted fellow Telly got to?"

Jack Telly was quite gone.

"But where can he have got to?" Temeraire said: there was not much of anything for several miles around, and even if the man had wanted to run away from them, there was nowhere he might have run away to; they had covered a good ten miles of country, even flying the tedious sweeps, since their camp that morning.

It turned out, however, that the last anyone remembered of him, he had gone down to get a drink at the water-hole, and had taken with him a canteen: one of the other convicts had seen him go with it in his hand.

"So he has deserted and taken to the wilderness," Rankin said impatiently, "—looking for this idiot notion of China reachable by land, no doubt; and we may consider ourselves lucky he did not steal anything more necessary than a single can of water. Do you propose to spend an hour hunting him out from under whichever bit of scrub he has secreted himself beneath, or do you suppose we might value a little more highly the prize that has brought us out this far, than preserving a fool from his chosen folly?"

"We cannot spare the time, surely," Temeraire said anxiously to Laurence.

"We can and shall spare the time," Laurence said, "at least to fly some passes overhead around the immediate countryside and call out to him: this man is in our charge, and one of our party. If he has deserted, that is one thing; but desertion would be strange indeed in our present situation, so far from any sign of civilization; far more likely that from an excess of heat or air-sickness he has grown disoriented and wandered into the scrub, and lost his way back."

"I don't see why we should care, if he is silly enough to go roaming around in the wild without coming back," Iskierka said. "He is not an egg, being dragged about wherever anyone likes who has a hold of it, and quite unable to manage for itself."

Temeraire would of course not quarrel with Laurence, but he inclined to Iskierka's view of the situation, particularly after he heard one of the convicts say to another, "Ask me, he is well out of it and no mistake; halfway to China, I warrant, and here we sit swinging like the dugs of a back-alley sixpence whore under this monster's belly," while they were supposed to be yelling out *Jack, Jack* as Temeraire flew his circles. Jack himself seemed to agree with them; at least he did not answer, or step out from behind a shrub and wave an arm.

"He must be choosing to stay hidden," Temeraire said, "surely, Laurence; we have made such a tremendous noise no one anywhere near-by could fail to hear us. I hope," he added, only a little reproachfully, "that the thieves have not, for they must be warned if they have."

He did not add, although he might have, that Telly had been quite a regular nuisance since even before they had left Sydney: had complained quite incessantly. It did not seem to Temeraire that he would be a very great loss, if he did not wish to come with them any further.

"I cannot account for it," Laurence said. "Pray go below and ask those men, Demane, what was his sentence, and his profession?"

Demane climbed down Temeraire's side, to speak with the convicts in the belly-netting; and swung back up again to report: Telly had been trained up as a carpenter, once, and had so called himself; but convicted of debt in the amount of £2 5d 7s at the age of sixteen had gone through a window in London to snatch a few goods to repay; finding this a more lucrative profession, he had given over hopes of respectability; he was, in short, a thief: a second-story man, sentenced to twenty years of transportation and hard labor.

"What business has such a man in the open wilderness, and running out into it?" Laurence said.

"I cannot see why you insist on crediting such a man with more wit than willfullness," Rankin said. "I am sure he imagines all will be charmingly easy: a man with prospects of a respectable profession, who runs himself into a debt ludicrous to his station, turns thief, and runs riot in London until he is seized for transportation, surely cannot be allowed to have the remotest powers of reason.

"Nor," Rankin added cuttingly, "any value to society; and meanwhile a beast priceless to our situation is being trundled away by, I gather your Chinaman friend suspects, some party of French spies. If you insist on pursuing this course of action, we will surely lose the trail; and you may be sure I will not stint in speaking my mind on the subject in my own report to their Lordships, or about Captain Granby's ill-judgment in yielding to your wishes."

It was very unpleasant to be in any way of the same mind as Rankin, particularly when he spoke in so offensive a way, and Temeraire thought *he* had not much value to society, either. But—the egg must be paramount, that was incontrovertible; and even as Temeraire steeled himself to speak to Laurence, Iskierka was swinging back towards them. Granby called over, "Laurence, I am damned sorry, but the fellow don't want to be found, if he hasn't broken his neck somewhere; and Iskierka won't stand for looking any longer."

"Very well," Laurence said, after a moment, "—let us go onward."

"You are not very distressed, Laurence, I hope?" Temeraire asked, as he and Iskierka fell again into the sweeping pattern he had worked out that morning: she flying slightly above, and the two of them interweaving, and looking in opposite directions always, that both of them should have cast an eye over the same ground, to be sure not to overlook anything.

"No," Laurence said, "only I must find it strange; I have known men desert, often enough, but only at the prospect of some immediate gain and a nearby harbor: with women, generally, and I would be the more likely to credit him with deliberate flight if he had taken a cask of rum instead of the canteen. I imagine Granby has it right, and the poor devil took a wrong step and fell into some crevasse; where he will likely die of thirst, if those wild dogs we have heard at night do not come on him first. This is not a kind country, and I cannot think very much of abandoning a man in it."

They did not find the smugglers that afternoon, nor that evening. They flew on through the deepening dusk, which took all the color out of the countryside, and their sweeps grew more narrow while they peered in every direction for the tiniest glow of a campfire; but there was nothing.

The ground cover rapidly thinned out further as the twilight advanced; even the shrubs had begun to diminish and crouch lower to the ground, small dark lumps as they flew. The only trees to be seen looked dark stick-like things against the fading sky, much like the brushes Mr. Fellowes used for scrubbing the harness-buckles or carabiners: long thin trunks like young saplings and a small lump of twiggy branches and small leaves atop. The stars were very bright and clear, above: cold and brilliant speckles of light, and the spray of the Milky Way pearly grey in a wide swath.

At last they had to give up again, and they settled for the night with somewhat diminished spirits. "And I am hungry," Iskierka said irritably: the hunting had not been as good.

But Temeraire could not feel quite so low as he had yesterday. "After all, we have nearly caught them twice now," he said. "At least, we have seen where they were, and it stands to reason we will get closer tomorrow, too, and we *do* know," he added, "that the egg is well: that alone is worth all our pains."

"Only if by *well* you mean, is not yet broken into bits," Iskierka said dampeningly, and curled herself up to sleep.

There was no water to drink here, either; the last gleam of water they had seen in the day's flying was some eight miles back in the distance, and three miles sweeping out from the line of the trail. The aviators rationed out cupfuls of water to themselves and the convicts; and smaller ones of rum, which were drunk up first, before the shares of biscuit went about.

While they ate, to Temeraire's great dismay O'Dea said, quite loudly, "I expect we won't find them at all, now we've left Jack Telly behind to starve and die, food for dogs in a strange country. Tisn't right, and I have a mind his spirit is following us while his body lies behind rotting. We won't smoke out their trail with a curse upon us; Jack wants company, fellows, in his lonely grave. We'll search and we'll look, and we'll never find another living soul, though we go until we are all grey and bent as widows."

"Laurence," Temeraire said, in high anxiety after overhearing this, "Laurence, you do not suppose that might be so, at all? I did not think of that, when we left; I should never have suggested we go away so quickly, if I thought he would curse us to stop our finding the egg."

"I do *not* suppose," Laurence said, "and I am surprised, very surprised, my dear, to find you grown so sadly superstitious," but this offered limited comfort. Privately, Temeraire was forced to admit that Laurence was unreasonably deadly on the subject of superstition, even though it did not make any sense, as he was equally firm on the subject of the Holy Spirit; Temeraire did not see how one could deny other spirits, when you had allowed *one*.

"Well, I don't think there is anything to it, either," Roland said, when Temeraire quietly asked her, after Laurence had gone to discuss their next day's course with Tharkay and Granby.

"I do," Demane said, examining his knives. "I would haunt us, too, if we had left me behind."

"He might *like* to," Roland said, "but if a fellow could haunt us, then he ought be able to do a little more to help us find him, in the first place."

"That don't mean anything; spirits aren't the same as bodies," Demane said, scornfully dismissive; and Roland did not seem to have an answer for this.

"Anyway, it ain't as though we flew off straightaway, or left him on purpose," Roland said, but this was not a settled thing amongst the men.

"Jack made a fuss, didn't he," Bob Maynard said, slurred with rum and not so quietly that he could not be heard, and rolling a significant glance towards Rankin where he stood speaking with Caesar. "Some as are high-in-the-instep didn't much like him saying what was what, when we are being hauled into the back of beyond; some here were mighty quick to hurry us off, and not a tear to shed for old Jack."

Though Maynard was given to persuading the other men to game away their rum to him, and while being nearly twice as large as most of the other poor thin convicts scarcely managed half the work of anyone else, he was endlessly ready to oblige with a song, in a fine deep baritone, or an entertaining story; not at all wont to complain, ordinarily, so the accusation struck with more than ordinary force, from him. Temeraire could not easily repress a start of guilt; he had himself thought—for just a moment, though, and not spoken aloud, he excused himself—that it would not be so dreadful not to have Jack Telly along always complaining.

"Still, it was *not* on purpose; no one asked him to go away and jump into a pit," Temeraire said, "and we did look, for quite some time," but he could not quite convince himself that Jack Telly would have accepted these arguments, and as it should be his decision whether to haunt them or not, Temeraire could not find any relief; he could only lie down curled very close about the last remaining egg, to make sure no malevolent spirits could creep in at it.

Chapter 8

*B*UT IT SEEMED to Temeraire that Jack Telly had indeed cursed them, for all their luck had run away. They searched and searched, and were always it seemed a little too late, or had gone a little too far; meanwhile the trail crept onward beneath them at the snail's pace of foot speed, offering only the most tantalizing bits of encouragement—today a scrap of porcelain; tomorrow another nest for the egg.

Temeraire passed an uneasy night, and woke even more uneasy; he raised his head in the first moments before dawn, while everyone else yet slept, and watched the line of the horizon growing sharper where it met the sky. It seemed very far away. The forest had broken up at some time during their last night's flight, and there was nothing to conceal the hard edge of the world but a handful of brushy trees looking a little like broomsticks stuck into the earth upside down, and low hillocks.

At first the dawn grey lingered, cast over all the ground, pale knotted clumps of grass and darker shrubs standing out against the dark earth. Then by degrees the blue washed over the vast bowl of sky in advance of the sun, and color began to come back into the world—but color terrible and strange. The sandy earth all beneath them was red as the exposed side of a freshly broken brick, as though someone had painted it. The grasses were hay-yellow, as if dead, but *all* of them; there was not a single green blade anywhere.

The stand of bushes along one side of their camp looked a little less unnatural: full of shining, dark green leaves; but they alone looked verdant, and the stand of trees which Temeraire had been looking at, between them and the horizon, were blackened as if by fire. The smoke-stains were dark up and down the bark, but equally strange, they had fresh green leaves put out at their ends, despite the curled-up, charred scraps of the old ones clinging still to the lower branches.

There were no clouds in the sky, no water on the ground; not a living thing stirred anywhere around. It was the queerest place Temeraire had ever seen: even the Taklamakan, which had been empty and barren and cold and of no use to anyone, had not looked so very *wrong*—at the oases, there had been poplar-trees, and proper grass; and where there was no water, there were no plants growing; and the ground had not looked so peculiar at all.

"Laurence," Temeraire said urgently, nudging him; Laurence was drowsing lightly against his forearm, sitting near the egg. "Laurence, perhaps you might wake up."

"Yes?" Laurence said, still asleep, and rubbed his hand over his face.

"I am not afraid myself, of course; but I should not like to alarm the men," Temeraire added, "and I am afraid we may have got into the underworld, somehow: I cannot account for it otherwise."

"—I beg your pardon?" Laurence said, opening his eyes, and standing; and then he was silent.

"I am sorry we should have pressed on during the night," Temeraire said, "but perhaps it was Jack Telly's spirit—"

"We are not in the underworld!" Laurence said, but the men when they woke were more of Temeraire's mind; until the meager breakfast of biscuit had been shared out, and then one very stupid person said, "I reckon there wouldn't be biscuit, in the hot place; we'm in China, I expect, and whoever would want to come here, I don't know."

At once the convicts all agreed: they had certainly reached China. They were not moved from this ridiculous opinion, either, even when Temeraire exasperated said, "But this is not China at all; China is across the ocean from here, and it is a very splendid place, not like this at all; there are thousands and thousands of dragons there, all over."

"There you have it," O'Dea said to the others with ghoulish relish, "a godforsaken place: we will see a horde of them fly out of the west, any morning now, coming to devour us; and then we will go down to Old Nick's country in the end." Temeraire put back his ruff in irritation.

"Some mineral in the soil gives it the color, I imagine," Dorset said, scraping at the earth with the end of a stick and peering inquisitively at the still-brighter dirt revealed below.

"We must backtrack in any case," Tharkay said, shading his eyes with a hand. "We must have overshot the turning of their trail."

"I can't see they would come into this countryside," Granby agreed, absently rubbing his arms as he looked around him yet again, as though he could not help it; Temeraire could see many of the other men doing so as well, and it made him look again also: it was indeed very odd to find oneself in the middle of this queer red landscape. "It *is* a godforsaken country; I don't suppose anyone can live here comfortably. Shall we go back to that water-hole we saw, last night? And we had better see the men all have a drink, before they come over ugly on us."

But when they had flown on three miles—still the endless sweeping in either direction, and all the while their eyes on the ground, so the tiny distance took the better part of two hours—Tharkay suddenly leaned forward on Iskierka's back, and Temeraire followed her to the ground: Tharkay leaped down in three bounds from her back to the sands, and he stooped at a mounded heap of red sand, exactly hollowed to that same eggshell curve, and beside it, stark and brilliantly reflecting in the sunlight, a white ochre handprint was marked freshly upon a jutting monolith of dark red stone.

Iskierka left them an hour later, winging her way back to Sydney, though not without a great deal of quarreling and dissension: she had not wished to leave, nor Granby; but there was no help for it. A smugglers' trail, which should by necessity come to a definite conclusion in some fixed harbor, was one thing; but the natives might go anywhere at all in their own country, and in circles if they wished.

"All right, maybe it isn't the smugglers; but what would the natives want with a dragon?" Granby had said. "I don't say they have any reason to love us, but they can't ever have *seen* a dragon before we landed in this country, and if you should tell me that a first glimpse of Temeraire, or Iskierka, or even Caesar, should make a man want to hatch a beast out for himself, I call it mad."

They were all at something of a loss from the new discovery: but besides the handprint the heavy red sand had taken all around the imprint of bare feet, and Tharkay had uncovered, too, some remnants of their meal: emptied seed-pods, roasted, and the stems of berries from a bush near-by; native, and certainly no smugglers would have made such a meal at the risk of poisoning themselves.

Tharkay shrugged a little. "I do not pretend to an understanding of their motives," he said, "but their tracks are reasonably clear, and I am afraid it answers a great many questions: I have already found it strange the smugglers should continue this far without making a turn for the coast, and such easy familiarity with their route was wholly unlikely even if the French had been colonizing this continent for a century."

"They have stolen the egg because it was precious to us," Rankin said impatiently. "We had it swaddled up as a great treasure; what more do you need? Likely they have not even realized it will hatch out a dragon, and think it some species of jewel."

Laurence could not be so easily dismissive. He would once have given as little credence to a native power sufficient to rival those of Europe, or as sophisticate in its organization and its forces. Although this was not a country, he rather thought, looking around the barren landscape, which should easily sustain and conceal an empire so large as the lush heart of Africa had concealed that of the Tswana; still he was not inclined to again make so dangerous an assumption.

"They have at the very least evaded us, despite the most urgent and enthusiastic search, over many days," Laurence added, "which ought command our respect and wariness. It would be a very unimaginative man who would look at a dragon egg and think it anything other than it is: they do have birds here, and snakes. Far more likely they should see us in company with Temeraire and Iskierka and Caesar, and realize the prize before them. They cannot be pleased with the usurpation of their territory by the farmers of the colony, and anything which offers them the power of resistance or of leveling the ground must appeal."

Rankin shrugged. "Very well; in that case we must fear at any moment that several thousand wild tribesmen, full of loathing, will leap on us in the night: splendid."

The greater danger of course was the far more certain one: that the trail might go on a long, cold time of searching; and it was this which necessitated Iskierka's departure. "We must grant them every power of hiding themselves from us in it, and knowing their way," Laurence said to Granby, "—and Riley cannot wait, weeks and weeks gone, and no word of us at all. We were already overlong, looking for our route through the mountains. By now he must be looking to see us return to Sydney every day."

"Well, I am not haring off to leave you here in the middle of the desert, if that is what you are getting at," Granby said.

"It is fairer to say that *we* are presently haring off, away from any reasonable course," Laurence said. "If the natives are not our friends, they are at least not the French; and one middle-weight dragon will not give them the power of doing us much harm even if they should wish to, when Temeraire is in the colony."

Fairer or not, Granby refused to like it, and Iskierka liked it still less. "Well, I am not going anywhere until we have found the egg," she said, dismissively, "so there is no sense discussing it: Riley must wait, and that is all."

But Riley would not wait, of course; they had already been gone nearly three weeks, on a trip that ought to have taken them one, and with no word sent back. Whatever misfortune could befall a party of two heavy-weight dragons and thirty men would not be lightly dismissed, and there was hardly anyone of the colony who could be sent in search of them, either. They would be written down as lost, victims of an unfamiliar territory; Riley might even leave the sooner, to bring the disastrous news back to England.

Even Temeraire was no ally, for once proving reluctant to see Iskierka go. "It is not that I am pleased with her company," he said to Laurence, "or that I cannot rescue the egg myself, of course; only it would be churlish to send her away, as though she were not worth having along. And she has been very handy at hunting; one cannot deny it."

"With as little game as this country looks likely to hold, from this day's flight," Laurence said, "if we must penetrate into it for any distance, that must argue rather for her departure, than her remaining: the two of you cannot as easily be fed as one in covering the same ground. But my dear, the greater concern must be their necessary imprisonment upon this continent: if Riley leaves, they are trapped with us for years perhaps, unjustly."

"Well, as far as that goes," Temeraire said, "I must say I do not see why it is just that I should be left behind, when Iskierka is not; for you cannot argue she is any more obedient to the Government than I am. But I do see the point: eggs are not always being stolen, and I am sure she would be tiresome again as soon as we had it back; and I dare say wanting to eat all the cows. For that matter, we ought to send Caesar back, also, I suppose?"

He finished hopefully, but this, of course, was by no means desirable: keeping Caesar and Rankin from interference in the colony's affairs was no longer their most pressing concern, but that scarcely meant they now wished to encourage it; and Caesar was not leaving with the *Allegiance*, in any case.

"We might go," Granby said reluctantly, "and come back, if you would build some cairns to show us which way you have gone. It isn't as though you would be moving very quickly, chasing a bunch of fellows traveling on foot: thirty miles in a day must be their utmost limit. We could catch you up if Riley thinks he can give us the time: I suppose he wouldn't mind that new mast, or at least it is an excuse. At this rate we will be chasing these fellows clear across the country, anyway, and we might well meet him on the other side, if he goes sailing around."

They did not immediately settle on this course: Iskierka continued to resist, and then there was the question of the convicts, and what was to be done with them. The men themselves were all for being taken back to Sydney, or at the least returned to the comfortable valley; Granby did not wish to leave Laurence so deserted.

"I know one can't call them reliable," he said, "but they are hands, and if you do find these fellows who have the egg, and need to work it away from them, you may need more than just your own and Temeraire's. It's precious easy to keep a dragon pinned down if you have an egg it is brooding: a little child could make Temeraire come to heel like a well-trained hound, with nothing more than a rock. And," he added in an undertone, "Rankin mayn't be good company, and he is a bounder, but in justice one can't call him a coward."

Rankin did not immediately offer his own opinion; Laurence was a little surprised to find him consulting quietly with Caesar, away to one side—he could scarcely have imagined an aviator less likely to inquire after a dragon's wishes. But Caesar's interests were the only ones aligned with Rankin's, of their company, which perhaps had driven him to such straits; and having conceded so far, no one could deny Caesar a great deal of sharpness, if he was too ungenerous for wisdom.

"Certainly I am not leaving," Rankin said, at length returning, when Granby pressed him. "If you are going, Captain Granby, I must necessarily assume command of the search; the recovery of the egg is our highest duty, and there can be no question of our returning to Sydney at present," by which he likely meant no value in finding himself again awkwardly committed to Bligh. "As for the men, for my part, you had better take this lot and deposit them back on the sufferance of the colony; they will hardly be of much use to us."

"Well, sir," O'Dea said to Laurence, "I do not mean to be quarrelsome, but we were offered our liberty for cutting a road: and I don't suppose we will get the one without the other."

"Those who wish to remain, and carry out their service, may," Laurence said. "Any man who prefers to return to the security of the colony, likewise; I prefer no unwilling hands."

Temeraire sighed a little, watching Iskierka go, after a great deal of urgent persuasion from Granby and only with the promise of returning, within the narrowest span of time. "And she is flying flat-out," he said, "and on quite a straight course; none of this tiresome sweeping. I do not suppose Tharkay might be able to make out their trail a little better, now that he knows they are natives and not smugglers, so we might not have to go hunting quite so wide?"

"First," Laurence said, "we must have water."

Water they might not have, however; not easily. The trees were quite misleading, and a patch of greenery did not seem to mean an oasis, as one might have expected. "They may be like succulents," Laurence offered as an explanation, "and have some reservoir of water to sustain them through the summer droughts, I suppose." But if Temeraire tore one up—rather difficult for all they were very skinny, as they had enormous nests of roots—it was quite dry all the way through, and there was not even a little cache of water which a person might drink from.

So they had to keep on with their sweeps, looking now always for some little trickle or gleam of water, and even more importantly for another sign of the thieves: who might easily go in any direction whatsoever. It was very distressing to look upon Laurence's maps of the enormous continent, so spread open, and so unmarked; they were already a way into the blank mysterious space at the center, and far from the surveyed coastlines. Now that Iskierka was gone, Temeraire felt still more anxious to be sure he did not overlook any movement, any small track which Tharkay perhaps could not see so well from aloft.

Caesar was flying alongside now, which limited their pace to his; as

Laurence had pointed out, that was even so a good deal faster than any person might have walked, so Temeraire tried not to be anxious, but he was nevertheless very soon annoyed, for even though it was Caesar who necessitated their going slower, he nevertheless felt justified in making many unnecessary remarks on Temeraire's own preoccupation, and his efforts to watch the ground.

"I can't see why you should be jumping down and up like a jack-in-the-box, every time you see some sand being stirred up by the wind," Caesar said. "You will get worn out, and then you will want more of the food and water when we get it, and precious little of either to start."

"Whatever there is," Temeraire said, "if I am the one catching it, I will take as much as I like; you might help look, instead of complaining."

"And if I happen to see an egg," Caesar said waspishly, "I will let you know of it; or anything worth seeing, but I don't suppose you would like it much if I began to say, *Oh look, there is something,* and then I would say, *sorry old fellow, I am mistaken, it is only a bush,* after you went flinging yourself at it."

Temeraire *was* a little hungrier than he might satisfy as they flew, over such a short distance: there were larger kangaroos here, with reddish fur, but they could move quite surprisingly fast, and the hopping made them a little tricky to catch when he must at once avoid too much jostling of the egg; he had only managed to snatch two all afternoon.

"There are a whole lot of them hopping away over there, Temeraire, if you like," Roland said, as evening drew on; and though it was not quite in the right direction, Temeraire was tempted; but as he pursued, it came clear they were hopping away from a narrow creek, and everyone was very thirsty.

"If you are not excessively hungry," Laurence said, "we had best stop: the light is fading, and we may not easily find our way back."

"Perhaps," Temeraire said, setting down very carefully, so as not to disturb the grounds, "perhaps, Tharkay, the aborigines should have been here, too? It is the first water we have seen since mid-morning."

"I can only inform you that there have been a great many kangaroos here lately," Tharkay dryly said, which was not at all fresh news. Temeraire tried not to be discouraged, but when they had dug a deeper hole for the water to collect, and he had drunk, he looked up and gazed with dismay around the wide-open country: low red dunes swelling and falling in all directions, a few outcroppings of rock, stands of bushes and of trees along the little creek which ran away into the distance, the bed gone nearly dry in places. There was nothing to distinguish one direction from another.

He sighed and closed his eyes for a little rest, while the men made their own small smoky fire, and cooked a little salt pork to eat with their biscuit, and they all disposed of themselves to sleep; the pleasant coolness of the night crept on, and Temeraire found himself half-drowsing, listening just in case the kangaroos should come back; the hopping ought to make a noise, he felt, and abruptly a short high shriek startled him up, wide-eyed and looking.

Dawn had not quite broken, but the sky was paling; the men were all sitting up around him, blurred grey shadows against the ground, not moving.

The yell had cut off as abruptly as it had begun. Laurence stood, walking amongst the men to count heads as the light crept nearer, and there was a spare hollow in the ground with empty shoes set beside it, where someone had been sleeping.

"It's them," O'Dea said, "—waiting out in the dark and picking us off one by one, taking us in the night. The egg is only bait to lure us on deeper into their country, so they can kill us all. We never ought to be able to follow them otherwise—"

"There's witchery in it, I say," another man muttered, not low.

The men were for leaving at once, at once; no-one proposed staying this time to search any longer for the luckless Jonas Green. "The ground at the creek has been disturbed a little," Tharkay said to Laurence quietly, while the hasty packing commenced, and the men warily filled their cans of water afresh, "but I see nothing one might expect, of a grown healthy man being dragged away, alive or dead; they cannot have swept the ground clean behind them."

"This *is* a strange country," Laurence said, low and puzzled, and came to swing himself aboard.

Temeraire was as pleased to be gone, quickly, not only so they might keep looking for the egg: it worried him a little that this mysterious snatching agency might seize on one of his crew. It seemed just as well to have Laurence and all of them safely away. But then in the air he paused, before he had even properly made any height, and stooped swiftly to the lee side of the rock outcropping.

"Oh, not again," Caesar complained, "and we have not even had breakfast," but Temeraire paid no attention, none whatsoever, as he thrust his nose into the low, half-hidden hollow in the stone, tearing away the covering of brush: and in the dirt lay a small heap of fragments of bright, red-glazed porcelain, the lemon-curd-yellow pattern of birds smashed apart.

Chapter 9

"*I* WISH YOU FELLOWS would make up your minds," Caesar said, "are we looking for smugglers, or natives, or the egg; and can't we go find something to eat, instead?"

"Pray don't be so thick," Temeraire said, "we are looking for all three, of course, and all three of them are one; and we will go get something to eat when Tharkay has worked out their trail and which way we ought to go."

This conclusion seemed quite self-evident to him, so he was puzzled to find Rankin utterly dismissive of the notion, and even Laurence saying to Tharkay, "*Can* the natives be responsible for the smuggling of the goods? I suppose the French might be supplying them, at some distant port—"

"It would certainly save *them* a great deal of labor," Tharkay said, "if I do not see how the natives could profit from the effort of carrying large quantities of goods across the width of an entire continent, only to the Sydney market."

"Why should they not like the goods for themselves?" Temeraire said, "—the porcelain is very nice; although they have been careless again." Anyone would have liked the piece, he thought, when it had been whole. "While I cannot really *wish* anything so nice broken, if they meant to break them anyway, it would be very useful if they should drop some others, as they go; and perhaps they may. Which way have they gone?" he asked, which after all was the real, the crucial point.

It was a little disheartening that Tharkay would have it that the pieces were older—had been here since the last rainfall, which certainly had not been in the last week, and of course that was far too long; but he insisted. Temeraire sighed a little, but after all, this was still a trail: if they had come this way before, then likely they had come this way again, or at least should end in the same place.

"And that would suit very well," Temeraire said to Laurence, tearing hungrily into his meat; they had gone on, and taken a few kangaroos to breakfast upon, "if we might fly on, and then wait for them to come to *us*, now that we know they will not be carrying the egg onto a ship somewhere, and over the ocean where we can never get at it again."

He looked for more shards or broken bits as they flew onward, now: if the ground had not been such an inconveniently bright color, it might have been easier; and also there were quite distinct sections, flying over, some of which were much more troublesome to examine. Temeraire preferred those where the trees and shrubs were scant and fire-blackened, and the grass very low to the ground, but in the afternoon when they had flown past a dry creek bed lined with the dark green shrubs, the vegetation flourished up again, huge straw-yellow mop-heads of grasses and pale green tender shrubs everywhere, trees spiking up.

Caesar did not help, either; he would have it that one could not hunt very well here, and they had very likely lost the trail, and the aborigines had gone quite another way, and so forth. And all the while the hot, dusty wind blew and blew into Temeraire's nostrils, and his eyes, and the red sand gritted upon his hide and collected in small pockets as his wings rolled through each stroke, and itched; and the men in the belly-netting muttered low and sullenly of home, and called out now and again to try and wheedle a halt for "a little grog, sir; it is downright inhuman, in this heat."

Caesar murmured and complained also, muffled by the heat and wind, until after an hour he said suddenly, "Hi, what is that there," and Temeraire halted mid-air and whipped his head around, hovering.

"I saw something there, I thought," Caesar said, but Temeraire flew back and forth and saw not the faintest gleam of foreign color among all the bushes and trees, not a track or even much of a clearing which could have been a camp, and Tharkay shook his head when he looked an inquiry back.

"Well, it wasn't color, so much," Caesar said thoughtfully, on being interrogated; he was flying in lazy circles while Temeraire searched. "Just I thought I saw something moving, but when I sang out it stopped. No, I can't tell you exactly where; this country all looks the same to me. I think it is pretty wonderful I should have spotted it at all."

"Very wonderful," Temeraire said, "when you cannot even say what you saw, and no-one else can see it."

"I am sure I don't need to bother, another time," Caesar said, bristling up his shoulders, and throwing out his red-blazoned chest, "if my effort is so unappreciated; just how I suspected it should be, and my fault, of course, that *you* can't hunt it out. If you want my opinion, if there were a hundred aborigines hiding about in this grass, you wouldn't know it, at all. We ought to fly somewhere else entirely; and at least we might set down and have a rest."

"I am not so lazy that I must have a rest before mid-day," Temeraire said. "We have already wasted enough time on whatever it is you *saw*."

Rankin was standing in his harness, on Caesar's back, looking behind them. "We will have to set down," he said, "in at best an hour: there is a thunderstorm coming on."

"Whyever should he think so?" Temeraire said to Laurence as he banked away, onto his course; the sky was clear, except for a little bank of blue clouds one might see if one looked around behind, but those were not coming on swiftly.

"I have been flying courier duty since I was twelve years old; I can damned well smell a storm," Rankin said flatly as Caesar came up with them, and twenty minutes later Temeraire was forced to concede, as the wind coming towards them began to die away in odd fits and starts, a suggestion of heaviness in the air, and as they flew on, the cloudbank behind grew long and turned a dark, essential blue striped a little with luminous grey and seaweed-greenish bands of color. The trees stood pale and white-limbed beneath it, lit from before by the sun.

"And it will surely erase all signs of passing," Temeraire said to Laurence unhappily. "Whatever can be done? I suppose we might fly on anyway, and try to keep ahead?"

"I am not flying on through that," Caesar said, looking behind apprehensively, as for emphasis the clouds put down abruptly a silent forked line of lightning directly to the earth, spidery and branching and flaring a moment in the dark. The roll of thunder came a long, dragging moment later; and a thin, wispy grey curtain of rain trailed down at one end of the cloud.

"We had better not," Laurence said, grimly, "and we ought not set down on higher ground, either; you are too large."

There was a little open space, of bare red earth and yellow grass, among some larger dunes and sheltered from the worst of the rising wind; the clouds were near upon them by then, and spattering gusts of rain which did not fill the eagerly outstretched canteens and cups, but only dimpled the softer loose dirt and left spots upon their clothing, and rattled the dry blades of grass. It was still hot and oppressive. The dark cloud came rolling up across the sky, suddenly quick after its long creeping approach, and the sun vanished.

More great long forks of lightning were tonguing down to the earth against the wide-open horizon, all around, and the voices of the thunder roared and groaned to one another from one side of the clouds to the other, so that one almost imagined meaning into it. Temeraire could not stop himself trying to make sense of it—he felt on the verge, over and over, as when he had learned only a little of some different sort of language, and thought he had just picked out a familiar word or two amid the sea of new sounds.

The wind shifted, coming hard into their faces: another thin spatter of unrefreshing rain thrown into his eyes and nostrils and flinging the dust upon him, so he had to blink and shake his head, snorting; a smell of distant smoke quite clear upon his tongue. Violet and orange haze spread across the sky, and Temeraire put out his wing a little further to shield the egg a little better from the wind.

"Peculiar sort of color there," Caesar said uneasily, sitting up on his hindquarters: he had grown a great deal, and when he stretched, now, his head might clear Temeraire's shoulder. It *was* a strange color: a vivid glow of red as though someone had painted a line across the horizon, and it was altering the color of the sky, casting that umber light on the clouds, so they were at once blue and muddied with orange-red, and still the lightning flashing against it, although now difficult to see.

"May I beg you to put me up," Laurence said, and Temeraire lifted him so he might see; Laurence opened up his glass and stood looking on Temeraire's shoulder, and then said, "Thank you; Captain Rankin, Mr. Forthing, I believe we had better get all aboard again."

The fire came upon them with shocking speed, a low hissing beneath the continuing crash of the thunder and dry wind, whispering with great malice and hunger, and Laurence shouting over the noise,

"Leave that, damn your eyes," while one of the convicts came reluctantly out from behind some bushes and through the grey wisps of drifting smoke, dragging a cask of rum which he had somehow stolen away after their landing, meaning to privately enjoy. The other men jeered and called, yelling at him, "Bring it on quick, Bob, and we'll be merry as grigs all this fucking flight for once; you won't have it all to yourself, you old sodden bitch, no you won't."

Maynard halting stooped to heave the cask up to his shoulder. The fire was in the distance yet, a broad and smoke-shrouded wall of glowing orange seen through the veil, but already the yellow tips of grass were igniting like red embers upon the crest of the dune behind him as he bent, and a wave of heat came shimmering almost palpable into Temeraire's face and stole his breath.

Maynard was staggering towards them, and the cask was dripping; small sparks of blue fire going up as the droplets struck the ground to meet the catching tinder of dry grass, and then the thickets were going up ahead of his feet, smoke rising in one thin column after another blown into spreading curtains. Temeraire could not see the fire at all anymore as a separate thing: all the world beyond the dunes was flame, and the smoke climbing into thick and stinging pillars around him.

The man let the cask fall, and began to run shambling and coughing towards them. Temeraire felt very strange; his head was thick and confused and his wings felt leaden. He breathed in deeply, and coughed and coughed also; his throat and chest were closing as though someone had wrapped chains around him, and was trying to draw them taut. "Aloft," Laurence was roaring, "Temeraire, go aloft," and Temeraire thought, but I must wait, and he felt quite tired; and then a sharp stab of pain caught his hindquarters, startling his eyes open: when had he closed them?

"Get that egg out of the fire, you damned beast," Rankin shouted, from behind him, and the egg, the egg: Temeraire with a great bunching effort launched himself up; as his wings spread a great shuddering gust of hot, hot, hot wind blew up from beneath him, catching him aback; Maynard was dangling from the belly-netting, being pulled in, and the cask below was a brief torch burning blue-white out of the smoke for a moment. His hindquarters yet ached: there was a little blood dripping, where Caesar had pricked him hard with his claws, which ran down Temeraire's legs as he beat upwards. His wings still did not wish to answer very well.

Caesar was ahead, stretched out long and flying all-out in a straight line, beating and beating: Temeraire fixed upon his grey body and flew as best he could. The smoke still climbed after them, in rising tendrils mingling into columns mingling into sheets, thickening along the ground as all the heaped growth was consumed. His breath whistled painfully in his throat, a particular effort every time, and the thunder roared abruptly very near, out of the huge building clouds overhead; he twisted away on instinct, quite uselessly: the lightning had already struck the ground, perhaps a quarter-of-a-mile distant, and another tree was burning like a torch on its hill of red and gold.

The cold air felt better on his hide, in his throat; but the wind struck him from one side and then the next. One great buffeting gust came rushing at them from above, wet and shockingly cold after the heat, and Caesar was tumbled over: his left wing and shoulder blown hard down, and turning his other directly into the gust, so he was blown every which way, and Temeraire with a laboring burst of speed came under him only just in time to right him; sharp painful sting as Caesar's claws scrabbled on his hide.

Caesar steadied a little, and then they were taken apart again by the wind, another dragging gust which pulled Temeraire suddenly fifty feet straight upwards, only barely managing to keep his wings from snapping against his back.

"Laurence, Laurence," Temeraire called, to be sure that Laurence had not been hurt, by Caesar's claws, nor any of his crew; or he tried to call, but nothing came from his throat, so far as he could hear. The thunder was going off again, like cannon or worse, beside him and ahead, all at once: the sky above blazing with great gunpowder-flashes of lightning which showed the clouds going up and up and up like mountains full of cavernous hollows, false promises of shelter, and the edges billowing and crawling out and in, like living things brooding.

He tried to look and nearly had his neck wrenched around for his pains, the only comfort that he could glance downward and see the egg against his breastbone, the oilskin wrappings shining wet with rain. But the harness did not look so tight, he thought with sudden anxiety, and then the wind struck and he was tumbling, his head bowed down nearly below his forelegs, the blazing orange of the fire suddenly become the sky, the ground yawning with blue cloud-canyons, and then turned over and over, blurring; he could not spread his wings.

He stretched his jaws wide and drew in all the breath he could; the wind cut a little as he fell back towards the earth and the heat rose up instead, and he felt lighter as his chest filled out. He managed to twist himself sideways, and open his wings out straight up and down, in the line of his falling, and banking just a little into the wind caught an up-draft back towards the blue-black heights of the storm, already reaching a talon towards the egg, anxiously, to try and see: he brushed it very gently and carefully with the edge of a knuckle; it was there, it was safe.

"Secure that rigging there, if you please, Mr. Roland," he heard Lieutenant Forthing shouting, and as the fire roared up in pursuit behind them, Temeraire might have heard Laurence's voice; but he was not perfectly sure. But he could not look, he could not turn; the fire was below, the storm above, blind and unmeaning ferocity in every direction, so vast one could not even see the limits of it. He did not see Caesar anywhere, anymore. The sky was so dark, so black, smoke and thunderclouds and no relief, and somewhere there might be sunlight, but so far as Temeraire was concerned there was none left in the world at all, and no direction, either.

He put down his head and flew on.

Laurence nodded his thanks as Roland gave him the small cup of water, and drained it off despite the bitter and acrid taste. Water was rushing with great violence along the once-dry creek bed and had collected in deep puddles over the flat baked surface of the ground, but all choked with ash and dirt, undrinkable until it had been poured through a handkerchief to strain it as clean as it might be gotten.

The landscape had been wholly altered: trees reduced to black-twig skeletons, the thick grasses all gone as if into vapour, leaving behind only scorched and blackened patterns upon the ground which in places still sent up thin lines of smoke. Only the thick dark green bushes yet survived, more or less; the fire had only skirted along their line, and on the other side a region of the sparser vegetation had escaped destruction. Distantly ahead, the fire continued on, a thick black smudge against the sky.

Temeraire lay sleeping, his breath coming in low, worrying rasps. He had landed and thrust his muzzle into the rushing stream to drink long and deep, despite the clots of debris; then had fallen into a stupor. Dorset had listened to his chest and his throat and shaken his head.

Caesar had flown limping into their camp perhaps half-an-hour

later, dripping-wet and exhausted from being tumbled about but a little less wretched: Rankin had steered him into the sheeting rain, far to
the west along the cloud, where the fire had not been able to take hold.
"I would not mind a bite, anyway," he said, drowsily, with his head
upon his forelegs; his grey hide was streaked and mottled with char-
coal.

Meat proved no difficulty, except for their fatigue. Many of the
desert creatures formerly hidden by the scrub had been robbed of shelter where they had not also been robbed of life; there were twelve kangaroos lying upon the earth near enough to be dragged back to the
creek, their fur already singed off and the flesh partly cooked through.
The aviators wearily set about the gathering and butchering, under the
direction of Gong Su. The best Laurence could say of the convicts was
that they were keeping quiet and out of the way, having been doled out
a reduced ration of grog. Maynard was forced to take his own glass at
the opposite end of the camp, alone and in disgrace.

"I shouldn't like to go aloft on this harness again, sir, not without
repairs," Mr. Fellowes said, climbing down from Temeraire's side with
a segment of leather, to show him a buckle which looked as though it
had been made of soft clay, pulled and stretched long and misshapen.
"Not the worst of it, either: all the buckles are gone ahoo: softened by
the heat, I think, and twisted up with all that buffeting we took."

"Do what you can with the supplies, Mr Fellowes; in any case we
cannot think of leaving tomorrow," Laurence said tiredly, running his
sleeve across his forehead; Temeraire would need the rest, and the pursuit should have to wait, if it were not now rendered quite hopeless.
"Mr. Forthing, Mr. Loring, we will have a little order in this camp, I
hope: let us have a couple of fires, and clear some of this debris; and
perhaps if these gentlemen will dig us a pit near enough the water channel, it will give us a little cleaner water for drinking."

"Yes, sir," Forthing said, and went to work upon the convicts,
sending those of them less greenish than the others to fetch their shovels; Laurence realized belatedly he had not thought anything of giving
an order, nor evidently the officers of obeying: the united power of cri-
sis and habit, he supposed, on both sides.

The sun was sinking, through the shredded remains of the storm
clouds and the haze of smoke: all the sky become true extravagant
splendour of purple and crimson and violent pink, gold-limned clouds
and shafts of light flaring out like beacons through their gaps. There

was not enough strength among them for any great labor. They managed with the shovels to rake away the worst of the smoky, stinking debris; the hole was dug in a curve of the creek and gradually began to fill up with water, filtered in through the dirt.

There was biscuit and the meat, thoroughly tasteless and without any scent and difficult to chew. "Can you stew them softer?" Laurence asked Gong Su, over the three kangaroos set aside for Temeraire; Gong Su nodded, but said, "They will be better in the morning," and Laurence nodding did not wake Temeraire to eat.

They slept uneasily, with a watch of four men all the night. The plains glowed with lingering embers all around, like a field of fallen stars burning gold, and a haze of orange-lit smoke hung in the west, as if the sun had chosen not to set but only to drop below the horizon. The creek's roar died away little by little. Laurence woke twice when Temeraire fell into a coughing fit, shudders rippling down his hide, and his head bent over; but Temeraire did not himself fully rouse, his eyes still closed to slits even as he trembled and spat grey-streaked phlegm.

"No, I am well, very well," Temeraire croaked out frog-like the next morning, although he swallowed the kangaroo, stewed into small half-disintegrated lumps, only very slowly and with visible pain, and reluctantly. "We must go on: we must find the trail again."

"My dear," Laurence said quietly, feeling a species of sneak, "I understand your feelings, but we must be practical: we must consider the egg which we yet have, and put its safety before the one which has been lost. Any strange territory is dangerous, wholly unguided as we are; we have already nearly come to grief one and all, and several of our company have suffered worse misfortune. We risk the last egg with every moment we continue: only your utmost exertions were sufficient to preserve it from this last disaster; if we should encounter a second such, could you honestly declare your present strength equal to the task?"

Temeraire was silent, his head bowed deeply over the last, the tiny egg. Laurence could not repress acute guilt: deeply unfair to use Temeraire's feelings so against him, perhaps even smacking of dishonesty, yet Laurence could not for a moment wish to withdraw, if by such a low method he might persuade Temeraire to take the rest necessary for his own health, even if a thousand eggs should be cracked upon the sands. "When you are recovered," Laurence said, "and the fire has died down, we will have more opportunity of finding the trail again. There is this benefit: the fire has quite cleared the landscape for our search."

"But also all the trail," Temeraire said sadly. "I cannot see how we should ever find them again if we wait at all; although I suppose I am being foolish. The trail *is* lost, and there is no help for it. Oh!" he cried. "I am glad we are never to go back to England again, Laurence: I do not think I should ever be able to look Cantarella in the face."

Temeraire cast his wings up and hid his head beneath them, afterwards, and did not care to speak; Laurence rested his hand on Temeraire's muzzle, for what comfort wordless sympathy might convey, and then fetched his writing-case and sat beside him in the dim shadowed cavern the wing-membranes made, pale bluish-grey light filtering in through their translucence. Laurence had been keeping a log of the journey, from the habit of service days; now he added the annotation,

> *Our present Location remains uncertain: we have been thrown thoroughly off any course, and we cannot be sure of the hour until we have made Noon, if the Sun should prove visible, at present it remains concealed within the extensive Haze. We are encamped beside a Creek, but this may as easily be the same dry bed of two days heretofore, or one entirely new, so I have not put it on the Chart. I hope we will retrace our steps towards Sydney, soon, when Dorset feels Temeraire is up to so much Activity.*

He wrote to Jane afterwards, a separate sheet to enclose with the letter he had already begun to her: he felt he could not put off so unpleasant a task on Granby as to convey the intelligence of the loss of the egg. If it had not been estimated so valuable in England, here it had been priceless, where the long journey would make any shipment of additional eggs all the more difficult; and if Jane had fresh hostilities to contend with, in Spain, she would all the less wish to spare more eggs to the very hypothetical breeding grounds of this new continent.

The camp was quiet, except for coughing. Laurence sipped at a mug of grog at intervals himself, the heat a little soothing against the rawness of his throat; there was a heaviness to his limbs, and despite all the game easy to hand, he did not wish to eat apart from a little biscuit soaked in water, which went down softly.

No one had much appetite. Aviators often did not set a regular meal hour, and lately the scarcity of water had made their mealtimes still more irregular, occurring when sufficient number of the party began to make a noise of protest; to-day no one spoke, even as the day advanced and the noon hour must have gone, even though the sun had not shown itself clear. The younger aviators only had any interest in their surroundings, more resilient: Demane had been foraging, and Roland had organized Sipho and Paul Widener—Rankin's signal-ensign, an anxious and fretful sort of boy—to butcher his findings and put out the meat to dry, sprinkled thoroughly with salt. For their immediate delectation, they roasted a brace of large lizards on sticks: Demane had found them alive but so dazed by smoke and thunder they might be taken by hand.

"It is quite good, sir," Roland said, offering some to Laurence, but what little of the smell he could perceive over the clouding of his senses was not appealing enough to provoke his deadened appetite.

They had already more meat than they would require for the return voyage; Demane went out again anyway, unable to resist the bounty, and coming back in the space of less than half-an-hour put down his latest trophy, a handsome-sized kangaroo, only a little singed, and then ducked under Temeraire's wing.

Laurence looked up; Demane said, "There are men there, on the other side of those dunes."

The men were for attacking at once, "before they creep away again, and come lurking upon us during the night, and steal away another," O'Dea said, presenting this to Laurence and Rankin, as a petition on their behalf. "Even the little one ought be able to do for them—" meaning Caesar, rather bloodthirstily, and Rankin said icily, "That will be quite enough, Mr. O'Dea; when your opinion is desired again it will be solicited."

A good deal of resentful muttering followed this, which the convicts did not trouble themselves to keep low; Rankin ignored it roundly, but Laurence shook his head a little: he had seen mutiny before, and with less motivation than the conviction of imminent murder. With Temeraire and even Caesar a little ill and groggy, there could be a real mischief done, if the convicts chose to try and seize upon himself or Rankin, or even another of the crewmen whom Temeraire valued.

"It is not them," Demane said, loudly and impatiently. "They do not have the egg."

Temeraire stirred, here, from his restless drowse, and raised his head: when he understood, he brightened and said, "But perhaps they may know where the others have gone—" and swinging his head towards the convicts asked, "Can no-one of you speak with them?"

"It is no good talking to them," O'Dea said, "what we want is some quick action: if they know we are here, they are sure to run off again, and steal back—"

"They do know we are here," Demane said. "They saw me taking the kangaroo."

"Well, he is a black fellow, though, isn't he; one of them," one man said; Demane was certainly of sable complexion, but hailing from the south of Africa had no more in common with the natives than this accident of coloration; although Laurence supposed doubtfully this might engender some common feeling, or at least defer the suspicion which their own appearance, so far different, might provoke.

"Are any of you gentlemen conversant with their tongue?" Laurence said, and after a little shuffling O'Dea granted that he had some experience; so, too, did a Richard Shipley, one of the younger of the convicts, not twenty and one, who said, "Though not much more than to trade some rum or some buttons for—well, sir, for a little company," with a blush.

"I cannot see how that will be any use here," Temeraire said anxiously. "I might make out a little bit, or they might know some other language: perhaps I ought to come as well."

"That must substantially diminish any hope of their receiving us in a friendly manner," Laurence said, and checked his pistols, instead, which if smaller were no less deadly.

He and Tharkay and Forthing took their two prospective interpreters, however inadequate, and Demane led them over the charred dunes perhaps a mile from the camp, near the far edge of the seared band where the marks of the fire ended and the vegetation had escaped. The aborigines had already collected their own supply of game, many dead animals strung together, and were standing near the unburnt ground, holding some discussion amongst themselves: four men, and a youth perhaps a few years older than Demane. Laurence was surprised, when they drew nearer, to see that the ground before them was burning, and evidently by their doing. They were watching it with narrow, careful attention, and stamping out flames which leapt back towards them.

The aborigines received them not unwarily but without open hostility, and when Shipley and O'Dea hesitantly spoke, they listened and made some reply. This at once exceeded the translators' limits; Shipley said, "It don't sound at all like, a word or two maybe."

Laurence turned instead to pantomime and sketchwork, in the conveniently empty canvas of the burnt ground which showed his lopsided figures red against the black of the ash; he tried to draw a picture of the egg, large, being carried away by small men—blank looks only—and then held out a fragment of the pottery.

This opened some species of communication: the aborigines nodded, and one held out a spear-thrower, which Laurence was startled to see decorated at the end with a string of porcelain beads in red and blue, and another of jade and pearls. He pointed at the pistol in Laurence's belt. Laurence shook his head and said, "No, I thank you," rather bewildered to be offered such a bargain in the middle of the desert. The hunter shrugged and equably accepted refusal, and when Laurence brought out his map and laid it out, they were willing enough to look down at the chart.

This, however, they did not seem to think meaningful; they touched the paper between their fingers appreciatively, and traced the colored lines of ink, but turned it upside-down and back without sign of recognition, even the territory lately traversed which Laurence pointed out to them, the newly marked creek beds and salt pans and hills which must have been familiar landmarks; but perhaps the aborigines did not have the habit of mapmaking.

Instead, Shipley pointed at the necklace and asked "Where?" in the version of the language which he knew, then pointing in each direction of the compass; the aborigines answered with "Pitjantjatjara" and "Larrakia," and pointed north and west, with almost a throwing gesture and another word—"Far, far," Shipley said. "I think that's what it means, anyway."

"And then what about the men they have been snatching?" O'Dea said, and drew in the sand several figures in stick form, and by them the water-hole and the rock outcropping where Jonas Green had vanished. He then crossed out one of his figures; the aborigines nodded without surprise and said, "Bunyip," and shook their heads vigorously.

"Bunyip," they repeated, and crossed the man out more thoroughly, and said a great deal more, which might have been excellent advice if they could have understood a word of it. But then, perceiving they were not understood, the youngest of their company proceeded to hold up his hands like claws by his mouth and made a hissing snatching gesture, with a growl, rather looking like a children's bogey; and Laurence grew doubtful of the proffered explanation: there had certainly been no monsters wandering about the camp.

But O'Dea proved more willing to accept this excuse, and, somewhat mollified, trying more of his limited supply found a few more common words: he drew the egg larger and showed a dragon coming out of it, wings outspread. The aborigines repeated their gesture towards the north-west, and then the oldest tapped the youth on the shoulder, demanding attention, and opening his mouth sang, in a low and gravelly if resonant voice; the other men clapping softly along, to add rhythm to the chant.

"No use to trying to work that out," O'Dea said, looking around. "They go off so from time to time, when you ask them directions, but it is only these stories of theirs: monsters and gods and the making of the world. It don't mean anything."

The song finishing, and the small smudgy fire also, the men bent to take up their strings of game and to move on to another patch of the grasslands; the youth stepped into the newly burnt section and took himself a branch still burning quietly at one end. Laurence would have liked to try and get a little more intelligence out of them, perhaps recruiting Dorset, who was a good hand at draftsmanship, and trying to with better illustrations convey more precise questions; but the hunters had evidently tired of a conversation of so little profit to themselves, and to restrain them could only provoke the quarrel which the men had formerly imagined.

"Bunyips," O'Dea repeated to Shipley with ghoulish satisfaction, as they walked back towards the camp. "So it is bunyips: and they must be man-eaters, did you see how those black fellows shook at the word? God rest their souls, Jack Telly and poor Jonas; in a bunyip's belly, it is a cruel way to end. Like tigers, they must be."

The story would certainly be all across the camp in moments, when they had returned, and the men undoubtedly as pleased to transfer all their fears to man-eating monsters, as to native tribesmen; or more pleased, for the greater hideousness of the threat. Laurence sighed, and climbed wearily up the dune ahead to wave a reassuring hand to Temeraire, who should be worrying; but when he came in sight, Temeraire was looking down instead at the egg, which Fellowes was hastily taking out of its wrappings.

Chapter 10

"I WILL THANK YOU for an end to this wholly inappropriate interference, *Mr.* Laurence," Rankin said, icily. "You have neither rank nor office, nor even proper training to recommend your opinion on the matter. Mr. Drewmore, I trust you are ready to stand the duty? Mr. Blincoln, I believe you are next in seniority, should Mr. Drewmore fail to secure the hatchling; you will prepare yourself as well."

"Yes, sir," Lieutenant Drewmore said after a moment, not displeased but only slow to grasp the offered advantage: a man of forty, heavy of body and of mind at once; he had shown not an iota of initiative, which Laurence had seen, and set himself apart only by a certain amiable willingness and basic competence. He had reached the rank of first lieutenant aboard a middle-weight, for no greater accomplishment than being the son of a distinguished and well-liked captain; but he had been grounded by the death of his beast, during the plague, and no equal post had been offered him.

And Blincoln, only a little second to him in both years and seniority, was similarly a nonentity; neither of them in any way worthy of the one, the last egg. Meanwhile Forthing, who alone among the aviators had distinguished himself in service, however meager his connections, was evidently to be set aside.

Laurence had grown up in a service where influence was very nearly all, in the way of promotion, but he had grown used to the very different mode in the Corps: if a man had much in the way of influence, he was not an aviator, as a rule. Rankin himself was an exception, and Laurence's former lieutenant Ferris: the only two such cases Laurence had so far met, in the service. Merit, and the lucky opportunity of demonstrating it, had in practice by far the greater reach. Personal loyalties might have their impact, but Rankin did not know these men; they had not been affectionate towards him. He had met them one and all, not a month ago.

Laurence had known the gesture was a futile one; but he had spoken anyway. "Sir, you may not be aware that Captain Granby had other intentions," he had said, quietly.

Rankin had rebuffed him in as offensive a way as possible, and without bothering to lower his voice; adding now, "I do not intend this covert should be conducted on the irregular and unsound lines of your own model of behavior."

"By which I can only suppose you mean that Mr. Forthing is not of a line of aviators," Laurence said.

"Your own example must be all that any man requires to appreciate the value of a trained, a trusted lineage: of men who understand what dragons are, and what their own duty is," Rankin said.

Temeraire, who had been anxiously watching the egg so far, lifted his head here and said, "Well, if the egg should prefer Mr. Forthing, it may have him; and I will tell it so whether you like me to or not: *I* do not care whether he has a trusted lineage."

Rankin wheeled to confront him, but meanwhile the egg was rocking; it cracked abruptly across its equator, or near enough, and all their attention was drawn over to it at once. Tipping over, it did not quite separate; with an evident effort, the broken upper half was slowly pushed forward over the sand, furrowing up the burnt patches, and the hatchling beast crawled laboriously out.

There was a brief, dismayed silence as it raised its head. It was a strange, misshapen creature, with none of the lithe, deadly grace that every other dragonet whom Laurence had ever seen had possessed instantly on cracking the shell. It was a long almost skeletal thing, uniformly mottled brown-grey, and bristling along all its shoulders and in patches over its back with spikes very like the barbs on the tails of the Chequered Nettle, one of which had produced the egg; it had, also, inherited the claws of its Parnassian sire, so long they bid fair to snag upon its own flesh.

Its wings were a little stubby and badly cramped together, draped loosely over the hatchling's sides, but as it tried to stretch them out, those sides were revealed—distended into swollen folds which bulged out over the dragonet's shoulder and hip-joints, as if its rib cage were shrunken in too small, and the hide too large for it.

Yet it was otherwise painfully thin to look upon, the bones of the shoulders and hip standing in sharp relief: long and narrow, and had been folded upon itself several times in the tight bounds of the shell. The dragonet had evidently suffered from the confinement, and moving palsied-slow unwound itself only a little at a time, and pausing every short while to gasp a few labored breaths. Laurence could only wince for its sake. It was scarcely the size of an underfed hound.

"Oh, I am hungry," the dragonet said, in a small piping voice which sounded very much as though it were being whistled through a reed; but none of the aviators moved. Drewmore and Blincoln shifted uneasily, and looked at Forthing, who already had edged back away. They, too, stepped back, from the hatchling, and a general uneasy silence began.

"Well," Rankin said after a pause, "it is a pity. Gentlemen, I assume you are one and all in agreement? There is no officer who would care to try the harnessing? Mr. Dorset?"

Dorset was already pacing around the hatchling, inspecting it; he shook his head absently. "I cannot speak either to the source or the effects of the deformity until I have opened it, of course; from the labored breathing I should imagine the lungs are constrained. Quite an interesting case."

No-one else spoke; Laurence did not immediately follow, until Rankin turned and said, "Mr. Fellowes, I believe you are our only ground-crew master; I must ask you to undertake the duty—I am afraid we do not have rifles. Would you prefer a sledge, or a pistol?"

Temeraire, Laurence thought, had also not yet understood; before he should realize, Laurence said sharply, "That is quite enough, sir; I wonder if you could have the temerity to call yourself a Christian. Mr. Fellowes, we will have none of that."

Rankin wheeled on him and snapped, "That you are ignorant of all principles of the Corps, and disdain those few you know, is no surprise; that you have the audacity to set yourself up as authority likewise— What can you, who received the privilege unlooked-for and unearned, understand of the feelings of any aviator on such an occasion, who has lived all his life in waiting for it? It is our duty—as much our duty as harnessing the beast would be, if it were fit for service; it is not. It is not, and there is nothing to be done for it."

"It is nonetheless one of God's creatures for its lack of usefulness," Laurence said, "and I will not see it murdered."

"Would you prefer to see it abandoned and exposed, to suffer slowly?" Rankin said. "A dragon comes out of the shell ready to fend for itself: do *you* imagine this hatchling could do so, if we should leave it here, unharnessed and alone?"

The dragonet, as yet mostly preoccupied with untangling itself, looked back at them wary and uncertain. Fumbling its long-clawed feet over one another and its tail, it tried to spread out its wings, and managed to flap and raise a little dust; but then it ceased the effort, and fell to gasping instead.

"Oh," Temeraire said sadly, to the hatchling, "you cannot fly?"

"I am sure I will manage it shortly," the hatchling said, in its small pale voice, "only I am so stiff; and hungry."

Rankin jerked his hand cuttingly. "It cannot live long in any case," he said.

"Then," Laurence said, "we will give the poor beast some food, and what comfort it can take, until the natural end should come; if that be quick or late, that does not relieve us of the obligations of humanity."

"And who do you propose should feed it?" Rankin said. "No aviator will do it and so bind himself, sacrificing his one chance; and I will be damned if I will allow you to impose a low convict upon us with a claim to call himself Captain—"

"I will feed it myself," Laurence said.

"What?" Temeraire said, his head swinging around sharply. Laurence paused, astonished, and Temeraire said, "You would—?" and his voice was trembling, thrumming with distress and wrath, an edge of the resonance of the divine wind to it.

"Have done," Rankin said, impatiently. "You cannot feed it; unless it has no sense at all, it will not take food from your hands: it can see you are Temeraire's, and it knows he would kill it at once. Which," he added, "would save us the difficulty, I suppose."

Laurence threw him a disgusted look; Temeraire might perhaps *dislike* the gesture, but as for murdering a small and helpless hatchling, he did not in the least believe it. He said, "Temeraire—my dear, what is this absurdity; you cannot imagine I would propose any substitution, ever." That Temeraire was distressed, however, was certain; Laurence added, "My intentions are only the most practical: and I beg you to feed the hatchling yourself, if you should have any objection to my performing the office."

"Oh," Temeraire said, his ruff smoothing a little. "Oh, well; I do not *mind* that, but, Laurence—" He leaned his head over and in a low and confiding tone said, rather hesitantly, "Laurence, maybe you have not quite understood—it cannot fly."

Laurence was very much shocked—shocked, appalled; he scarcely knew what to say. Rankin said, "There; will this convince you to have done enacting us this thorough Cheltenham tragedy?"

Temeraire snorted at Rankin. "I am sure I do not see why you must speak if all you wish is to be unpleasant," he said, "and Laurence, if you should feel very strongly, of course I will give the hatchling some food. Only, it does seem a little strange."

"More than a little strange," Caesar said. "Why, what's it to do when you aren't about, and it is hungry? Anyway, we are still in this desert, and it has been scraps and string all week; there may be a bit of extra food about now, but it's a long way back to the cows. You might have a little sense, instead of wasting it."

"Perhaps it might come to be able to fly, after all," Temeraire said, "if it is only tired, from being shaken a great deal—although—then it might have stayed in the shell to rest—"

He trailed off, not very convincingly; and Laurence found himself abruptly unsure—adrift; what he had supposed a certain mooring had shifted, and was floating with him in an unknown current. If the hatchling *should* linger—deformed, helpless, without any means of sufficiency—rejected by the Corps, and its fellows also—

"Temeraire, you will oblige me greatly if you would give it something," Laurence said, nevertheless; there was no alternative which did not appall the worse: which was not full of barbarism and cruelty, and must be rejected out of hand.

He turned, and stopped: the hatchling was feasting slowly but with great determination in the gutted innards of the kangaroo, with a loop of belt around its neck for token harness, and Demane looked up and said, "I am naming him Kulingile."

"It means, 'all is well,' " Temeraire said to Caesar, "and I do not see what business you have complaining, when Demane was of my crew. I do not see why I must always be losing some one of my officers or my ground crew whenever an egg should happen to hatch; it is become quite unreasonable."

And almost enough to make one *not* wish to go and find the other egg: a certain anticipation of injury which made Temeraire feel not so delighted as he ordinarily would have been, with the intelligence which Laurence and Tharkay had brought back from the natives.

Not really, of course; it was not the fault of the egg, and in truth Temeraire was deeply, profoundly relieved, even to have the little scraps of direction; but—he might admit he was not quite feeling himself. He would not have minded a few days more of quiet rest, and stewed meat. Temeraire did not mean to complain aloud, but his throat was so very uncomfortable, and it seemed very hard he should have to go to all this trouble, and suffer indignities, only to be robbed of yet another crewman. He sighed.

"I beg your pardon; he *is* an officer," Laurence was saying to Rankin, "and not merely a personal servant: Demane has been rated nearly two years, and served as acting-captain on Arkady—"

"A feral beast, which could not be controlled in any case," Rankin said, dismissively. "No; if you imagine I will submit this to the Admiralty, you are thoroughly mistaken. Your servant has made a pet of the creature, and so far as I am concerned, they neither of them have anything to do with the Corps at all; he is welcome to ship back to England if you imagine he will fare better with recognition there. Not that the beast will survive long enough to make that necessary."

"Only long enough to eat up the best of everything," Caesar said, disapprovingly; and Temeraire did think the hatchling was being excessive. Kulingile did not eat very quickly, but he had not stopped eating since he had begun, and was now nearly inside the carcass.

"The kangaroo is bigger than you are," he said, "and you seem to be eating all of it; you might leave some for tomorrow."

Kulingile pulled his head out of the kangaroo, having torn free another fresh gobbet of meat, and tipped back to swallow down the lump, which traveled as a visible knot down his skinny throat. He panted a few times afterwards, his very peculiar-looking sides heaving out and in, and then said thin and piping, "But I am still hungry now, and my captain fetched it for me, so it is mine, and I will eat it; I will," and he pushed his head back inside.

Temeraire sighed, and supposed he could not be mean enough to grudge the hatchling its meal; it must, he thought, be very distressing not to be able to fly. He looked at it critically: it was those sides, so queerly bulging and heaped on one another, he thought, which were likely the problem. "I do not suppose you might cut a bit of them out, and sew it up again," he suggested to Dorset, who was sitting cross-legged by the hatchling's side and listening to the chest with his ear-trumpet.

"A little quiet if you please," Dorset said absently, "and it would be of the greatest use imaginable if he would stop eating," he added to Demane, "—the digestive processes are drowning out the action of the pneumotic system."

"He will sleep when he isn't hungry anymore," Demane said, a possessive hand still on the dragonet's neck, stroking. He looked over at Roland with a rather triumphant expression, which faded when she turned her back and with a set face went to the other side of the camp, to busy herself with packing away the gear for their departure.

"I didn't think you would be so jealous," he said to her, when the dragonet had gone to sleep a little later.

"Yes, very jealous," Roland said without turning, "you ass: I will be taking Excidium in seven years or so, when Mother is ready to be grounded." Temeraire silently swelled with indignation, overhearing this.

"Then—" Demane said, and she rounded on him, and said, "What business have you, dragging it out for the poor thing and everyone, only to make a show of yourself? Half these fellows are grounded because their beasts died, d'you think anyone likes it, watching it fight just to get its breath? It'll outgrow its lungs in a week—"

"You don't know!" Demane snapped. "The captain doesn't think it's going to die."

"Of course he does," Roland said, "we all do; listen!" The dragonet, breathing, was quite audible from across the camp; long effortful hissing breaths, which distended its sides. "And the captain wasn't looking to save it for himself, was he? Only he'll go through fire if he thinks he ought to; he's churchy. You aren't; so I think you are a perfect selfish beast," she added, and stalked away.

"I am not!" Demane said, and looked up at Temeraire. "He might not die," he demanded.

"Well, I do not see any reason he should *die,*" Temeraire said; he was not at all inclined to see the hatchling die, it would be very distressing, "except I do not quite know what he is to do for food, if he should ever have to hunt for himself."

"I can hunt for him," Demane said.

"And he is so very small, that perhaps he will not take a great deal of feeding," Temeraire agreed, and added encouragingly, with a burst of inspiration, "and perhaps he will turn out to be a scholar, and not need to fly at all—or a poet."

Demane did not look very happy at this suggestion; it was always a little difficult to persuade him to sit to his books, and he was already grown deeply disappointed in his brother, who could hardly be got away from them. Temeraire felt however that he had hit upon an ideal solution, "and after all," he said to Laurence, "I do not find that anyone asks a fresh-hatched egg to hunt, when it is a person; Harcourt's egg could only lie about and flap its arms and wail, and at least Kulingile can speak, and eat without someone else putting food into his mouth a bit at a time."

On this philosophy, he tried to begin teaching Kulingile his characters, when he had woken up, but Kulingile only pulled in his wheezing breath and said, "But I am hungry."

"It is only two hours since you ate," Temeraire said, "you cannot be hungry again."

"I am hungry," Kulingile repeated sadly.

"Well, at least learn these first five," Temeraire said, with a sigh, "and then you may have some lizard."

Kulingile looked at the scratched characters, then looked up and said, "I have learned them."

"You have not," Temeraire said, and swept the marks clean from the dirt with the smooth curve of his talon. "Draw them over," but he was forced to yield in the end, for the long claws would not allow Kulingile to write.

So Kulingile was permitted to devour two—three—of the large lizards, which had been cut up and preserved, earlier. Caesar watched disapprovingly, and Temeraire himself could not be exceedingly happy to see them go. He liked the flavor extremely, but he could not at present enjoy very much of it: his throat ached unpleasantly if he tried to eat anything that was not very soft, and the water tasted still ashy and bitter, even where it had been filtered into the small hollow. Anything which Gong Su had tried to stew for him was tainted with the flavor. He ate as much as he could bear, until the worst demands of hunger were satisfied, but sadly that left a great deal of room in his belly afterwards; he would have been glad to look forward to something better, when he could eat again, but at this rate Kulingile would have

eaten up all the salted meat before anyone else could have more than a
bite.

"I am very ready to go," Temeraire said, however, when Laurence
asked: Temeraire could not help but feel that the egg must be found
very soon, or not at all, and now that there was no other to worry
about, his duty was clear; and oh, he so wished to redeem himself—he
had almost thought, for an instant, when Laurence had talked of feeding the hatchling—

Well, it did not bear thinking of; Laurence had said everything
which could be reassuring, and he had not after all done it—his explanations were entirely sensible, and after all, Temeraire could not really
think that anyone would prefer Kulingile to himself, no matter what;
Kulingile was very small, even if he did not mean to die. But, Temeraire
could not help but be conscious—he had already lost Laurence his fortune, and his rank, and his home; to conclude that sequence by losing,
also, an egg—

"I do feel almost perfectly recovered, Laurence," he said, strongly.
"I know I do not quite sound like myself, but that is only a bit of smoke
still in my throat; let us go at once."

Temeraire indeed did not sound like himself, and the pace he set was
considerably lowered from the extremes to which he had formerly tried
to press: Laurence had been obliged to ask him to rein in, a dozen times
in an hour, to keep to a speed which Caesar could match; now not at
all. Kulingile clung on to Temeraire's back flattened low and strapped
on, Demane sitting beside him, the recipient of cold disapproval from
every aviator who looked over at him; the boy's head was held up
proudly in defiance, and Laurence said, "Mr. Blincoln, we will have a
little of the dried meat brought up for the hatchling, if you please," by
way of reproof to the others.

Kulingile devoured what was offered him almost at once, and
sighed for more, although they had only been in the air half-an-hour:
they were obliged to feed him twice again mid-air, before a water-hole
offered itself below and Temeraire descended for a rest—without requiring much persuasion, Laurence was concerned to note.

The landscape was yet blasted in all directions, save where the
thick green bushes had acted in some manner as a fire-break, or a barren patch of earth had offered nothing to the hunger of the flames.

Fringed with both of these protections, the water-hole had only a thin coverlet of ash resting upon the surface, which they were able to skim off with their cups and buckets; it was however not very deep, for the most part, and they were obliged to keep most of the water they had obtained at the creek in their jugs and cans, and use the better and fresher supply only to satisfy their immediate thirst.

Temeraire drank and drank, when they had done, until the hole was nearly down to a damp recession in the earth; fortunately the water began to seep out again when he withdrew, so they might have a prospect of more when they had rested through the heat of the day. "Can we spare so long?" Temeraire said, wistfully.

"We will do better to conserve your strength," Laurence said. "My dear, you are not yourself yet; I beg you do not try and push on through this heat. At least here we have a little shade, and I do not think Kulingile ought to be exposed to the sun's worst violence."

However, Kulingile did not at present seem to care anything for the sun, or for anything but food: he stood waiting out in the open at the edge of their makeshift camp nearly quivering, until Demane came trudging back with a fresh load of game for him to eat, and fell upon the provender without a pause.

He was done very quickly, and looked for more with a hopeful air; Demane stared at the wreckage—there was very little left but scraps of hide of the four small animals he had brought—and then pulled himself up to his feet again, despite the heat. "You may have another hour," Laurence said, glancing upwards: the sun had made noon and was beginning its descent; soon, he hoped, they might leave again.

Another pair of lizards and a smallish kangaroo were found amid the burnt wreckage, only a little torn by birds, and they vanished into Kulingile's gut with the same ravening speed while Demane knelt at the water-hole and cupped water into his mouth with his bare hand, panting, his arms shaking with fatigue; then he crumpled beneath one of the bushes and slept. Having devoured all there was, Kulingile licked his jaws and muzzle and every bloodstained talon clean, very carefully, and then looked around again: he crept to Demane and curled against him in the shade, and fell into a fitful, wheezing slumber beside him.

Sipho watched all this resentfully. Being both younger and easier in temper, he had acclimated with far less hesitation to the upheaval of their life, and the new society in which he found himself had become his home, where Demane, warier by nature and experience, yet held aloof. Sipho had begun, Laurence thought, to dislike a little his brother's overzealous and smothering attention, the last year; but he was far from approving its transfer to the new recipient, and too proud to compete with open demands instead put himself in the deep shade of Temeraire's body, and opened again his book, a Chinese text, to demonstrate his perfect unconcern.

"Well?" Laurence asked of Dorset, quietly, when the surgeon had risen from his inspection: he had gone to look over the sleeping hatchling yet again.

"It is certainly a pity, from the scientific standpoint," Dorset said.

"You have no hope of his surviving, then," Laurence said.

"On the contrary, I must now expect him to last some time, as he has lived this long," Dorset said—several of the aviators, lying hangdog in the shade nearby, looked up abruptly—"and at his present rate of increase, there will shortly be no chance at all of an effective dissection. I would learn a great deal in his current state, but if he should live another month, there will be no working out the original deformity."

Laurence paused and compressed his mouth; then he said, "Perhaps, Mr. Dorset, you might consider the patient's feelings in the matter, before making your laments. Can you determine what is inhibiting his flight?"

"The air-sacs are malformed in some fashion, certainly," Dorset said. "I imagine they have collapsed, and are pressing upon the lungs. The constraint of the shell very likely also injured the development. I hope I am not heartless," he added, albeit without sounding very much concerned by the accusation, "but without the supportive action of the air-sacs and the vessels between them, his weight will crush the remaining organs as he grows; unless he should remain stunted. That I am afraid is unlikely. I can only guess at weight, but he has already put on ten feet in length."

"Mr. Dorset, I assume there is no chance the dragonet should last much longer than that; nor ever fly?" Rankin interjected abruptly, having roused himself at the intelligence that Kulingile evidently did not mean to die at once and conveniently remove himself—and Demane—from consideration.

Dorset shrugged. "The vessels are functioning to some small extent, or else the weight of the skeletal system should already have crushed his remaining organs beyond use. It is not wholly impossible."

This opinion produced a good deal of stirring amongst the aviators, and low conversations. "Not impossible," Temeraire repeated to Laurence, with equal parts optimism and satisfaction, "I am very pleased Dorset should say so: that would be much better. There is no reason why he should not live, although he does eat a great deal; if only he can work out how to fly."

"I hope you will not set your heart on his survival," Laurence said, low, and looked with some concern at Demane, who yet slept, with an arm now curled over the dragonet's shoulders: determination as much as affection would drive him hard. "We cannot rely upon it; certainly it forms no great part of Dorset's expectations. Will you not eat a little more, before we go?"

"Oh," Temeraire said, "no, perhaps not; but I will drink a little more."

He drank, and they began the laborious process of loading him again, dragged out with reluctance: the convicts had all eaten heartily of the preserved meat themselves, and weighted down by food and the sun were in no great mood to continue the journey still further into the barrens, now without any guidance or promise of success but the ill-understood recommendation of the aborigines. "Three dragons ought to be enough for one town," one man muttered, "without looking to get more."

Laurence could muster no great enthusiasm himself, and particularly when Temeraire was so visibly unwell: his voice croaked raggedly, and even the smallish portions of meat, cooked a little while in water, were beyond his endurance to swallow. But with the hatching of Kulingile, there was no egg remaining to be a lever which could turn Temeraire aside; there was nothing now but to continue onward, until time should make it certain the lost egg was hatched.

"I must hope the egg is waiting," Temeraire said, "and trusts that we will rescue it; I am sure it must be very anxious. I could not blame it, of course," he added sadly, "if it did not like to wait, with as long as I have taken to find it. Pray, Laurence, can you repeat over anything of what the hunters said? Perhaps I might understand a little more."

"I cannot," Laurence said, "and I doubt O'Dea or Shipley could do so, either; and while I admire your gifts in this area greatly, my dear, I cannot allow you to suggest that you might form an understanding of a language of which you have never heard a syllable."

"Well, I did hear the singing," Temeraire said, but sighed, and did not press further.

*   *   *

He pushed himself up standing with an effort, when it was time to get
the belly-rigging on him; and now several of the convicts made excuse
for not climbing in, and abruptly had small personal errands which required their attention, or needed to refill a can of water; Laurence
rounded several up and sent them aboard, and went down to the water-
hole after another handful of stragglers—they would not stir save in
pairs, anymore—who insisted they were coming, only they were taking
turns filling their cans: they had drunk them all dry, and he could not
ask them to sit aboard for hours in this heat, without so much as a
drop.

"That will do," Laurence said, "fill your can on the other side, and
enough of this malingering, Mr. Blackwell; if tomorrow you cannot
provide yourself with water over the course of a pause of three hours
without delaying us, you will fly thirsty; and if that is not enough we
will consult the lash," with more acerbity than his usual wont; he was
in no spirit to spare sympathy for the men who were dragging out
Temeraire's discomfort.

"Aye, sir," Blackwell said, tugging at his forelock, and stepped
across to the other side of the water-hole, and was gone: a red flashing
of jaws, talons, tremendous speed—then he was jerked down and
away; the bushes rustled over him once and were still.

Laurence stared; Jemson and Carter stared; the unreality of it—
"Temeraire!" Laurence bellowed, as the men backed hastily scrambling away, their canteens tumbling and water spilling over the
dirt—"Temeraire!"

Temeraire lunged over the dune and nearly brought half of it down
spilling into the water-hole, and when Laurence pointed at the bushes,
he seized them in his talons and began to tear them away. "What is it?"
Temeraire said. "I do not understand, where did it come from?"

"It was concealed beneath them," Laurence said, "or so it seemed;
I scarcely caught a glimpse."

Forthing was hastily organizing the aviators: they had their pistols
drawn, and swords, and stood warily back while Temeraire dragged up
the bushes one after another, their long spidery roots dangling red dirt.
When he had cleared them, there was nothing there: only the dirt, and
grass, and stones, and Laurence would have thought himself mad, if

only there had not been Jemson and Carter to swear to it, also; but Jemson said, "I didn't see it; only Blackie was there, and then he weren't," and Carter said, "It was big as a house, it was. It et him whole in one big bite, and then it went into thin air."

"Perhaps it did," Temeraire suggested, sitting back on his haunches; he nosed at one of his talons, abraded by his struggles with the tough bushes, "like a spirit? That would account for why we have not seen them."

"No," Laurence said, "whatever it was, the creature was perfectly corporeal, and it took him: can it have tunneled away?"

Temeraire raked his claws through the dirt, and they caught: with a heave he brought up a ragged mat of dirt and branches and a knot of grass atop it, which when thrust aside showed a gaping hole descending into the earth: narrow and rough-edged, dug out of the loose sand.

The sides were packed with stones, and plastered also with some yellowish green matter, flecked with larger bits of leaves and of grasses, as though these had been mulched, all to give it stability, although not very much. The walls yielded easily as Temeraire dug into them, and Caesar was now helping, too: they made rapid progress into the depths, but the tunnel crumbled as they dug. In a little while, they broke through into something like a junction: Laurence, crouching by the side, had a glimpse of many passages branching; then the walls collapsed inward and the whole fell in upon itself. Caesar nearly slid forward into the depression.

"That is certainly where he was taken, but if the bunyip has retreated, perhaps we may find some other entrance to come at its lair," Laurence said, pulling himself free from the heavy sand, which had buried him nearly to the knee in collapsing, and they began with shovels and talons to scrape at the ground around the water-hole.

"I think I have found one," Roland said, thrusting the handle of a shovel deep into the earth, a little way back from the water-hole beneath some more of the bushes. These did not need to be torn up, they discovered: when Temeraire had set his claws in the mat, he might lift it up, and the bushes would go with it: evidently their roots had grown around and through the mat, a clever way to disguise the lurking trap.

But they dug a little way down, and this passageway, too, collapsed: designed for its maker, and not the weight of dragons or shovelwielding men, or perhaps only ever intended to be temporary. If there were more permanent chambers, far below, no quick excavation would reach them: the bunyip had undoubtedly fled as deep and as far as it could go, with so much noise and upheaval upon the surface.

"Well, are we going to dig forever," Caesar said, shaking dirt a little fastidiously off his claws, "or are we going? I am sorry for the fellow, but I don't think we are going to get anywhere at this rate: it can dig, too, and while we are going at it here, it is probably digging itself halfway across the desert and away."

While blunt, there was no denying the practical truth of the matter; and Laurence could not call Blackwell's survival likely: he had made no sound, and any man would have shrieked, dragged away by such a creature, if still alive. The very speed and silence of the attack which had made it so otherworldly, to be missed even if one was standing directly by, argued for the creature's instantly killing its prey, even as it whipped its victims away to be devoured in quiet and safety.

They considered and delayed a little longer, while Temeraire dug in a half-hearted way around the opened holes, trying if by chance he should find a deeper chamber, but these efforts collapsed the passageways even before he broke into them, and the only result was to leave behind a wreckage of sand-heaps and torn-up grasses, and the dunes assembled into new shapes, a deep valley marking where Temeraire had labored.

"Very well," Laurence said finally, drawing his sleeve across his face. "We can do no more."

Temeraire's belly-netting had grown choked with sand, during the first efforts, the desperate rush to try and retrieve the taken man. They did not wait to clean it, but only shook and brushed off the worst of the clumps. The men boarded silently and with alacrity; all were glad to be gone.

Chapter 11

⬦

THEY HAD LOST MUCH of the light. "If we find any sign of the trail, we will find it at water," Tharkay said quietly to Laurence, as Temeraire flew on towards a mid-point between the purple and golden splendour of the beginning sunset and the haze of fire yet clinging to the horizon to the north: the orange light more a faint tinge of color flung up against the sky than real illumination. They were nearly free of the scorched landscape: patches still of burnt ground beneath them, but these faded into the low scrub like paint-strokes brushed too long.

"And these bunyips also, of course," Laurence returned, grimly.

Tharkay nodded. "The camps we have seen have all been some distance back from the water, or upon rock: an example we perhaps ought to have had the sense to follow before now," he said dryly.

"Now that we know of them, I will clear the bunyips away," Temeraire said over his shoulder, "when we have landed: I cannot see what business they have sneaking about so, hiding under bushes, and I am not going to have them leaping out and snatching away any of my crew; or anyone else, either. I think they must all be very great cowards."

The sky behind them was already gone to cold-water blue when they found another water-hole, and Temeraire and Caesar drank deep and thirstily while they yet all remained aboard; except Demane, who slipped his carabiners and slid down to go hunting at once, and was already out of ear-shot before Laurence could notice and reprove.

"There," Temeraire said, lifting his dripping muzzle, and shaking his head to throw off a little of the dirt and sand which had accumulated upon his ruff and brow as they flew, "that is very refreshing; and now we will see about these bunyips, if there are even any of them here."

He set upon the bushes, tugging, and almost at once uncovered another of the trap-door openings; Caesar likewise found another, and pushed the mat clear of it. "Well, I don't see anyone in it," he said, poking his snout inside, and then drawing out, "so I expect they have run off."

Temeraire tossed aside the covering and said, "We had better make sure there are no more, however, before any of you should come down," and raking his claws through the knotted, clumped grass hit upon another.

They went scarcely a few strides before they had found a fresh opening after this, and throwing aside the vegetation in great heaps began to tear up all the border of the water-hole: the gaping dark holes began to show themselves everywhere, as they worked, and the oasis began to have a strange, nightmarish ant-hill quality, as the full honeycombed extent of the tunnels became clear. The bunyips never showed themselves, but their presence was everywhere: as though the water-hole itself was but a shining lure in the midst of a vast and malevolent trap, its real nature concealed beneath the earth, and they had haplessly been throwing themselves within all along.

Some of the tunnels further from the water's edge were in worse repair, disused and half-crumbled; in other places the concealing mats had dried up and were thin and fragile things that broke when Caesar and Temeraire pulled upon them. Others however were fresh and strong, requiring real effort on Temeraire's part to drag them loose: this was no abandoned complex. "How many of the creatures could there be, to build to such an extent?" Laurence said, a little horror-stricken to envision armies of the creature which he had glimpsed so briefly; and if they should survive here, in the desert, he wondered, what of their possible presence within the countryside nearer the colony—?

Temeraire stopped to turn his head aside and cough raggedly; they had stirred up a great deal of dust and dirt, in tearing up the mats and the stubborn clinging roots. "I don't suppose we must keep going," Caesar said, pausing to take another drink himself. "We might fill these in, what we've found already, and then we can have a rest if we only stay on this side of the water-hole. It is getting dark, and it will be too hard to spot them soon."

They all warily disembarked, and unloaded the dragons; then Temeraire reared up on his hind legs and set his claws into the side of the rising dune and pulled it down, cascading sand and the narrow trees sliding askew, to bury all the dark gaping mouths: the tunnels vanished beneath the spill of darker red earth, and they all beat down upon it with the backs of shovels, to trample it flat and smooth, and then without any orders, the men began to roll over whatever rocks of any size they could find, and the toppled trunks, to make an entrenched border around the site.

They posted a watch of four men, holding pistols: not much use, Laurence privately thought, against the sort of creature he had seen, unless a man should be exceedingly lucky in his shot; but comforting to the spirit nevertheless. He stood by the water's edge with his own pistols drawn and ready, while they filled their water-jugs by twos and threes, and when Demane came back over the ridge, Laurence said to him, "You will not go away without permission again and alone: we do not know how far from the water-holes these creatures may travel."

"But I have to hunt," Demane said, "or else he will eat everything we have: he has already eaten half the salted meat I found the day before."

Laurence had not realized that Demane had given Kulingile still more food during the flight, but a consultation of their stores confirmed the truth. "Well, I call that greedy," Caesar said, disapprovingly, "and a waste, too. Now what are we to eat, and when we have been doing all the work?"

"*I* have done the work of finding the meat," Demane flashed, "so I may feed it to anyone I want."

"That is enough, Demane," Laurence said. "All our stores are held in the common interest, and we must ration a little better than this; if you permit him to gorge in excess to-day, he is too likely to starve to-morrow, when we are in strange territory with such uncertain supply."

Demane subsided, and his latest gleanings were shared out. Temeraire at least did not quarrel over his portion, but as his restraint came from lack of appetite, Laurence was not disposed to be glad. Gong Su dug out a cooking-hollow in the earth, lined with the oilcloth, and brewed a profligate vat of tea which Temeraire drank eagerly; but this at once consumed nearly all their store of tea, and was no adequate substitute for food.

"Pray do not be anxious," Temeraire said, "I am sure I will be better soon; only it is so very dry, all day long," and he coughed again.

"I will make soup," Gong Su said, "and we will let it cook overnight, so more of the virtue will go into the water," and three times during the night, Laurence roused to see him depositing more hot stones from the fire into the cooking-hollow, clouds of rich steam billowing out from under the oilcloth, soft hissing smoke as the rocks went into the water: Kulingile woke with him, his small head rising on the narrow slender neck from under Demane's protective arm, to watch very intently, and sniff deep.

By morning, the meat had been wrung nearly grey and the cracked bones clean and white with all the marrow gone, a thin gleaming layer of flecked white fat floating on the surface in the slanting early sunlight, when Gong Su had uncovered the whole. This Temeraire ate, and then drank off the soup to the dregs and professed himself very satisfied. The meat he would have abandoned, with the last few feet of the soup which were too awkward for him to extract; Kulingile waited only until Temeraire had turned his head away to pounce, tipping himself nearly entirely inside the hollow, and very shortly had consumed all that was left.

He certainly would have cared for more breakfast, but there was none; Laurence shook his head when Demane would have gone hunting. "When we stop at mid-day, you may go," he said. "We must use these early hours for travel," and, he hoped, thereby ease Temeraire's labor.

Dorset had persuaded Temeraire to tip his head back, angled towards the sun, and had crawled nearly into his throat to perform an inspection further aided by the light of a candle. "There is a great deal of general aggravation to the tissues," he reported, his voice echoing out queerly. "Hmm."

This last came stretched long and hollow, and Temeraire said interrogatively, "Ammnh?"

"It appears particles of ash entered the throat: the flesh is burnt in a speckled pattern," Dorset said, and did something.

"Aaahm!" Temeraire protested, and when Dorset had emerged added reproachfully, "That was not at all pleasant; I do not see why I ought let you look if you will only be hurting me."

"Yes, yes," Dorset said, callously, and informed Laurence, "There is some blistering as well; I should advise against any roaring, and only cold food, henceforth. It is a pity we do not have any ice." The sun was climbing; soon it would be near enough to a hundred degrees. It was indeed a pity.

They rigged up again the oilcloth canopies on his back, for what relief both they and Temeraire could get thereby, and settled within the artificial shade as he leapt aloft, only stirring to look over the side for some track or sign; or to sip from their warm canteens. There had been no trace of the aborigines at the water-hole though they had inspected around the near-by rocks which should have offered shelter from the bunyips.

"I am still hungry," Kulingile piped from behind them.

Laurence sighed. "Demane, he must be patient."

"Yes, sir," Demane said, but when the bell was rung for the half-hour, Kulingile asked with great anxiety, "Now may I have something?" and again before the next bell sounded. At last Laurence permitted Demane to swing down and fetch him a little of the salted meat, but this did not stifle the pleas for long, and they possessed an edge of real misery which made them very difficult to endure. Kulingile did not whine, but only grew more desperate, and when he fell silent, Demane said suddenly, "No! You cannot chew that—" and Laurence turned to see Kulingile had begun to gnaw upon the harness.

"I did not mean to; only it is hard to be quiet when it aches so," Kulingile said, small and miserable, leaving off and trying to hunch himself tighter around his belly.

"Temeraire," Laurence said, with equal and warring parts pity and exasperation, "if you should see any game, we must stop, I think." Happily the kangaroos proved to yet be active in the relative cool of the morning, but Temeraire did not quite so easily catch them as before: he made several attempts, while Caesar took two one after the other, and plainly did not mean to share his bounty.

There was a quiet indignation in the makeshift camp, when Rankin did not order Caesar to do so; Caesar remarked, "I am sure I would be happy to share with anyone who could not catch their own, if they did their part; but as for throwing good food after bad, no, thank you."

"Oh!" Temeraire said, coughing, "I should like to know why he has deserved to be fed, ever, in that case; and I certainly would not like any of his catch: they look very skinny and tasteless to me. If I wished a kangaroo of *that* sort, I am sure I might have taken two myself."

"I would not mind one like that," Kulingile said indistinctly, swallowing.

"What are you feeding him?" Laurence said, looking over.

"Snake," Demane said, despairingly, "and also two rats, but I could not find any more."

Temeraire gathered himself and leapt aloft once again, going after the small herd of kangaroos which were yet fleeing, and this time he did not try to snatch one or another as they hopped: instead he flung himself down among them and returned with eight: more than their appetite could require, and the herd likely smashed beyond recovery by so brutal a culling; he was plainly embarrassed by the clumsiness of the maneuver, and looked away when Caesar sniffed.

"Pray eat as much as you can now," Laurence said, "and when we have reached water, Gong Su can stew the rest for us to carry: it will save us similar pains should we have enough to feed him tomorrow."

Kulingile dispatched an entire kangaroo alone, by no means the smallest of the catch; Temeraire could scarcely manage as much, despite all his exertions, before the pain of his throat once again overcame his appetite. They loaded the remaining carcasses, cleaned a little, into a sack to hang below the belly-netting.

"Only," Temeraire said, a little low, "it is quite unaccountable why I should be so tired when we have not been flying very long; it feels as though I cannot properly get my breath, and if I should try and breathe deeply, it aches." He stretched his wings, and rolled them through their range of movement, a few times, and refused Laurence's suggestion they should rest a little longer. "No; we have already lost too much time," he said, "pray let everyone come back aboard."

Temeraire flew now with the sun climbing over his shoulder and his neck, so that he felt uncomfortably warm upon the one half, and lopsided; a grinding flight which seemed very long. "I suppose it is not mid-day yet," he said eventually—he did not ask for himself, really; only Laurence had urged a break from the heat of the day, for all their sakes. But it was only eleven.

He put his head down and flew doggedly onward, thinking of nothing but the next wingbeat, until Laurence said, "I think we will stop a little while here, my dear, if you will agree," and Temeraire raised his head to see the shining blue-white stretch of water, rolling out before them and stretching northward, covering all the ground.

The lake's shore was peculiarly crusted, seen from aloft: blue and shallow water, and very white sand, which when they had landed proved instead to be salt: a thin crust over the earth, and the lake full of fish; too small to be worth catching for dragons, Temeraire noted with regret, but the men made a hearty meal of them, and it was pleasant to dip into the deepest part, some distance away, and come out wet.

There were not very many trees or shrubs, although fresh grasses grew in abundance; but despite the lack of shade, Temeraire found it a great refreshment to sit upon the half-green shore and look away from the red sand and rock everywhere; and there were no bushes to hide lurking bunyips. It only lacked, to make the respite complete, Tharkay's returning in a little while with a tiny scrap of blue silk he had uncovered, half-buried, near some rocks a distance down the shore.

"It has been here some time," Tharkay said, spreading out the ragged strip to show them: one corner exposed to the sun had gone quite white, where the rest which had been buried was yet a dark blue when it had been brushed free of sand. "There is no reason to expect their latest visit was recent, but we are on some track which they have used."

"And which should lead us back to their home," Temeraire said, jubilantly, "and there we may wait for them to come out of the desert with the egg, or perhaps if there is someone there, they will tell us which way to go to find them."

So he might rest easy in his conscience: he flew out for another swim and drank deeply, gratefully, from the cool water; he did not mind at all that it had a faint little taste of salt, and it was pleasant running down his throat.

He was sorry to leave again; the lake seemed a true oasis at last, the first they had found in so very long. When they had built the cairn of stones, for Iskierka to follow back, and Laurence had tucked a note for Granby beneath it, Temeraire looked over the gleaming expanse with a little sigh.

But Caesar said, half under his breath, "We might stay a little longer," so Temeraire might even feel virtuous in saying sternly, "No; the egg is still somewhere ahead, and we must keep going," and he flung himself aloft over the silver water with a leap.

They made good time, after the rest, and Temeraire thought that his breathing was not quite so embarrassingly noisy as before; certainly he could get his breath a little easier, and if he did cough a little, it was nothing so unpleasant as before, he told himself, and managed not to be overcome.

Tharkay counseled against crossing the lake directly: instead they skirted its limits, ragged and imperfect, with long spurs of land protruding deep into the lake, miles wide, which they crossed, landing briefly to scrape together a few more cairns. Long hours and not a sight of the smugglers, or their trail; at least there was game, and Temeraire took more than one kangaroo from the air, neatly, to his satisfaction.

They landed for the night at another stand of trees and shrubs around a watering-hole of fresher water, a little distance onward from the lake, although the ground was still pale with salt. Temeraire put down the kangaroos to be cleaned properly: Gong Su meant to salt down a great quantity of the meat, to sustain them through the desert. The men began to rake together a heap of the salt under his direction; meanwhile Temeraire set upon the vegetation with a will, happy to clear away the bunyips' concealment.

He had an additional cause to be satisfied with this labor, too, for many little rodents fled from the wreckage, and also some birds, and Kulingile sat by as he worked and snatched them up as they tried to dash.

"You see," Temeraire said to Caesar, quite pleased, "he can hunt, even if he cannot fly; so there is no call for you to always be sneering."

"I don't call it hunting," Caesar returned, tugging up a shrub beside him, "when we are running them out towards him, and he is only sitting there picking them up. Why, you might as well call it hunting to take a drink of water from a hole that is right before you."

Temeraire snorted, dismissively; water did not try to run away, so it was not at all like. "Perhaps you might care to try flying, again," he suggested to Kulingile, as he threw down another heap of bushes.

Kulingile shook out his wings and drew a deep breath and reared up on his hindquarters; he flapped a little; his sides quivered, jelly-like, and then he tipped back down panting thinly and said, "Maybe I will manage it tomorrow."

Temeraire sighed.

Demane was plainly glad for the respite, also; he had gone out hunting at mid-day again, to take advantage of the bounty of game at the lake, and as soon as they had disembarked to the security of the rocks, he collapsed almost enervated in what shade they offered. Temeraire thought he might say a private word to Kulingile: he was not taking very good care of Demane, and one might be hungry and still think of these things.

Temeraire, and Caesar, had cleared away the brush and once again filled in all the wretched tunnels—there were so very many of them; Temeraire did not see why they should be necessary. If the bunyips were as quick as Laurence said, it seemed to him they did not need to be hiding underground and leaping out on some unsuspecting person, only to eat; they might hunt respectably. There was something unnatural and unpleasant in it, he felt—and when they had cleared all away, and made safe the camp, the rest of the men shifted over: but Demane lay where he was, asleep.

"If he does not want anything to eat, he can stay there," Sipho said, rather coldly. "I am surprised he has not gone out hunting again; won't Kulingile be hungry?"

"You are saying it wrong," Temeraire said, "it is Kuling*i*le, and you know better, so there is no excuse."

"I don't see why it should matter to anyone," Sipho said, and stared down at his book mulishly.

But Roland pushed herself up, after she had drunk and rested a little, and trudged over to Demane with her canteen. He struggled up and hanging limply over his crossed legs drank and drank, and then drooping followed her to the camp and fell asleep once more, as far as he could be from the little fire which the aviators had put up, for comfort and cooking. Kulingile crept over to him and nosed at his shoulder anxiously until Demane blindly reached out and patted him; then slumped back.

Kulingile sighed, reassured; then looked up at Temeraire and said, in his thin voice, "May I have another kangaroo?"

"After all those rats you ate, anyone would think you had put away enough," Caesar said, but as Caesar had taken two kangaroos earlier and not shared a bite, Temeraire was quite out of temper with him, and it pleased him to say, in what he felt was a particularly gracious way, "Certainly you may; *I* do not believe in being stingy," and Kulingile fell with so much gratitude upon the meal that it gave Temeraire a glow of lordly satisfaction.

"If he is going to smother himself with his own weight," Caesar said, "it seems to me you can't call it friendly to help him do it quicker," but this was only spiteful meanness, Temeraire felt; although Kulingile would eat too quickly, and then stop and gasp to catch his breath, and then begin again; and when he was done and had collapsed in slumber beside Demane, his breathing *was* a little worse.

"Another ten feet," Dorset remarked, winding up his knotted cord again as he stood from Kulingile's side. "The rate of growth is exceptional. I will have to make a note of it for the breeding journal, and perhaps for the Royal Society."

"But when will he be able to fly?" Temeraire asked, and Dorset had no satisfactory answer to give.

But this was only a small and vanishing shadow on his general complacency of spirit: his throat did not hurt quite so much, and Gong Su was now making another pot of soup, which Temeraire expected to enjoy a great deal in the morning—flavored this time with the small yellow fruits of one of the bushes which Temeraire had torn up; Tharkay had pointed it out as having been harvested a little by the aborigines, he thought, and an experimental taste had not caused any discomfort: a little sweetness, and a strong flavor rather like tomatoes, although they looked more nearly like raisins.

"Will you try and eat a little now, before you sleep?" Laurence said. "We can cut some kangaroo small, if that would ease the passage; you cannot heal quickly or well when you are straining to your limits, and not eating."

"I think I can," Temeraire said, feeling optimistic, and if he only managed perhaps one kangaroo, and none of the bones, those went directly into the soup and so would not be wasted, and he did not feel quite such vivid pangs when he at last settled upon the sand.

To cap his evening, Laurence read to him a little; when their patience for going over the by-now-familiar material had faded, he put the book down, and Temeraire said, "I have been thinking, Laurence, of the valley: perhaps we might take some of this red stone out of the desert with us, as we return, and use it in building a pavilion: would it not make an interesting pattern, with the yellow stone there?"

"I cannot quarrel with your taste," Laurence said, looking at the red earth, "although the labor in bringing back so much stone must be great. But we will have the time, I imagine."

He was silent a little while: night had come on fully now, clear, and with the moon out and shining, cool and pleasant after the sun's heat.

The desert beneath was endless shadows of clumped grass and the thin scrubby trees, dunes rising and falling away into the distance, and the water a silvered reflection gleaming out at them from the ground. Temeraire thought perhaps Laurence had fallen asleep, but then he said, softly, "I had not quite felt the vastness of this country, until we had come into it all this way, nor its strangeness."

"Laurence," Temeraire ventured, holding his breath for the answer, "are you very sad to not return to England?"

"I must be anxious for the sake of our country," Laurence said, "and our friends left behind; it is difficult to know them in dire straits, and feel we might be of more use elsewhere, and yet remain helpless to assist. But in a personal sense, I have left very little behind, my dear. I have long been used to rely upon correspondence to sustain the intimacy of friendships: it is a necessity for a sailor."

He paused, then, and said low, "You must be more constrained than I am, by our remaining; I have not forgotten Tharkay's proposal, only—" He stopped.

"Well, I must say that privateering seems quite splendid, to me," Temeraire said, unable to conceal a touch of wistfulness, "but I do see, Laurence, that you do not quite like to think of it; and I should not at all wish to do it if you did not feel perfectly satisfied, also; only I thought perhaps you might miss the war."

"The war? No," Laurence said. "To be of use, yes; but there is no sense in thinking of it. I am very sorry, my dear, but I hold out no hope for a pardon."

"But I am sure we need not be useless here," Temeraire said. "We have found our valley, after all."

"It would be something, indeed," Laurence said, "to build for once, instead of tear away; yes."

So Temeraire might lay his head down with some degree of relief, and the pleasant occupation, before he slept, of working out in his head a design for a pavilion of adequate magnificence to console Laurence for any remaining regrets, patterned in stone of red and gold.

He woke gradually, very cool and comfortable, except for a little smacking of sand at the corner of his jaw; he raised his head and spat it out, and startled: he was overbalancing, and his hindquarters went tipping away underneath him as though he were on the deck of a ship plunging unexpectedly down into a trough. "What has happened to the ground?" he said, and tried to stand, and could not: there was nothing solid for his feet to grasp, and his limbs dragged very strangely if he moved them—everything seemed very low—"Laurence?" he said: the moon had set, and the sun was not yet risen, and he could not make out much of anything but the small glow of the fire's embers, down within the camp, and the rearing outcrop of rock some distance away.

"Yes, my dear?" Laurence said drowsily, from his back, and then looking over raised his voice and called, strongly, "Mr. Forthing! A light there, if you please—"

The aviators came with torches, and then abruptly stopped, scrambling back with exclamations: their boots sinking in the sand, thick sludgy noises like the bubbles of a porridge slowly boiling as they pulled them free. In the light, Temeraire saw he had sunk into the earth, nearly up to his breastbone; the folded edges of his wings were plunged deep and his tail was half-submerged, his legs wholly so—

"But I was only sleeping," he protested, and tried to rear out, but he could not pull his forelegs free, though he exerted all his strength: one would come a little way out, rising, wet sand dribbling from his hide as he pulled, but the effort required grew, and grew, until he could not continue, and sank forward again.

He panted and found this raised him perhaps half-a-foot, not unlike bobbing in the water, but he could not get out: he could not move. He tried again, more vigorously thrashing his limbs—he might move them a little side to side, he found, if he did not try to pull free—until Laurence sharply said, "Temeraire, stop! You are sinking further—"

The sand had crept up higher on his chest, and was lapping at the edges of his back. "Laurence, perhaps you had better climb off," Temeraire said, turning his neck around to inspect Laurence's position with some concern. "I am sure I can reach to the others, if I stretch my neck."

"No, I thank you," Laurence said.

"I would advise against moving, or lowering your neck to where it may be entrapped," Tharkay said; he was crouched down inspecting the pit, and setting broken-off twigs into the sand to mark its border. "I am surprised the quicksand should go deep enough for you to have sunk this far."

"We cannot have overlooked this last night," Laurence said.

"Temeraire and I were sitting here an hour before we slept; the earth was perfectly solid."

"I only do not understand why it will not let me out," Temeraire said, unable to resist trying again to draw his foreleg free, very slowly and carefully, only a little way at a time, but it dragged and dragged and dragged, and at last halted: he could draw it no further, and it sank gradually back away as soon as he stopped his efforts.

He was not uncomfortable, precisely: it was quite pleasantly cool, and when Laurence asked, Temeraire said stoutly, "Oh, I do not mind it of itself, only I would like to get out of it, now," but that did not address the clinging, sticky quality of the stuff: sand was squirming everywhere under the edges of his hide, and there was something dreadful in not being able to get out: it was not at all like swimming in water, which did not try and drag you back down, like chains which you were not allowed to take off.

"Well, I don't see why you didn't get out of it when you first noticed," Caesar said, having roused up, and yawning tremendously against the early morning: he was not yet done with a hatchling's usual tendency to sleep endlessly.

"I was asleep," Temeraire bit out, annoyed, "and so I did not notice, until I had woken; and I do not think it is at all wonderful I should not have, as no-one would expect perfectly ordinary sand to turn into something like this. How are we to turn it back?"

"The sun's heat may burn off enough of the moisture to allow you to dig free, when it rises," Tharkay said, after a moment. "Perhaps some underground spring feeds this place."

"If we can remove some quantity of the sand, you may be able to free yourself more quickly," Laurence said. "Mr. Forthing, shovels, if you please—"

"What's over there, then," one of the convicts said, pointing, and Temeraire looked: on the ridge of the dune rising above his precarious position, a narrow angular head was up and visible as a black silhouette against the lightening sky, watching.

Another rose up beside it, and then another: until there was a line of them, long muzzles with rounded snouts, and small black eyes which caught the reflections of the torches and gleamed yellow back at them. They had queer tufted heads. "Steady, there," Forthing said; the aviators had out their pistols.

The light was increasing: the bunyips were shades of red and brown, the very color of the earth, with pebbled hides, and the tufts were yellow as the grass; if they were not poking up from the hill, they would have been very difficult to see at all. "Oh," Temeraire said, indignant, "I see now how it is: they are even more cowardly than I thought. This must certainly be their doing; they did not care to fight me properly, or defend their territory, but instead they have made this wretched sneaking trap."

Rankin snorted. "How a gaggle of lizards are to have produced anything of the sort, I should care to know," he said. "More likely they have come like vultures, to wait."

Laurence would rather have liked to knock Rankin into the quicksand. "Mr. Forthing," he said, tightly, "let us begin digging: I doubt the beasts will make any direct attempt while we have Caesar here, nor come near enough for Temeraire to reach them with his jaws."

The row of spectators was nevertheless unpleasant to endure: those gleaming pupil-less eyes, malevolent even in their immobility, while they worked and dug heaps of wet sand out from around Temeraire's body to pile up dark and wet into piles like the misshapen sand castles of small children, towers crumbling as they dried in the rising sun.

"Laurence," Temeraire said, as the sun grew higher, "I would not mind a drink of water, if it were at all convenient," which it could not be, given his size, but Forthing sent men down to fetch back all the largest jugs of water, under a pistol-wielding guard.

They returned empty-handed. "There isn't any," O'Dea said, "—any water, it has all run away in the night."

"We drank it nearly dry last night, but it ought to have refilled by now, surely," Forthing said.

Tharkay had slipped silently away at their announcement, drawing his own pistol; he returned shortly and said, "The spring is no longer flowing to the water-hole. It has been diverted; underground, so far as I can tell."

Laurence paused, looking up at the row of sentinel bunyips, and said, "Tenzing, do you mean they *have* done it? Deliberately?"

"Certainly they have done it deliberately," Temeraire interjected. "You cannot imagine they have done it to be friendly; oh! How I should serve them out, if they were not such cowards, and hiding all the way over there where I cannot get at them, thanks to all this sand."

Tharkay said, "I see no reason to doubt it. They would find it still more convenient to their hunting to make the water-holes, rather than merely take advantage of whatever natural ones the countryside should offer. If they can divert a natural spring to suit one purpose, why not this one?"

"Why did they not make the pit deeper then, and sink him entire?" Laurence said.

Tharkay shrugged. "It is no great difficulty to avoid drowning in quicksand," he said. "He is too buoyant to sink so far. The difficulty is in getting out."

And whatever difficulties should entail on extracting one man, trapped in such a quagmire, were as nothing to the problem of extracting Temeraire, Laurence dismayed realized—and Temeraire was already thirsty.

"This excavation is nonsense," Rankin said. "We cannot hope to get him out without Granby returns, and that is scarcely likely."

"If you have any better solution to propose, Captain Rankin, we may hear it at any occasion," Laurence snapped: he *had* been looking to the east, vain and unlikely though the hope was, of course, when they had been blown so far off their course and their line of cairns broken by the storm.

"We might rig some ropes as well," Forthing said, "and do what we can to pull him—"

Rankin snorted, and there was indeed very little to be hoped for, from such an effort: thirty men to drag him out when Temeraire himself could not even presently free one limb. "If you will try and drag him nearer one edge," Laurence said grimly, "perhaps, Temeraire, you may then draw yourself out."

The ropes were hurled over, and Laurence secured them about the base of Temeraire's neck, and through the rings of the harness which he was devoutly glad they had not removed, the previous night. But there was not very much purchase, still, for such an operation; with only a handful of passengers, and no expectation of combat, Temeraire had barely been rigged out with what harness was necessary to support his belly-rigging.

Thirty men hauling, the rope resting upon their shoulders, their hands wrapped around the length: Temeraire did move, a little, trying to help as best he might, with a sort of paddling; but they gained a few inches with the best they could do, and needed perhaps fifty feet. "Sir," Forthing said to Captain Rankin, "I believe we must rig Caesar up," politely but firmly: Rankin hesitated, but could scarcely refuse under the circumstances.

"I will help, also," Kulingile piped up, watching, and seized onto the rope near the edge with his jaws, to pull; Demane said, "Wait—" and to Mr. Fellowes said, "Can you put him into harness?"

"Precious good that will do," Caesar said, ungraciously submitting to having the ropes secured to his own harness, as Kulingile was hooked in to a makeshift affair of a few straps and buckles: he had grown at least to the size of a respectable cart-horse and, while he might not be anything to Temeraire, or to Caesar, was not wholly inconsequential.

Mr. Fellowes said, "We might send the ropes around a tree, or some of these rocks, to make a bit of a pulley, sir."

They took up the oilcloths and folded them together to make a pad about an outcropping of rocks, and stretched their two hawsers around it; Caesar and Kulingile were put at the end, and the men hauled on wheresoever they might. The bunyips made an excellent overseer, their small eyes gleaming: if Temeraire were taken so, Caesar could not carry all the men out of the desert; and if any were left behind, there was hardly any doubt of the death-sentence to be read in those eyes.

Muscles strained, and groaning they all pulled together; Temeraire bracing back his neck so the pulling would act upon his body instead. The quicksand glubbed around his breastbone and eddied away, curling in upon itself in thick slow-moving rolls like pudding batter being stirred, and he moved—a little, only a little, but he moved. "Heave, there!" Forthing shouted, and, "Heave!"—one enormous effort after another, each one winning a little more space.

Temeraire tried to paddle a bit, to move himself along; another united heave, and he slid a few more inches through the muck. A few men fell to their knees, panting; all but hanging from the rope. Caesar snapped, "There's enough of that, we are all pulling, aren't we? Get up, then."

They crawled back up. Forthing sent Sipho down the line with a swallow of rum for each man—the last dribbled end of their supply, with nowhere to look for more; but he did not mix it with water, and the taste of the hard liquor heartened them, more a memory of satisfaction than a reality with the sun still beating upon them, but with a great straining effort they drew again upon the ropes, and Caesar, for all his complaining, threw his powerful shoulders fully into the effort.

Kulingile, too, strained; he drew great heaving breaths, and his long claws scrabbled into the earth as he leaned into the harness, and then abruptly his slack and crumpled sides belled out very like sails catching the wind into smooth roundness. He gasped in his thin fragile voice, and clawed furiously at the ground again; Demane was by his head, encouraging and pulling also. "What is the matter?" he said, then catching sight of the swelled-out sides said, "Dorset! Dorset, what is wrong with him!"

"Not now!" Forthing snapped, "all together, heave—" The ropes slid upon the oilcloth and putting their heads down they one and all pulled: feet dug into the sand, driving up dark red hillocks of the damp sand below. One man started to sing, "There were two lofty wyrms from Old England came," and one after another took it up: awkward voices, dry and cracked with the heat and lack of water, and tuneless; but their feet crept on, little by little the ropes crept after them, and Temeraire was moving.

Then abruptly someone yelled, "Christ, the buggers are coming at us," and the ropes were falling. Caesar turned in the yoke and was instantly in a tangle as men dropped all the slack of the ropes and began to run, as a couple of the bunyips made a sudden darting-quick lunge down the slope, lean and serpentine, broad splayed feet webbed a little between narrow clawed fingers to give them purchase on the sand.

Roland was too short to get more than her fingertips on the rope; she had her pistol out already, and her first shot caught the advancing bunyip in the thigh. It flinched back, its mouth opening on a peculiar and incongruous sound, a low throaty howl more like the coughing of a hyena than the hiss of a reptile, and then it came swarming on again.

"Roland!" Temeraire called, very anxiously, and Laurence found his hand uselessly clenching upon his sword hilt. "If I should roar," Temeraire began, but he could not—the divine wind would as surely have killed Roland herself, or more likely brought the whole slope down upon them and buried them bunyips, men, and dragons all together into a single common grave. Temeraire strained his neck, but he was too far to reach.

She held her position coolly; she was already reloading, the cartridge tearing in her teeth, black powder into the barrel and then the wadding and the bullet rammed down hard, powder in the pan, and she took aim and fired again as it drew nearer.

The second shot took it in the throat, and the howl was choked; blood ran deep, near-black from the wound, very like dragon blood, dripping upon the sand and making small wet pockets in the red earth; the bunyip curled over itself coughing. Young Ensign Widener had his small single pistol drawn now: he fired also, though the recoil nearly staggered him, and the second bunyip flinched from the noise; then instead of continuing after the fleeing men, it darted for the ropes themselves.

It moved a little awkwardly, perhaps, over the sand: a quick but skittering motion, the hind legs small and the forelegs enormous and disproportionate, and two strange half-circle stubs rising between the shoulders, small webbed ridges. Seen in profile, it had an enormous lantern-jawed head, built to crush and grip, and the talons of the forelegs were short but hard gleaming-black horn; it seized upon the rope and took a length between its jaws and began to pull.

"Damn you all for cowards!" Roland yelled over her shoulder as she reloaded, "come back here and stop them; or they'll pick us all off," and she fired again; Forthing had dragged himself free of the ropes, and Demane, who had been at the end: he dived for Laurence's pistols, in amongst his things, and fired again at the bunyip.

The shots took chips off the rock, and one struck home; the second bunyip howled and let go the rope, retreating; it stopped only to nose the first, still bleeding, and they together skittered limping back up the slope to rejoin the rest of the watchful band, the others more patient, more prepared to wait.

Their effort had not been in vain, if it had cost them: the ropes hung slack and all ahoo, Caesar only making matters worse with his efforts to work loose, and the chewing had worn through a couple of strands of the cable. Forthing inspected the damage grimly, and then he said, "Back to the work, gentlemen," and detailed off Roland and Demane with pistols to stand guard.

The men straggled back from their panicked flight, but not all of them: two did not return, and Laurence looking up at the ridge noted that there were fewer bunyips watching than before; they had not failed to take advantage, then, of the confusion which they had created. "It is not at all fair," Temeraire said stormily, "that they will do such things where I cannot even try to fight back; low, and sneaking, and they ought to be ashamed. I am glad that we have drunk their water, and wrecked their territory; I will do it again, whenever I am loose."

They resumed their effort. Caesar was untangled; the damaged rope was mended, a little, as best it could be, and Fellowes wrapped some oilcloth about the gnawed section and sewed it down with waxed thread. The men spat upon their hands, and rubbed them with dirt, and took hold.

No one sang. Inch by inch, Temeraire shifted. "If you should exhale, just as they heave," Laurence said, "you might make a little more slack in the sand," and the trick helped, a little. All together breathed in, and took hold, and exhaling pulled; Temeraire breathing out opened a small gap of softness in the quicksand, into which they might drag him a little further.

"Oh," he said, abruptly, "pull! Pull harder, I think I can feel a little rock—" and with this encouragement they all threw their backs into another throw, and then all were stumbling onto their knees with the ropes gone suddenly slack, as Temeraire gave a low struggling hiss and managed to pull himself nearly a foot further along.

He was obliged to stop, panting, but he did not sink back; they drew the ropes slack again, and with another heave, now all their efforts united, his breastbone rose several more inches from the clinging mirk.

Laurence swung down onto Temeraire's shoulder and said, "Mr. Forthing, if you will fetch me a shovel, I think we may begin to do some good clearing some of this away," and they detailed away some five of the men to the work: shoveling away the quicksand from before Temeraire's body, to the sides, while the hauling teams yet strained to assist him in the effort of climbing free.

The evening was coming on a little; the watching bunyips one after another began to disappear, as Temeraire made his slow and creeping escape. When at last they freed his first foreleg, coming loose with a gargled sucking noise like a choked drain running clear, the last of them were gone, and when Roland and Demane warily went to look over the edge of the slope, they returned to report no sign of the bunyips anywhere upon the flat plain of the desert: likely they had gone somewhere beneath the earth, to brood upon the failure of their attempt, and perhaps to envision another.

With his forelegs free, Temeraire might more easily exert force, and they restrung the ropes around his mid-section, behind the foreleg joints, to better pull; he began to drag himself onward, little by little, and they dug around the ends of his wings to free them. Then around the hindquarters, as little by little he crawled the rest of the way out and crumpled exhausted upon the solid ledge of rock, free at last, and caked thickly with red sand dried onto him by the sun.

"Oh, how tired I am," he said, and closed his eyes; they were united in thirst and hunger, but exhaustion commanded still more of their spirit, and the men were dropping where they stood.

Laurence sat down and leaned against Temeraire's side, heedless of the red sand crumbling over his coat, and closed his eyes; then he opened them again, and looked up as Iskierka came spiraling down from the clouds and demanded, "Whatever have you been doing? You are all over sand; and where is the egg? You might have found it again by now."

Chapter 12

❧

ISKIERKA DID at least go hunting for them, when she had understood what had happened, and helped to dig a channel from the quicksand pit which drained the water into a rock basin, where they might drink; so she was not useless, but she was still inclined to be critical and particularly of their having lost the trail.

Temeraire informed her with some asperity that he would have liked to see her do better, with a firestorm and a typhoon to be managed, all at once—if it had not precisely been a typhoon, it seemed far too mild to call it only a thunderstorm, and not at all reflective of the experience—and added, "And there was the third egg to be managed, also, at the time."

"Which was nowhere near as good an egg," Iskierka said disapprovingly, "as anyone could tell, only looking at it, and now you see what has come of it. Finish eating and hurry up, then, as we are bringing you along," she added to Kulingile, "which I do not understand."

Kulingile could not really be accused of eating slowly: he was taking everything which had been left, in gulps the very limit of his capacity. His sides had collapsed into their odd folds again only a little while after they had first swelled out; but twice more during the effort they had inflated and then crumpled once more. Demane was anxious, but it did not seem to have hurt the dragonet, Temeraire thought; at least, Dorset had not said anything dire, though he had examined Kulingile closely afterwards.

"So he might yet fly, after all, even if he cannot just yet," Temeraire said. "I did not always have the divine wind. Anyway, Laurence wished it: it would be immoral to leave him behind, as I understand it."

"I don't see what morality has to do with carrying about someone who cannot fly," Iskierka said.

"We have been carried about by the *Allegiance*, ourselves, when we could not have flown all the way," Temeraire said, "and if we did leave him, he would have to starve, as he cannot hunt; or what if those bunyips tried to snatch him? He was small enough, when he hatched, that they might have managed it."

"I don't see why you always want to dwell on and on about what will happen with things that are properly none of your affair, and far away," Iskierka said, dismissively.

Even Granby, to Temeraire's dismay, did not seem to wholly approve; he looked wincingly at Kulingile, and Temeraire overheard him saying, to Forthing, "I don't need to be told how it was: I am sure Rankin was a brute about it, and set his back up instead of explaining properly; I only wish I had been here sooner."

To Laurence he made no reproach directly, but said with excessive heartiness, "Well, one never knows in these cases what may happen, after all; although, we cannot be too slow—Riley can give us a little more time, he must wait for something to do with the monsoon, but—although, it is just as well, for there was still no news from England about Bligh, so perhaps . . ." and then trailed off in a very awkward way, and began instead to speak of the bunyips.

It was very irritating, and Temeraire was still tired, and sore; there was sand everywhere sand could be, and nothing like enough water to be properly washed, or even to drink as much as he liked; so he was by no means in a happy mood as the men boarded him again. "I wish," he said to Laurence, "I do wish that other dragons were not always thinking me peculiar; not that anyone would value Iskierka's opinion, but it makes one doubtful."

"I hope you never doubt the value of charity," Laurence said, "regardless of any contrary opinion which you should meet: do you imagine Iskierka would have concerned herself particularly with the fate of the French dragons, as a consequence of the spreading of the disease?"

"No-o," Temeraire said, and looking slantwise asked, "Laurence, then you are quite sure that we have done as we ought?"

"Very sure," Laurence said. "And consider, my dear: a week ago his imminent death was certain, and now he is eating well and steadily gaining weight, and he was of material use in extracting you from the quicksand. I must think his prospects of further improvement are high."

That was not precisely what Temeraire had meant, but he was very cheered to know that Laurence felt the two acts were connected in such a way, and equally necessary; he had wondered sometimes if Laurence might have had some regrets—some feeling of disappointment, that Temeraire had asked so much of him. He did not at all mind bringing Kulingile along, or carrying him forever, if it should mean Laurence were not distressed.

And, he suddenly realized to his consolation, if he were doing so, then it was not really as though Demane was not his own anymore: if Kulingile was to be always riding with him, then it was more as though *he* was part of Temeraire's crew himself. "And," he told Kulingile, who listened intently, "if we should see some action, I think you might be of very real use, as no one might board while you were on my back: if only you can contrive not to grow very much more."

"Well, I will try," Kulingile said, but then he took the second half of the lizard in front of him and threw his head back and swallowed the whole thing at once, so that it traveled down his throat as a distended lump, as much as to say, *Look how much I have eaten.*

"That is not going to help," Temeraire said, exasperated.

There was not very much more water to be had, either, as they flew onward: the water-holes which they found were almost all drying up, in the heat of the day, in a suspicious manner. "I expect they are telling one another to dry them up for us," Temeraire said, rather disgruntled, as he lapped a little water up from a rocky basin; he could not take nearly as much as he wanted, as it should have to serve for all.

"Well, let us dig up some more of these coverings, and then I will breathe fire in at them," Iskierka proposed. "That will bring them out, and they will soon learn not to be causing trouble for us."

"I don't see why you must be so quarrelsome," Caesar said. "I suppose if you want to be dragging up their houses all over, you can't be too angry if they don't like it, and I don't much fancy waking in the middle of the night up to my neck in sand, either. We might leave them a kangaroo or two, and see if that sweetens them up to give us water."

"As if we were going to give them presents, after the way they have behaved," Temeraire said, revolted, and Iskierka snorted her disdain; but much to their shared dismay, Laurence and Granby thought the idea sound.

"Consider, my dear, the very real difficulty we should have in constantly facing the objections of so widespread and hostile a force," Laurence said, "if indeed they are communicating, as you imagine not without grounds."

"And we are not here to pick quarrels with bunyips or anyone else, for that matter," Granby said. "We are here to find that egg, and be shot of this wretched desert; if they like to live here, there is no reason we shouldn't leave it to them, if you ask me."

To make matters still worse, Rankin alone disagreed. "You will only encourage the creatures by bribing them," he said, "and induce them to think humans more worthwhile prey: they ought to be eradicated one and all."

If he did concede so far as to not at once fire all the bunyips' lairs—which was a pity, as it seemed to Temeraire an excellent strategy, particularly as the bunyips should also have to flee the smoke, and come out for a proper fight, instead of hiding away—Temeraire could not quite see his way clear to leaving the bunyips a kangaroo.

"It is no more thrown away than letting that one stuff it into his gullet," Caesar said, meaning Kulingile, but for his part, Temeraire felt he should rather feed Kulingile twenty kangaroos than see the bunyips profit from one, when he had hunted it down.

"If we had begun by tearing up their homes," he said, "I might see the justice in it, but after all, we did not; we did not even know they were there, until after they had stolen some of our men, and eaten them, which is barbarous anyway. If anyone were to be apologizing and giving presents, it ought to be them and not us; instead they are only quarreling more, by stealing the water, now, too."

"If they have brought the water there in the first place, it seems to me they aren't the ones doing the stealing," Caesar said, but that was plainly absurd; it was not as though the bunyips had made the water. The water was there, and they had only moved it to a place most convenient for themselves, to trick people into coming near their traps; another part of a low sneaking strategy which deserved not the least bit of credit.

"Anyway, they might have said something if they did not like us to drink. They set the water out on purpose, and make it look as though it is not theirs, so it does not seem to me they can complain if we treat it like any other water," Temeraire said.

But it was very tiring and inconvenient to have to stop, over and over, to drink what little they could get at any one water-hole. It was not even restful, for one could not feel refreshed with so little to drink, and his throat ached all the worse. Temeraire still felt a deep unpleasant ache in his forelegs and hindquarters after his ordeal, and it was more of an effort than it ought to have been to spring aloft every time.

He sighed a little; and they must again fly sweeps, to watch for any fragment of pottery or silk or anything else which might have been brought from China; of course he was glad to have found the trail again, but there was no denying it was pleasanter flying when they could only guess, and go on flying straight.

However, watching the ground as they drew near yet another half-dry water-hole, he did at length near the end of the day catch sight of a little movement: a shadow which did not quite fit the rest of the ground, and Temeraire realized all at once it was one of *them*, the bunyips. He dived at once, stretching, and the bunyip burst suddenly into motion, skittering away across the sand towards a bare patch of ground, and as Temeraire reached, it squirmed itself madly beneath the earth, casting up a cascade of sand at its heels as it burrowed.

It was astonishingly quick: Temeraire landed and stuck his claw inside the freshly dug tunnel, and could not reach it; he sat back on his haunches and hissed in displeasure. "Come out, you wretched craven thing," he called into the tunnel, and looked back. "Laurence, are you quite sure you would not like us to smoke them out? I am certain we could quite easily manage them, if they did not squirm and run away so."

"And so ensure an endless sequence of attacks," Laurence said, "further delaying our search for the egg; pray let us continue on, my dear."

"You may consider," Dorset said, peering over, "that it is in their nature to hunt from their burrows, and the consequence of our own venturing into a country we do not know; and after all, you are eating the game on which they depend for sustenance. We are as foolish to resent their predation as cattle would be to despise you."

This argument swayed Temeraire to some extent; at least he was persuaded to fly onward without further molesting the bunyips. Later in

the evening, Temeraire said thoughtfully, contemplating the stew which
Gong Su was brewing, with the meager haul of kangaroos, "I have
never before considered the feelings of a cow: I suppose they must not
care for us at all."

"They are only dumb beasts," Laurence said, "and such thought
surely beyond them; any animal will defend its life and young, but that
is not in the same vein as a thinking, reasoning creature."

"Only, how could one be certain?" Temeraire said. "After all, if
one wishes to be particularly dull, one might be like that fellow Sal-
combe, and say that dragons are also dumb beasts. And I am quite sure
the bunyips are not, though they do not seem to talk at all: they are
only *nasty* thinking creatures. It is not very fair, though, that I should
allow them to have sense because they will contrive one unpleasantness
after another; what if cows are very clever, only they do not like to
make a fuss about it?"

"If they dislike fuss enough to tolerate being eaten," Laurence said,
with rather an amused expression, "surely it need not matter one way
or another."

"Perhaps they think they will be eaten anyway, as they are so delicious," Temeraire said, and sighed. "I would give a great deal for a
cow, Laurence; not that I wish to complain, and I am very grateful that
Gong Su will go to such lengths: only they are a bit thin, the kangaroos,
I mean."

They posted a watch that night, and twice Temeraire and Iskierka
were obliged to shift their places, as the ground beneath them grew odd
and unsteady to a probing stick; Caesar was nearly buried when
abruptly a sinkhole opened beneath him, tumbling him down in a cascade of pouring sand. He roused all the camp to his cry of alarm, and
several pistol-shots were fired uselessly into the dark, spending some of
their precious store of munitions for panic.

"Keep your head raised," Rankin said, his hand on Caesar's neck;
he had leapt clear as the sand poured in, and then jumped in to keep the
young dragon steady. "Fetch a light, there, and bring shovels; we will
have to clear some of this off him before he can scramble out."

It was near enough two hours before he could be resettled, now
safe if uncomfortable upon an outcropping of rock; they none of them
passed a very quiet or a restful night, and in the morning, all of Gong
Su's stew had leaked away, the consequence of a smaller but equally

malicious shifting of the earth beneath the cooking-hollow. Temeraire was obliged to eat the gummy and nearly leached-clean kangaroo or go hungry, as he had not eaten the night before; they might be soft, but were scarcely palatable. They had all to contend with thirst as well as irritation.

Iskierka was all for waging a thorough war upon the enemy: all their shelters were to be fired, or filled with smoke, despite the dreadful hazard of open flame in this dry country, and the utter impracticality of fighting who knew how many of the creatures there were with a force of four dragons, one half-grown, one stunted, and no supply whatsoever. Temeraire at least was grown more willing to be sensible, perhaps under the preoccupying influence of hunger, which drove out some quantity of pride.

He said, "I do not like it in the least, but we do not have the time to serve them all out now, and they *can* make it so very uncomfortable: we had better wait until we have the egg back safely, and then we may settle them; or," he allowed, "I suppose we may give them a chance to show they can behave better," and that afternoon, when they had taken half-a-dozen kangaroos and stopped at another half-dry water-hole, they laid one before the first trap-door which they found, and did not molest the covering after all.

Iskierka eyed it darkly and brooding; Kulingile eyed it, too, with a very different, a yearning expression, but he turned to his own portion instead, and Iskierka grumbled under her breath and did the same. Temeraire was hungry enough to ignore the pain of his throat and eat the kangaroo unstewed, only roasted a little, and crunching the bones for the marrow, though Laurence was sorry to see him forced to it, and Termeraire winced as he swallowed.

"It's gone, then," someone said abruptly, and Laurence realized that while they had all been engaged in their own meals, the kangaroo offering had silently vanished—rather a dreadful reminder of the speed and stealth of their enemies, and their omnipresence. But they were at least not harassed the remainder of their halt, although they did not tempt fate: no man ventured anywhere near vegetation, and they drank their share of water under guard.

The experiment was repeated that evening, when they paused again at a fresh spring with a larger outcropping of harder, stony ground near-by where Laurence thought they might encamp safely;

whether for this reason, or the accepted bribe, they did not suffer further attacks that night, and Temeraire declined to risk his supper again, and ate his portion of game once more only seared.

They might also by now have been outstripping the speed of the bunyips' communications, whatever method they used. Tharkay was not particularly sanguine of their chances of finding still more traces of the smugglers' route, and did not encourage the fervent searching for scraps which Temeraire and Iskierka would have indulged in, left to their own devices.

"If they are not going to some central location lying in this direction we have been given, as limited as it may be," Tharkay said, "then we have no hope of catching them: a few shards of five years of age and half-buried samples do not make a trail worth following. We may as well hope for a more cooperative fate, and make the only attempt which has a hope of success."

So the dragons flew on with much less investigation of the countryside, and quicker: the red miles were eaten up swiftly with Temeraire's wingbeats, the unvarying dunes rising and falling, vanishing away beneath the leading edge of the black wings, only to be exposed once more, falling behind them like waves receding. The desert might have gone on forever: everywhere one looked, the world was flat and barren and strange to the curving blue-hazed edge of the horizon. Occasional taller hills would swell out of the low dunes; salt pans stretched pallid white; a trickling stream or a hollow full of water. These fell away and rode the earth over the horizon and disappeared, one after another.

The shapes were at first easily mistaken for clouds, low on the horizon; but they remained, and grew, and grew, until the brick-red stone was struck by the sunset and glowed fiercely against the sky. They reared up from the flat plateau, enormous and uncanny domes clustering together in the absence of all other company, their surfaces pitted and streaked in grey, a faint clinging fuzz of greenish moss upon a few of their heads. Temeraire slowed, as they approached; Laurence did not know what to think of the peculiar construct, so alone.

It was not possible even from the air to encompass the whole: at different angles it had a wholly different appearance, even as that first intensely glowing color faded, and a twilight cast of violet dampened the domes' presence, blurring them into the sky. Though the stone would have offered a certain refuge from the bunyips, they did not land upon the rocks. They had from habit and the fatigue of extreme toil begun, Laurence thought, to grow used to the alien and rust-red landscape; but in their strangeness, the monoliths made all else around them once more strange, a reminder.

They encamped instead upon a few dunes, not far removed; a little trickle of water came past the camp, not very much to drink from, and with no sign of bunyip management, which they now had a little cause to regret. They dug out a hollow in the curve of the creek, and it gradually filled; meanwhile Laurence stood with Temeraire watching the strange monumental stones blur and fade away into darkness, as all the stars of the Southern Hemisphere came wheeling out above.

They were all quiet that night, in the unseen shadow of the monoliths. In the morning Temeraire said, "Laurence—Laurence, there is another one, over there; look," and Laurence rising saw one last monolith standing at a distance: alone, wholly alone, even without a separated hillock for company: pink and palest orange cream in the early sunrise, and then Temeraire said slowly, "—is that a dragon?"

Iskierka roused up looking, and Caesar said, "Well, what else would it be?"—to be glimpsed at this distance, standing beside the monolith and casting a shadow against the smooth red wall, of wings outspread. Huge wings, even half-furled: and there were tiny dark figures of men to be glimpsed, moving around the dragon; there were bundles upon the ground, bales tied up with string, boxes, which they were taking off the beast: and still others, smaller bags, were going up to be stowed in replacement upon the dragon's back.

Iskierka said, "Whyever are we only sitting here? Let's go and have a look, and see if it has seen—"

"Oh!" Temeraire cried, "the egg, the egg!" and indeed, a round swaddled bundle was being handed carefully up to the men aboard the dragon, easing into a sling across its breast.

Laurence had barely a moment to seize upon the chain of Temeraire's breastplate, and get himself latched on, as Temeraire lunged aloft in a burst of speed, Iskierka with him. They had not been seen, Laurence thought, by the company on the ground near the other monument: there was no visible hurry, no move to self-defense. Instead the strange dragon rose and leisurely unfurled its wings the rest of the way—going on and on and on, twice the length of its body and more—and with a tremendous spring of its hindquarters was aloft; one wing-stroke, two, three, and then it spread those wings and was swinging away to the north, gliding on the air.

"Come back!" Temeraire called, flying quicker. "Stop!" and he paused, hovering mid-air, and began to draw in his breath, his chest expanding with the divine wind, that shattering roar which should reach even across that distance.

"Temeraire," Laurence said sharply, "Temeraire! You ought not, your throat is not—"

"Hurry, hurry," Iskierka said, circling impatiently; she could not get into its path. "She is getting further away, and with the egg!"

Temeraire flung back his shoulders and pulled in one more heaved breath, and then he opened his jaws, and roared—and broke, the thunder barely begun and the resonance dying in his chest, so Laurence felt the tremors come rippling through the flesh. Temeraire's voice cracked like strings upon some instrument breaking, and he clenched upon himself coughing—coughing—wracked and gasping, and he sank abruptly to the sand, his head bowed forward over his breast.

III

Chapter 13

✦

HEY GAVE CHASE ANYWAY: Kulingile and Caesar left to
trail behind, the men packed into the belly-netting with haste; Temeraire and Iskierka stretched themselves lean and straight and flew and
flew, at the limits of their speed. They made progress; little by little the
dragon grew larger in Laurence's glass as he watched, the immense
wings protruding past the edges of the lens. Onward through the panting heat of the sun, always keeping the dragon in their sight; then the
dusk a welcome relief, but there still might be no respite: their quarry
did not stop to rest, so neither could they.

The night came on, and the moon spilling silver: Laurence had to
struggle to keep his eyes on the dragon now, a moving inkblot crossing
the stars, and still it did not pause. The wings scarcely moved; one beat
or two now and again to catch a draft of wind, and otherwise nothing,
like one of the great sea-birds, an osprey or an albatross, hanging
peacefully aloft and more at rest in the sky than on the ground.

It was drawing away. Temeraire's breath labored more gratingly
than before, and Iskierka's speed was dying. They had flown already a
long day, and without halt for anything but a little game snatched on
the wing, a few gulped swallows of water at a creek. "There's another,"
Granby said at last, his voice faint but clear across the gulf of the empty
air, and Temeraire and Iskierka landed by the gleam of water to drink,
their legs trembling and wings drooped nearly to the ground.

Granby leapt down. "Mr. Forthing," Laurence said quietly, "let us
disembark, and see about a camp; by those rocks, if you please, clear
away from the water."

"Yes, sir," was all Forthing said; failure lay heavy upon them all.

Temeraire and Iskierka did not speak a word; they drank heavily and thirstily, and fell upon the sand asleep as soon as they had been unburdened. Forthing marshaled the aviators and they formed a phalanx of pistols and knives bristling while in that shelter the convicts hastily filled canteens and jugs, and they all drew back to the security of the rocks to eat their dry biscuit and a little hot tea.

"Do you know, the worst of it is, I don't think they were even trying; I don't know that they ever saw us," Granby said tiredly, stretching his legs one after the other out and then in again, working out the stiffness of nearly twenty hours aloft. Laurence did not yet trust himself to sit at all; he thought once he had gone down he would not come up again very easily.

"No," Laurence said. "The crew all kept below and out of the sun, and so far as I saw them they were sleeping. The dragon did not look around once." He shook his head. "She might have been sleeping on the wing, herself; I have known Temeraire to do it, on a long flight."

"Half-sleeping, anyway," Granby agreed. "Did you see those wings? I suppose she could go around the world on them twice if she wanted to. I have never seen the like. That is no feral beast; that's breeding, if you please, and I should like to know what they have bred her out of, when we haven't seen a single other dragon anywhere in this country."

"Their own lack of concern argues there may be none to be seen," Tharkay said quietly. "They did not see us because they did not look; they did not imagine any pursuit."

"You think they have her from somewhere else?" Granby said. "I suppose there might be something like her in Java, with all those islands to fly amongst; but how we have missed ever seeing one of them, I would like to know. I suppose I wouldn't value an egg of hers much over half-a-million pounds."

"I should value more," Laurence said, looking over at Temeraire, so exhausted his head had lolled to one side, and he had not stayed awake even to have his muzzle cleaned of the red dust of their travel, "some way to catch her up."

The quarry already lost, they waited the next day until Caesar caught them up, himself exhausted and deeply disgruntled: "Well," he said, "and you haven't got the egg back, with all this mad peltering, and meanwhile I have had to slog on all day with this lump hanging on to me; and he has eaten everything."

Kulingile ignored him in favor of swallowing yet another kangaroo nearly whole. Caesar's complaint was not without some justice: Kulingile had grown visibly in the short span of their absence, and would have made an increasingly heavy burden. Caesar had made by now some eight tons in weight, but Kulingile bid fair to make near enough a ton in weight himself by the end of the day.

"I will not have Caesar carry him again," Rankin said. "We are not going to stunt his development to carry a spoiled beast along."

"I have said I am sorry," Kulingile said, piping, "but I cannot help it I am so very hungry. I think I might fly to-day, though, and then I need not slow anyone down."

"I don't see why you should fly to-day, when you did not fly yesterday, or the day before," Iskierka said dismissively, "so it is no use saying anything like that; but *I* will carry you, since I am not a complainer."

Kulingile looked at Iskierka's bristling sides a little sadly, and it did prove something of an awkward puzzle to fit him aboard, as his own armament of spikes was by no means insubstantial, and were beginning to harden into solid horn, so that as he squirmed into position they clacked noisily against Iskierka's own. "That will have to do," Iskierka said, "now strap him down; and you had better not squirm."

Dorset climbed out of Temeraire's throat after a final inspection. "I can hardly overstate the damage. There are burst blood vessels throughout, and what blisters were half-healed are now raw. It was wholly inadvisable."

Laurence nodded but only briefly; there was no sense in dwelling on what was done. "What would you recommend?"

"Rest," Dorset said, "rest, and a soft diet of fat salt pork; but under the present conditions I must settle for absolutely no exertion of the throat. I will not answer for the consequences should he attempt to roar again until he is quite healed; and if it can be helped, he ought not speak at all."

Temeraire did not much like not being able to speak: it was very irritating to always be thinking of something, and then unable to tell anyone. And if he should turn his head round to say something, as he flew, Dorset would pick up his head and glare from behind his red-dust-coated round spectacles, quite like a gimlet—Temeraire did not know what a gimlet was but had the impression it was a disapproving, narrow-faced creature that was sour and unpleasant—and anything Temeraire might have been about to say died away.

His throat did not hurt so very much more when he spoke as to make him feel the necessity of the restriction, although he very much did wish the condition to improve—apart from the endless soup and gruel which was now his portion, he had been very distressed to find himself unable to roar. It was not so bad as being unable to fly, of course, so he could not really complain around Kulingile, who could do neither, but Temeraire did feel instinctively that roaring was of particular significance to one's existence as a dragon, even apart from the divine wind, which of course marked him as a Celestial.

He wondered a little dismally if it were perhaps some sort of retribution, although he did not have a very good idea whence this might have originated; the men spoke of a vengeful deity quite often but Laurence had thoroughly refuted the notion of God dealing out either reward or punishment in life, even if Temeraire did not see the point of passing judgment on people when they were dead and could no longer either enjoy or dislike the consequences.

Only, it did seem to Temeraire that it was somehow fair in a dreadful and unpleasant way that having lost Laurence his title and his fortune, he should now lose the divine wind, himself. It made him anxious, and he formed the habit, in the evenings, of asking Roland quietly to bring out his talon-sheaths, so he might inspect their condition, and watch her polish them over; and he would glance several times down at his breastplate during the day, as they flew.

There was one small saving grace to lighten the unpleasant restriction: there was nothing very much to talk about. The wide-winged dragon had flown quite away; they did not even find a camp, although occasionally there would be a few bones or a scrap of bloody fur left on the ground, or gouged lines in the sand where a dragon had stooped from above with claws outstretched, and once at one of the water-holes there were a few claw-marks where she had stopped to drink, and footprints showed where the men had come down, too. Tharkay looked at them and said, "Four days old; or five," and that was when they had flown only a week: she had already got so far ahead of them.

She was flying in a straight line nearly directly north, only a few degrees off to the west; Laurence had plotted the course on his maps and it appeared—they were not wholly certain of their present location in the great empty space of the map, which made it a little difficult to conclude—but it seemed as though the course might end in a convenient bay upon the farther coast of the continent, which had been lately surveyed. "It has been marked out, I believe," Laurence said, "for further investigation; the proximity to Java should make it of great value for shipping among the archipelagoes, and thence to China and to India."

So they knew their destination, very likely, and there was nothing to be done but to fly towards it, far-away and tedious as it was. Laurence did suggest a little tentatively that the egg might well have hatched, by now, or would do so any day; and that it was in the keeping of another dragon.

"But we cannot turn away now," Temeraire said. "After all this time we have seen the egg with our own eyes; we cannot let some strange dragon steal it unchallenged, as though it did not matter."

"That is enough talking," Dorset said sharply, so Temeraire could not go on to explain further: she was a strange dragon, after all; they did not know her, or whether she had managed eggs successfully.

And Temeraire did not quite understand this business of only staying in the air, endlessly; it did not seem very interesting or practical, although when he looked at the maps, he did think—privately, without spending his voice upon it—that if one could stay aloft so long, then it was not after all such a long way to the next land over. It looked to him only two hundred miles perhaps to Java, or to Indonesia. Even without particularly wide wings, one might make such a flight, if one really wished to, and after that everything else seemed to be closer; one might fly from Java to Siam without going out of sight of land, and then one was really very close to China, if one had wanted to pay a visit.

That afternoon—they flew now only during the evenings and the cool, dark nights, navigating mostly by the stars; occasionally Laurence would touch his shoulder and murmur some small correction, working with his compass by the light of a hooded lantern. They slept instead during the sunlit heat of the day, and that afternoon as they looked over the maps, Laurence said to him quietly, "I am sorry; I beg you to put the thought of such a flight out of your mind."

"But, Cape York," Temeraire protested in brief, referring to the northernmost spar of the continent: on the map, there was scarcely a gap between it and the southern coast of the large island marked NEW GUINEA; the distance could not have been more than a hundred miles.

"By what few reports we have, Cape York is surrounded by nearly impenetrable jungle," Laurence said, "and even having reached it, New Guinea would not offer much improvement in our position: it is nearly two hundred miles across open ocean to any sizable island, and that much again to reach Java, a journey which must be attended by the greatest danger. Any small error could so easily be magnified into disaster—the day clouding over, missing the passage of time, a stronger headwind—and all estimates, all planning, might be for nothing, and leave you without a glimpse of land. Only imagine the desperate quality of losing any sense of place, and knowing that in that very moment, you may be flying further from your only hope of landfall, and yet unable to turn away from the plotted course."

Temeraire sighed a little; he had not said anything at all, but Laurence had known anyway. Laurence put his hand on Temeraire's muzzle, and stroked him gently; Temeraire puffed out a little breath against him, and he did try and put it out of his mind, although he still did not think it could be quite so dangerous as Laurence suggested, if one waited for a clear day. He had flown two hundred miles in a day before; though over land.

They did not cover so much ground here, however: it was too hot to fly so far, and they were all carrying quite a lot of weight. Iskierka did complain about Kulingile, despite her fine, boastful remarks of before; and not without some justice. He was still eating tremendously and growing on and on, whatever one might say to him, or however one would prod him warningly away from the food which one was still eating oneself, even if a bit slowly because one's throat ached.

Temeraire was weighted down with all the men and their things, although at least they had put a few of the aviators off onto Caesar: Rankin had taken some of them for his crew, now that Caesar was getting big enough to manage it, and he had even after some consideration—and discussion with Caesar—taken a few of the more steady convicts for ground crew.

Temeraire had expected more complaining, but quite to the contrary, Caesar instead made himself unbearably smug about it, when Mr. Fellowes had rigged him out with more harness straps, and he made a point of learning the names of all his crew and saying such things as, "Mr. Derrow, my third lieutenant, has done good work today: very handy managing the distribution of weight across the hindquarters," whenever they landed, or, "It is a fine thing to have a proper ground crew, instead of only one or two unofficial attendants, I will say that much: a great advantage, if one would like perhaps to be scrubbed a little, or to have a harness-buckle adjusted just a touch."

Caesar did complain about Kulingile, endlessly: every bite of food which Kulingile took might have been snatched from his own mouth, and he would have it that they were robbing him, even though he had a perfectly fair share himself, and really, Temeraire felt, more than quite justified by his size and prospects. Caesar had begun to slow down growing, it seemed, Dorset thought: he was now three months out of the shell, which startled Temeraire to think; had they really been traveling so long?

"Longer than that," Laurence said, tiredly, dragging a sleeve over his forehead, "and a fortnight more to reach the coast, at this pace."

"Laurence," Granby said quietly, "we had better think about how we mean to get back, too. I don't like to ill-wish, but—Kulingile is nearer to being a real difficulty every day. I know he is the size of a rabbit, as dragons go, but without the air-sacs doing their share, he is getting to be as heavy as though he were carved out of gold. I think Iskierka could take Caesar on her back more easily than him. If it keeps up in this way, I don't see how we can manage him on the way back."

Demane overheard enough of this to look rather desperate, and Temeraire saw him saying to Kulingile, "You cannot eat so much: you cannot. Promise me you will only eat half-a-kangaroo today."

Kulingile said sadly, "I will try not to; only it is very difficult to stop after half of anything, as the other half is right there," which Temeraire had to agree as an argument possessed a great deal of justice.

At least Kulingile would eat almost anything, without pausing; if they took some more of the cassowaries, he would have them with the feathers on, so they did not need to spend the effort to butcher them. Temeraire tried a small wing just to have a taste—of something, anything, other than soup—and found it very awkward getting a proper bite: the feathers would cushion his teeth, and they tasted wrong in his mouth, as though he were trying to eat something like rope or sailcloth.

He gave up and set it down for Gong Su to put into his vat of soup after all, and shook his head. Kulingile shrugged and said, "I only swallow it anyway," and tipped his head back and sent down all the rest of the bird, squirming a little to work it down into his belly.

"I suppose it does make it easier to take it all for yourself," Caesar said, "before anyone else can get in a taste; but what use you are going to make of it, I would like to know."

Temeraire snorted, wordlessly disapproving, as Caesar had eaten two himself, and did not need any more; but it was true he did not see how Kulingile could enjoy his food at all, taking it so quickly.

Temeraire found that his thoughts drifted easily as he flew, with the stars unchangeable slowly turning above their heads, and through the afternoons; when he could not speak there was not even conversation to break the stillness. The days crept onward and blurred, one very much like another; and with a quality of strangeness. The country rolled away beneath them, and dust whispered against Temeraire's wings when he tucked his head beneath them to rest in the hot wind.

He found he did not really mind the soft haze of one day to the next: it was a relief of sorts from the weight of anxiety, and he certainly preferred to fly at night and to lie down afterwards in the middle of the day, when the heat of the sun might be a pleasure, as one did not have to work. Each morning a little before noon, when they found water, they landed and encamped. Temeraire would make sure that Laurence and all his crew were safely established upon the rocks, and that there was someone patrolling the sand, just in case the treacherous bunyips decided to make some other attempt, and then he would stretch himself comfortably and sleep for several hours in the steady, baking heat.

To-day he yawned after some time, raising his head, and squinted at the shadows: it was a little while past noon, and still very hot; he was glad not to be flying. He pushed up and went over to the hole for a little drink of water, and returning frowned at Kulingile, who looked very strange: his sides had swelled out again, and he was sleeping in an improbable posture, crouching low to the ground with his head and limbs dangling. Temeraire put his head down and nudged him, and Kulingile did not tip over or lie down properly, but bobbed away over the ground.

He raised his head and blinked reproachfully. "I am sleeping," he said.

"What are you doing?" Temeraire said, unable to resist asking. "Are you trying to fly?"

Dorset was roused from his own nap, and irritable and vague with drowsiness said, "It was not wholly unexpected, given the growth rate. Tether him," and would have gone back to sleep without further explanations.

"What do you mean, not unexpected?" Rankin said. "I believe we have had enough of this evasion, Mr. Dorset: what is his prognosis? I do not recall that I have heard of any dragon floating away without its own accord. If he is to become still more of a burden, I will hear of it now."

"The phenomenon is seen occasionally," Dorset said in his most biting tones—he did not like the heat, and most days came out unevenly red and speckled in the afternoons, if he did not stay always in the shade—"in Regal Copper hatchlings: it is an indicator he will make twenty-four tons, at the least, when he achieves his growth."

The response silenced Rankin entirely. Temeraire did not mind that, but everyone else was gone quiet, too, and he could not help but eye Kulingile dubiously: the dragonet was certainly growing very quickly, but that was not saying very much, when he had begun scarcely the size of one of Temeraire's talons, and now was perhaps a quarter the length of his tail.

"Dorset," Granby said after a moment, equally doubtful, "I don't suppose you are quite sure of it?"

"That he will make a heavy-weight, yes, now that the sacs have inflated permanently," Dorset said. "As for the particular weight, I will not swear to it; but the extreme disproportion of the air-sacs to the rest of the frame exceeds any other recorded to my knowledge, and any hatchling which has exhibited a negative total weight at any point in their development has achieved that size or more."

No one said anything much afterwards; except Roland gave a sort of squeaking noise and pounded Demane on the shoulder—he looked wary and dazed at once, and said, "He is not going to die, then?"

Temeraire was a little torn over the whole matter: so he would be losing Demane, after all, but on the other hand, there was the very great, very real satisfaction of being proven right, or rather seeing Laurence proven right; but Temeraire might have the credit of trusting Laurence, as anyone else ought to have, and also of having been charitable, with so pleasant a result for once. To further add to the glory of the coup, Rankin was not at all pleased, and now Caesar might not make any more noise about it, either, as Kulingile would outgrow him.

"I will believe it when I see it," Caesar said, loftily, and then would have tried to sneak another of the cassowaries which Gong Su was cooking for Temeraire to eat, later, if Temeraire had not warned him off with a snap near his hindquarters.

Kulingile took the news more equably. "I did not mean to die, anyway," he piped—the inflation did not seem to have altered his voice— "but I am glad, if it means I may eat more, and no one will poke at me for it." He put out his wings and flapped a little, which sent him going up alarmingly quick; Temeraire had to reach out and catch him by the tail-tip, and even then he stayed in mid-air, floating. "Look, Demane, look at me," Kulingile said, and flapping only one wing managed to spin himself about in a circle.

"It is certainly better than being a great solid lump upon the ground," Iskierka said, "and I do not mind if I do not have to carry you anymore, but that is a ridiculous thing for a dragon to do; you ought to come down or fly properly," but Kulingile's spirits were not depressed by this criticism, and Demane did indeed have to tether him with a rope, which Temeraire allowed to be secured to his harness, as the only rocks about were flat and inconvenient for the purpose.

The only other person displeased by the situation was Sipho, but as he had retreated into the solace of his studies, Temeraire selfishly did not mind that: it was a great satisfaction to him at last to have someone who might read the Analects to him aloud, correctly; if Sipho happened to find a character which he did not yet know, he would scratch it out large and Temeraire could give it to him, which served very well. It went a good deal quicker, and also Temeraire did not need to feel quite so guilty as if he had forced Roland or Laurence to write out a stretch of it for him large enough to see.

"You are getting hunchbacked," Demane said, disapprovingly, and poked Sipho between his shoulders; Sipho flailed an arm resentfully at his brother and spat, "At least I am not only spending all my time stuffing a fat dragon's belly, who can't bother to hunt for himself, even if he can fly, now."

It was not quite fair to call what Kulingile did at present flying: he had grown so used to dragging about on the ground that Dorset said he had failed to properly develop his instincts, so that now he had it all to learn from the beginning. Quite to the contrary of any natural assumption, it seemed that being so light did not help him at all. He might get off the ground very easily, but he would then float off in quite the op-

posite direction to the one he desired, and if he flapped too vigorously
he would go caroming off anything around, and wrecked several trees
in the process. Certainly he was not yet ready to hunt, although no-one
could possibly have doubted his enthusiasm for that eventual day; he
could not dive effectively at all.

Demane fetched his brother a clout across the ear. "You ought to
be helping me, instead of sitting here wearing out your eyes," he said
severely. "You are being very stupid: now we have a dragon, of our
own, don't you understand? When he is grown a little bigger, he will be
able to hunt, too, and fight; and then they cannot do anything to us we
don't like."

"Who?" Sipho said; Temeraire wondered if perhaps Demane
meant the bunyips.

"Anyone!" Demane said impatiently.

"Why would anyone do anything to us we don't like, unless we are
going to war, and fighting them," Sipho said, "and if that is what you
mean, then having a great huge big dragon will only mean you have to
fight more, and the enemy will try and hurt you anyway, so that doesn't
seem very safe to me at all."

Demane said, "I don't mean the enemy. The law has made the captain a prisoner, and taken all his property; what if they would try to
take us, too? That is what I mean."

"Then we would run away," Sipho said, "except now we have a
dragon following us around it would not be hard to catch us. And anyway," he added, spiteful and contradictory, "I expect they will not let
you keep him, now he is going to live and be very big; they will want
to give him to somebody else. And I don't care if they do."

Demane clouted him again, and stalked away, but later that afternoon he said to Roland quietly, "You don't suppose they would; take
him away from me?"

"In half-a-second," Roland said absently, without looking up from
the pistol which she had taken apart to clean, "if they had any chance
of it; I think I heard that scrub Widdlow going on to Flowers about trying something of the sort." Demane did not say anything, and she
looked up. "Don't be an ass," she added, "it don't work that way; ask
Temeraire if he would have swapped Laurence, himself."

"Certainly not," Temeraire said, "although," he could not resist
adding very quietly, so Dorset should not hear him, "I suppose

Kulingile might be more fickle, but if he were, you might find anyway you prefer to remain among my crew; and you would certainly be welcome."

"That is quite enough murmuring; and inappropriate besides," Dorset said, without looking up, although Temeraire's throat felt much better by now, except when it was particularly dry, or they had not found very much water in a day or so. "I would hope that a grown dragon might have a little more restraint than to so resent a hatchling, I might add; I must consider it particularly shameful."

"What have you been saying to my captain?" Kulingile said suspiciously, picking up his head from his nap, which movement brought him back up off the ground, and trying to swim himself over to Demane managed to accidentally knock him and Roland both over into the sand.

"Nothing," Temeraire said, because he could not talk any more: Dorset had said so; and anyway he had only been trying to console Demane in case Kulingile should have proven false. If Kulingile remained steadfast, certainly no one would ever interfere, although Temeraire did think it was not quite so bad as Dorset painted it, when one considered that Demane had been his, first.

Laurence found that the resentment towards Demane, which had already been pronounced, easily transmuted itself in form: where the aviators had formerly criticized his daring to preserve a useless beast and thereby slow and threaten the recovery of the final egg, they now without any difficulty objected to his possession of that same beast as undeserved and unsuitable. There was a particularly strong understanding amongst aviators which held in contempt any sort of intrusion into the relationship between captain and beast, but as Laurence himself had known, this understanding might become flexible when the captain was not considered properly an aviator himself.

He remembered with distaste the coarse effort which had been made to separate him from Temeraire early in their relationship and prefer a proven lieutenant into his place, wholly disregarding all that the aviators had known of Temeraire's likely feelings on the subject, and even resorting to outright falsehood. Laurence himself had been too uninformed to object, at the time; he was now not so, but had no standing to speak even when he heard men muttering enviously and, past convincing themselves that it might be permissible to interfere, well on the way to embracing the idea as a duty.

Demane's temper was not one which would lightly brook such an insult, either, and he had also the means by which to resent it: though Laurence thought he was not yet fifteen, and a little short perhaps from the inadequacy of his childhood diet, he was filling out rapidly; and he had taken to sword and pistol and rifle with bloodthirsty appetite.

"I will not tell you to swallow it," Laurence said, "but I do tell you that any gesture, any act, which should demonstrate an uncontrolled temper, or a disdain for the rules of the Corps, can only create a worse prejudice against you, and make all the more unlikely that an official recognition will come; it will not come quickly, that much is certain."

"They none of them wanted him before," Demane said, glittering-eyed and angry. "They would have knocked his brains out, and left him to rot, or taken his food—"

"That is quite enough, Demane; they did their duty as they saw it," Laurence said; while perfectly accurate, Demane's resentment needed none of the encouragement of approval. "They misjudged, and you did not; that satisfaction ought to hold you against the natural murmurs of regret which any man might feel on seeing a boy advanced so greatly ahead of his years, and with so few opportunities as remain to them."

"They would not mind so if it were Widener," Demane muttered, meaning Rankin's hapless young signal-ensign, but subsided when Laurence regarded him sternly.

"Widener is a lump, so of course they would," Roland added to Demane scornfully, after he had slumped back sitting next to her in the shade. "Stop being so ungodly prickly. Of course they are all jealous now; they will get over it when you have been in a proper action."

"It is easy for you to say," he flared. "No one would ever say you are not an aviator, and talk of sending you back to Africa."

"And I suppose you have had to knock a lieutenant over for putting his hand in your shirt, then," Roland said, which brought Laurence's head up sharply, appalled. "No, I don't mean to say who," she added to Demane's immediate demand, before Laurence had even made an attempt, "he was drunk, and sorry after: really sorry, I mean, not just being a weasel. A weasel would have been afraid to try, I expect, now Mother is a lord admiral. Anyway," she went on, too candidly, "I don't know if I should have minded, if he had not been so drunk."

Much to Laurence's dismay, however, Demane showed as alarming and visible a predisposition to resent *this,* as the other; the whole business of which gave Laurence fresh cause for concern: he had been neglectful of his duty by Roland. She might not officially be under his command any longer, but certainly she was still his responsibility, and he had left her without sufficient evidence of protection. He had allowed her to run wild with the other ensigns and runners, though they were plainly reaching an age to make that inadvisable; it suggested a lack of care which could only encourage improper advances.

As there was not a single other female in their company, however, he would be hard-pressed to manage a chaperone at present; and he rather dismally felt Roland would not take with much kindness to supervision, in any case.

"What for?" Granby said, with that perfect disregard for reputation which Laurence could no longer be surprised by, and yet sigh for. "If she does decide to fancy Demane, or anybody else, it would be just as well if she got it out of the way early. Lord knows we would like to keep Excidium in harness at least two more generations, if he will have it; by now he knows our formations better than any ten officers put together. And you can see with Harcourt, there is no telling what may happen; it might take half-a-dozen tries to get a girl.

"No, but I will tell you," Granby went on, "I am a little worried about this business with Demane: I'll put a word in where I can, when I have got back to England, and I don't expect Admiral Roland will have any truck with this business of saying he isn't in the Corps. But that still leaves you with a good year and a half to manage, and I think Rankin means to encourage it, the rotter."

"So far as that goes, if need be we will remove to the valley, or find another," Laurence said, "and have done."

With Rankin's encouragement or no, Blincoln—evidently feeling that, as he had originally been offered the egg, he had some right now to try again—did make an attempt; he was a former rifleman, and while they were encamped took one of the guns and went out, in a surreptitious manner, to return with a fresh-killed cassowary, which he brought back and offered to Kulingile while nearly all the rest of the camp were sleeping. Laurence roused only in time to see Kulingile fall upon the carcass at once with evident pleasure, while Demane rolled up to his feet, his hands clenched by his sides, rigidly angry.

Blincoln did not look over, but in a low voice suggested, as he put out a hand to stroke Kulingile's side, that perhaps the dragonet would like another captain, with a proper rank and standing in the Corps, who might provide for him not only raw meat but the chance at real service.

"No," Kulingile said, eating unconcernedly, "I have Demane."

Blincoln paused and said, "Surely this is a very nice cassowary; I am glad you are enjoying it," beginning on another tack; but Kulingile said, "Yes, although the one which Temeraire gave me yesterday was a bit more fat; and the one Lieutenant Drewmore shot the day before had a better flavor," and indeed he had been used to be fed by so many, lacking the ability to hunt for himself, that it was not surprising he did not attach much significance to the gift.

The first attempt having failed, Blincoln would have withdrawn, but Demane confronted him: a head shorter than the lieutenant and some fifty pounds at least lighter, a slim dark figure trembling with rage, and he said, "You are a coward, and if you try and steal Kulingile again—"

He stumbled to a halt, not so much reluctant to threaten as unsure precisely to what degree, and Blincoln said, "I hope," with an air of stuffy superciliousness, "Mr. Demane, that you have better sense than to indulge in histrionics and unreasonable expectations: no heavyweight can be managed by a young boy. Your passion is understandable, however, and I am sure if you should demonstrate perhaps some more sense—some cooperation—that you will find it a good foundation for future expectations, and a more steady and rational advancement in the Corps—"

Demane spat, comprehensively. "That for steady advancement, as though I would trust any of you cheats," he said, "and if you think I will ever help you take Kulingile from me, you are a great fool; as if he would have a lying sneak like you anyway, after you wanted to let his brains be knocked out with a sledge. As for being a boy, at least I am not a useless old scrub sent away because he did not deserve his old post—"

Blincoln slapped him across the face, which Laurence, on the point of intervening, could not call entirely unmerited, even if there were no shortage of blame to be credited to Blincoln's account in the situation; but the noise was crisp and loud in the dry air, and Kulingile's head snapped up from his repast to see Demane stumbling back under the blow.

Kulingile did not precisely spring: the motion was more peculiar, as he launched himself and landed against Blincoln still floating, but then he exhaled in a sharp, hissing way, and the swelled air-sacs began to deflate, so his real bodily weight at once began to tell, and Blincoln stumbled and went down beneath him. "You have hurt him!" Kulingile said, shrill and furious. "You have hurt him; Demane!" and opened wide his jaws to push out still more air, and Blincoln coughed and struggled to push himself free, gradually being crushed.

"Demane!" Laurence said sharply, turning to rouse Temeraire, who had just cracked open a sleepy eye; but Demane was already there at Kulingile's head, seizing the tethering-rope and tugging.

"No, come away, you mustn't kill him," Demane said urgently, "or there will be trouble: look, I am all right, you can't even see a mark."

"That is only because you are dark," Kulingile said, "and not squashy and red like him," but with some reluctance he allowed the sacs to inflate once more, and himself to be pulled away, leaving Blincoln gasping and wretched upon the ground, curling around what proved on inspection to be several broken ribs. Dorset bound these up without great gentleness. There were no further attempts; at least, none where Demane might see and object to them, and as he made a determined sentinel, this ruled out nearly any such slinking efforts.

The end of the endless journey came abruptly and unexpected: though Laurence had marked off each day their progress, and written estimates of distance and position in his log. This was for some time their only account, as neither Granby nor Rankin nor any aviator had any notion of keeping records which Laurence could even call barely adequate to serve as a proper second to his own, and Dorset kept voluminous and wholly useless notes on individual leaves, or berries, or the paw of one animal, and could not tell which way was west if the sun were going down at the time.

Laurence put O'Dea to the work experimentally, as the man at least could write a decent hand now that the rum had been sweated out of him; which did produce somewhat more successful accounts, if Laurence would have preferred to do without such descriptions as the Blighted Crimson of the earth here, which surely has drunk the Blood of the Heathen and unwary Traveler, and yearns to taste still more, and the wholly unnecessary dramatization of—

*. . . the loathesome Creature gazed upon us long and
meditatively, as if considering which to single out as its lawful
Prey, tho the Carcase of the Offering lay before it limp and
bloodstain'd from the Slaughter, ere it chuse the easier Course
and withdrew beneath the Sands to devour the Flesh of the
Kanga-roo and only dream instead of the Satisfaction to be
found in a Repast accompanied by the piteous Cries of a
more sensible Victim.*

They had come now more than five hundred miles from the strange
monolith through the endless desert landscape, shifting only a little to
be yet more parched; they were drawing nearer the equator, and the
heat scarcely to be believed: strange clouds racing overhead, and the
sunsets vast and spectacular. They saw once in the distance two more
plumes of fire, and endured half-a-dozen thunderstorms which sent
water sheeting in violent cascades over the hard-baked ground, so the
dragons had to leap aloft out of the torrents.

They could not be sure of their position: one single survey could
not necessarily be relied upon; there were no landmarks known, or any
way to be sure of their approach. Their progress upon the map showed
them steadily nearing the coast, however, and one morning they came
upon a broad band of verdant green, stretching away in either direction
along the banks of a riverbed, flowing vigorously.

They cut its course again, some two days later, and after this each
day the countryside grew less dry: the red earth slowly vanishing from
sight as the trees grew closer to one another, and water now more plentiful. They were flying through the night, the cool wind rushing in their
faces familiar and pleasant against Laurence's eyes, half-closing, and
then Temeraire was descending, suddenly, to land upon the top of a
low hill.

Laurence roused: the air was salt, and below them the moonlight
was running silver across the water, a thin shimmering road stretched
out vanishing to the dark horizon, far away. The sound of the ocean
came lapping clear and liquid up the slope towards them. There were
some lights down below—an encampment perhaps, but there were
many of them; and Laurence thought perhaps even one or two out on
the water, from the bobbing motion—night fishermen in canoes, most
likely.

"We had better camp over here, and have a look in the morning, before we go blundering in," Granby said, his voice kept low not to carry, and Laurence nodded; there was not much chance of hiding Temeraire or Iskierka, but they found a heap of rock which the dragons might curl themselves around, and so have at least a little camouflage against a quick glance in the dark. They put up the small tents around them.

"It is something to think we have crossed the whole continent," Granby said thoughtfully, while they drank their tea, "but Lord! What a waste of time it will have been, if the egg has already hatched."

"If it has *not* hatched," Rankin said, "I wonder what you propose to do to find it and extract it; you seem to imagine that only because we have found some native village, we have found the end of our search." He stalked away to Caesar's side.

"Whether we have found the egg or not," Laurence said, "I think we have found the end of our road: it must be hatched, or very soon, and when we have reached so clear a terminus I hope they will not demand further pursuit, so vainly." He looked where Temeraire lay sleeping, silent but for the rasp of his breathing.

He slept by Temeraire's side; in the morning roused and said tiredly, "Yes?" before he realized he was being looked over by a native man: tall, with a curly beard gone a little to grey; he was otherwise built like a much younger man than his face would have had him, sinewy and muscled, with a spear held casually in hand; he wore a braided belt, from which was slung a loincloth, and nothing else. Two younger men, rather more wary, hung back a little way behind him.

"Laurence, perhaps he has seen the egg, or the other dragon?" Temeraire said, peering interestedly down, which despite the proximity of his teeth did not seem to disconcert their visitor. "Have you?" he asked, and began to repeat his question over in French and in Chinese.

"We will have to try and manage it with pantomime, and whatever O'Dea and Shipley can work out of their language, if anything," Laurence said, pulling himself up to Temeraire's back to see where the men had got to. "Mr. O'Dea," he called, and that gentleman turned and came down from the ridge, where he had been standing with several other of the convicts, looking down at the sea.

"Sir," O'Dea said as he scrambled down, "we should like to know if we have got to China properly at last."

"Certainly not; we have only reached the coast," Laurence said. "I had not thought to find *you* turned credulous, O'Dea; you can read a map."

"Well, Captain," O'Dea said, "I can; but I have seen Chinamen, too, and there are four of them down the hill there."

"What?" Laurence said, as the native man answered Temeraire, in fragmentary but recognizable Chinese.

"Galandoo says there are *two* dragons here," Temeraire said, turning his head around.

Laurence caught hold of the harness and scrambled down from Temeraire's back, and went to the top of the hill. Below in the harbor, a small, narrow-hulled junk was floating at anchor with lanterns at her stern and bow, still lit in the early-morning light. A small open pavilion of wood and stone stood some distance up the shore, all the corners of the roof upturning towards the sky, with small dragons carved and crouching on every one.

Chapter 14

※

$\mathcal{L}$AURENCE COULD NOT HAVE IMAGINED any more awkward and inconvenient period to their journey than to be kowtowed to in his plain and travel-stained gear by a dozen men better dressed, on the damp sand of the shore, when Temeraire had said, "I am Lung Tien Xiang, and this is the Emperor's adopted son, William Laurence," in Chinese, before Laurence could forestall any such introduction.

The adoption had made a useful and face-saving diplomatic fiction at the time of its promotion, on both British and Chinese sides; to use it for personal gain in the present circumstances felt to Laurence at once dishonest and wretchedly embarrassing. Now these men could not fail to perform any of the formal obeisance which their court etiquette demanded—however visibly, however plainly inappropriate when directed at Laurence—without showing disrespect to their own Emperor, a crime punishable by death.

The ritual had for audience Galandoo and several other of the native men, who looked on with interest. What structures of a permanent sort stood upon the shore all looked to be of the Chinese style, amongst which however the peripatetic natives seemed to be entirely comfortable: there were several younger men, hunters, bringing in game to cooking-pits; and women could be seen working in the enormous courtyard of the pavilion, and also peering down with interest at the ceremony.

If the Chinese gentlemen found the act objectionable, they concealed their feelings, and having risen from the sand invited them into the pavilion, where Laurence halted on the threshold, dismayed: a Yellow Reaper, perhaps a week old, was sleeping comfortably on the stone beside a small fountain, and there were several native women sitting beside it and working with some rocks.

"Oh, here you are," the dragonet said, lifting its head, and turning said something to one of the women in what sounded like their tongue. "I am Tharunka," the dragonet added, and a little critically, "you have been quite a long time coming after me."

"So long as you are hatched, I do not see you have anything to complain of," Temeraire said, having put his head inside the pavilion. "Who are these people, and what did they mean by taking you, I would like to know?"

"These are the Larrakia," the dragonet said, "who had me from the Pitjantjatjara, who had me from the Wiradjuri; and pray do not be angry, for they needed me quite badly. You see, we are sending goods so far that all the directions are in different languages for all the different tribes, and of course all of you in Sydney, and there is no one who can speak to all of them; but now I can, as I have heard them all in the shell," she finished, with some complacency, "and I am learning Chinese, too, as much as I can; and they have given me a great many jewels."

"Where?" Iskierka instantly demanded, and Tharunka nosed over a large basket, filled near to the brim with glowing, burnished opals, and the women working around her were polishing still more.

"I do not see much use in just a basket of jewels," Temeraire said later, in private, drinking a bowl of light fragrant tea prescribed for its cooling properties. "If one had them strung, on gold wire perhaps, there might be something to admire; one cannot wear a basket. At least, not without looking silly."

"Well, I want some," Iskierka said. "I like the way they shine, the dark ones. Granby, I am sorry we did not bring more gold with us; do you think there are any prizes we might take, hereabouts?"

Granby very emphatically did not.

The chief of the outpost was Jia Zhen, a gentleman of perhaps thirty years of age, young for so isolated a position of responsibility, and full of energy; he had presented to them with earnest satisfaction, all the details of the pavilion, established for the comfort of dragon visitors, and beside it across the courtyard stood a large and comfortable house in the Chinese style, offering an excellent prospect upon the harbor.

Laurence disliked extremely feeling inadequate to his social occasions, and all the more so that the Chinese might have expected him, by the grace of his rank, to be more versed than he was; but the courtesies had baffled him in his short stay at the Imperial court, and he had not improved in the intervening time. He did not know how to tactfully inquire after their purpose in being here, nor how far that purpose went: did they think to establish a colony of their own? It did not seem very probable—the Chinese did not have anything like a merchant marine; the little junk in the harbor looked to him a wallowing death-trap, and he was astonished they should have survived the journey: a matter of sheerest luck.

"I suppose you could not have been very comfortable: it must be two thousand miles of ocean and more," Laurence said to Jia, doubtfully.

"The journey was tiresome, of course," Jia agreed, "two weeks nearly without land! But one must endure," which became comprehensible to them that afternoon, watching as the great-winged dragon came in landing before the pavilion, and yawned hugely before dipping her head to the courtyard's fountain to drink.

"They cannot colonize very well by dragon, at least," Laurence said, after a dismayed silence: two weeks to China! He did not suppose one could make it in under two months by sea, even if the monsoon were cooperating.

"No," Granby said judiciously, peering down at the beast, "she's prodigious, but it is all in the wings now I see her closer; I don't think she could carry more than a ton and go anywhere."

"Which I am afraid begs the question," Tharkay said, "where several tons a week of smuggled goods are coming from into Sydney, unless they have an army of these beasts," but this theory Temeraire was able to discount, though scarcely with less disquieting news: the dragon, Lung Shen Li, was one of barely four beasts extant, of a wholly new breed.

"The crown prince gave orders they should be bred," Temeraire explained, "to travel long distances: she says it took them almost three years to manage, and she is still the only one who can conveniently fly so far: her year-mates cannot stay in the air longer than two or three days at a time."

"In three years?" Granby said, watching covetously: the dragon was stretching herself out in the sun, the massive wings glowing amber with a fine branching tracework of darker veins and tendons. "It can't have been done; it is twenty, at the least, to work out a halfway sort of new breed, if you don't mind it being half-blind when you are done."

"Oh; it is not that they did not know *how*," Temeraire said. "She says that her kind were bred by the Ming, before, and there is a record of the matings."

"Then why the devil shouldn't they have done it before?" Granby said.

"Because," Laurence said slowly, realizing, "they did not wish to; or more to the point, the conservative faction would not allow it. — This is the consequence of Prince Yongxing's death."

They were silent, considering the implications for Britain's empire—China choosing to reach beyond, and with the means to do so. "Do you suppose we will have to quarrel with them, over the place?" Granby said dubiously. "I don't know how much of the country we have claimed; or where we are, for that matter."

Laurence laid out the maps on the floor of their chamber, but they were uncertain enough of their position to make the determination more than a little troublesome. "I think we are somewhere near One Hundred Thirty East," he said finally, "which would put us outside the border: Cook's claim begins at One Thirty-five. The Dutch might have something, of course; although I cannot recall."

"Well, the politics of it all are past me," Granby said, "but someone in Whitehall will want to know this; and I dare say they would like to know it quicker than eleven months from now, too."

There was more they would like to know, also: Tharkay slipped out, that evening, and returning could report that the dockyards were not so simple as they appeared: there were pulley wheels upon the jetty, and along the shore paving-stones had been laid down in clean lines marking out a road, very broad, in the Chinese style, to accommodate dragons. "With two foundations marked along it," he said, "I imagine for warehouses; or barracks if you care to be pessimistic."

Laurence could not but be grateful for their presence, whatever the larger political questions: there was a physician of some skill among them for the benefit of Lung Shen Li, out of caution for any possible complication which might threaten the health of a new breed, and he had with great courtesy discussed Temeraire's condition with Dorset, and suggested a course of treatment which their supply had further made possible; and besides this, Jia had with great generosity flung wide their stores, and Gong Su had applied himself with great energy: Temeraire had eaten better in one week than in the past two months, and already seemed to Laurence much improved.

There was food enough to meet even Kulingile's appetite, which they saw properly satisfied for the first time at last when he had eaten a heap of fresh-caught fish nearly the full size of his body; and in a smaller and more personal vein, there was something near paradise in finding after so long and grinding a journey, so civilized and gracious a welcome, familiar even if foreign.

But this same gratitude could not but make Laurence all the more sensible of the very real danger of conflict which this outpost represented. It was not merely the presence of the Chinese, or their cooperation with the native Larrakia: two days after their arrival, several Macassan praus appeared in the harbor, come to harvest trepang. Shortly their small flotilla of canoes were plying the coast, Malay divers plunging from their sides over and over, and in the evening bringing in their haul to be counted up and prepared: enormous vats of boiling seawater stood on bonfires, and after boiling the trepang were hauled out and laid upon frames in huge dark ranks for drying in the intense heat of the sun.

Apart from this freshly gathered haul, the divers brought up also from time to time pearls; to these the native tribesmen had the supply of opals and heaps of dried spices, to exchange for Chinese goods. The market which was forming among them might be small only for being so new, and for the limitations of the harbor, but it was taking shape with remarkable speed.

Jia had set aside all the southern wing of the building for their use and comfort; it was not adequate to the full size of their party, but the lower officers and the convicts put up light tents upon the ground behind the building, as yet undeveloped, and so filled out their shelter. The building was in a light, unfamiliar style well suited to the humid and tropical climate, allowing the winds to bring coolness through the thin walls.

The men were certainly in no great hurry to leave: four had fallen sick, and Laurence felt himself strangely enervated, the natural urgency of so extraordinary a discovery deadened by fatigue and by the peculiar and isolated circumstances: their return journey would devour another two months almost certainly, and then whatever intelligence they might send would require six more at the least to reach any authority who might act. A full day's idleness seemed without meaning, when matched against such stretches of dead time, and almost difficult to avoid when so abruptly they had been relieved of the necessity or even the opportunity to fend for their own care; one after another unspooled into a week, and when they had only begun to settle it, that they must shortly depart, Jia interrupted their plans by visiting to invite them formally to a banquet, to be held at the night of the new moon, a week hence.

The invitation could not be refused, after so much generosity on the part of their hosts, and so much slothfulness on their own: to suddenly find it necessary to leave at once could only be, it seemed to Laurence, the height of rudeness. "I scarcely see how it can be more suitable to attend some barbaric feast," Rankin said, "given by encroaching agents of a foreign power likely soon to be at odds with our Government, and undermining our trade; but certainly we will wait if you insist upon it," he finished, with cool sarcasm, "and a pretty figure I am sure you will cut on the occasion."

"We are pretty ragged," Granby said, "but I suppose that is better than behaving like a rudesby; I don't see you saying no when they are offering you dinner, and bringing a tunny for your beast."

"At the least," Laurence said to Temeraire afterwards, privately, "the intimacy of such an occasion may prove an opportunity to broach the subject of their position here—the awkwardness such a situation must produce between our nations—"

"I do not at all see why," Temeraire said. "We have come so dreadfully far, Laurence; whatever can it matter to anyone in Sydney that the Chinese are here? And it must be very pleasant for us," he added, "to at least have the opportunity of visiting, if we like to make the journey; and Mr. Jia has already very kindly informed me that if I should like to send letters, he feels it quite his office to send them express. He sees no reason that Lung Shen Li should not visit us even in Sydney to deliver them, when that should be convenient. I have shown her our valley, on the map; she does not think it would be more than a week out of her way, flying from Uluru, so she can manage it now and again."

"Uluru?" Laurence asked.

"The great rock," Temeraire said, "where we saw her: that is where they deliver goods to the Pitjantjatjara, who have been sending them onwards to the other tribes; it is easy to make out from aloft. I suppose she might also bring some goods to Sydney herself," he added, quite the opposite sort of encouragement which the British Government should have liked.

Laurence was determined to make some attempt, however: this outpost was new enough, and the market yet so small, that it might not be an entrenched enterprise; some agreement might be found, some compromise, if he could understand better the purpose of the settlement, and it occurred to him in a dawning hope, that if Jia would forward letters, he might send one also to Arthur Hammond, the envoy established in Peking, who had negotiated the treaty which had left Temeraire in British hands and secured them certain advantages in the single open port of Canton.

"If we could not rely on the letter's remaining secure and unread," Laurence said, "at least it would not take the better part of a year to arrive; and I suppose I would trust Hammond's sense of the situation better than ours."

"Better than Whitehall's, also," Granby said, and looked at Tharkay, "unless you know more of that than we do?"

Tharkay shrugged noncommittally.

Laurence struggled to form some plan of attack, some approach not hideously clumsy in execution, and to further complicate the matter, he would have to rely on Temeraire to translate as his own Chinese was a limited mess and half-forgotten. The occasion could only be uncomfortable; it must seem in some sense almost a threat, or at least interference. Laurence thought it nearly certain he should give offense, and to gentlemen who could not resent it, very nearly the worst solecism he could imagine for his own part; but he had in some sense an obligation to both parties, which demanded the effort of reconciliation: however inadequate he might be to the task, he and Temeraire at least were present, and there was no better interlocutor to be had.

Certainly the Government would likely wish to challenge the encroachment on Britain's trade, if not the mere existence of what might be termed a colony, although the Chinese seemed less particularly interested in peopling the territory than in forming relations with the native tribesmen, and profiting by the extension of their trade. China's strength was in her aerial forces, but one light-weight dragon, or even four, if all the other of Lung Shen Li's breed were brought hence, could not withstand the full force of a British naval expedition, nor modern weaponry, if brought to bear against them.

But all concerns Laurence might have had and all his planning were by the next morning overturned: on the tide, a small fleet of vessels began to come into the harbor: more of the Macassan praus armed with their narrow sleek canoes, but these bringing in great heaps of ripe tropical fruit and carved wooden vessels to be carefully unloaded onto the shore and added to the other stores already under shelter. Several seeming officers of this company were met with some ceremony upon the shore, and invited into the other quarters of the house: and Laurence realized belatedly that the dinner would not be a private event, as Gong Su came and asked if he might offer his assistance with the burgeoning preparations.

Jia was now quite unavailable for any private conference, either, consumed with attentions to his rapidly increasing number of guests: the next morning, Laurence woke and saw in the harbor a launch rowing to the jetty, from a neat little merchant sloop of six guns, an American; and a Dutch vessel came in on the next tide, in the evening.

"The flow of goods to Sydney begins to look incidental," Tharkay observed: by the evening of the dinner, a Portuguese barque had joined the increasing throng, and without wishing to play the spy, Laurence had seen some dozen small and heavy chests brought onto shore, carefully, and set into the dragon pavilion under guard: almost certainly coinage, and in enough quantity judging by the size to pay for holds full of silk and porcelain and tea; where these goods were to come from, however, Laurence did not see.

"I cannot see why they should not be delivering them by air," Temeraire said, a little absently; he felt anyone might have been distracted, with chests quite full of gold and silver only sitting there in the corner of the building, and such splendid smells as were rising from the cooking vats upon the shore. Oh! the smell of roasted sesame; and the women were hulling exquisitely ripe longan fruits directly inside the pavilion, and heaping them into enormous bowls: the greatest self-restraint was called for, and Temeraire was not sure if he could have managed it, but for the coming occasion.

"But I will ask Shen Li," he added, "when she comes back again, although Laurence, I will tell you privately, I was quite right: there is something very peculiar about her, and I am sure it is all these long stretches aloft. She is perfectly pleasant, no-one could ever complain of her; but unless one speaks to her she will only sit quite still without say-ing a word, for hours and hours, and if one should ask what she is thinking, she says she is trying to *stop* thinking."

The magnificence of the coming dinner did make Temeraire feel a little awkward and anxious. He was privately conscious he did not look his best himself, as he had grown a little thin over their journey, and all the sea-bathing in the world had not yet sufficed to clear all the red dust from his hide; his scales were not quite so glossy as he might have liked, and he was sadly conscious that the edges of his wings were ragged. His breastplate had collected several scratches and dents, which Mr. Fellowes with all the will in the world had not quite been able to correct—Temeraire sadly missed having a proper blacksmith.

But at least he did have his talon-sheaths, and Tharunka had of-fered him some of the oil which she was using upon her own hide, against the dry, hot climate; the effect, Temeraire thought, would be particularly elegant on his black scales.

"I don't mind sharing at all; I *am* sorry you had to come all this way," she said, in what he felt was a handsomely apologetic manner, "especially as no, I don't suppose I will come back. It is no reflection on the Corps, I am sure, as your captain seems a fine lot; but I can't be fond of any of these officers you have brought along. They are all too pushy by half, and there is no really good fellow-feeling, as anyone might like to have around. Maybe I don't have a particular captain of my own, but I am pretty sure of good company any time of day or night if I want it, here with the Larrakia or anywhere in the country; and I don't have to sleep in a covert, or on a ship, or in some lonesome valley."

Temeraire could see the sense of her decision, if one cared to have quite a large circle, as most Reapers did seem to. Although he himself could be perfectly content with no other society so long as he had Lau-rence, certainly none of the other aviators was nearly as good, as Tharunka showed good judgment in recognizing; and the aviators might stop going around muttering and complaining of waste, if they did not choose to be better.

However, in one respect Temeraire did have to blush for Laurence, and for himself: there was no possible consolation for the appearance which Laurence would have to present at the coming dinner, the most particular and notable occasion they had met in this whole country since arriving. Temeraire struggled with his pride, and then yielded: when next Jia Zhen came by the pavilion, Temeraire dropped his head and deeply conscious of embarrassment began to try and explain— the length of the journey—the unsettled state of England after the invasion—the minor technical irregularity of their situation—

Before he had gone very far, however, Jia Zhen forestalled him and said, in the most delicate way imaginable, "I have been meaning to ask you if it would be considered excessively bold to offer a gift of robes on behalf of our small and unworthy outpost, when we have only the most limited of skill and our materials are scarcely suitable."

"Oh, how happy I should be," Temeraire cried, deeply grateful, "and I am sure Laurence could not but be honored by the gesture—" which proved even more splendid than Temeraire had ever hoped it might be: there was still some deep blue silk held in the stores, and green, and yellow thread to sew it with which looked almost golden; and it proved that Mr. Shipley had formerly been a tailor. Given the pattern of Jia Zhen's own formal robes and offered a small sum of golden coins, Shipley worked with great speed and energy, and even went so far as to try a little embroidery, at Temeraire's suggestion.

To cap his satisfaction and his feelings of deepest good-will, Tharunka said, when it was nearly ready, "Temeraire, the Larrakia have considered the circumstances, and believe that according to the law, it was not *quite* proper for the Wiradjuri to take my egg from you, even though you were in their country, as I am not anything which one would hunt. As they cannot give me back now, of course, they would like to know if you would accept instead some of these opals? That bit," she added aside, "was my own notion: I thought they might be very fine on those robes: how lovely they do look!"

"Now that," Temeraire said, feeling as though he must be aglow, "is what I must call civilized; and I am *very* glad, Tharunka, that you should have hatched with people of such consideration; if they have not any other dragons amongst them, that is not their fault, after all; certainly no-one could say they do not deserve to have them."

So the opals were sewn tightly onto the sleeves and the borders of the robe with fine thin thread, and Tharunka was quite right, they shone beautifully upon the dark silk; and when the whole was held up for inspection, no-one could have found any fault in it at all. "I will say it is something like," even Caesar grudgingly admitted, when he had nosed his head around it, and Iskierka jealously jetted some steam and said, "It is very unreasonable that Granby will not let me take any of these ships; if only I had any more of my treasure here!"

Laurence was stricken perfectly silent by their magnificence, when Jia Zhen presented them—at Temeraire's request, in the pavilion, so that he might observe. "Pray put them on at once, Laurence," Temeraire could not help but urge, as Laurence held their luxurious weight across both his arms and looked upon them, "for perhaps they might not fit perfectly; there is still time to alter the size, I think, before this evening."

Temeraire need not have worried; the robes fit without any alteration, and Laurence said, "My dear, I am very sensible of the effort—the consideration which should have gone into—" and stopped.

Temeraire said delightedly, "It is nothing, Laurence; nothing but what you ought to have had always, and how happy I am! I have not been easy about it, since I knew that I had lost your fortune; but I suppose anyone would rather have these than only some money in a bank. I do not think anyone could buy anything nicer anywhere."

"And—" Laurence said, "—and you are certain that this should be appropriate for the occasion—not, perhaps, excessive—"

"No; how could it be?" Temeraire said. "When Jia Zhen himself proposed them; and after all, Laurence, you *are* the Emperor's son: it is only suitable that you should have the grandest appearance."

"Oh Lord," Granby said. "Well, Laurence, you may call me a scrub, but I will be an honest scrub: I will swallow my gold buttons and silk coats and count my blessings. But at least you don't look a fool," he added, trying to be comforting, perhaps. "You look as though you might say *Off with their heads!* at any moment; but not a fool."

"Thank you," Laurence said, rather austerely: he *felt* a fool enough, and furthermore an outrageously false one, counterfeiting the appearance of an Oriental monarch and making, as it must seem, the most absurd pretensions to a station at once far beyond his own and utterly foreign to it.

And he could say nothing: if Temeraire's plain joy had not forbidden it, simple courtesy towards his hosts would have done as much, when so much effort and expense had been spent in the creation of the garments, and when they had been so ceremoniously presented. But

Laurence was perfectly certain he had not put them on correctly, and also unable to persuade himself he would not look ridiculous both to his fellow Britons, and more surely to his hosts, who knew better; he was reduced to only the meager hope that they might not fall down while he ate; which event if it occurred should certainly draw the attention of the entire assembly, as he realized with dismay he was to be seated at the head, beside Temeraire.

The tables had been put out in the large and sprawling courtyard of the house: it was a little crowded for the servants to maneuver in around the five dragons who were all welcome guests, but if a few of the Dutch and Portuguese sailors did look anxiously at the large and well-toothed neighbors, no one protested aloud. Rankin had in the end condescended to make one of the party, at Caesar's earnest persuasion—"When there are so many foreign visitors," he had said, "it must look very strange for the senior, the most official representative of His Majesty's Government to absent himself, and perhaps convey a misleading impression of the relative authority of such representatives as will be present."

Laurence would gladly have sacrificed all false impression of the authority that he wholly lacked. Instead he was obliged to seat himself upon a large and elevated bench, which he suspected of being the Chinese notion of a throne, while beside him Temeraire gleamed as though he had been lacquered in paint, and displayed what fraction of his jewels he had not seen fit to load onto Laurence instead. He was seated on the other side beside one of the Larrakia chiefs, the oldest of their company, who regarded Laurence's attire with the unconcealed pleasure of a man enjoying an excellent joke.

The other aviators were a ragged and untidy crowd after their long journey and wore whichever garments they possessed that offered the least embarrassment; saving only Rankin, who had somehow kept with him untouched across an entire continent his formal evening rig. He cut the only elegant figure among them, down to his spotless stockings and the high polish upon his buckled shoes, with no decoration but his small buttonhole medal for valor and a simple, discreet stickpin of gold in his cravat.

"Only look how plain Rankin is," Temeraire whispered, with satisfaction, and Laurence sighed.

Jia Zhen began the event with a toast delivered in Chinese, of which Laurence understood only enough to blush still more for his own audacity, and which Temeraire unfortunately saw fit to comment upon in perfectly audible whispers, such as "—the generosity of Heaven in bestowing upon our humble outpost the presence of the most noble Celestial Lung Tien Xiang and the emperor's son Lao-rentze—that is a particularly nice turn of phrase, Laurence, *the generosity of Heaven in bestowing,* do you not think?"

At least after this, the worst of Laurence's mortification was at an end: the wine came around, the food was carried in, and a gathering of men more likely to be sticklers would have been hard-pressed to care anything for social niceties before the largesse of the hospitality. One might have anticipated some awkwardness from the motley company: the Larrakia elders, the Macassan fishermen, merchant captains from three countries and their first mates, all in their respective best; their hosts in their formal robes.

But these very extremes of appearance and manners in some wise made less difficult their meeting; if only through pantomime might most of the guests communicate with those not of their party, smiles and nods seemed to serve universally, and a raised glass required no explanation. The perhaps natural consequence was overindulgence, so that by the second course, the volume of laughter and conversation was rising steadily, and what formal etiquette any of the participants had preserved began to vanish quite.

With the increased potential for disaster. Demane, unfortunately, had been seated next to a younger Larrakia man, with Emily Roland on the stranger's other side; the young man was interested in her dress-sword, a fine blade with an elaborately engraved hilt, a gift from her mother. He managed through his scattering of Chinese and her own to make his admiration evident, and as she was no more proud of the sword than a cardinal might be of his office, she was by no means reluctant to show it away; and having displayed it, she tapped her chest and informed the young man, "Emily," to which he returned, "Lamoorar." From this the acquaintance proceeded swimmingly through several courses and eventually to the offer, on his part, of a braided wristlet; on which Demane, whose feelings had followed the progression with a visible increase of surliness, gave vent to a hissed demand that Roland reject the gift, on the grounds of impropriety.

"Stuff," she said. "I don't see why I ought to be rude; and you needn't be unpleasant, just because this fellow likes to be friendly," and when he would have remonstrated further, she turned her back, and offered Lamoorar a trinket of her own: a few glass beads she had acquired in Istanbul, strung upon a cord, which he accepted with a glance at Demane that a jealous spirit might sadly have interpreted as triumph.

Laurence observed the resulting spark in Demane's expression with alarm, and tried to think how he might intervene without disrupting his own awkward position. But the event was saved: at that moment, Kulingile managed to overset his emptied dish with the wreckage of the fish carcass upon all three of them. Forthing, sitting on Roland's other side, prudently changed places with her while the damage was repaired, and shifted Demane with Sipho, who with an air of smug and deliberate maturity offered Lamoorar a few words in the Larrakia tongue, which he had troubled himself earlier to acquire, while Demane tried to glare from Kulingile's other side.

For the convenience of all, it had been decided that Iskierka should take the second position of honor, at the leeward end of the table, so that her occasional jets of steam should not be blown upon everyone else. Granby was seated beside her, of course, and while she sighed in satisfaction over the elaborately layered dish of cassowary and crab and fruit, the American sea-captain leaned over from his own place, three seats down, and said to Granby, "I don't suppose you ever go wanting a tea-kettle. She's a big one and no mistake: what sort is she?"

"A Kazilik," Granby said, perfectly glad to brag, "a Turkish breed; fire-breather, of course," he added, proudly.

The American introduced himself as a Mr. Jacob Chukwah, of New York; his peculiar name was evidently of Indian extraction. He added, "My brother has one; but more along these lines," jerking a thumb at the smaller Kulingile, who was stretching out his neck yearningly to the whole tunny being set before him, stuffed to spilling-over with some sort of roast native root, and fried.

"I hadn't heard you had your own Aerial Corps, yet," Granby said.

"He is signed on with the militia, and they go in when they are called up, of course," Chukwah said, "but no, they are on the run from New York to the Ojibwe: dry goods out, mostly, and furs in."

None of the merchantment officers, with whom he might have shared a tongue, similarly made bold to speak across the table to Laurence: the dreadful state in which he sat precluded such familiarity even from his increasingly free neighbors, and when it occurred to him on the next pass of the wine that shortly the conversation would be past any real exchange of information, Laurence with some little struggle jettisoned his own sense of propriety, and leaning over asked the Portuguese captain, some few seats down, "You have French perhaps, monsieur?" in that language.

A little exchange sufficed to determine that Laurence shared with Senhor Robaldo, a native of Lisbon, a familiarity with a particular inn, which was enough to promote further conversation, leading as soon as Laurence could manage it to a discussion of the state of the war; he was anxious to know more of the attacks upon the cities in Spain, and Robaldo, he hoped, might know if the British had entered the field.

"Oh, the dog, the dog," Robaldo said, meaning Bonaparte. "Do you know, Mr. Laurence, what he has done? He has made allies of them, and ten thousand corpses still unburied in Spain and in France both."

"Sir," Laurence said, blankly, "your news runs too far ahead of me; I am lost. He has made allies of—?"

"The moors!" Robaldo said with fervent, furious energy, not unaffected by the glass of wine he was gulping to wet his throat. "Dogs, dogs all of them; and he is shipping them to Brazilia."

"Are you talking of Brazil?" the younger American sailor asked across the table in English, Mr. Chukwah's first mate. "They have burnt Rio to the ground. We spoke to a whaler out of Chile a couple of weeks ago who had heard it in Santiago."

Robaldo groaned, when Laurence had translated this, and covered his face: he evidently had significant interests in the colony, lending his wrath a very personal intensity. "You would think his heart could not allow it! He was anointed by the Pope; but he is a heathen in his heart, a demon, a demon," and slid into his own language.

Rather less intimately concerned and better able to command himself in the face of the wine, being some six feet and more in height and solidly built, the American sailor, a Mr. David Wright, could offer Laurence more intelligence. "I'm afraid I don't know anything about what your redcoats might be up to in Portugal," he said, "but as I hear it, these fellows came out of Africa, the ones as burnt up the slave ports, and started in on some cities on the Med. They had a run at Gibraltar, too, but that went badly for them, so there's that for you."

Laurence was not much comforted to hear it. That the Tswana had intended some more thorough pursuit of their stolen tribesmen, the victims of the slave trade, he had learnt during his brief captivity among them; that they should have with such speed already realized their goal so far as to reach the coast of Europe was more than he would have dreaded. "Then it was not the French who sacked the cities?"

"No," Wright said. "The Africans went for Toulon, too, after they had done with Spain, and I guess that is where Boney got hold of them, somehow—caught some of them, or bribed 'em; but in any case he worked out some bargain with them, and he has been shipping them across the Atlantic since, on transports—by the dozen, I hear, and they are happy to go."

"He is setting them on our colonies," Robaldo said bitterly. "—the inhumanity is beyond words. No civilized nation could abide it."

"Well," Wright said, when Laurence had conveyed the sense of this remark, "I am sorry for them, but it puts pretty well paid to this stuff I have heard fellows say about the business, that the black fellows don't mind it. I would; I don't reckon I would sit at home quiet if I heard someone had taken my Jenny over the ocean and put her on a block, so I don't see anyone has a right to complain if they don't, either."

"I do not, either," Temeraire said, putting in, "and it seems to me that if anyone in Brazil did not like to be attacked, they would only need to give back the slaves, and then no one would wish to hurt them, either."

"I am afraid," Laurence said grimly, "that the better part of the kidnapped are gone beyond anyone's reach and are now in the grave; that news is not likely to appease the Tswana when they have crossed the ocean to hear it."

"I wonder how this gentleman will like it," Robaldo said, having gathered that Wright did not perhaps feel the full degree of sympathy which he felt appropriate, "when these African monsters have worked their way up the coast, and begun to pillage *his* cities: there is no shortage of slaves in his country."

"I don't mean to make light of the gentleman's trouble," Wright said, conciliatory, when he had understood. "There aren't any in my state, and we haven't missed them, either, so perhaps I don't see why folks can't do without. But I guess it would be hard if you have gotten used to it, years and years, and suddenly there is someone knocking down the door."

Chukwah leaned over the table and said, "Davey, you can tell that fellow, if you like, the Iroquois hatched thirty-two in New York alone this last year, so if these African fellows come to us looking for a fight, they can have one; and so can anyone else who likes, I expect.

"I've surprised you, I guess," he said with some perhaps pardonable complacency, looking at Granby, who had nearly choked upon the prawn which he was eating; all the other aviators at the table had brought their heads up from the profound attraction of their plates and cups. "Yes, the chiefs have come around to proper cattle farming, and it is working pretty well. I am thinking of jumping ship for it myself: they have more dragons than men to work them these days. A steady man, who doesn't get the jitters or lose his head aloft, can have a beast of his own in three years."

To punctuate this remark, Ensign Widener dropped his chopsticks entirely into his bowl, splattering himself shamefully.

"My brother says it is the course of the future," Chukwah continued. "What does it matter if you can't ship more than a ton, when you can get it from Boston to Charlotte in a week, hail, sleet, or storm? I am taking this load straight to Californiay, myself, to see if the Chumash riders will carry it over the Rockies for a share: and if they will, no bother with the Horn for us."

As deeply interesting as the development of the American aerial shipping should naturally be to himself and to every other aviator, Laurence was preoccupied and yet again baffled where Chukwah meant to get sufficient cargo to justify his making so obscure a voyage, and not only him but every other captain present.

He was on the point of speaking to inquire, when Temeraire leaned over and whispered, "Laurence, as we are nearly at the end, it would be very courteous if you were now to offer a toast yourself, and I have thought of a few remarks, if you should wish to make them." These Laurence had to parrot without comprehension; what little he might have understood, the liquor haze had by now consumed. They were received with utmost politeness and applause, but as he was mortally certain the same would have been true if he had inadvertently insulted the families of all the attendees, he took no great comfort here.

The toast completed, and the wreckage of the meal beginning to be removed, Jia Zhen rose—himself not a little wavery—and invited them to recline in more comfort upon makeshift couches which had been arranged along the wall of the courtyard; the tables were pulled apart and lifted and carried out, to open more room within the court, and the lights were put out. In the absence of the moon, the night was very dark, and the jetty was lined with red lanterns that glowed brilliantly both in their own right and as reflections upon the water.

A peculiar sound began: down upon the sand, one of the Larrakia men was sitting with some sort of an instrument, an enormously long pipe it seemed, which produced a deep, low, droning noise that resounded ceaselessly; he somehow did not pause even for breath. Two of the younger Chinese attendants were now standing at the jetty's end, holding long poles with lanterns at the ends, which they dangled over the water; a crowd of the younger Larrakia men were waiting upon it.

The company had grown quiet, muffled by the steady droning of the instrument and a sense of anticipation; no longer restricted to their seats, the guests gravitated towards the society of those with whom they could converse, but voices remained low. The tide was lapping in swiftly, high upon the shore, and the waves slapped at the jetty audibly.

"I suppose they might be showing a path to land," Temeraire said, peering up vainly into the night sky, but then the instrument ceased; in the sudden stillness, a low churning gurgle might be heard, traveling up the slope towards them from the bay, and the illuminated waters about the jetty shivered suddenly with many colors: gold and crimson and blue, rising up, and the great lamp-eyed head of a sea-serpent broke the surface and rose up and up, water streaming from its fins and in rivulets from the knotted brown seaweed which throttled its neck, like heaped strings of pearls.

There was a smattering of applause from the guests, a murmur of appreciation; although one of the Dutchmen said to one of the Macassan captains, in French, "I don't care; it makes any sailor's blood run cold to see one, or he is a liar."

The men on the jetty were heaving a tunny into the serpent's waiting, opened jaws; it closed its mouth and swallowed with evident pleasure, and they reached for its sides: beneath the seaweed lay chains, running through a network of golden rings piercing the serpent's fins and sides, and forming a mesh. The ends of these strands were now being drawn up onto the jetty, a heap of untarnished net, and being wound upon the capstan which Laurence had seen before.

Twenty men put hands to the capstan bars, and heaving together were bringing up a chest: carved of wood in a stretched egg-shape and banded with more of the gold, the size perhaps of the water-tank of a first rate; when it had breached the surface, another party of men set pulley hooks in it, and with a great effort it was swung up and onto the shore. The sea-serpent, watching, was fed another tunny; a second chest was drawn up, and then a third, of equal size, with the same maneuver.

The netting was flung back off into the water. Trailing it behind like a skirt of gauze, the serpent turned away and plunging into the water swam to the far side of the bay: a pair of yellow lights gleamed and a bell was ringing from another distant jetty which Laurence had not formerly noticed. As the serpent cleared away, the great head vanishing into ripples and froth, the red lanterns were lowered again to dangle above the water; all fell silent once more, and yet another serpent broke out of the water, blinking slow, garlanded with gold and gleaming kelp.

Chapter 15

⟨✦⟩

THE SERPENTS WERE HAVING a frolic in the sunlight, out past the edge of the harbor and where the water was dark and deeper; one could see them even from the shore as their shining curves breached the waves and plunged again, glittering with scales and their golden nets. There were a great many of them, thirty perhaps, although they were difficult to count and would not stop to even try and talk, when Temeraire had flown over to speak with them.

"They do not seem to care for anything but fish and swimming," he said, landing again discouraged at the pavilion.

"I don't see what else you expected," Caesar said. "My captain says they are a menace to shipping, and they will get themselves caught in fishing nets and break them, which oughtn't be hard to miss if they were not very dull fellows."

The pavilion was now the scene of many and intense negotiations, among the various captains and Jia Zhen as well as his lesser officials, who it seemed were responsible for working out the various arrangements, and then presenting them for his final approval. The rows and rows of containers upon the shore had been opened up for inspection, very like, Temeraire thought wistfully, heaps of splendid gifts arrayed for one's delight. It was a little saddening to think they should all very shortly be going away, and one might not keep any of them, although he was well aware this could only be classed as rampant greed when he had already come out of their visit with so much good fortune. No-one, he felt, could deny that Laurence had been by far the most gorgeously arrayed of anyone present, the evening before, and the exquisite robes, at Temeraire's suggestion—he did not find that Laurence was quite so careful of his clothing anymore as one might really wish—had now been packed away in oilcloth and in some scraps of silk, and were in a box among Temeraire's own things, safe and protected.

He would have even been very happy to possess one of the sea-boxes quite empty, and had sniffed them over several times to make a note of their design. They were so very ingeniously crafted that they had scarcely leaked, all the long way from China: on both top and bottom, a sequence of long wooden lips and trenches interlocked with one another, and these had been lined with pale creamy beeswax. It was indeed quite a struggle to open them at all: Temeraire had been only too pleased to oblige with a little assistance, and even he had found it hard going to work his talon-tips into the notches and lever the two halves apart.

Some few seals had failed, but only perhaps three of the lot, and two of these contained porcelain which was only dampened and not spoilt. Although it made for tedious work to take out each piece and inspect it and dry it again, Temeraire could not be sorry in the least, as he and Iskierka and Caesar and Kulingile and Tharunka might all sit at the edge of the pavilion and watch each lovely glowing piece come out, to be wiped and set out upon cloths upon the mowed grassy verge, in the sunlight, and there were hundreds and hundreds of the pieces to be seen.

They were crowded, though, and at first they were distracted by a little squabbling among the little dragons: Caesar was still the largest of those three, but Kulingile had eaten nearly four times as much last night, with all that Caesar had been able to do, and was not so very far off; and Tharunka, who of course was still very small, had the very reasonable contention that as this was in her country, the pavilion was more nearly hers than anyone else's, and so she ought have the best place.

"I do not see why you must all make such a fuss," Iskierka said impatiently, "and look, they are bringing out some platters: that one could hold an entire cow."

"Oh, oh; how marvelous," Temeraire cried: it was painted with a great phoenix, in yellow and green; of course it would have been the very pity of the world if it had been hurt in any way, but Temeraire did wonder if, perhaps, the salt water had faded the color a little, whether they might decide it could not be sold after all, and they might as well put it aside. "That is enough," he added to the squabbling, turning his head, "Tharunka, you shall come and sit between Iskierka and me, up

on the steps, and Kulingile, you may sit upon me: if you are not floating anymore—"

"—which I am very glad to see," Iskierka put in, "as it is not reasonable, and looks very strange."

"—even if you are not floating, anyway you are still very light; one
would hardly know you were there," Temeraire finished. "And there is
no reason, Caesar, why you cannot fit on Iskierka's other side, if I
should turn myself a little so Kulingile can see, and then Iskierka sit
straight back; but I must say it is time you gave over pretending
Kulingile is not going to be bigger."

Harmony thus re-established, they might all enjoy the remainder of
the spectacle as it unfolded before them: there were even some plates
which had gold upon their rims, so they flashed in the sunlight, and
Temeraire did not even mind Iskierka sighing damply; it was impossible to blame her.

"I should like a whole set," she said, "and I should eat off them
every day."

"It doesn't seem to me that it is proper to get anything like that
dirty," Tharunka said, and Temeraire was of her mind, but Iskierka
pointed out that the plate would be clean at first, and when one had finished eating one's food it would be cleaned again, so one would have
all the pleasure of seeing it cleaned fresh every day, and also of having
it uncovered little by little as you ate.

This seemed almost excessively sybaritic, Temeraire thought, but
after all, it was true the plates were intended for the purpose, and one
ought to use them so, if one were careful not to let them be broken.

At last the plates were all dry, and packed away again, this time in
an ordinary crate: they were going to Holland, it seemed, or at least the
Dutch captain was taking them away after some intense conversation
with one of the officials, who consulted his records and shook his head
a few times, and then at last reached a bargain: one of the chests which
had been kept under lock and key in the pavilion was opened up, and
oh, it was full to the brim of bars of gold, of which ten were carefully
counted out, and then each separately wrapped by the officials in
paper; another, with an ink-pot and a brush, wrote upon them in large
characters.

"What does that say?" Iskierka said, craning, quite to no purpose,
as she could not read a word even of English.

"It is a name," Temeraire said, squinting a little. "It says, the house of Jing Du, who I suppose is a merchant, and that this is the third of ten bars, in payment for the shipment of five hundred pieces of porcelain," and the bars were carefully wrapped again in oilcloth, over and over, and set back into one of the other containers: he supposed those would be returned to China.

Mostly the remaining porcelain was not unwrapped, to all their disappointment; each piece was taken out wrapped in paper and shaken a little, and if no pieces came out they were put away into the new crates; a few did drop some shards, and were opened up, and whichever piece had broken was put aside and marked down upon the accounts; but it was more melancholy than satisfying to only see the ones which were smashed.

One of the flawed containers, alas, had contained great bolts of silk; the leak had penetrated also into the oilcloth wrappings and stained several of these wholly beyond repair, and Temeraire bowed his neck in wincing sorrow when they were lifted out and unrolled in the sunlight: great sprawling white-crusted splotches all over the pale-spring green and deep crimson bolts. But the officials only shrugged, philosophically, and put them aside in a heap with the rest of the ruined goods; a note was written and wrapped in oilcloth, to be set with the rest of the payments.

As the morning advanced, the speed of the exchanges began to increase; the rest of the goods came out swiftly, were repacked, and one after another rowed out to the waiting vessels, where the crews loaded them aboard as more and more payments went into the waiting container. Before the sun had reached its zenith, the smaller of the ships were leaving: the Macassan fishermen singing as they put their backs into their rowing and loading the dugout canoes back onto the praus. Their small white sails went up as they drove past the sea-serpents and vanished into clouds upon the ocean, sculling away.

As the other containers were emptied of their deliveries, many of the goods which had been left and unloaded over the past week were now transferred within, in their place: the heaps of trepang now dried and smoked; the sweetly fragrant ripe fruit, each bundled separate into a little wrapping of paper—

"They mean to ship fruit?" Laurence said, doubtfully; he had come to watch.

Temeraire inquired of one of the officials, who had come hurrying inside for a fresh pot of ink. "Yes," the young man said, "the deep water keeps it cold, and only half of it will spoil. Of course it is all for the Imperial court. Six silver," he added, when Temeraire asked the cost of a piece.

"Good God," Laurence said, comprehensively, and Temeraire had to feel that for his own part, he should have rather had six silver coins than one piece of fruit, which might as easily be spoilt as not, and in any case would not even make a bite. "But," he said wistfully, thinking of the great treasure-chambers at the Emperor's court, which his mother had shown him on their visit, "perhaps if one has so very many silver coins that one cannot look at them all and enjoy them, one might rather have a piece of fruit; and then one might eat it and think, that is the taste of six silver coins."

One entire container, one of the newest judging by the color of the outer wood not yet as stained by the ocean waters, was thoroughly lined with oilcloth, and into this were laid bundles upon bundles of furs from the American ship: they were not gold, or brilliantly colored, so Temeraire found it a little peculiar that so much care should be taken with them, but when one of the bundles was spread out, it did glow very richly in the sunlight, a sort of warm red-brown color, and Laurence evidently thought them very fine: beaver, he said, and seal, and mink, which would go to make winter coats of particular warmth.

"Perhaps I ought to have one made for Granby," Iskierka said— showing away, Temeraire thought with some superiority, out of jealousy over Laurence's robes; it certainly could not compare in beauty, although as a practical matter, it might not be a bad notion; but it did not seem as though it was ever cold in this country.

Not all the furs were laid into the container, either: Mr. Chukwah and Senhor Robaldo were not allowing anything on the order of a philosophical difference to stand in the way of their making a separate arrangement, and a crate of furs was exchanged for a casket of gold and silver, to the satisfaction of both parties.

At the very last, a final few containers were opened: and within them inside oilskin wrappings a second nested container, and within that another layer of oilskin, which folded back revealed at last rows upon rows of sealed wooden casks marked with characters upon the top: Silver Needle, White Dragon, Yellow Flower, and when one of these was breached, the lovely fragrant smell of tea wafted nearly to the pavilion.

"How many tons would you say this delivery has made?" Laurence said to Tharkay, as the tea was bargained out among the captains, for really astonishing amounts of gold, Temeraire wistfully noticed.

"Twenty at the least," Tharkay said, and flicked a hand at the smaller pile of goods set aside at the end of the beach, those which had not been taken by anyone; Temeraire had been wondering with increasing interest what should be the fate of those neglected goods, as he could not see anything wrong with any of them. "I imagine the leavings are all they send to Sydney."

"It is ours: it is part of the payment for using Larrakia country," Tharunka explained, looking up. "Whatever they cannot sell, we keep, and whatever we don't want we trade to the Pitjantjatjara, and the Yolngu, and I think the Pitjantjatjara trade it to the Barkindji and the Wiradjuri, who take it to Sydney, and trade it to you. So everyone may have something they like, and no one has to travel anywhere they don't want, and by the end of it, no one gets left with anything they don't care for," which seemed to Temeraire an eminently sensible arrangement through and through.

Laurence did not seem quite so sanguine. "How often do the serpents come, with such a load?" he asked.

Tharunka consulted with Binmuck, the chief of her companions: a woman with a soft and peculiarly deep voice. With the women's habit of silent labor, this had encouraged the aviators to think her shy: but she had quite established her authority after Maynard had attempted, with an offering of rum which he had somehow once again filched out of the stores, to wheedle one of the younger women out behind the pavilion.

This conversation, which had been carried out in a combination of coaxing whispers and covert pantomime—to evade Laurence's attention, as he had made quite clear his opinion of such behavior—went forward for some ten minutes, with the woman's attitude passing from initially a half-flirtatious fascination to withdrawal, as Maynard tried to put his hand upon her arm and draw her out.

Temeraire had just been wondering if he ought perhaps say something to Laurence, even though the young women were Tharunka's and not his; but Binmuck had silently risen up, taken one of the logs from the fire, and coming over to Maynard clouted him solidly across the back, with so much force that he was knocked flat to the ground on his face, the rum spilling beneath him. He sprang up red-faced and wet, which Temeraire felt served him right; the women all laughed with great enjoyment, pointing at the spreading dark stain upon his shirt—they none of them wore much in the way of clothing—and Maynard slunk hurriedly away in the face of Binmuck's unsmiling and censorious expression, and her substantial cudgel.

Now she listened thoughtfully to Tharunka's translation of their question, then answered at length: "This one was particularly good," Tharunka said, "but Binmuck says that they have been bringing more and more, as they get more of the serpents trained: the Chinese don't like to put goods on any one of them until it has swum the route back and forth three times without, you see, because it is such a long way; sometimes a new serpent will change its mind and just go another way, and then all your goods are lost. They come once a month," she added, "because there are two schools now trained to come here and return to Guangzhou; when one leaves here, another leaves there, and they go in opposite directions."

"And they may add more, I expect," Laurence said grimly, "and with no great delay," which Temeraire supposed was true; after all, if all one wanted was fish, and one did not mind where one swam, why ought they not swim here where they should be given so many: the Larrakia had been feeding them all day, whenever they swam up to the bell.

"They won't like it above half in Whitehall, I suppose," Granby said. "How soon do you think they will hear of it? It can't be long."

"No," Laurence said. "These gentlemen," indicating the ships yet riding at anchor, "are adventurers, following nothing much better than a rumor in hopes of finding a profitable run; but each one of them will make that rumor into news, wherever they put into port, and I cannot imagine no British captain has yet heard those same stories: we have any number of Indiamen running all over these waters, and going on to China as well."

Temeraire did not see how it should be anything to the British, even so; but Laurence and Granby and Tharkay all seemed not even to doubt that it should be provoking in the extreme, and that there was only a question when an angry answer should come about it.

"The absence of those tariffs which drive up the price of Chinese goods must wreck the trade in and out of Canton, as soon as it reaches a sufficient quantity," Laurence said, "as also must the lower risk: a serpent cannot be sunk, and if they will from time to time wander afield, or lose a container, each single one is not on the scale of a full merchantman.

"But that must now be scarcely the worst of the situation," Laurence added. "This is no smugglers' cove; this is a port city and a growing one, under the auspices of a nation which if it is not our enemy, is not our ally; a port here upon the very rim of the Indian Ocean must represent a very real strategic threat to the security of our shipping and to British mastery of the seas."

Temeraire privately felt that it seemed a little unreasonable for a country as small as Britain to want to rule an ocean halfway around the world, and to complain if China, which was much larger and nearer anyway, wished to only have some sea-serpents coming by, with splendid things which people wanted to buy. "I am sure they would not mind if British merchants should come also," Temeraire suggested.

"They have never objected to taking our silver before," Laurence said, "but that will only lead to the same complications as before which our government have already been protesting, and the deficit between our nations will only be increased by a greater flow of goods: they are not likely to take finished goods, or anything else which it profits Britain to trade."

"Except opium," Tharkay said, a little sardonic, "which manages its own popularity. The public inspection of the goods might offer some difficulties, but I think one must have faith in the ingenuity of man."

Laurence was silent; he did not approve of opium, although it was so very useful for managing cattle and sheep when one wished to carry them along and eat better than whatever one could hunt; Temeraire was rather sorry they had not had some of it with them upon their journey, as they might have taken along some of the cows, from their valley.

"Even that trade is not likely to be sufficient consolation in Whitehall," Laurence said finally, "for the establishment of a port which, at the discretion of the Emperor, might give safe harbor to the French to prey upon our shipping, or at his will lock out British traders and none others from the profits of the trade, whatever those may be."

Rankin was particularly insistent, but Granby and even Laurence were also firm in agreeing they must return to Sydney at once with the intelligence they had acquired; although Temeraire did point out that if as they assumed, Government would shortly learn of the port without their doing anything, the news would no longer be news by the time they had brought it. Nevertheless, it was their duty, it seemed; and so

Temeraire sighed, and supervised Roland and Sipho in packing up the robes along with his other treasures. He felt wistfully how long it would be, before they might once again enjoy such hospitality, and such comfort.

Of course, he did not say so; that was he felt a very poor-spirited reason for not wishing to go, if duty were involved. Only, it was a little hard to know there would be so long a journey, through the uncomfortable desert, hungry and too-hot all the long way—and the hunger would be all the more difficult to manage this way, now that Kulingile was eating more and more—and nothing at the end to hope for but the very awkwardness which had caused them to leave in the first place.

"By now some answer must have been received from Government," Laurence said.

"But what if they have sent to put Bligh back in?" Temeraire said. "That would not suit us at all, and I am sure he would be unpleasant about it."

"If they have," Laurence said, "we must endure him early or late," which Temeraire thought an excellent argument for *late*.

But he consoled himself with the prospect of visitors: Shen Li might come, and Tharunka had already promised she should do so as well, one day. "And even if we don't wish to go so far very often, it is a cheering thought," she said, "that we *can* go visiting, if we only can manage the trouble of finding food and water. My people tell me you have been lucky, and it has been a very wet year; ordinarily it is not nearly so green, and the water-holes nearly all run dry by this time of the year."

Temeraire sighed to hear it; while he would be happy to see Shen Li, too, who could more easily make the journey, one could not look for much in the way of conversation from her.

She returned to the port one last time shortly before they were to depart, and there was something of a stir, for when she landed outside the pavilion, she said, without even having folded her wings, "Jia Zhen, pray ask everyone together at once; I have a letter from the Emperor, for Lao-ren-tze," so of course everyone had to put down whatever they were doing, and assemble in the courtyard, which a brief discussion established as the most appropriate place, and kowtow to the letter.

"To the *letter?*" Laurence said, in dismay, when Temeraire explained.

"It has the Imperial seal," Temeraire said, "so it is as though the Emperor himself is here in part, or at least, I gather that is the notion. Perhaps you would wish to put on your robes again, for the occasion?"

"No, I thank you," Laurence said. "If I am going to be bowing and scraping to a letter, at least I may do it without fearing to trip and fall by accident."

"My captain says he would not do it for anything," Caesar observed, and Temeraire snorted.

"Of course not; there is no reason whatsoever why the Emperor should ever be writing to your captain," Temeraire returned smartly, "who is of no particular account."

With this splendid rejoinder he went with Laurence to the ceremony, and afterwards the letter with its magnificent red seal was handed to Laurence, who broke it and looked without comprehension: Temeraire was sorry to admit it, but Laurence had not mastered an adequate number of characters to read very much of anything; and the letter was too small for he himself to quite make it out very well.

"Sipho may read it, however," Temeraire said, "and inquire of me if he cannot make anything in particular out, by drawing it large."

It was not a very long letter, but full of great kindness: the Emperor sent wishes for the health of Laurence's family, and inquired if Laurence had yet married—Sipho paused and added, "and he says if not, there is a young noblewoman of the fourth banner come of age who has not yet been married, which would be very suitable," which made Temeraire put back his ruff, and Laurence said, "What?"

"I would of course not quarrel with the Emperor," Temeraire said, "but it does not seem to me that Laurence must marry anyone if he does not like to. Pray what else does it say?"

"We have learned that you were responsible for widely conveying the remedy for—coughing fever, I think it says," Sipho said, reading on, "when certain unenlightened and disordered individuals within the government of the nation of England would have guarded this blessing for themselves, at the cost of many lives. We commend your behavior: as all know, loyalty to the state is founded upon filial loyalty, and upon the proper observance of the will of Heaven: faced with a difficult situation you have acted in accordance with right principles, and we are pleased."

Laurence did not seem quite so flattered as Temeraire thought he might have been; certainly the young official who had been appointed

to guard the letter and carry it upon its golden tray looked deeply impressed by this mark of favor, reading the letter upside-down even as
Sipho worked through it. "Any praise and reward for the act are
rightly yours," Laurence said, "and in any case I cannot take any satisfaction in being thanked by anyone whose feelings did not enter into
my consideration at all, whether that should be Bonaparte or the Emperor of China. Does he say anything else?"

"Only that he hopes you will call upon Jia Zhen for anything
which you might require," Sipho said, and Laurence paused and said,
"Do you mean to tell me this letter has come from him direct?—he
knew that we were here, in this outpost?"

Temeraire looked at Shen Li; she said, "Having delivered the news
of your arrival, I awaited the reply and then came, so there should be
no unwonted delay: this answer came to Guangzhou in two days by
Jade Dragon, and so did your letter."

For Temeraire had also a reply to his own letter, written much
larger upon a scroll of parchment, from Lung Tien Qian, his mother,
and she wrote to hope that he was well.

> It is a great comfort to me that you are so much nearer:
> although the distance is very great still, at least one need not
> endure such inconveniently long delays for correspondence.
> Your letter of last August had only just reached me, which
> cannot be considered satisfactory. I am all the more happy to
> hear of your safe arrival in this part of the world, as I have
> suffered great consternation upon hearing of the recent
> upheaval in the country of England, from your friend Mr.
> Hammond.
>
> I am charmed by the description of your valley, and await
> with pleasure a view of the landscape. Will you be settled here
> a long time? You would make me very happy to hear that it is
> so. I have enclosed a copy of the Songs of Chu, also, which
> you may enjoy if your studies have advanced.

"And you may read it with me as well, Sipho," Temeraire said,
very pleased. "How kind my mother is! Perhaps we will save the poems
and read them out only one a day, as we make our way back, and that
will make the journey go more quickly."

Laurence seemed silent and rather thunderstruck by the letters' having come so quickly; although Temeraire thought that it was more peculiar and embarrassing that they should take quite so long to come from England.

"They might at least bring letters by courier to somewhere that does not need so much flying across the open ocean—perhaps from Macassar, where those fishermen were from," Temeraire said, "and then they might row it across, and Shen Li bring them to us in Sydney; that would not be quite so fast, but it would not take eight months! What good is a letter eight months late, when everything must be changed? One might as well write stories that were quite made up— one might say, oh, I have just received a bag of lovely pearls, and if ever a reply came asking to see, one might say, why that was a year ago: they are all gone, now."

Laurence began to write a letter himself, to Arthur Hammond, the envoy in Peking; Temeraire did not remember him very fondly, as it had been very clear that Hammond would have been perfectly delighted to trade him away for any advantage he might get in the way of ports, or of shipping, and Temeraire had felt this was not merely a great misjudgment of his value to England, but also more than a little rude.

But in the end, Hammond had proven very useful, and had worked out the very many confusing details of the adoption, and Temeraire had grown quite reconciled to him; so he was telling Laurence to send Hammond his best wishes, when Mr. Chukwah came into the pavilion, in search of Jia Zhen.

"I am sorry to run out before dinner, more for myself than for you, to tell the truth," he said, "but I had better: a frigate has just heaved up over the horizon, and she isn't flying any colors, but I think I know British handling when I see it; and I don't care to have half my best men pressed. No offense to you, sir," he added, giving Laurence a small bow, "but the Navy has been getting a little unreasonable about it: we objected in 'seventy-six, and we'll object again if we have to."

"Why," Temeraire said to Laurence, "surely that means we do not have to hurry away at all; now they must know for certain."

"Yes," Laurence said, grimly. "Now they know."

Chapter 16

❧

THE FRIGATE MIGHT BE SEEN from shore before dusk fell, and a little after a sloop-of-war, sailing in company. "That is the *Nereide*, I think," Laurence said, looking through his glass for what he could glimpse of the bow. "She was sent with the expeditionary force to Île de France, by my last *Gazette;* under Corbet." He did not share what he had heard of that officer: a hard-knocks captain, court-martialed for brutality; anything might have changed in half-a-year, and rumor might be mistaken.

"I suppose—" Granby said, reluctantly.

"Caesar is the only one who can go," Laurence said. "Neither Iskierka nor Temeraire could land upon the ship; and I have no confidence they would listen to Demane—or for that matter to me; the captain can scarcely have failed to hear of my case."

"I don't know I wouldn't rather wait until he was close enough to row out to," Granby muttered, but there was no help for it; they could not with any conscience at all allow a British company to approach without speaking them, so Rankin must go with them; in any case, he was scarcely waiting for their opinion on the matter, and had already gone to dress. Caesar was arranged upon the shore waiting, preening with self-importance.

"Well, we are glad enough to find you," Willoughby said—Nesbit Willoughby, captain of the *Nereide*, having supplanted Corbet in that position after, he said, the successful taking of Réunion, which had been undertaken, under Commodore Rowley, to secure a port in place of the lost Capetown; but Laurence could not take any great comfort in the substitution: Willoughby had himself been charged with cruelty before a court-martial, in his previous command, and the ship did not

have a happy air; there was a lowering stiffness everywhere, and Caesar was looked upon with a wariness more intimate than mere reflex-
ive anxiety: these were men who feared punishment, and feared it
might grow worse.

"Not," Willoughby continued, "that I imagine we will have any
great difficulty. I wonder at them, indeed: planting themselves here cool
as you please, not a single possession nearer than four thousand miles
and only that one floundering mess of a junk to defend it; other than
the dragons, of course, and I am relieved to hear they have only the one
they stole. I believe we cannot expect to recapture her?" he inquired.

"Sadly," Rankin said, "I am afraid the beast has been too thoroughly suborned to permit us to entertain any such hope: several of my
officers," some effrontery in that, which Laurence controlled himself
from remarking upon, "have attempted to entice her back, but she has
rejected wholly all the lures: her egg was in their possession too long."

Willoughby nodded. "Well, it is a shame," he said, "but at least we
cannot be too worried about her, new-hatched and untrained. I suppose they will strike their colors at once when we have made clear the
situation, in any case."

"And what is that situation?" Laurence said, a little sharply, and
Willoughby looked at him with disfavor.

"I do not much care for your presence at this conference in any
case, Mr. Laurence," he said, "and I will thank you to keep silent. I do
not propose to answer to the inquisition of a convicted traitor."

"Captain Willoughby," Laurence said, too impatient to tolerate
this, "I must beg you to imagine my own interest in either your feelings
or your opinion of myself, when I have allowed no similar consideration for those who had greater claims by far to alter my course; and if
you dislike my company, you may be shot of it all the sooner if you will
not stand upon some notion of preserving ceremony, in circumstances
so wholly irregular and unexpected: unless you imagine that a twenty-
ton Celestial will have any more patience for it than do I."

Rankin looked away, as though to express silently his mortification
at Laurence's crudeness; Captain Tomkinson of the *Otter* covered his
mouth and issued a cough, soft and uncomfortable. Granby only did
not see anything awkward in the speech, and added, "And speaking of
whom, if you do mean to make some noise, you oughtn't be glad to
have found us; Temeraire won't in the least sit still for your having at
these fellows, and I don't suppose any of the other beasts would care to

disoblige him. I don't know what Captain Rankin may have said about seniority, which is a right-enough mess between us presently, but he knows very well that it don't make a lick of difference to them. What *are* your orders?"

Willoughby frowned: he was a narrow-faced man, whose hair had already crept back along the curve of his skull, and he was not particularly well-dressed: his clothes were those of a man who had been at sea for eight months, and lodging in irregular shelters. But Granby had given him an excuse, and it was to Granby he answered: "*Our* orders," with emphasis, "are to take the port. And if it will not be surrendered, gentlemen, I will take it; I will take it if I have to shell it to the very earth."

Willoughby's authority was quite real: the orders, which he allowed Granby to read, were from Commodore Rowley and indeed specific: the port, if it existed, could not be tolerated, and must be taken before it were fortified; the grounds for doing so a mere bagatelle of a technicality: the Regent had ordered the remainder of the continent claimed on the basis of Fleming's circumnavigation, which might as easily have given France a claim by the journeys of La Pérouse.

"There's no sense arguing it with him, anyway," Granby said, when they had flown back to shore. "He has the bit in his teeth, and the orders are clear enough, to be just."

"If we must choose between starting a war with China now," Willoughby had said, "and starting it a year from now, when they have cannon here and are letting the French romp merrily through our trade, we will start it now. And I say it has been too long in coming, myself, when they have been giving Bonaparte one plum of a dragon after another. One despot likes another, I suppose."

This was a wholesale misunderstanding of the original intention of the Chinese in sending Temeraire's egg to Napoleon, which had been done for purely interior purposes and merely to avert a question of succession; and even more so Lien's presence amongst the French: she had fled the country an exile, suspected in treachery against the crown prince, and had gone to Napoleon seeking only revenge.

But this was not Willoughby's deepest objection; he had added, more vehemently, "And when I think of the way they snatched our East Indiamen, and all of us forced to be meek as milk to them after, I avow it must make any man worthy of the name want to put his hands to his gun. It is time and more we blacked their eye for them."

Laurence remembered well his own feelings on learning that the Chinese had confiscated four British ships: confiscated them, and forced the sailors to sail their envoy to England, with neither cargo nor payment and only peremptory demands. It had been a gross violation of sovereignty, and he had felt, with every other sailor who had heard it, the most violent fury, not lessened in the least by the cringing behavior of Government—more anxious then to prevent the entry of China into the war, or at least more sanguine that it was to be prevented.

Jia Zhen might of course have felt a similar sense of outrage when Rankin presented to him the demands for surrender, through Temeraire's dubious translation, to which Temeraire added as commentary, "I do not see how this is reasonable: after all, it is stuff for the Regent to say we have claimed the country, when the Larrakia are right here and have been for ages and ages. Why, what if I were to land in London and say, *Very well, because I am the first Chinese dragon to land in London, now I will claim it for the Emperor*—that has as much sense as this does."

Rankin snapped, "That is enough: these are our orders. You may question them if you must in private, not in front of the agent of a foreign nation."

"That is a very handsome way to talk," Temeraire said scathingly, "after you have been sleeping in his house, and came to his dinner; it all seems to me like the sort of thing that Requiescat would do, when he was behaving like a scrub. And anyway," he added, "if Jia Zhen could understand whatever I was saying in English, I would not have to translate, so I do not see why I ought to be any quieter about it in front of him."

Whitehall claimed a violation of the treaty of Peking, the agreement negotiated by Hammond, wherein China had granted to Britain an equal access to any of her opened ports under the same terms as any other Western nation. Jia Zhen with great courtesy pointed out that this agreement said nothing whatsoever about China's granting her own merchants other and more favorable terms for export, as should be natural to any nation, and further that the port was not after all a Chinese port, but the possession of the Larrakia, if they had been so kind as to grant the Chinese the use of much of the land.

"And certainly British merchants must always be welcome, in any case. The *Pomfrey*, I believe," he said, "was here in the spring: her captain a pleasure to deal with, and most reasonable. I hope that Captain Willoughby will reconsider his position. Any disagreement or quarrel between our nations must be a most painful circumstance, and I fear could scarcely help but grieve the Emperor."

Laurence ignored Rankin's black looks to say, "Mr. Jia, I hope that you might agree that the terms of the treaty are somewhat unclear, and the possession of this port itself open to dispute: certainly left to their own devices, the Larrakia had not opened such a trade. Perhaps if the trade were suspended for a time, while our respective governments should discuss such amendments to the treaty as would satisfy them both—"

But Jia Zhen was not to be persuaded, not without reason; he did not refuse outright, but spoke in a calm and roundabout fashion of the difficulty of managing the sea-serpents, the impossibility of interrupting their peregrinations without causing their training to founder, and the expense of providing their food, which must be supported by the trade; he also, to Laurence's dismay, spoke of the warehouses which were to be constructed, and added, "By the order of the Emperor, several craftsmen have already been commanded to prepare themselves and their families to make the journey: Lung Shen Li will bring them hence on her next journey." This of course was very like throwing tinder onto a fire, and likely only to stir further enthusiasm on Willoughby's part for immediate action.

"There was no real hope, of course," Laurence said, low and bleak, when they had ended the fruitless audience.

"If it is any comfort," Tharkay said, "I doubt whatever concessions you might have wrung from them would satisfy Willoughby. He is here to take the port; nothing less will content him, and he does not strike me as that political sort of creature who might be persuaded by an appeal to his caution."

"But he is wholly unreasonable," Temeraire protested. "It is not as though Britain had built a port here, and the Chinese were taking it away; we had months to travel only to reach here at all."

That the port was strategically placed so as to easily wreck all of Britain's shipping, and her mastery of the Indian Ocean, did not appease him. "I do not see how one small country can complain if it does not rule all the oceans of the world, even those which are quite upon the other side," he said, "and after all, have we not heard that Java is only on the other side of the water here, and the Dutch are there, and our friends? Why does Willoughby not go there and say, *Those are yours, and hand them over.*"

"He would," Tharkay said, "but they are defended with modern guns and modern navies, which can raise the price of making such a demand."

Granby was kind enough to make one final attempt: they flew over with Caesar once more, and he remonstrated with Willoughby, who if he heard, did not show any particular interest in listening. When Granby had finished, he nodded, and then said, "Well, I have heard you out, and now, Captain Granby, and Captain Rankin, I am giving you a damned order: you will get your beasts and all these others out of the port. We scarcely need your help to secure the place, so you need not involve yourself, if you do not choose to—I will be happy," he added coldly, "to forward your reasoning to Whitehall. All I require is that you do not interfere with my orders, and we will manage the thing ourselves."

"So he means to smash up all the port," Temeraire said, "and maybe kill Jia Zhen, who has been so kind to us, or the Larrakia: when I think of the tremendous, the extraordinary generosity which has been shown us—oh! what a wretched little worm this Willoughby fellow must be; it is no wonder he should like Rankin so."

Laurence said somberly, "I am afraid the fault was ours in accepting that hospitality when we had so little information on the position which our nation had taken, or might choose to; there was reason enough to know the Government would dislike it, if not to guess they should risk a war over the matter. They may," he added, "suppose that a sharp rebuke here will warn China off from any similar attempts."

He looked up at Temeraire and said, "I do not say I like it, my dear; I do not, in the least, and Willoughby is the last man I would wish to see entrusted with the power to offer so great an insult to any foreign power not already our enemy. But he has been entrusted with that power, and this is an open and honest act of warfare. The enemy has been offered terms, and however little I think of Willoughby, I know of no reason to suspect he will refuse quarter when surrender has been given. I hope a warning shot will be sufficient to persuade Jia Zhen not to prolong the engagement.

"If it is any comfort to you, I ask you to consider that we ought have left before now, in any case, and we might already be on the track back to Sydney, wholly unaware of anything which occurred in our absence."

"But we have not left," Temeraire said, "so we are not unaware, and that is not comforting at all."

He brooded after, when Laurence had gone to pack his things; he did not mean to make things still more awkward for Laurence, or for Granby, but it seemed very wrong to allow this Willoughby person to destroy the pavilion only because the Government wished to quarrel; after all, the Government had sent Temeraire away here, and did not want him in the service anymore, so he did not see that he owed the Government anything; meanwhile Jia Zhen had been perfectly splendid.

Temeraire was not quite sure what he might do, but while everyone else made ready to depart, a little surreptitiously he went behind the pavilion, and experimented with clearing his throat and trying to take the deep breaths which were required for the divine wind. Dorset paused going by with his instruments, frowning, and when Temeraire in a roundabout way inquired he said disapprovingly, "I cannot recommend the exertion of the throat yet in any way. The strain has been very great, and you have not kept quiet as you ought to have."

Temeraire thought this was hard, when he had been so silent on their journey—he had not talked above half-a-dozen times a day, except on special occasions, or if he needed to explain something, or if he had seen something of interest which he wished to mention to Laurence or one of his other crew, or had needed to consult on their direction. His throat did not feel so unpleasant anymore, either: it did not hurt when he spoke, and at dinner he had eaten a couple of tunny spines, roasted deliciously, without suffering the least difficulty or soreness.

And he certainly must have the divine wind, to do anything very useful: if he were only to claw away at the ships, he could not do much to both at once. Of course, he did not mean to do anything excessively unpleasant to the ships, either, or at least not to the sailors; but he thought perhaps he might wash them some distance out to sea, so they were too far away to do any shelling; or he might make the seas high enough beneath them that they should be forced to stop working the guns.

Temeraire had tried a little, on their long sea-voyage, to work out how Lien had built up the tremendous wave which she had used to drown the British squadron at the battle of Shoeburyness, but it had to be admitted he had not had very much success. He understood vaguely how she had done it—she had built many little waves, and sent them sculling on, and then had built one last and sent it sweeping along to gather up all the smaller. He had mastered the trick enough to manage perhaps four or five little waves, compounded into one great, and this one he had certainly made more substantial than the ordinary waves all around, but by this Temeraire meant he could achieve a crest of ten feet, perhaps, above the swell; scarcely enough to do more than rock a frigate for a minute or two.

He had thought of his former trick upon the *Valérie,* where he had struck her with the divine wind directly, but the ships in the harbor had their sails furled: they were riding at anchor, and built solidly of oak; the divine wind had nothing to grip upon. It would not do, so that night he determinedly shook out his wings and flew from their new camp—out on the sand across the bay, exposed to all the weather, with meanwhile the pavilion standing empty but for little Tharunka—and he flew out to the ocean and began doggedly to practice once more, trying to work out how quickly each wave should go.

"For that is the difficulty," he said to Kulingile, while he scratched calculations in the dirt—he quite missed Perscitia, who would have done the mathematics in her head for him—to try and work out how many breaths he should take between raising another swell. "They do not keep apart the same distance, and some are further apart, and so when the large one goes, it reaches a larger gap, and then by the time it reaches the next wave it is already breaking, and it only falls upon the rest of the waves and does no good to anyone."

Kulingile ate another bite of his raw cassowary, which he had managed to catch for himself that morning—they were now obliged to fend for their own meals again, without the very material assistance of the Larrakia hunters, who even if they had not brought something pleasant back would at least reliably be able to tell where one might find game—and piped, "But if it takes so long to make, and you do not sink the ships, won't they only wait until it is gone and then shoot afterwards?"

"Well," Temeraire said—but it would at the very least disrupt any immediate attack, and very likely make them confused. "And anyway they will have a time beating back up into position; if only the wind should not be in the right quarter, that is, but I do not see why it should be."

"What are you working on?" Iskierka said suspiciously as she came landing with her own dinner, and looked over the figures; of course she did not understand a thing of mathematics, but only to be safe, Temeraire swept his tail-tip over the diagramme.

"It is none of your affair," he said loftily; he did not intend to confide in Iskierka, of whom he felt a little wary; one could not rely on her to have the right sort of opinions in such circumstances as these; Granby was still in the service, of course, and so their interests might not be perfectly aligned.

He felt rather more uncomfortable over having so far also avoided the subject with Laurence; but he thought they might better discuss the matter a little later, once Temeraire had already worked out how to make the great waves—after all, so long as he could not do it, then there was nothing really to be spoken of; and when he had, he might then demonstrate the technique to Laurence, which would certainly be a source of great relief and pleasure to him. Laurence had not said anything on the subject directly, but he had encouraged the experiments, and asked Temeraire to consider how one might defeat a similar effort, another time. And if Temeraire should happen to demonstrate it somewhere the ships could also see, perhaps this Willoughby person would be afraid, and Temeraire would never even need to use it directly upon them at all.

He did not just yet think over what he would do otherwise—what else Laurence might say. It seemed after all a great waste of time—one might even consider such ruminations to be an attempt to shirk the certainly very difficult work of learning how to make the wave. And there was no time to be wasted: the ships were almost surely only waiting for the tide to come in that night, so they might come further into the harbor, and do their worst.

"I am going to go find something more to eat," Temeraire announced, therefore, and flew out to make another attempt. It was not after all false: if there were any fish about when he worked the divine wind upon the water, they often came directly up, dead already or at least so confused that one might just collect them without any difficulty. He had already made a handsome meal of them on his first pass, and the sea-serpents had been pleased enough to take the leavings; he could see their heads breaking the water in the distance, peering at him in anticipation of more, even if they did stay properly and respectfully clear.

He had more success this time in regulating the interval between the waves, and having sent out a series of them pursued with one large final roar: which did make his throat ache dully, and he was forced to stop and cough a little, but oh! what was any of that, for abruptly a great glassy hill was rising up out of the water. The swell went rushing away from him, eating every one of the little waves—climbing higher and higher, until it would certainly have gone to the topmasts at the least, thirty feet and shining pale green, and Temeraire was compelled to fly around in several circles to express his delight as the whole struck upon the hidden reef half-a-mile further out and crashed in a thundering, foaming roar very like an entire broadside firing off.

There was no time to be lost: the boiling white seafoam was tinged pink with sunset, and Temeraire flew flat-out to the shore and landed by the tents, calling, "Laurence—Laurence, pray come and see—"

Laurence looked up from the letter which he was writing—to be carried back to England by the ships, about Demane, although privately Temeraire thought there was no reason why anyone should wish to be a captain in the Corps anymore. If the Corps did not want Laurence, their judgment was plainly unreliable, when even the Emperor had approved of him so highly, and Qian; Temeraire had not mentioned to Laurence, for fear of seeming an excessive brag, but her letter had mentioned him as well, and informed Temeraire that she felt he had made a most auspicious choice of companion.

"If you please, Laurence, would you come and fly out with me?" Temeraire said, "I should like to show you something," and Laurence looked at the water lapping high upon the shore and said, "I will have my harness in a moment," and spoke to Granby briefly as he shrugged into the leather straps.

"My dear, I know the situation must give you great pain," Laurence said, as Temeraire beat out—not so very far this time, still in eyeshot of the harbor. "I cannot like asking you to bear an insult to the nation of—not precisely your birth, but your origin, and certainly of intimate concern to you: I beg you to believe I do it with the utmost reluctance."

"Laurence, you do not like it yourself at all, though, do you?" Temeraire said. "You do not think that Willoughby should behave so badly to our hosts—*you* do not approve."

"No," Laurence said, "—but I find there is very little to approve of, particularly, in war or in the relations amongst nations. There is no secret of our colony in New South Wales, my dear; China certainly has known of it, and of our interests in the Indian Ocean trade. They cannot even pretend ignorance when they have been sending goods to Sydney herself, and there is certainly a degree of provocation in seizing upon a location so strategic, and so very near the boundary of Cook's claim to establish their own holding."

"But that does not excuse destroying the port," Temeraire said, "and perhaps killing our friends. I do not see that Cook had any business claiming anything anyway, but even if one should make allowances for that, he has *not* claimed this, so it is not as though one could call it a real challenge.

"But," he added, stopping to hover, "I do not mean to argue, Laurence; I have something splendid to show you."

Laurence paused and said, "We might fly further out."

"Well," Temeraire said, "I particularly thought it might be useful if Willoughby might see it, also, from where he is—"

He turned and looked, and the ships were making sail: the great billows of white spreading to catch the wind, and come about into the harbor; and the guns had rolled out of the portholes, black tongues. "The tide is not wholly in yet," Temeraire cried in protest.

Laurence laid a hand upon Temeraire's side. "My dear, pray let us go further; there is no reason you should be witness here."

"But you do not understand," Temeraire said. "I have done it: I have worked out how to make Lien's wave—" and on his back he felt Laurence go very still.

"No—no, Laurence. I did not mean—of course I did not mean that," Temeraire said, into that awful silence. "But if only they should see it, I thought—I thought they might not persist."

Laurence paused, very long, and then he said, "A threat rarely suffices which you do not mean to carry out. And regardless—no. I can have, I will have, no part of even issuing such a threat against the Navy. To prevent an officer of the King from performing his duty and from the commission of his orders would be equally grievous a crime whether committed by violence or mere intimidation. No. I have committed treason once, but in the service of a higher cause than nations, not the lower one of mere personal sentiment; I must beg you to excuse me."

He spoke with hard, bleak finality, and Temeraire shuddered with distress. He had not seen it so, at all; he had not thought—"It need not be treason, surely," Temeraire said, "not just to let them see?" but as he spoke, the protest shriveled small upon his tongue: he had known, of course; he had not spoken to Laurence.

He coiled around himself in distress, mid-air, and said, "Oh—I am so very sorry; Laurence, I beg you will forgive me. You cannot think I would ever mean to ask anything like of you again, after everything so dreadful which has occurred—not just to defend a pavilion," and he was very relieved to feel Laurence's hand upon his neck, and added, to try and explain himself, "Only I cannot see how it can be right to only watch, as friends are hurt, who have been so generous—and when the Government, after all, has taken so much away."   ·

"By this argument you should soon reduce all loyalty to a mere competition of bribery," Laurence said. "If I had thought for one instant that those robes should so secure your affections as to make you wink at treason, I should have thrown them on the fire directly, regardless of what distress you might feel; and," he added, with a degree of heat, "I am growing inclined to think Jia Zhen knew precisely what he did when he made you so extravagant a gift."

"I do not mean only the robes," Temeraire protested weakly, but he was very much shocked that Laurence should even consider so hideous an act, and added, "and I hope you would never really do anything so dreadful. Of course I cannot help but feel kindly towards them, and the Government is always behaving like a scrub; that is not any of their fault, and certainly it is no fault of the robes."

He looked back at the pavilion in much distress: the *Otter,* small and quick, had already turned broadside to the harbor, and as he watched, and flinched, the roar of the cannon echoed across the water. The ball went sailing high—they had the cannon elevated—and came down upon one graceful high-pointed corner of the pavilion's roof, in an instant carrying away the elaborately carved dragon and smashing through the tiles. A distant shriek of wood breaking, which sounded queerly as though it came from somewhere to the east, and a cloud of splinters bursting away; a clatter of more red tiles went sliding down into the gap, and the dark hole stood dreadfully jagged against the elegant line.

"Oh!" Temeraire cried in distress, "Laurence, only look; and if anyone should have been below—"

He darted a little closer—of course he would not do anything, not now he did see it must be still more wrong; but he could not help it—

"Temeraire," Laurence said.

"No, of course I will not," Temeraire said, despairingly. "I suppose I might not even knock down the cannonballs, as they flew?" He did not know if the divine wind would allow it, but—

Laurence's answer, whatever it might have been, was entirely lost to Temeraire; instead all the world went spinning round and full of noise, roaring, and he was driven in a tumbling rush down into the ocean swell, green foaming light everywhere, choking into his nose and into his throat. Temeraire struggled wildly to right himself, belling out his sides, and he burst back up through the surface, coughing and coughing. "Laurence," he managed, choking, twisting his neck around in panic—but Laurence had not been snatched: he was there, streaming wet and short one of his boots, but dangling safely from his harness and pulling himself back into position.

"There," Iskierka said, beating back up and away, looking down at him, "so much for your scheming; as though you were so very clever, and no-one had any business making out that you meant to do something to the ships, behaving like a sneak."

"I did not, at all!" Temeraire said, calling up at her wrathfully, because that was a wicked lie; he had never meant to hurt the ships, "and I think you have been a great deal more of a sneak than I might have been in ages, jumping down upon me like that with no warning."

"You may complain all you like," Iskierka said, "but it is no more than you deserved; I will not let you hurt Granby in the service any more than you already have. He is going to be an admiral, and a lord, too; like Roland's mother."

"Pray be quiet, you wretched selfish creature," Granby said, calling through his speaking-horn. "Laurence, are you all right? She would have it he meant to do something—"

Laurence was occupied with a wracking cough, but he managed reassuringly to say, "I have had a ducking before now—perfectly well."

"Temeraire did mean to do something," Iskierka said, "whatever he may say; and I have stopped him, which I hope you will tell that captain when he goes back to England; I am sure they will be glad to hear of it," she added, in a very self-satisfied manner.

"Oh!" Temeraire said. "If I *did* mean to do something, you should never stop me," and he took a deep breath and flung out his wings and beat them wildly, swelling out his sides as much as he might; with a lashing of his tail and hindquarters, as though he were trying to lunge back onto the *Allegiance* after a swim, he managed to get back into the air.

He meant to teach Iskierka a sharp lesson, despite Laurence's protest, but gunfire called his attention back to the ships, the spattering of rifles going, and not the great guns. Tharunka had come flying out from the pavilion with a couple of men in belly-netting, who were holding great dripping sacks. Temeraire could smell the stuff even at the distance, as they upended it over the *Otter* and then the *Nereide* in turn: a clotted, dribbling mess of half-spoiled fish and rotting seaweed, black as tar. As Tharunka stayed quite high to be clear of the rifle-fire, it splattered all over the sails and the poor sailors high up in the crow's nest, whatever did not miss the ships entirely and land in the water. It was not less than the ships deserved, for their attack, but it seemed quite useless to Temeraire; the bow-chasers were perhaps splashed a little, and the carronades on the quarterdeck, but the gun-deck of course was not touched at all.

The harbor bell was ringing, as Tharunka flew hurriedly away to the shore, and then the waters of the harbor began to churn as one and then another, the sea-serpents breached the stained water and began to claw their way up the sides of the ships and onto the decks, stretching their long necks up towards the slurried sails.

The speed with which the serpents moved was appalling—the massive beasts were struggling one against another to get a purchase on the ships, pushing and shoving to get at what was evidently pure delectation, and meanwhile beneath them the deck pitched and heaved as their weight threw the ship all ahoo. The unfortunates in the rigging, coated in the slime, were immediate victims, snatched like particular tidbits even as the men tried in desperation to flee down the ropes. Wide jaws tore at the cables, and the spars yawed wildly and went tumbling down, throwing more of the slush upon the men on the deck, to draw the serpents' attention.

A smaller of the serpents had managed to wriggle itself onto the deck of the *Nereide* entirely almost, only its long tail dangling back over the side, and it began to pursue the sailors with such enthusiasm that it thrust its entire head into the fore ladderway. The axes were coming out now, however; axes and the great guns firing, and as Temeraire and Iskierka flew to the ships, beating urgently, Laurence saw a tall man leap forward and swing down upon the small serpent's neck, directly behind the head which had been thrust below.

In two strokes he had cleaved the spine, and the body went into furious convulsions that tore the head the rest of the way from the body, spurting dark blood in torrents across the deck. It ran orange-red over the ship's white-painted rail and down its side, and the smell of dragon blood mingled with the fish-rot and kelp.

Temeraire dived and seized hold of one serpent by the shoulders, dragging it away from the ship as it lashed and flung back its open maw to try and snap at him, the coils and coils of its great length twisting and the small forelegs clawing at the air. Laurence could see directly down into its jaws and throat, looking over Temeraire's neck, and a pallid hand within desperately clinging to the tissue of the gullet, a face bloodied but not yet senseless gazing up at him in utter horror before the serpent's thrashing shook the man loose and he vanished still whole deeper into the creature's belly.

. The serpent was unmanageable with its enormous mass drawn out of the water and so violently clawing—"I cannot keep hold of it," Temeraire panted, struggling to drag it still further; but then Iskierka called, "Only a moment, keep clear!" and dived in. She blasted its dangling length with flame, the skin and scales crisping up and roasting with a dreadful stink; the serpent made a high thin shrieking noise and curled around itself like a beetle as Temeraire dropped it at last back into the water.

"That does for that one," Iskierka said, satisfied, but Tharunka had just darted in and flung yet another sack of the fish-refuse all upon the disordered deck of the *Nereide,* closer now that the riflemen were all in disarray, and still more of the serpents came boiling out of the water in a frenzy.

There were dozens of them, ripping, tearing—nothing coordinated, only a maddened and savage fury which did not know even their own kind: as the axes and cutlasses bit into their flesh, they began to snap and tear at their injured fellows, at the rigging, even at the guns slick with fish-scraps—a cannon breaking free of its moorings and running riot across the deck to smash through the railing, taking half-a-dozen men and a serpent with it. The deck was slick with their blood, and the guns roared: cannon tore into their flesh and flung them back into the water.

But more came, and the injured, only still more frenzied, clawed in blind, mad rage at the source of their hurt; and one of the greater monsters, perhaps now recognizing the ship itself as prey and danger, pulled its huge forequarters to the far side and plunging down over into the water began to loop the whole vessel.

Laurence had seen the maneuver attempted once before, on the *Allegiance*—a vessel nearly twice the draught of the poor *Nereide*—and only the greatest effort had kept it from succeeding. "We must stop her, that one," Laurence shouted to Temeraire, who dived and set his claws into the traveling length, the spine itself too protected by a vast and razored network of hard spiny fins.

He strained back, beating; but as they began to drag the serpent clear, above them one of the spars tumbled loose and tipped towards them, and Laurence was half-blinded with the muck as it splattered from the sail upon Temeraire's back and wings. He wiped the stuff from his eyes only to see a great pink saw-toothed maw coming lamprey-wide towards him, unblinking orange eyes fixed on him with intent greed.

Laurence jerked his sword loose—pistols useless after the dousing—and managed to bring it down into the approaching lower jaw, opening a deep purplish gash into the creature's lip, which made it recoil; only a little, but Temeraire noticed, and snapped at the beast. It snapped back, and then turning its head bit at his wings, seizing the pin-joint in its mouth and wrestling back and forth while it tried to pierce the tough, resilient membrane. Temeraire roared at it, the great startling thunder of the divine wind resonating painfully in the bones of Laurence's ears, and it let go and fell away with that high shrilling cry.

But more were lunging at them, and the great serpent beneath them was all the while marching on; the noose was drawing tight, and abruptly the port rail snapped like matchsticks beneath it, and the starboard gone an instant later. The bulk of it slipped Temeraire's claws and fell to the deck heavily as the support was taken away; he darted down again to seize a fresh hold, and four serpent heads reared up feeding from the deck, one tipping back to swallow the better part of another victim.

Temeraire twisted away from their stretching mouths, and Laurence had managed to pack his powder fresh; he pistoled one of the creatures directly in the eye, and saw the sclera cloud with dark blood as it recoiled shrieking. But Temeraire had to beat away again: they were biting at him from all sides, and he had not won a fresh grip; he had only brought away one sailor, snatched from the deck, and now twisted to hand him up to Laurence: a midshipman, perhaps fourteen, hair and face thick with slime.

"God save you, sir, and him," the boy said, glazed with horror and polite by reflex; with shaking hands he laced his belt through a harness-ring when Laurence showed him, and wound his arms through the straps to hold on; then Temeraire was making another plunging attempt.

He attacked lower down on the side this time, and between the squirming press of the serpents' bodies managed to set his claws again into the great one. But he was fighting now against the ocean, too: the swell slapped at his tail and the lower edges of his wings as he sought to hover and pull, and then he was windmilling back, his grip lost: another great serpent, surging suddenly up from the depths, had seized hold of the deck and pulled all the ship groaning askew.

The *Nereide* was tipping, and the serpents scrabbling up her far side, still trying to reach over to the deck, tipped her further yet; there were cries audible within, and the cannon trying to roar, and then abruptly the loop was drawing tight and tight: the decking began to crack and splinter, and the water pouring over the rail was rushing into the gaps.

She was sinking. Laurence looked out in desperation: Iskierka had seized on to the *Otter*'s anchor and dragged it deliberately aground, into the shallow water on the shore, where the serpents might not follow: men were leaping from the sides to escape those which yet clung on, while Caesar and Kulingile worked to tear them away: even Tharunka was now helping them, picking men out of the water to carry one after another to shore, and the Larrakia had come down to help pull out the staggering survivors.

There was nothing better to be done. "Temeraire," Laurence called, "can you drag her onto the shoals, or push her?" and the looped serpent proved an unlikely and bleak hand-hold for Temeraire to use. Kulingile diving came to join him, setting his own long claws deep into the flesh, and they together dragged the hulk even as she splintered and cracked still further.

The deck was nearly empty now of men, pillaged clean, and waves slapping flat against the tipped deck washed clean the muck with seawater. She was settling lower in the water every moment, but they were moving steadily in towards shore as well, and as the water grew more shallow the less-maddened serpents dropped away. The second enormous serpent looked up at them with what Laurence in an unpleasant fancy thought for a moment was cool deliberation, and then it, too, let go and slipped away into the clouded water.

They pulled the *Nereide* at last onto a small reef, near the *Otter;* and there with Temeraire's claws and the tearing of the coral managed at last to carve away the looped serpent, already dead and slick with blood; Demane was already rescuing men from the hatchway, standing in his straps to help them crawl out onto Kulingile's back while the dragon clung on to the railing, his sides belled out hugely to support him.

There was no hope of setting her to rights: the keel itself had cracked, and great seams opened all along the hull. Already it was growing dark; Laurence sent Demane back to shore, and Temeraire hovered to receive what other men could be saved: Willoughby was handed up with his eye bandaged over and one leg gone below the knee, the surgeon climbing up after him; the gun-crews crawling out grimed with smoke. They could only hold on to whatever harness they could reach, and though Temeraire flew slowly and carefully to shore to set them down, some lost their grip and plunged down into the surf, only slowly to drag themselves out, crawling the last few feet upon the sand.

They made another journey, and then a third, picking men out of the water. The sun was sliding away behind the pavilion, glowing red upon the lacquered roof; in the water, the corpses of sea-serpents rose and fell with the lapping tide. Temeraire sank upon the sand, heaving breath and his neck bowed deeply with fatigue.

The Larrakia were watching; the young men who had been helping to carry the half-drowned survivors had drawn back and taken up their spears again, standing loosely ringed along the shore: many of them, quiet and watchful, and others joining them; several of the younger Chinese men also, with swords which looked awkward in uncertain grips: they were none of them soldiers. "Mr. Blincoln," Rankin said, from Caesar's neck, "if you please, let us have a little order here; Caesar, if you would," and Caesar reared up onto his hindquarters, making himself however more imposing could be managed, and thrusting out his breast with the bright-blazoned red stripe.

The aviators began loosely to form an opposing line. Laurence slid down from Temeraire's neck and laid a hand on the soft muzzle, feeling Temeraire's breath going in labored rasps: aggravated again, no doubt, by the excessive use of the divine wind. Whatever they had in the way of supply remained back in the camp, further along the curve of the bay and out of reach. "Roland," Laurence said, low, "go and tell Demane; if it comes to fighting, you are to go back to the camp and fetch out powder and shot, and whatever guns might have been left."

She nodded and ran to join Demane on Kulingile, who despite fatigue was perhaps among all the beasts the nearest to wide-awake, his eyes bright with hunger. Some of the Larrakia had come fresh from their hunting: a brace of small kangaroos were roasting on a spit behind their line, and this had all of Kulingile's attention.

The sailors lay inert upon the sand, spent more even than the dragons and worn past exhaustion by the wreckage and the horror of what Laurence hardly knew how to call a battle: a struggle against some elemental force, invoked too unwarily, and as swiftly gone when its bloodthirst had been appeased. Out past the edge of the harbor, many of the serpents were at play again, heedless like children who had already forgotten a reproof.

The Larrakia men were speaking amongst themselves, spears held low and ready; the elders in convocation with and the younger men interjecting occasionally. There was a hesitation on both sides: no one was unshaken by the violence of the eruption.

Galandoo came forward out of the men, and beckoned to Tharunka to translate; and to Laurence he said simply, "It is time for you to go."

Chapter 17

❧

$\mathcal{T}$ HEY AT NO TIME saw any of the natives during the long tedium of the return voyage, which even on dragon wing consumed half
the autumn: the desert creeping by slow, and their passage wary and
hunted. They found tracks and signs enough, in the mornings, to know
that they were watched; at the water-holes they drank swiftly, and left
what small offerings they could spare for the bunyips from their hunting with the country grown still more spare and ungenerous in the
waning of the year, and four dragons, one of rapacious appetite, to be
fed.

The beasts were all four of them thinner than Dorset liked before
they reached at last the marker, the great monolith standing up out of
the red desert with all its vegetation now burnt yellow by the sun; and
began their turn for the coast. "At least there will be the lake, soon,"
Temeraire said wearily lapping at another water-hole, too shallow to
put his muzzle in to drink properly.

It was all their hope that long fortnight's flying: though they were
yet only halfway home, they were now moving at a pace wholly different than during their first journey, flying straight instead of in pursuit
of an unknown foe, and the prospect of the lake's refuge invited them
onwards. When at last they sighted it in the distance as a faint brilliant
gleam stretching over the curve of the horizon, catching the sunset,
Temeraire's wings quickened; all the dragons' pace increased, and they
came landing by the shore not an hour later: to the stench of rotting
fish, and a shore crusted with a rim of pink-stained salt; the lake had
receded to a long narrow stretch of water.

The water of the shrunken lake could not be drunk: it was become
more salty than sea-water, pinkish in hue, and the dead fish floated

half-eaten in clumped masses on its surface. The birds had deserted the shore.

They managed to find a small water-hole, sufficient to give the dragons a few swallows, although the requisite bribe drew down too much of their stores; in anticipation of the game at the lake, they had not paused so often for hunting. What little they had left, they ate in silence, huddled close around their small fires. It was not merely inconvenience; the disappointment felt something of a parting slap, contemptuous, from the wild back-country: a reminder they were not welcome.

And yet Laurence felt little more so as they limped finally back into Sydney, a ragged and thinner band, and set down upon the promontory already once more overgrown in their long absence: grass and weeds and small prickly shrubs beginning to re-establish a hold. They arrived late, the *Allegiance* riding at anchor in the harbor, a small flotilla of merchant ships clustered nearer-in to the shore; the sun hung low in the sky, throwing orange flame across the water, and at the mouth of the harbor, where it emptied out into the ocean, the light glittered on the hides of a dozen sea-serpents, rising and plunging from the water at their play.

"The question only remains how it is to be done, not whether," Governor Macquarie said: Bligh's replacement, finally arrived a little while after Granby's second departure. In the intervening months of their journey, an elegant house had been raised on the spur of land overlooking the harbor, with a clear prospect from the office stretching all the way to the open ocean. Even a small rug lay upon the floor, and the furniture neatly joined; Laurence and Granby stood raggedly out of place, and Rankin for all his efforts was not much better arrayed.

They had not been afforded any opportunity to acquire new clothing; the summons had come last night before they had even sent a runner to formally announce their arrival, and called them at first light to the governor's mansion, to find the new governor waiting urgently, pacing across the floor of his study.

"I can see no reason to have them here," Bligh was saying scarcely under his breath, meaning MacArthur and Johnston, on the point of being shown in; MacArthur came across the room to shake Laurence's hand.

"I find you have been a prodigiously long way, Captain," he said, throwing a look at the dust-stained and faded maps which had been laid out across the broad desk. "I am glad to see you returned safely," although there was perhaps some enthusiasm lacking: he and Johnston were ordered to England with Bligh, to stand trial for the rebellion; Granby's return meant the *Allegiance* would sail at last, and she would make their natural transport.

"We must first however resolve what is to be done with these serpents: their presence was ominous enough before the report we have had from you, gentlemen," Macquarie said, interrupting the private greetings, and waving a hand to the chairs at his table.

The serpents had not appeared alone: another of the wide-winged dragons, not Shen Li, had been sighted lately off the eastern coast, on one occasion not thirty miles distant; the serpents shortly thereafter had begun to make their sporadic appearances, evidently being trained upon some new harbor, near enough that in their frolics they from time to time came past Sydney. Shipping went still to and fro without incident; the serpents had not been incited against them, and seemed sufficiently well-fed that any natural inclination which might have led to attacks was suppressed; but this was scarcely much comfort to those who had seen the devastation they might easily wreak.

"They must be eradicated, at once," Captain Willoughby said harshly, his wooden-leg stump stretched out awkwardly before his chair; he had insisted on accompanying them, though his injuries yet left his face grey and drawn with pain. "We must trace them to their harbor and put them to the sword; them and their masters."

"Sir," Laurence said, "we have already suffered a repulse from one attempt at taking a harbor so guarded, without sufficient preparation and, Captain Willoughby must pardon me, without sufficient provocation for the consequence we court. Surely there can be no justification for spurring on a war with China which, we now know, they have the means to carry against all our shipping. Even without the direction of intelligence, the serpents have been a constant peril to sailors before now; they need neither wind nor current in their favor to maneuver, and may strike wholly unexpected from below."

"Yes," Bligh said belligerently, "and there are a dozen of them outside our harbor this very moment. If the Chinese meant to teach us to respect their power, they have succeeded; if they meant to teach us fear, sir, they have failed and will always do so."

"Hear, hear," Willoughby said, glaring at Laurence, who compressed his lips at this ludicrous enthusiasm; he could scarcely fault Willoughby's courage, having already lost both an eye and a leg to the serpents, but his sense offered more to criticize.

"The Navy gentlemen must forgive me," MacArthur said, "but I cannot help but wonder if we could not manage to think of something better to do with these fellows who can, I gather, bring in twenty tons of goods from China to our shores in a month."

Bligh might have purpled himself into an apoplexy in response; Macquarie raised a hand. "If you please," he said: he was quiet-spoken, and his face drawn in craggy but warm lines, with deep-set dark eyes. But he would not allow the possibility of negotiation. "Our last orders, by Commander Willoughby's report," he nodded to that gentleman, "are plain enough: we are not to tolerate any foreign encroachment on this continent. If efforts to dislodge them from this northern port have failed, that is only more cause to repulse them before they can establish another, nearer."

He was bent upon the eradication of the serpents; it was left only to discuss how it was to be done. "Bombs must be our surest method for disposing of the creatures," Rankin said, "delivered from aloft: if they have been trained to come to fish-slops, we can easily bait them to their doom."

His suggestion was adopted with enthusiasm, despite the obvious difficulties of delivering bombs upon creatures which could plunge to the ocean depths, and whose size alone would make them difficult to kill; Willoughby applauded regardless, and Macquarie approved. Granby, who had more experience of aerial warfare than Rankin, whose former experience had been in the courier service, looked doubtful, and said, "We had better try it on one, first, and at a good distance: if you drive them mad and it don't work, they might do for all the shipping in the port."

"Perhaps we ought to clear out some of the most valuable ships," MacArthur suggested. "If we will be dropping on them from above, I cannot see there is any need to keep the *Allegiance* in port for them to gnaw on her anchor-cables."

There was something disingenuous in this proposal: he had already offered his services and Johnston's to arrange the manufacture of the bombs, which should give them excuse to postpone returning to England. But Riley had already once seen his ship nearly brought down by a sea-serpent, and could not be said to be eager to repeat the experience: he was only too pleased to second the notion, and Governor Macquarie did not disagree.

The plan of attack was agreed upon; the conference dismissed, not before Laurence was given his long-delayed post: three letters bundled together from Jane, and another two for Temeraire; and one to be passed on to Tharkay. He put them in his pocket as they departed; MacArthur caught him at the door of the governor's office.

"I suppose they aren't to be reasoned with," MacArthur inquired, "—these Chinamen, I mean. Do they wish to have us all thrown into the harbor and fed to the things?"

"I will beg you, sir, not to entertain the sort of absurd fancies which I have grown used to hear from raw hands," Laurence said, too exasperated to be courteous. "They are men, like any others, and like any others possess full measure of folly and vice; but I cannot say their portion is greater than our own."

"Ah, well," MacArthur said, "then we may all go to the Devil together."

He touched his hat and they parted, Laurence to join Temeraire upon the promontory, to share their letters. The correspondence did not go any length to reconciling him to the imminent attack, devastating almost equally in success or failure: Bonaparte had indeed made alliance with the Tswana, according to Jane.

> *Put them on every Transport he has in his Pockets and shipped them straight across the sea: twenty-six Beasts delivered direct to Rio, nine of them heavy-weight, and two fire-breathers; you may guess what it was like, and I will spare You the Particulars: they don't make Comfortable Reading, I will tell you.*
>
> *The Portuguese are howling for Help, and we must do our Best, before they swallow their Pride and bend the Knee to France, but I have no Notion how we will keep these fellows from tearing all the Colony to Rubble if we cannot persuade the Inca to take an Interest. We must have Iskierka back at Any Price, and I would give an Arm for one of those Japanese fellows, the waterspout-makers.*
>
> *Ten million pounds lost they say so far in Property;*

ludicrous, ain't it? So far the Tswana only seem to care about the Plantations and the Slaves, but if they get a taste for War, as Dragons will if you give them half a Minute, and want More, you may be sure Boney will find some to offer them.

Laurence laid the letters down, bleakly: in such circumstances, to be opening another front against an enemy far better equipped than the Tswana to wage war upon their shipping, seemed still nearer to madness. He sent Sipho for pen and paper, and began to add to his own letter, however late and useless it should be, to advise Jane of these new circumstances, and of his fears.

"At least they have made some progress here," Temeraire said, meaning on the quantity of cattle, and Governor Macquarie was proven very reasonable, he felt, having allowed them each two cows after the ordeal of the journey, despite the expense to the colony. With the shortage, it seemed hard to see so many cattle and sheep loaded aboard the *Allegiance* for her provisions: Iskierka would at least be at sea, and might eat fish if she chose, in all their variety; there was no reason she ought not take instead some kangaroos, and perhaps some of the grey cassowaries, and there would be seals at New Amsterdam.

She was unswayed by this argument. "And I do not see that I owe you anything," she added, with a flip of her tail, "when I consider how long the journey, and how many pains I have taken over it. You might at least have given me an egg, for all my trouble."

"You have caused a good deal of trouble, yourself, and no one wished for you to come from the beginning," Temeraire retorted, but guilt smote him painfully when he had said it: Iskierka *had* been of material service, he could not quite deny it in the privacy of his own conscience. He squirmed with discomfort, but he thought rather despairing that Laurence should never approve if he permitted selfish interest to outweigh justice, so Temeraire drew a deep breath and heroically said, "You might stay, I suppose, if you wished to."

Iskierka snorted, disdainful, "As if anyone would wish to stay in this wretched country, where there is nothing fine to eat, and the only battles one can get, one is covered in stinking fish. No; and if you ask me, you are a great gaby to stay," she added. "Granby says we will likely go from Madras to Rio, instead of home, and have a splendid battle against those African dragons who ran you off before. I am sure we will do better."

Temeraire flattened his ruff, from equal parts annoyance and envy; Madras—he had never seen Madras, or any part of India, although many pleasant things were always coming from there; and he understood all of Brazil to be thoroughly littered with gold, from what sailors said. Nor could Temeraire have any enthusiasm for the coming battle: as he understood they would only be dropping bombs, from aloft; and while he would be perfectly happy to clear away the serpents, who had proven to be so wretchedly difficult and stupid besides, Laurence thought it should certainly mean war with China.

But there was no choice: when the *Allegiance* had gone, and the latest frigate, and those of the merchant ships whose draught was too deep to bring them into the safety of the shallows, they would attack. Laurence also was making his farewells. "Pray give my best to Harcourt," Laurence said, and then belatedly added, "—I mean to Mrs. Riley, of course; I hope you will find her much recovered, and the child well."

"I suppose he will be talking by now," Riley said, "if he hasn't been dropped from dragon-back mid-air; I shan't be surprised to hear it if he has." He took the letters which Laurence had prepared, and those which Sipho had taken down for Temeraire.

"Captain Riley," Temeraire said, "I know you are not very fond of each other, but if you please, I hope you will tell Lily that I send my regards, also; and she is very welcome to visit, she and Maximus, if they should ever choose to."

"Oh," Riley said, a little dismally; Temeraire did have to allow that Lily had been a little unreasonable towards him, but then, in a way one might say it was Riley's fault that poor Harcourt had suffered so much, with her egg. "Yes; certainly I will convey your wishes."

"I call it damned stupid and a waste besides," Granby was saying to Laurence meanwhile, low, but not very low. "To leave you here, and with Rankin to command the covert; if one can even call it a covert when there are three dragons in it, and two as likely to throw him in the ocean as obey him."

"I wish him very great joy of the command," Laurence said dryly. "It is not likely to demand much initiative, and he may as well be here as anywhere; he cannot do very much harm in the position, and he is welcome to the politicking. In all honesty, we would be at more of a standstill if Demane *were* confirmed in rank; from what we have seen of Governor Macquarie, I cannot imagine he would be in the least inclined to listen to a stripling, quite apart from his birth."

"As far as that goes, Demane is as much an officer as he is a fish; so I don't know you are worse off with Rankin, either," Granby said. "No; but it is still a crime to leave you here to rot along with him, and I expect he will make a nuisance of himself; I don't think he knows how to otherwise. *And* a prime heavy-weight," he added, with still more frustration, "with not a prayer of getting him off the continent when the *Allegiance* has gone."

Kulingile had outgrown Caesar a short way into their journey, to Temeraire's private satisfaction, but it seemed to him Kulingile did not need to continue growing at such a pace now, when it plainly consumed so much of the available stores. Even if Iskierka was going away, that still did not leave them with so very many cows, and the hunting grew a good deal more tedious when anyone was taking half-a-dozen kangaroos at a time; soon they should have to fly several hours afield to find herds which could be culled.

"And you have surely heard several of the officers say that there is no use for a really big heavy-weight here in this colony," Temeraire had said to him, when they had at last returned to the valley, and Kulingile had insisted on a portion of cattle just as large as those which Temeraire and Iskierka had commanded.

But Kulingile remained unimpressed by the hints which Temeraire dropped, and continued both to eat and to grow. "Of course he will not outgrow Maximus," Temeraire murmured to Dorset interrogatively, when the second cow had vanished, and Kulingile was eyeing the rest of the herd with a sad, speculative gaze; Temeraire did not really see why Kulingile should outgrow *him*, either, but one did not wish to sound self-centered, or as though one would mind any such thing: it did not signify, of course, if one were a Celestial, even if Kulingile was also coming into a quite handsome pattern of golden scales, as he grew.

"Very likely he will," Dorset said, writing in his log-book; he had been making a record of everything which Kulingile ate, and doing a great deal of measuring with his knotted string, at least until Kulingile had grown so large that only his talons might so be measured in any reasonable amount of time.

Dorset added, "We will know he has begun to reach his growth when he ceases to be quite so rounded: that is when the body will have overtaken the air-sacs, and so begin to approach the limit." But it was now more than a week later, and Kulingile still had a tendency to roly-poly, and if he was not quite as long as Temeraire, it would have been a little difficult to say he was decidedly smaller, if one should compare their shadows on the ground.

MacArthur was certainly very impressed by his appearance when he came up to the promontory that afternoon, presumably to speak with Laurence; but Laurence had gone down to the *Allegiance* to dine with Riley and Granby one final time before their departure, and so there was no one else to meet him. MacArthur paused at the edge of the hill, and asked Temeraire, "So this is the new one, I gather? Something prodigious, I see, for a few months out of the shell; he will have your measure if he goes on a little longer this way."

"I suppose, if one is only concerned with *weight*," Temeraire said, a little repressively.

"Ha ha," MacArthur said, although Temeraire saw nothing very funny in it. "And does he have a captain?"

"He is mine," Demane said, belligerently, having already raised his head to listen from where he and Roland were sketching out the proposed plan of attack upon the serpents, and arguing over its merits; Demane was inclined to dislike it only because Rankin had proposed it, and so was finding fault, where Roland had said impatiently, "Yes, he is a scrub, what has that got to do with fighting? If Laurence said to jump in the water and fight them, would you like to do it?"

MacArthur eyed Demane more than a little doubtfully, and then said something to him which did not make any sense: it was a little like the aboriginal languages which Temeraire had now heard bits of, mixed together with a great deal of English peculiarly pronounced. "What?" Demane said, justly baffled.

"He thinks you're one of their natives!" Sipho said, without looking up from his book. "We are from Africa, and we aren't stupid, either; you needn't talk like you are babbling to a child."

"Well, that is handy," MacArthur said. "It is a shame more of you black fellows cannot speak better English."

"It is a shame you can't speak better Chinese, too," Sipho said, not quite under his breath, to which MacArthur said, "Why, I cannot say I would mind it these days," and laughed again, ha ha, and said to Demane, "Now then, how did that come about: you are never an officer?"

"I am, too," Demane said defiantly, "whatever Captain Rankin may have said; he wanted to have Kulingile killed, when he was hatched, so," he spat, "that, for him, and anyone else who likes to deny me, I am happy to meet them anytime they like."

"Well, for my part you may keep your sword in its sheath," MacArthur said, "and I am happy enough to call you captain if the dragon does; there's the real sticking-point of the business, after all. I suppose the other fellows are being sticklers over it?" he added shrewdly, and Demane looked mulish.

"You will be sticking here with this big fellow, I gather: what do you mean to do, stick here in this covert?" MacArthur went on. "A little uncomfortable, with a grousing pack of envious fellows about; you might do better to go it your own way, after all—with your own piece of land, and raise cattle of your own."

Demane took a low startled breath; there was nothing more highly valued in his childhood society than cattle, at once survival and currency: orphan and impoverished, he had risked his life willingly to become the possessor of a cow, which yet remained in some corner of his spirit a standard of wealth. MacArthur might as well have said, that Demane ought to dig up a chest all full of treasure, and pointed him in its direction. "I might," he said, attempting to be a little cool about the matter, and sounding merely wary.

"Well, keep it in mind," MacArthur said. "There is no need to make any hasty decisions; only you might think it over, whether it would suit you."

He asked after Laurence, then, and hearing he was at dinner touched his hat and went away, not without promising another pair of cattle, "With a yearling beef for the littler fellow," he said, meaning Caesar, "and that way you don't need to squabble it with this— Kulingheelay, did you say?" as though Temeraire would have squabbled anyway, in some undignified manner. "Give your captain my regards," he concluded, and so departed, leaving Demane to say to Roland in an undertone, "It would suit me better than scraping to Rankin."

"As though you would, anyway," Roland said, rolling her eyes.

"Don't be an ass; he probably wants to see if you can be persuaded to fetch and carry for him, or something like, at a bargain price."

"Do you suppose he might like something carried at *not* a bargain price, if he could not get better?" Temeraire inquired; though Roland abjured the idea scornfully, as beneath the dignity of an aviator to consider, Demane was of very like mind when Temeraire said to him privately, afterwards, "But if he or some other person were prepared to pay in cows, no one could object, *I* find, to doing him some service."

There would be time yet to consider; at present, the question and MacArthur's visit both were driven quite from his mind, for the wind had shifted: not very strong, but enough to rattle the spars a little, and in the ideal quarter. There was a consultation going forward on the deck of the ship, which Temeraire could see in the fading light: the young officers on duty peering up and calling questions to the crow's nest. They were a little while at it and resolved not too soon: below in the street, the doors to the inn opened, where the men had gone to dine, just as the ship fired away a blue light and the small blue pennant rose up on the mast to summon all her officers aboard.

Laurence came up the hill slowly and rested his hand on Temeraire's side as the ship's launch rowed back out, the guests from dinner crawling up the side one after another; the men were already at the two massive capstans, marching around, as the sails billowed out in sheets of rolling white.

"Good-bye!" Iskierka called from the dragondeck, her voice carrying over the water. "Good-bye! I will tell Granby to write you whenever anything interesting should happen."

Temeraire sighed a little, and put his head down upon his forelegs as the *Allegiance* began her slow and stately progress: the evanescing light orange-pink and steam wreathing her foremast from Iskierka's spikes, spilling up the belled sails and trailing away; shouts, calls, the bell rung at the quarter-hour came distantly. The ship was moving towards night, away, and the curve of the land gradually concealed the hull so that one saw only the sails gliding; a little longer, and then only the lantern-gleam high up, if Temeraire sat upon his haunches and stretched his neck. Then even that faded to just the gleam of the stars coming out, and between one blink and another, Temeraire lost the track, and she was gone. The *Allegiance* was gone: the first he had ever sat upon the shore and watched her leave.

The harbor looked strangely empty and smaller with her out of it, as though one could not quite imagine that any ship so large had been in that place, and all the other ships which had looked so small beside her now seemed ordinary in size and respectable. "There is no reason she should not come back someday," Temeraire said to Laurence, "of course; after all, a ship may go anywhere it likes, and she was sent here once. They might like to send some other dragons. And oh! it would be so very tedious to be sailing another eight months, as Iskierka is likely to do—if she is not sent to Brazil, that is," he finished rather despondently. He was sure Iskierka *would* be sent to Brazil, it would be just the sort of thing which happened to Iskierka; it did not seem very fair that anyone so careless should have acquired heaps of treasure, and all the ship's stores of cattle to herself, and also have a great deal more fighting, and everything pleasant.

But he was determined not to be dismal: he would not be a weight upon Laurence, who had also been left behind to manage with Rankin, and this new governor; Temeraire had been forced sadly to reconsider his feelings towards Macquarie. Laurence certainly thought better of him than of Bligh, and Temeraire would not quarrel on that point, but it seemed Macquarie was rather given to consulting Rankin, and not Laurence, and Laurence had not been invited to several of the conferences to further discuss the plan of attack.

Instead Rankin would return to the covert after these were held, and present the plan to the aviators in a very officious manner; and if Laurence had a point to make, or some question, Rankin would address him very pointedly as *Mr.* Laurence, and the others as *Lieutenant,* such as Lieutenant Blincoln; he only ever addressed the midwingmen so, as Mr. Peabody, or Mr. Dawes, so it was all the ever more sharp.

"That scarcely concerns me," Laurence said, when Temeraire had expressed his very great irritation. "He might as easily refuse to share with me any intelligence from the conferences at all, and try and put another man aboard with us to govern the course of events during the battle; he would be within his rights."

"As though I should allow any such thing," Temeraire said, "and I am sure he knows it; he might fight the battle without me, then, and I expect without Kulingile, too."

Kulingile cracked open an eye at his name and asked drowsily, "Is it time to eat again yet?"

"No, but I imagine you have not long to wait; I passed a butchering on my way," Tharkay said, coming up the hill.

He shook Laurence's hand; to Temeraire's dismay, he had come to also take his leave. "The master of the *Miniver* informs me he means to make port at Bombay," Tharkay said, "and I know the road from there to Istanbul." He smiled a little, twistedly. "Much of my intelligence may be a little old by the time I have got there, but I have promised to deliver it."

Temeraire did not see why Tharkay should have to go so far, only to deliver news; and particularly when he did not seem as though he wished to go, very much. "But if you must, you might come back," Temeraire said, "and if you see Bezaid and Sherazde, pray tell them that their egg hatched quite safely; I have often thought that I ought to send them word. It is not their fault, of course, that Iskierka is so very irritating."

"I think we must expect to regret you a longer time," Laurence said. "—there can be very little to call you back to this part of the world anytime soon."

Tharkay paused, then said, "We spoke some time ago of endeavors which might call *you* away from it, however. I would have opportunity to make inquiries, if you have decided."

Laurence did not answer immediately; then he said, "No; thank you, Tenzing. I cannot see my way to it. I am very grateful—"

Tharkay waved this away. "Then I will hope some other occupation finds you; you do not seem likely to me to lie idle." He drew out a handsomely embossed card from a case in his pocket. "My direction is likely to be, as always, uncertain; but you may write me care of my lawyers: if they cannot find me, they will hold the letters until I have called for them." He gave Laurence the card; they clasped hands once more and agreed on dinner, the following day, before Tharkay went down the slope away.

"I certainly hope that he is right," Temeraire said, with a little sigh; privateering did seem to him a splendid occupation, and it was a great pity Laurence felt it was not quite the thing. It did not seem to him that anything of interest should ever happen here, nor fair that everyone but himself and Laurence should go.

Tharkay and Laurence were away at dinner the next afternoon when the gunfire erupted, late in the evening. Temeraire had just woken to enjoy the cooler hours, and had been contemplating whether he might call it worth the effort to fly a little distance to the more shaded water-hole and have a cold drink; as the crack and whistle of musketry went off, Kulingile opened his eyes and sat up.

"Is it time to fight the serpents?" he inquired hopefully: his voice had not grown lower, but a great deal more resonant in an odd, echoing manner, so that when he spoke it seemed as though several people were talking at once, saying the very same thing.

"Of course it is not time to fight the serpents," Caesar said, peering down the slope, "my captain would have come for me, and my crew. There are men fighting one another: perhaps it is duels."

"It is not duels," Temeraire said, "no one fights duels at night, and with dozens of people against one another; one fights them at dawn. I do not see why there should be so much disorder in this town, and why Laurence must always be in the midst of it, somewhere I cannot see him; oh! they are firing again."

There were a great many men in uniforms in the street, struggling now against one another with bayonets and wrestling, their rifles held like staves and battering away. Temeraire rose and peered down the hill anxiously, looking to see if he could make Laurence out anywhere at all in the melee, but his brown coat would have been difficult to see in better light than they had, so that Temeraire did not see him was no comfort; if he had seen Laurence, he might at least have had the opportunity of snatching him away to safety.

"I am going to go down there," Temeraire said, decisively, "—no, Roland, I cannot wait; plainly Laurence might be anywhere, and perhaps they will stop if I should land among them—I will only knock over that low building, which is very rickety-looking anyway, and perhaps the one beside it."

"You are not to go anywhere," Rankin said, panting up the hill, in his heartlessly plain evening clothes and great disarray, with Blincoln and his second lieutenant behind him. "Mr. Fellowes! You will rig Caesar out at once; it is a rebellion. You are to remain here," he added to Temeraire. "Laurence is in no danger whatsoever: they are advancing on the governor's mansion, and nowhere near the inn where he was dining."

"As though I were likely to take your word for it," Temeraire said scornfully, "or listen to you; I am not under your command, and if someone is rebelling, who is it, and why?"

"That," Rankin snapped, "is none of your concern; if you do mean to go blundering in, and likely crush Laurence yourself in reckless abandon, by all means do so, but you will keep out of our way. Caesar, does all lie well? That breast-band does not look secure to me, Mr. Fellowes, you will see to it."

"It is a little loose there over the shoulder, as well," Caesar reported, puffing out his chest tremendously, and then Demane said, "I don't see why *we* should—ow!"

Roland had kicked him soundly in the shin, and as he bent towards it caught him by the ear, twisting it painfully. "Don't be an ass," she said, "and don't you yowl at me, either," she added, when Kulingile had reared up his head in bristling protest. "It is for his good, and yours."

"Let go!" Demane hissed back at her, but she was managing to dance around him and keep hold, so he could not easily wrench loose without hurting himself worse. "Why should we let him decide, who is ruling the colony and everyone in it—"

"We shouldn't," she hissed, "but you aren't the son of an earl with twenty thousand a year and half the Lords in his pocket; if you look a rebel, someone will just shoot you, you ass, and not bother with trial about it, either; you haven't a scrap of influence. And anyway," she added, "if he hasn't any business deciding, you have less; you don't even know who it is rebelling, or why: and I dare say they are all just drunk."

"They are certainly not drunk," Temeraire said, "for they have got off three volleys: and it is no joke to reload a gun even when one is sober; it was the greatest difficulty for our artillery company to manage it, with seven men to a cannon, so it must be even more trouble for one person with a musket, it seems to me; and I do wish I knew who they were—"

"It is the New South Wales Corps," Lieutenant Forthing said, panting; he had dashed up the hill. "Mr. Laurence is coming, Temeraire; he says to tell you he is quite well, and you are not to come in search of him."

"Where is he, pray?" Temeraire said, still a little wary; Laurence, he knew, thought a little better of Forthing after their journey, but Temeraire did not see that he had done anything of particular value; he would much rather have had Ferris back, or perhaps his midwingman Martin; except of course Martin had given them the cut direct, after the trial.

It was grown too dark to see, but there was a lantern coming up the hill, and then Caesar said, "All lies well, Captain Rankin," very satisfied with himself, and stood waiting while the company of officers began to go aboard with their rifles and their pistols, and as they mounted, he added aside to Temeraire and Kulingile, in a tone of unpardonable condescension, "Well, fellows, we will settle this in a trice, and be back; pray don't trouble yourselves over it."

"I do not see why we do not get any fighting, and you do?" Kulingile said queryingly, which Temeraire felt was a remarkably appropriate question. "I have been very sleepy, but no one can sleep when there are guns going. And if it is the New South Wales Corps, have they not been giving us those sheep? and the cows?"

"Well," Temeraire said judiciously, "so far as that goes, Governor Macquarie did provide us with some cattle." One ought, he felt, be scrupulously fair in such circumstances. "But he does mean to start a war with China, which no one would like; Laurence," he said, swinging his head around, "I am so very relieved to see you: I had meant to go down, but Forthing came sooner. We are discussing whether we ought help Governor Macquarie, or the Corps, who are rebelling again."

"Yes," Laurence said, grimly, "—Roland, my glass."

The battle, if one might call it that, had gone all the distance to the governor's mansion now, and seemed so far as Temeraire could see it to be quite reduced in scope; there was very little fighting, and the soldiers who had stood in the way now seemed to be walking with the rest, except for the small company of Marines, who had fled. There was singing going on, and a great many of the townspeople had come out with lanterns and also flagons and bottles: one could see the light shining on the glass as they drank and cheered, and pistols were shot off into the air.

Laurence closed the glass and gave it to Roland. "Caesar," Rankin said, "put me up."

"Temeraire," Laurence said, "you will not permit him to go aloft, if you please. Sir," he said to Rankin, "the event has run past you: you will not turn your beast against a crowd of civilians. God knows there has been enough of that in this war: I will not see it done again."

Rankin's face went very pale with anger, and his hand clenched upon the straps of his carabiners, which he held ready. "Mr. Laurence, if you should dare interfere—"

"I do," Laurence said flatly, and whatever Rankin might have said foundered: there was no threat he could offer.

"If you had the least ambition of pardon," he said after a stifled, furious struggle briefly contorted his narrow, aristocratic mouth, "you may leave it aside forever; if you think the account I shall give of you will not suffice, Governor Macquarie will surely damn you as thoroughly."

"I have no doubt of it," Laurence said, and turned away; he did not care to give Rankin his face.

Epilogue

"OF COURSE it is not a real rebellion," MacArthur said, handing Laurence a glass of the cool sillery; the heat had broken at last, and the autumnal air was pleasant as the small bats cried and flung themselves among the trees along the border of his gardens. "I don't see any reason we ought to behave like those Yankee Doodles, cutting off our nose to spite our face; but it is unreasonable to be governed at eight months' distance and guesswork. Their Lordships cannot have known they were asking for a war we cannot win: what should we do if China sent over a dozen of these albatross creatures, which they do not even know existed, and ran them over our heads with sacks full of bombs? No, plainly we must manage ourselves; but certainly I do not mean to forswear my loyalty to the King. Never that."

By which, Laurence supposed, MacArthur meant that he did not mean to forswear himself for at least the next year and a half, before some fresh answer came; if the ministers should not choose at that time to recognize his new self-declared position as First Minister of Australia, Laurence suspected MacArthur's feelings on the matter would prove somewhat more malleable.

"Now then," MacArthur said, "this Rankin fellow: I cannot see how he can continue the commander of our little aerial force here—"

"I should be surprised if you had much success in persuading him to undertake it," Laurence said dryly. He had rather expected Rankin to return to England, with Macquarie: the deposed governor had no notion of lingering as Bligh had, but meant at once to leave by the same frigate which had brought him, when that ship was ready.

"You *would* be surprised, I think," MacArthur said. "He is a little stiff-necked, there is no denying it, but his beast is a reasonable creature; I have found it work well enough when I have a word in his ear beforehand to any discussion with his captain. But it is no use saying Rankin has charge of the covert, under the circumstances: you are the man we want for the business. I have written you a pardon; there may be a little irregularity about it, of course, but it must do for now—"

"Sir," Laurence said, "I am obliged to you; I must call it more than a little irregular."

"Well," MacArthur said, waving a hand to leave this minor quibble in the air, "we are all irregular here, more or less, and we shan't grow less so for a good long time: I do not think, sir, you are inclined to sit in a corner until we get back some word: you are not made to moulder in some forgotten corner of the world. And why ought you? You were sent here, after all, and with the intention of your doing work for the colony. I cannot see how it should in any way contravene the terms of your transportation."

There was a special sort of gall in proposing that Laurence's life-sentence for treason did not preclude his taking command of the nascent covert and its aviators; the same sort of gall, of course, which had staged not one but two separate coups d'état. Laurence rather thought MacArthur and Bonaparte were cut from the same cloth, spiritually speaking, if they did not have the same gifts.

"And I do not mind saying," MacArthur said, "you cannot help but be damned useful in this whole China business. They turn up remarkably sweet as soon as they have clapped eyes on you and this fellow, no one can help but see that."

For this MacArthur's evidence was a pair of young Chinese officials, who had been brought to the colony the last week: Temeraire at his request had managed to intercept Lung Shen Gai, the dragon previously sighted so near to Sydney, and invite discussion of the territorial issues. MacArthur represented the general sentiment of his citizenry in embracing with great enthusiasm the prospect of Chinese goods entering their market in considerable quantity: *free trade* was the byword on every man's lips who had an opinion, which was everyone. The reports from the north of the haul of treasure brought in by the serpents, of tea and luxury, had by now diffused very widely among the populace from O'Dea's reports: which he recounted nightly in the taverns for his grog, the accounts losing no allure in the transmission and gaining much.

"I dare say if you should not care to be the commander of the covert," MacArthur added, "you might take on the foreign ministry: why, that might do better, indeed."

"You would do better to hire Temeraire for that post, if he were inclined to serve," Laurence said. "No: I thank you for the compliment of your confidence, but no." He set down his glass. "Pray give my compliments to your wife."

Temeraire was drowsing in the field behind the house: filled out a little better after a month of recovery, and the scales of his hide beginning to regain some of that particular glossy sheen. He raised his head as Laurence came nearer, and yawned. "Is your dinner finished? What did he wish to say to you?"

"To offer me the earth, or at least a portion of it, if we would take charge of the covert," Laurence said, swinging himself up and hooking on his carabiner straps. "He would like to make me an admiral, or a minister; and of course he has pardoned me, for whatever that is worth in a British court: perhaps another twenty years on the sentence, I would imagine."

"It is a kind thought, of course," Temeraire said, his ruff pricking up. "You are sure you should *not* like to be a minister?" he inquired. "That is very like a lord, is it not, for you are always saying *their Lordships* when you should mean the King's ministers."

"Very sure," Laurence said.

The deposed governor was at the promontory when they returned, speaking with Rankin, low; a small guard of New South Wales Corps soldiers stood a little way off, his escort—or gaolers, nearer the truth.

"If I cannot approve your reluctance to act, I am glad to hear you have not wholly acceded to MacArthur's rebellion," Macquarie said heavily. "The Crown will wish to remove you at once, with Captain Rankin and the loyalist officers: if we can catch the *Allegiance,* we will return for her to serve as your transport. Some arrangement can be made for your sentence to be carried out in India—"

"You must forgive me, sir," Laurence said, "but if you have no better use for us than to trundle us over the ocean to a pen in India, only to keep us from MacArthur's powers of persuasion, I will forgo the pleasure."

Macquarie was by no means easily reconciled to this position: he protested, and commanded, and came as near cajolery as a man so sensible of his dignity, and wounded in it, could do; but Laurence found himself wholly unmoved even by the final, grudging offer. "You are impatient with your lack of use; some honorable work surely can be found—will be found," Macquarie said, "which perhaps may even render suitable a pardon—"

"There is an ugly character to the work which has heretofore been found for us," Laurence said, "and I think I have done trying the patience of my commanding officers."

"Laurence," Temeraire said tentatively, when Macquarie had gone away frustrate, "it is not that I mind, for I had just as soon not have anything more to do with Government and their orders; but are you quite sure you would not like to go back to the war, if they will have us?"

Laurence was silent a moment, waiting for the sense of duty to answer; but it did not speak. They would not be asked to defend England, or liberty, or anything worthy of service: only to assist at one spiteful destruction or another. He found in himself only a great longing for something cleaner. "No," he said finally. "I am sick of the quarrels of nations and of kings, and I would not give ha'pence for any empire other than our valley, if that can content your ambition."

"Oh! It can, very well," Temeraire said, brightening. "Will we go there tomorrow, then? I have been thinking, Laurence, we might have a pavilion up before the winter."

ABOUT THE AUTHOR

NAOMI NOVIK is the acclaimed author of *His Majesty's Dragon, Throne of Jade, Black Powder War, Empire of Ivory,* and *Victory of Eagles,* the first five volumes of the Temeraire series, recently optioned by Peter Jackson, the Academy Award–winning director of the Lord of the Rings trilogy. In 2007, Novik received the John W. Campbell Award for Best New Writer at the World Science Fiction Convention. A history buff with a particular interest in the Napoleonic era, Novik studied English literature at Brown University, then did graduate work in computer science at Columbia University before leaving to participate in the design and development of the computer game Neverwinter Nights: Shadows of Undrentide. Novik lives in New York City with her husband and six computers.

www.temeraire.org